Reform Acts

Reform Acts

*Chartism, Social Agency, and the
Victorian Novel, 1832–1867*

CHRIS R. VANDEN BOSSCHE

Johns Hopkins University Press
Baltimore

© 2014 Johns Hopkins University Press
All rights reserved. Published 2014
Printed in the United States of America on acid-free paper
2 4 6 8 9 7 5 3 1

Johns Hopkins University Press
2715 North Charles Street
Baltimore, Maryland 21218-4363
www.press.jhu.edu

Library of Congress Cataloging-in-Publication Data
Vanden Bossche, Chris.
Reform acts : Chartism, social agency, and the Victorian novel, 1832–1867 /
Chris R. Vanden Bossche.
pages cm
Includes bibliographical references and index.
ISBN 978-1-4214-1208-5 (hardcover : acid-free paper) —
ISBN 978-1-4214-1209-2 (electronic) — ISBN 1-4214-1208-X (hardcover :
acid-free paper) — ISBN 1-4214-1209-8 (electronic) 1. English fiction—
19th century—History and criticism. 2. Social classes in literature.
3. Chartism in literature. 4. Literature and society—Great Britain—
History—19th century. I. Title.
PR830.S6V36 2014
823.009'355—dc23   2013016722

A catalog record for this book is available from the British Library.

Special discounts are available for bulk purchases of this book.
For more information, please contact Special Sales at 410-516-6936 or
specialsales@press.jhu.edu.

Johns Hopkins University Press uses environmentally friendly book
materials, including recycled text paper that is composed of at least
30 percent post-consumer waste, whenever possible.

To Laura

Contents

Acknowledgments   ix

1 Social Agency: The Franchise, Class Discourse, and
National Narratives   1

PART 1   MAKING PHYSICAL FORCE MORAL:
THE DILEMMA OF CHARTISM, 1838–1842

2 Social Agency in the Chartist and Parliamentary Press   21

3 Egalitarian Chivalry and Popular Agency in *Wat Tyler*   37

4 Unconsummated Marriage and the "Uncommitted"
Gunpowder Plot in *Guy Fawkes*   50

5 Class Alliance and Self-Culture in *Barnaby Rudge*   60

PART 2   "THE LAND! THE LAND! THE LAND!":
LAND OWNERSHIP AS POLITICAL REFORM, 1842–1848

6 Agricultural Reform, Young England's Allotments, and the
Chartist Land Plan   75

7 The Landed Estate, Finely Graded Hierarchy, and the Member of
Parliament in *Coningsby* and *Sybil*   85

8 Agricultural Improvement and the Squirearchy in *Hillingdon Hall*   102

9 The Land Plan, Class Dichotomy, and Working-Class Agency in
Sunshine and Shadow   113

PART 3   THE SOCIAL TURN: FROM CHARTISM TO
COOPERATION AND TRADE UNIONISM, 1848–1855

10 Christian Socialism and Cooperative Association   129

11 Clergy and Working-Class Cooperation in *Yeast* and *Alton Locke*   142

12 Reforming Trade Unionism in *Mary Barton* and *North and South*   164

Coda: Rethinking Reform in the Era of the Second Reform Act,
1860–1867   189

Notes   201
Works Cited   233
Index   245

Acknowledgments

I want to express my gratitude to the many interlocutors in dialogue with whom I have written this book. These include the students in my undergraduate and graduate courses in which I posed, and we vigorously discussed, the questions explored in this study. My colleagues and thesis and dissertation students at Notre Dame contributed in many ways, in particular in discussion of portions of this work in the Eighteenth- and Nineteenth-Century British Area seminar. Countless scholars encountered in books and articles, conferences and classrooms, have contributed to my knowledge and understanding of all things Victorian and literary, whether as provokers, challengers, or affirmers. I also thank the Institute for Scholarship in the Liberal Arts at Notre Dame for financial support of this project.

I made my first public presentation of ideas that I would eventually develop into this project at the first meeting of the North American Victorian Studies Association, and it has continued to be a fruitful venue for presenting the work in progress. Interdisciplinary Nineteenth-Century Studies has been especially important as a model for intellectual dialogue and exchange; I am grateful to it not only for intellectual stimulation but also for the friendships that have developed over the years at its meetings.

I have spent many a pleasant dinnertime recounting the chapters of this book. Always listening intently, questioning, responding, and helping me to think through problems that stymied me was my colleague, companion, and wife, Laura Haigwood, to whom I dedicate this book.

Social Agency

The Franchise, Class Discourse, and National Narratives

The title of this study refers to the Reform Acts of 1832 and 1867, which expanded the electoral franchise and altered the system of parliamentary representation in Great Britain. The First Reform Act raised the number of eligible voters in England and Wales from 366,000 to 653,000, an increase from 11 percent to 18 percent of the adult male population (figures for Scotland and Ireland were similar). This modest increase meant that, even after passage of the Act, four out of five adult males—and, of course, all women—did not have the right to vote. The intention of the Act, as understood by contemporary politicians, was to enfranchise the newly risen middle class. It did so by altering property qualifications for the franchise and redistributing parliamentary seats to provide better representation of the industrial midlands. Working-class radicals supported the Act as a precursor to further change, but they discovered after its passage that a Parliament still very much dominated by the upper classes had no intention of expanding the franchise any further and, moreover, that the reformed Parliament was no more inclined to legislate on behalf of the working classes than the old Parliament had been.

Over the next few years working-class discontent continued to grow, and in 1838 radicals began circulating a National Petition advocating passage of the People's Charter, in effect a new reform act. The movement focused primarily on universal adult male suffrage, but the Charter also demanded annual parliaments, the secret ballot, payment of MPs, abolition of the property qualification for MPs, and electoral districts of equal size, measures that were meant to ensure representation of the working classes. There was nothing new about either petitioning Parliament or the six demands, both of which had been staples of radical politics since the late eighteenth century. What was new was that the movement was national—a single "National Petition" replaced scores of local ones—and the name of the People's Charter, with its allusion to the Magna Carta and the tradition of political rights with which it was associated. As Malcolm Chase points out, the resulting movement was the "first (and arguably the greatest) mass political movement in industrial Britain" (*Chartism* 7). Employing tactics developed by radicals earlier in the century, the Chartists mounted a series of massive public demonstrations in support of the Charter, culminating in huge processions to Parliament to present the National Petition, which they did three times, in 1839, 1842, and 1848.

Although they were highly successful in mobilizing the working classes, the Chartists never came close to persuading Parliament to accept their National Petition. Following the rejection of the petition of 1848, the leadership became divided about how to proceed, and by the early 1850s Chartism no longer operated as a mass political movement. Nonetheless, Chartism did alter public discourse about the right of political representation, and many former Chartists took part in the campaign leading to passage of the Reform Act of 1867, which was widely regarded as the first step toward enacting universal male suffrage and fulfilling the aims of Chartism.

⌒

This study seeks to demonstrate how the Victorians thought about agency—the capacity to act—as reform. When, in 1831, the Whigs introduced their "Ministerial Plan for Parliamentary Reform," they used the term *reform* to indicate that they did not propose a revolutionary change that would overturn the British constitution but merely to institute reforms mandated by it.[1] The debates that ensued repeatedly returned to the question of whether the bill would amount to revolution or reform.[2] In part because they mounted their campaign as the ministerial party from within Parliament, the Whigs ultimately prevailed not only in passing the bill but also in establishing public acceptance of their representation of the bill as a reform measure.

In 1837, when the Chartists inaugurated their campaign for universal male suffrage using the language of reform, they had no such advantage. Newspapers like the *Times* and the *Morning Chronicle*—speaking for the Tories and the Whigs, respectively—concurred that "whoever has attended in the least to the language of the Chartist orators and publications, must be well aware that 'revolution,' not 'reform,' is the object in view" (*Morning Chronicle* 23 Apr. 1841: 2). Although the radical press insisted on the reformist intentions of Chartism, its campaign took place outside of Parliament and the political domain defined by the parliamentary parties. A very small number of MPs supported the Chartist cause, but the party leadership and party organs, branding it as revolutionary, overwhelmingly opposed consideration of the Chartist petitions. Even as some Chartists insisted that these circumstances meant that insurrection was their only option, the very nature of the movement—a campaign for the electoral franchise—manifested its commitment to constitutional reform and to the principle that changes in the socioeconomic domain could best be effected through acquiring political power. As Charles Tilly and Sidney Tarrow have shown, the repertoires of contention— mass demonstrations, petitions, boycotts—through which the Chartists sought to gain the franchise and so reform society have remained in use ever since, in the March on Washington, antiwar protests, and most recently, the Arab Spring.

The Reform Acts were also *actions* that sought to change society for the better and thus they reflect this study's concern with social agency, by which I refer to the capacity to change the social order. I distinguish social agency from individual agency and questions of free will, but I do not mean to refer only to the socioeconomic domain in contradistinction to the political. On the contrary, I work from the premise that in the first half of the nineteenth century, public discourse defined social agency in political terms. Precisely because I am exploring the ways these discourses sought to envision new forms of agency, however, I do not use the term *political agency* but instead use *social agency* to refer to the full spectrum of possibilities for improvement of the social order.

This study approaches agency historically rather than theoretically. Instead of assuming that meaningful social change must take a particular form, it seeks to investigate how the Victorians themselves envisioned such change. Literary criticism has taken up questions about agency in response to theories depicting individuals as subjected to ideological or discursive structures that dictate the possibilities for action.[3] Accordingly, what literary criticism calls agency involves the possibility of acting in ways that are not constrained by, or at least have the possibility of reshaping, these structures. Seen in this way, acting within social structures is not acting at all, for acting requires overturning the structures, at least conceptually; it requires, in other words, revolution. Rather than adopting such an a priori theory of agency and then analyzing how literary texts conform to it, this study conducts a historical analysis of the conceptions of social agency texts employ and produce. It therefore begins from the premise that the most widely circulated conception of social agency in the first half of the nineteenth century was not revolution but reform of society through possession of the franchise and the power to legislate, and it examines how Victorian novels envision social agency in terms of this conception.[4]

While I focus on how novels represent social agency, I implicitly treat the novel itself as a social agent. I contend that while novels can only imagine agency in terms of existing discourses that produce contemporary ideology, they can also reframe or re-function those discourses. This approach reflects what I take to be the proper understanding of ideology as a process in which the cultural and material reshape each other and not as a fixed set of discursive relations within the cultural domain that mask or legitimate the economic domain.[5] Consequently, the primary method of operation in this study is to engage in what Sharon Marcus calls "just," as opposed to symptomatic, reading (75). Just as critics like Amanda Anderson, Lauren Goodlad, and David Wayne Thomas take seriously the Victorians' thinking about detachment, cultivation, and liberalism, I take seriously their thinking about agency and reform. Like symptomatic readings, my analysis discovers contradictions in the texts, but rather than claim that I have discovered something that the text itself does not know (its subtexts), I ask how these contradictions arise from the novel's attempts to engage with existing discourses of agency. This approach is in keeping with the main concern of this study, which is to learn how public discourse and novels that employ public discourses of social agency seek to come to terms with these contradictions by reordering the relationships within them so as to envision possibilities for social change.

Unlike other studies dealing with the working classes and reform, this one focuses on the political rather than the social and economic.[6] This emphasis is not a theoretical investment but derives instead from the decision to make my investigation historical rather than theoretical. That is to say, my approach brackets theoretical questions about how social change must take place (i.e., the assumption that all meaningful change must originate in the socioeconomic domain or must be revolutionary) in order to examine how the Victorians themselves thought about the nature of social improvement. Nineteenth-century British discourse, at least in the first half of the century, located social agency in the political sphere. As Gareth Stedman Jones and others have pointed out, this explains why Chartism, as well as earlier nineteenth-century radicalism, operated on the assumption that change in the political domain would lead to change in the economic, not vice versa.

In this respect, I seek to broaden the domain defined by the term *social-problem novel*, which literary criticism has tended to equate with the industrial novel, and to focus instead on the Chartist, or political, novel.[7] Because these are not hard and fast categories, there is inevitably some overlap between them, but even when I take up a novel like Disraeli's *Sybil*, my attention is on the political rather than the industrial. Thus I also discuss *Coningsby*, which does not deal with industry, but which in its political concerns is closely linked to *Sybil*. In this respect, I read not only *Sybil* but also *Mary Barton* and *Alton Locke*, as well as *Sunshine and Shadow*, as Chartist novels or, to be more precise, as novels that take up questions about social agency raised by the Chartist movement. Moreover, because I am concerned with parliamentary and Chartist discourse at least as much as I am with the representation of Chartism and the working classes, I have in some cases selected novels that employ contemporary political discourse but do not explicitly represent contemporary politics. In addition to examining novels such as *Coningsby* and *Hillingdon Hall* that do not focus on working-class life but deal with politics, I also discuss novels — *Wat Tyler*, *Guy Fawkes*, and *Barnaby Rudge* — that depict popular uprisings antedating Chartism but engage with contemporary discourse about it.

The discussion that follows establishes the context for my examination of how novels take up questions about social agency. In the first section of this chapter, "The Franchise, Class, and Social Agency," I examine how the constitutional discourse employed in the Reform Bill debates made the franchise and legislation the dominant forms of social agency and the social class the privileged form of social agent that exercises the franchise. I demonstrate that the resulting parliamentary discourse constructed social agency in terms of the contest between the aristocracy and the middle class over which was best equipped to disinterestedly exercise social agency and that Chartist discourse in turn articulated its claims of agency for the disenfranchised lower classes by taking up and reworking this parliamentary discourse. Both discourses, I argue, constructed national narratives of reform that legitimated particular political agendas by projecting a future in which the privileging of one class as a disinterested social agent produces a more harmonious social order.

The second section, "Imagining Agency through the National Marriage Plot," explains how Victorian novelists revised the historical novel by drawing on these constitutional narratives in order to produce narratives of reform. These novels employ parliamentary and Chartist discourses to translate the historical novel's and national tale's narratives of cultural or national conflict between Saxon and Celt into narratives of conflict between social classes. These national narratives envision a future achieved through a companionate marriage that privileges one class as social agent and resolves class conflict by reordering the relations between classes to produce a new class structure defining new social agents who in turn employ new forms of social agency.

THE FRANCHISE, CLASS, AND SOCIAL AGENCY

That reform in what has been called "the age of reform" is most closely identified with the franchise—there were many proposals for reform but only those dealing with the franchise were known as reform bills—reflects the constitutionalist discourse that in the early nineteenth century defined social agency in terms of parliamentary representation. Both the proponents of the Reform Bill and the Chartists defined the social agent as a political constituency and action as electing legislators and legislating. As one speaker at a Chartist demonstration put it, the object of the Charter was to enable the disenfranchised to become "political agent[s]" (*Northern Star* 11 Aug. 1838: 6). This discourse marked the dividing line between reform and revolution in terms of whether a particular action was mandated by, or a threat to, the constitution. Similarly, it defined those who possessed social agency as members of a constituency whose position in the social structure ensured that they would act in accord with the constitution.

The status of the British constitution as a "founding national myth" made constitutionalist discourse a powerful means of legitimating political positions, which is why by the beginning of the nineteenth century it "provided a strong sense of historical agency to those who used it."[8] By constructing constitutionalist histories that legitimated particular political positions and constituencies, a wide range of political groups could depict themselves as advocates of reform rather than revolution. As James Vernon has pointed out, "Competing political groups sought to construct their constituencies of support by appropriating and using the 'shared' language of constitutionalism in different ways" (*Politics* 296; see also *Re-reading* 12). Consequently, as James Epstein concludes, "during the first half of the nineteenth century, the constitutionalist idiom was distinguished not so much for being the ideological property of any one class or political tendency, but as defining the contested terrain between different social and political groups" (*Radical Expression* 27; see also 24, 28; Stedman Jones 111).

These histories focused on the right of representation. Gareth Stedman Jones traces constitutionalist discourse to the development in the 1770s of a "vocabulary of grievance" derived from a "critique of the corrupting effects of the concentration of political power and its corrosive influence upon a society deprived of proper means of *political representation*" (102; emphasis added; see also Epstein, *Radical Expression* 27). Because social problems were the result of the "monopoly" of political power by particular constituencies that promoted their own interests, the solution was the acquisition of the franchise and parliamentary representation by legitimate interests that had been excluded from political power.

Consequently, radical discourse in the early nineteenth century made political reform the means to achieve social reform of all kinds.

Proponents made the case for the Reform Bill by arguing that it was needed to provide social agency to a "new social constituency," the middle class, which required parliamentary representation because its interests were distinct from those of enfranchised landowners (Wahrman 267; see also 306, 328). This rhetoric enabled Thomas Macaulay to claim that the Reform Bill would "repair and modify, not . . . destroy and reconstruct, our political institutions" and that the new constituency it would create wanted "Reform," not "revolution" (quoted in Wahrman 309). Opponents did not challenge the idea that a constituency with interests distinct from those of the aristocracy deserved parliamentary representation but instead argued variously that no new constituency existed, that it was already well represented, or that the bill would enfranchise individuals who did not belong to it.

This construction of reform in terms of class shaped the way the Chartists employed constitutionalist discourse to argue for universal male suffrage (see Vernon, *Politics* 301). They persistently argued that the problems of the disenfranchised people could be traced to "class legislation" enacted by the enfranchised elite.[9] The parliamentary elites responded to these Chartist claims by contending that the people were not a constituency requiring representation and that they were incapable of exercising social agency responsibly — in short, that they did not seek constitutional reform but revolution.

As their origin in political debate makes clear, the discourses of class that emerged in the Reform Bill debates and Chartism were political rather than socioeconomic. Class became central not because the rise of capitalism produced the middle and working classes but because Reform Bill discourse made classes the privileged agents who exercised the privileged agency of the franchise. As Dror Wahrman concludes, "The triumph of the 'middle class,' then, was achieved less in the Reform Act itself than in its immediate aftermath; and it had to do less with people's choice of parliamentary representatives than with people's choice of representations of society with which they framed their mental vision of the world" (333). In other words, we need to distinguish the discourse of class the Victorians employed to explain and debate the problems and conflicts that arose from the material stratification of society from the actual material conditions of that society. What matters for the purposes of this study is that the discourse of class became the means through which individuals and groups understood and sought to respond to those conditions.[10]

As David Cannadine points out, while depictions of society divided into ranks or classes had long been in existence, in the aftermath of the Reform Bill "these visions of society were . . . more consciously and contentiously politicized than before" (60). Even though the majority of Whigs belonged to the landed aristocracy, they became, during the Reform Bill debates, advocates of the "middle class" (see Wahrman 306; Cannadine 75–79), while the Tories in turn depicted themselves as advocates for landed property. This was a matter not merely of the parties allying themselves with social classes but of parties using the discourse of class as a means of conducting political debate and advancing political objectives. Consequently, the Chartists opposed the upper classes not as the possessors of industrial capital but as the monopolizers of parliamentary power. As Stedman Jones puts it, they saw class conflict in terms not of "employer and employed" but of "the represented and the unrepresented" (106; see also *Northern Star* 28 July 1838: 3). When, for example, the Chartist London Democratic Association contended that "the masses are socially—because they are politically slaves," they meant that economic exploitation results from the lack of political power (*Northern Star* 13 Oct. 1838: 3).

In the post–Reform Bill era two forms of political discourse—parliamentary and Chartist—developed, each of which defined a field of class contestation and hence of the social agents who took part in this conflict. In accord with the arguments that prevailed in the passage of the Reform Bill, parliamentary discourse defined a contest between the aristocracy and middle class over which could best govern the nation and which, therefore, should control Parliament. While each class discourse constructed a different picture of itself and the opposing class, the two together formed a single discursive field because both shared the assumption that only these two classes could possess social agency. Chartist discourse contested the latter assumption and construed class conflict in terms of the opposition of the enfranchised and disenfranchised. The question in this case was whether those currently enfranchised should act on behalf of the disenfranchised or all adult males should be enfranchised so they could act for themselves. In keeping with the constitutional idiom, however, the two discourses concurred in defining agency in terms of the franchise and parliamentary legislation.

Both parliamentary and Chartist discourse depicted class conflict as a conflict between opposing political interests. Earlier in the century, political discourse had envisioned the constitution as balancing the various interests of the nation (Wahrman 90–96). After passage of the Reform Bill, however, political discourse depicted class interest as the pursuit of self-interest at the expense of the interests of others and thus at odds with the responsible exercise of social agency. In its characteristic form, this discourse defines the conflict between classes—the aristocracy and middle class on the one hand, the enfranchised and the disenfranchised on the other—by depicting the political opposition as pursuing class interests while claiming that the class for which it speaks does not act for its own interest but disinterestedly for the interests of the nation as a whole. In this way, those who possessed political power sought to legitimate their right to exercise social agency and to deny it to others. The enfranchised elites claimed that they did not possess power merely because of their wealth or status in itself but because wealth and status enabled them to act disinterestedly. While parliamentary discourse used these standards to construct either the aristocracy or the middle class as deserving privileged social agency, Chartist discourse made the claim that the elites were not disinterested on the one hand and that the working classes did possess the capacity for disinterestedness on the other.

Parliamentary discourse defined the possession of disinterested agency, and thus which party or class should control Parliament, through forms of property. The right to exercise the franchise was, of course, defined by property ownership, the rationale for the property qualification being, as Blackstone had explained, that property owners are "individuals, whose wills may be supposed independent" and therefore are "free agent[s]," whereas those who do not own property "are esteemed to have no will of their own" because they are "under the immediate dominion of others."[11] In order to legitimate the Reform Bill, its proponents had defined the middle class as a new group of property owners whose property consisted of liquid capital rather than landed estates.[12] While these arguments suggested that both the aristocracy and the middle class as property owners are free agents who can be trusted to exercise the franchise responsibly, the assumption that the interests of one group of property owners were distinct from those of the other opened up the possibility that each would exercise agency to its own advantage and not for the good of the nation as a whole.

Consequently, parliamentary discourse articulated the claims of the aristocracy and the middle class in terms of their particular forms of property ownership. Middle-class discourse, drawing on earlier criticisms of "old corruption" (Vernon, *Politics* 305), depicted an idle aristocracy that pursues its self-interest by exploiting family influence and social status obtained as inherited property rather than as property acquired through one's own efforts. By contrast, the entrepreneur disinterestedly achieves his status through self-culture and merit, a path open not to a select few but to all. Aristocratic discourse countered this rhetoric by portraying the entrepreneur as ruthlessly pursuing profits in the marketplace, his self-making nothing more than the pursuit of self-interest. Landowners, it claimed, were not idle but leisured and so possessed the detachment to cultivate a disinterested moral sensibility untainted by the marketplace (Vernon, *Politics* 304).[13]

Even as they sought to distinguish between forms of property and the attendant right to legislate, the parliamentary parties agreed that those who did not own property could not be trusted with the franchise. Indeed, the property qualification provisions of the Reform Bill had served not only to define a new middle class (Wahrman 332–33) but also to exclude the lower classes (Vernon, *Politics* 305). The Chartists did not challenge the principle of the property qualification but instead sought to redefine it by claiming property in their own labor (Stedman Jones 109–10; Vernon, *Politics* 312). Just as the need to protect one's land or capital gives one an interest in the rule of law, so too, they argued, the working classes need to protect their ability to obtain a just compensation for their labor. In other words, their interests were distinct from and could not be served by the Whigs and Tories, who promoted the interests of the middle class and the aristocracy. Contrary to the principle of propertied disinterest, they insisted, the Whigs and Tories promoted "class interests" through "class legislation." As the National Petition itself put it, because "the few have governed for the interest of the few," the "interests of the people" must be "confided to the keeping of the people" (reported in *Times* 18 Sept. 1838: 6). In opposition to this argument, the Whigs and Tories, invoking Blackstone, united in claiming that only property owners had an interest in maintaining the laws and thus the interests of the nation as a whole, while the propertyless working class did not possess "free agency" and would only pursue their short-term self-interest (*Times* 29 Dec. 1842: 4). As we see in chapter 2, this claim soon modulated into an argument that the lower classes lacked the rational capacity to exercise social agency disinterestedly.

We can observe the operation of these two fields of discourse in the debates about the Corn Laws and the New Poor Law that were so prominent in this era. The Whigs alleged that the Tories supported the Corn Laws because they benefitted the landed aristocracy, while the Tories alleged that the Anti–Corn Law League aimed not to lower the price of bread for the sake of the lower classes but rather to reduce demands for wage increases. The Tories responded to claims that the Corn Laws harmed the poor by attacking the Whigs' New Poor Law, and the Whigs in turn replied that the Tory critique had little to do with concern for the poor but was prompted by its own party interest. Both parties solicited the support of the Chartists in opposition to these laws, but in spite of the fact that they did favor their repeal, the Chartists rebuffed these appeals because they regarded them merely as attempts on the part of the aristocracy and middle class to protect their own interests. They argued, rather, that they alone could protect their own interests, that obtaining the franchise "would enable them," as the Chartist leader Henry Vincent put it, "to destroy the corn-law and every other bad law" (*Examiner* 30 Oct. 1841: 696).

These discourses constructed narratives that envision class conflict giving way to a more harmonious social order through a particular class's disinterested exercise of social agency. These narratives rewrote in terms of class the constitutional histories that were a key element of constitutionalist discourse (Vernon, *Politics* 298; Epstein, *Radical Expression* 27). Not only did various groups use these histories to legitimate their claims to political inclusion and power, but they also used them to envision a future in which they would "transcend class identities in the wider interest of the nation" (Vernon, *Politics* 325). This transcendence of class does not mean eliminating class divisions (at least not initially) but the establishment of a particular class structure or model in which the classes no longer come into conflict. Consequently, these narratives imagine a future in which the privileged social agency of one class fashions a new class structure in which it can operate disinterestedly.

The dominant narrative of the rise of the middle class adapted the Whig constitutional narrative of the restoration of rights lost at the time of the Norman Conquest, a process it depicts as beginning with the Glorious Revolution and reaching completion with the Reform Bill (Vernon, *Politics* 304). On the one hand, this narrative privileges a tripartite model of class in which an emergent class takes its place in the middle between the upper and lower classes. On the other hand, the narrative of what Wahrman calls the "ever-rising" middle class depicts it as continuously gaining power until it ultimately displaces the aristocracy (chap. 10). In this respect, it moves toward a model of class in which the middle class governs the lower classes. However, in its utopian form, this narrative imagines a future in which class divisions disappear as everyone becomes middle class by adopting the ethos of self-making.

Aristocratic constitutional histories depicted the Glorious Revolution and the reform movement as disrupting the traditional hierarchical order to which it sought to return (Vernon, *Politics* 298–303). Translated into class discourse, this narrative depicts the rise of the middle class as splintering into conflicting classes a harmonious society that had been organized as a finely graded hierarchy. We can see a version of this narrative in Catherine Gore's *The Hamiltons; or, Official Life in 1830* (1834), in which the town of Laxington, which had once been of "one mind" and so was content to allow Lord Tottenham "to take the trouble of thinking and acting off [its] hands, by finding gentlemen to sit in parliament, and think and act *for* [it]," becomes divided between adherents of the Whigs and the Tories (52.355, 353). As the older term *station* suggests, the model of finely graded hierarchy envisions not a society organized in terms of classes with conflicting interests but rather a social order in which the aristocracy and members of various social stations are knit together through a system of deference and obligation (see Cannadine 51, 64–65). In envisioning a future in which this hierarchy is restored, these narratives simultaneously depict the conferral of privileged social agency on the aristocracy and the elimination of the class divisions in the tripartite model of class, with the middle and working class classes dispersed into a variety of social stations.

Radical discourse, employing the myth of the Norman yoke, depicted the Glorious Revolution and the Reform Bill as minor adjustments in the constitution that did not address the fundamental problem that the liberties of the people had been lost during the Norman Conquest (Vernon, *Politics* 312–19). Consequently, radical narratives depicted the continuing existence of a dichotomous class structure divided between the enfranchised elite and the disenfranchised "people" and a future in which class conflict ends because the people possess the franchise (Cannadine 67).[14] Like middle-class and aristocratic discourse, however, even as it envisions a people comprising all (male) citizens—the nation as a whole—it privileges the social agency of the formerly disenfranchised working classes and defines "the people" as the working classes.

In sum, these narratives seek to envision the end not so much of class as of class conflict. They do so by privileging the social agency of one particular class that will govern disinterestedly on behalf of the nation as a whole. However, this class cannot achieve this privileged status unless the social order is reformed. Thus in order to fulfill their utopian aims, these narratives link the triumph of a particular class with changes in class structure that enable them to act disinterestedly.

These changes in the composition of the social agent coincided with but did not dictate experiments with alternative forms of action. From the beginning, the Chartists were compelled to develop alternatives to the franchise, precisely because they did not possess it. Even as they sought to work within the constitutional framework by employing "moral force" to persuade Parliament to enact universal suffrage, circumstances led them to countenance the use of "physical force." While the possibility of using physical force arose repeatedly throughout the history of Chartism, debates about its use were especially prominent between 1838 and 1842. After the rejection of the petition of 1842, the Chartists shifted their focus, seeking to achieve acceptance of the Charter through the Land Plan, which, while still aiming to obtain the franchise, began to formulate an alternative conception of agency in terms of economic reform. In 1848, with the rejection of the third petition and the collapse of the Land Plan, radicals further developed this reconception of agency by taking a "social turn" in which they sought to intervene in the social sphere through cooperative associations and trade unionism. As with the campaign for universal suffrage, the Chartists developed these projects in dialogue with the elites, who developed their own plans for land reform and cooperation, the projects of each tailored to their conception of the social agent.

While Victorian novels for the most part did not intervene directly in these debates, they employed parliamentary and Chartist discourses in order to envision new forms of social agency. Although they employed these discourses in their representations of the social order, they did not merely reproduce the forms of social agency constructed by them. Just as parliamentary and Chartist discourse each adapted elements of opposition discourse—parliamentary discourse, for example, adopting and reframing the Chartist term *class legislation*—Victorian novels imagined alternative social agents and forms of action through dialogic use of parliamentary and Chartist discourse.[15]

IMAGINING AGENCY THROUGH THE
NATIONAL MARRIAGE PLOT

These novels envisioned new social agents by revising the national marriage plot of the national tale and the historical novel, transforming it from a narrative of conflict and resolution between nations and cultures into a narrative of conflict and resolution between classes.[16] The constitutional histories discussed above developed in tandem, and probably in dialogue, with the national tale and historical novel. Just as constitutional histories depicted a present in which society is divided between conflicting classes and a future in which those conflicts are resolved, so national tales such as Sydney Owenson's *Wild Irish Girl* (1806) and historical novels such as Walter Scott's *Waverley* (1814) resolve conflicts between cultures—between the English metropole and the Celtic periphery—through "a wedding that allegorically unites Britain's [Celtic and English] 'national characters'" (Trumpener 141; see also Ferris 48).[17] Following passage of the Reform Bill, novelists translated culture and ethnicity into class, so that the opposed nations of Disraeli's *Sybil; or, The Two Nations*, for example, are no longer England and Ireland but the "rich and the poor." Similarly, even as the title and structure of Gaskell's *North and South*, like national tales and historical novels, "spatializ[e] political choices" (Trumpener 138), it locates these spaces within England and links them to class—in this case the southern gentry and the industrial middle class—rather than to ethnicity.[18]

The marriage plots of these novels are able to imagine the resolution of conflict because they invoke the companionate model of marriage. The Irish national tale was a response to the Acts of Union (1801), which subordinated Ireland to England. The power differential in this union, as in the earlier union of Scotland and England (1707), characteristically manifests itself in these narratives through the gendering of the metropole as male (Horatio or Edward Waverley) and the periphery as female (Glorvina or Rose Bradwardine). The marriage plot thus represents a union that, in terms of contemporary law and cultural practice, involves the subordination of the female/other to the male/metropole. In this respect, these novels would seem merely to affirm the subordination of the periphery to the metropole. However, as Mary Jean Corbett points out, while such "family thinking can imply hierarchy and naturalize gender inequality," it may "also chart relations of intimacy" (3; see also 53–54). More particularly, the companionate marriage ideal assumes an equality between male and female that is essential to envisioning the union as achieving the resolution of conflict.[19]

The novels that I discuss—like most Victorian novels—not only depict resolution through companionate marriage but also trace the conflict requiring resolution to attempts to promote kinship marriage.[20] They depict kinship unions as hierarchical and patriarchal, exterior to the individual, and coercive, in contrast to companionate marriages, which are egalitarian, unite interiorities, and involve free choice. Characteristically, they portray a situation in which kin, most often a parent or guardian, promote a marriage as a means of obtaining or preserving wealth and status, while the hero and heroine seek to form a union on the basis of affection that arises from the encounter between two interiorities. Precisely because the hero/heroine seeks a companionate union, those promoting a kinship marriage often resort to psychological and even physical force that subordinates the marriage partners, most often the female marriage partner, to the kin as well as to the partner. By contrast, the fact that the partners recognize one another as equal interiorities enables them to enter freely into companionate marriage.

While there are many variants of this plot and the ways that novels map it onto social conflict, their resolutions consistently hinge on the premise that the companionate marriage accords agency to both partners. If, on the one hand, the gendering of the metropole and the periphery in national tales and historical novels implies the subordination of the latter to the former, on the other hand, the depiction of the marriage as companionate implies that both partners freely act on the basis of their interior convictions and thus are equal to one another. When Victorian novelists adapted these narratives to the depiction of class conflict, they similarly employed the companionate union as a means of envisioning new possibilities for social agency. Moreover, many of these novels associate kinship marriage with a homosocial rivalry and companionate marriage with the formation of a homosocial bond between men from different classes.

In the years following passage of the Reform Bill, novelists depicted the displacement of the kinship by the companionate ideal as a transition from the archaic to the modern. As Trumpener has shown, Scott transformed the national tale into the historical novel by emphasizing the distinction, already implicit in the national tale, between the archaic periphery and the modern metropole (142–48). In novels like *Waverley* (1814) and *Ivanhoe* (1820), he constructs marriages that join the virtues of an outmoded archaic culture with those of the modern culture that must inevitably displace it.[21] In the 1830s and 1840s, novelists adapted this narrative structure to the dominant rise-of-the-middle-class narrative by depicting an archaic aristocracy that adheres to the kinship ideal being displaced by a modernizing middle class that embraces the companionate model of marriage. These novels correspondingly depict the aristocracy as promoting kinship unions as a means of maintaining political power that in turn sustains their wealth and status, while their protagonists, by contrast, embrace the entrepreneurial ideal of self-making and adopt the corresponding companionate ideal.

However, just as various constituencies constructed constitutional histories that rewrote the myth of the Norman yoke, so novelists could construct narratives in which the displacement of kinship by companionate unions served to envision a range of different possible social agents. Benjamin Disraeli employed such a narrative to depict the reform rather than displacement of the aristocracy, while Thomas Martin Wheeler inverted the Disraelian narrative by depicting the rise of the middle class as merely producing a new form of aristocracy. Even novels that affirmed the rise of the middle class worked variations on this narrative, such reframings in each case serving to envision alternative configurations of class and possibilities of social agency.

These national marriage plots draw on parliamentary and Chartist discourse not only to envision changes in social agents through changes in class structures but also, through the ways they position these plots in relation to Chartist discourse, to envision changes in the kinds of actions that constitute social agency. As discussed above, the Chartists were from the beginning forced to consider alternative forms of social agency to supplement the franchise that they did not yet possess. Consequently, by the end of the 1840s, the slogan "The Charter and nothing less" became "The Charter and something more" (Chase, *Chartism* 336). The fact that the Reform Bill did not produce substantial social reform led many even among the upper classes to conclude that the conception of social agency in terms of the franchise was too restrictive. Thomas Carlyle, whose influence on Victorian novelists was broad and deep, contended that Chartism arose from a legitimate feeling of injustice but challenged the assumption that gaining parliamentary representation would bring about reform by accusing Parliament of "Donothingism" and dismissing the "right to vote for a Member of Parliament" as merely the ability "to send one's 'twenty-thousandth part of a master of tongue-fence to National Palaver'" ("Chartism" 7.167, 9.187). While many novelists followed him in this view of Parliament, they did not adopt his solutions but instead used their narratives to envision a range of possible forms of agency.

⁓

Each of the three parts of this study focuses on a major conception of action employed by the Chartists. Part 1 is concerned with the first phase of Chartism, from its beginnings in 1838, through the presentation of the first Chartist petition in 1839, to the presentation of the second petition in 1842, a period dominated by debates about the use of moral versus physical force. Part 2 focuses on the period between 1842 and 1848, which was dominated by the Chartist Land Plan. Part 3 deals with the era following the rejection of the third Chartist petition in 1848 and the collapse soon thereafter of the Land Plan, when many Chartists, embracing the "social turn," shifted their emphasis to cooperative associations and trade unionism. The coda moves forward to the passage of the Second Reform Act in 1867.

Each part begins with a chapter in which I discuss the dialogic development of discourses of social agency. Chapter 2 examines how the press representing the parliamentary parties contended that working-class agency is inevitably violent and thus illegitimate and the Chartist press legitimated Chartist agency by moralizing physical force. Chapter 6 is concerned with how proponents of the Chartist Land Plan, of Young England's land allotment schemes, and of the agricultural improvements of the Royal Agricultural Society of England (founded in 1838) took up traditional discourses linking the franchise, and thus agency, to the land, while also using these schemes to envision alternatives to the franchise. Chapter 10 examines the relocation of agency to dialogue between the professional intellectual elite (in particular the clergy) and Chartists envisioned as cooperative association and between manufacturers and laborers in trade unionism.

The ensuing chapters in each part examine how novels use these discursive fields to construct national narratives envisioning new social agents and forms of agency. Pierce Egan's *Wat Tyler* (1841) and Thomas Martin Wheeler's *Sunshine and Shadow* (1849–1850) attempt to envision the process by which the working classes achieve social agency, in the former through moralized physical force and in the latter in relation to the Land Plan. Harrison Ainsworth in *Guy Fawkes* (1841) and Charles Dickens in *Barnaby Rudge* (1841) adopt the dominant narrative of the rise of the middle class, with Ainsworth focusing on the problem of moralizing physical force and Dickens on self-culture as an alternative form of agency. Similarly, Benjamin Disraeli in *Coningsby* (1844) and *Sybil* (1845) and R. S. Surtees in *Hillingdon Hall* (1843–1844) envision social agency in terms of a finely graded hierarchy, the former through the paternalist model of Young England and the landed estate and the latter through a squirearchy committed to agricultural reform. Finally, Charles Kingsley in *Yeast* (1848) and *Alton Locke* (1850) and Elizabeth Gaskell in *Mary Barton* (1848) and *North and South* (1854–1855) envision dialogue between the working classes and governing elites, the former depicting a Christian socialism based on cooperation between clergy and workingmen and the latter depicting a reformed trade unionism. In the coda, I take up two novels—William Howitt's *Man of the People* (1860) and George Eliot's *Felix Holt: The Radical* (1866)—that, during the agitation for the Second Reform Act, look back to the era of the first; there I examine how the construction of agency as self-culture takes us back to the debates about revolution versus reform with which this study begins.

Although the three parts of this study proceed chronologically, they do not trace a linear progression or define a teleological development toward some ultimately successful form of social agency. Nor do I mean to suggest that the forms of agency on which I focus were the only ones available during this era. My aim is not to discover *the* Victorian conception of social agency but to write a history of the various ways in which the Victorians engaged with questions about how to effect social change. By exploring how they envisioned such change as reform rather than revolution, I also hope to recover an understanding of the possibilities for social agency in our own time.

PART I

Making Physical Force Moral

The Dilemma of Chartism, 1838–1842

Social Agency in the Chartist and Parliamentary Press

In 1839, during the lead-up to the first Chartist convention, the *Northern Liberator* published *The Political Pilgrim's Progress*, which retold Bunyan's popular allegory as the story of how Radical flees the City of Plunder and journeys to the City of Reform, passing along the way through Vanity Fair, in which newspapers touting their "independence" and claiming to "labour . . . only for the happiness of the people" are in fact "the property of political partizans" belonging to the ruling elites (44–45).[1] This allegory manifests the Chartists' awareness that the elite press sought to define political participation and social agency in ways that confined it to the enfranchised parliamentary parties, each of which sought to turn the rise of Chartism to its own advantage. The Chartist press in turn developed a rhetoric that opposed this parliamentary discourse, as we can see in the inaugural issue of the *Charter*, which asserted that it aimed to counter an elite press that was almost as responsible for the state of the working class as Parliament itself (27 Jan. 1839: 1). To understand how Chartist and parliamentary discourses conceived social agency, therefore, we must examine how each dialogically reframes the other in order to define both social agents and forms of social action.[2]

From 1838 to 1848, this rhetorical contest between the Chartist and the parliamentary press centered on the question of whether the Chartists would achieve their aims through moral or physical force. The Chartists' campaign for parliamentary reform required them to confront a paradoxical dilemma. Both the parliamentary and the Chartist press understood social agency in terms of the capacity to enact legislation that benefits the entire nation. On the one hand, therefore, the Chartist campaign focused on obtaining the right to elect legislators by obtaining universal suffrage. On the other hand, this conception of social agency dictated that they must obtain this right by an act of Parliament, but so long as they did not have representation in Parliament, it was not likely to grant it to them. In other words, they lacked the form of agency—the franchise and parliamentary representation—that would enable them to obtain social agency. Consequently, almost from the beginning they considered the use of "ulterior measures"—a repertoire of supplementary forms of action including mass demonstrations, strikes, and boycotts—through which they sought to pressure Parliament to enact the Charter. This led to a debate among Chartists about whether they could legitimately employ not only moral-force suasion but also physical-force tactics, possibly even armed insurrection, to obtain what they regarded as their constitutional right.

In this chapter, I examine how Chartist and parliamentary discourses sought to envision social agency in terms of this moral- versus physical-force dilemma. The principal aim of Chartism—obtaining universal suffrage—accorded with the dominant nineteenth-century conception of social agency, but through their use of ulterior measures, including physical force, the Chartists began to develop alternative conceptions of social agency. The events of 1839 and 1842 revealed that physical force was no more effective than moral force, but until 1842 the Chartists sought to legitimate these supplemental forms of agency by moralizing physical force. As the popular slogan "peacably if we can, and forcibly if we must" suggests, they sought to portray their actions as moral by reserving the use of violence until the moment when the resources of moral force had been exhausted (e.g., *Northern Star* 6 Apr. 1839: 6).

To situate my analysis of these discourses, I begin with a brief overview of Chartism from its beginnings in 1838 to the aftermath of the rejection of the second Chartist petition in 1842. I then proceed to examine how Chartist and parliamentary discourses constructed their versions of legitimate social agents by privileging particular models of class, which they in turn depicted in terms of class interest and the capacity for disinterest. The chapter concludes with a discussion of how these discourses envision the actions of social agents in terms of the moral- versus physical-force debate.

In 1841, when Dickens, Ainsworth, and Egan published the novels I discuss in the next three chapters, the first phase of the Chartist movement had passed, and a second was in the making. The movement had taken off in the autumn of 1838 with a series of mass demonstrations culminating in the meeting of the National Convention in the spring of 1839 and the presentation of the National Petition to Parliament on June 14 of that year. When, as the leadership anticipated, Parliament voted, on July 12, not to take the petition under consideration, riots broke out in Birmingham. The Chartist leadership called a national strike for August 12 but, unsure of its success, subsequently canceled it. That November a small group of Chartists in the Welsh town of Newport attempted an armed uprising that the authorities quickly suppressed. The Chartists had begun the year with considerable optimism that their efforts would have the same success as the agitations for reform in 1832, but by the end of 1839 the movement was in disarray, with many of its leaders in jail on charges of rioting, sedition, or treason.

The movement began to regain momentum when the economy slipped into recession in 1841. The following year, the Chartists brought forward a second National Petition, which on May 3 was roundly rejected by Parliament. That summer, labor unrest spread from the mining country to the industrial midlands. In August, striking workers in Manchester and the surrounding region marched from factory to factory, urging fellow workers to go on strike, breaking windows, and, in a few cases, looting provision shops. Although the Chartists did not initiate the strikes, they soon joined in and sought to persuade striking workers that making the "Charter . . . the law of the land" was the best means of attaining their goal of a "fair day's wage for a fair day's work" (Chase, *Chartism* 214). As with the Newport uprising, however, the government responded by sending troops, and by the end of August most of the strikers had returned to work. That neither the Newport uprising nor the Manchester strikes represented a concerted, organized insurrection together with the fact that both events demonstrated the superior armed strength of the government made clear from this time forward that the Chartists were not likely to gain their ends by physical force, but until 1842 it remained a key element of their rhetoric and, in turn, of parliamentary discourse.

⌒

Both Chartist and parliamentary discourse sought to reframe discourses of class in order to define a particular class as a social actor possessing the capacity to act for the good of the nation as a whole. In order to do so, these discourses of class employed an existing language that defined classes as groups of individuals with shared interests and in turn defined a class that acts for the nation as a whole as disinterested. As we have seen in chapter 1, these discourses privileged competing models of class as a means of defining a particular class as possessing the capacity for disinterest and thus the capacity to exercise social agency.

Because the Chartists and the parliamentarians were responding to one another and because parliamentary discourse ultimately was concerned with the contest for political power between parliamentary parties, each at times employed the class models of its opposition, reframing them to construct their own privileged model of the social agent. As Dror Wahrman has demonstrated, because the purported rise of the middle class legitimated the Reform Bill, parliamentary discourse in the years following its passage employed the tripartite model of class, depicting the question of which party should govern the people as a contest between the aristocracy and middle class. Chartist discourse reframed the tripartite model as a means of contending that neither Tories nor Whigs—neither aristocracy nor middle class—were disinterested, and it set forth a dichotomous model opposing the enfranchised elites, who sought to protect their class interests, to the people, who served as a proxy for the nation as a whole.

In response to Chartism, parliamentary discourse reframed the dichotomous model of class by employing the principle of virtual representation to invert its depiction of the people as disinterested and the elites as self-interested. The Tories, reviving the argument they had made during the Reform Bill debates, argued that their status as property owners endowed them with disinterestedness that enabled them to act on behalf of those who do not own property.[3] The *Times*, for example, contended that whereas previous alterations of the "representative system" had been made on the "principle . . . of securing and obtaining for the State the free voice and opinion, in things political, of every one qualified for and capable of the exercise of *free agency*," universal suffrage would produce a "polity of the savage tribe which votes man by man" (29 Dec. 1842: 4; emphasis added). While the Whigs rejected virtual representation in name, they nonetheless made a similar claim to govern on behalf of the working classes, merely expanding the concept of property to include capital as well as land.[4] For example, the *Morning Chronicle* (quoting the *Scotsman*) claimed that the aim of the Reform Bill was to produce a legislature that was "limited in numbers, but large enough to embrace the interest of all classes" and so to "put the franchise into the hands of those who are most intelligent and most deeply interested in the general weal. . . . If the electoral body is so composed as not to be the organ of any special interest, but to embrace all interests, the Legislature chosen by it will watch over the good of the whole people as faithfully and as impartially as if it had been returned by the suffrages of all the grown men in the kingdom" (5 Sept. 1838: 3). Elsewhere, they contended, like the Tories, that the Chartists were incapable of such disinterestedness and that, if given the vote, they would "exercise the privilege to the ruin of our best interests" (*Morning Chronicle* 1 Sept. 1838: 2).[5]

In keeping with their contention that they would govern in the interest of the nation as a whole, each of the parliamentary parties responded to Chartism by employing an idealized model of the social order under its governance. As I discuss in chapter 1, the Tories envisioned a "return" to a finely graded hierarchy in which people are not divided into opposing classes but knit together in a harmonious whole through the agency of a benign patriarch. The *Times* for example suggested that the Tories would restore the "old English system" of a hierarchy that aimed to "*govern* the working classes, and to *take care of them*" (*Times* 29 Dec. 1840: 4). In keeping with the rhetoric of virtual representation, they would achieve this social harmony precisely by privileging within this structure an aristocracy that would paternalistically act on behalf of those beneath it.

The Whigs employed the tripartite model in a similar fashion to project a future in which the middle class displaces an outmoded aristocracy and members of the working class earn their way into the middle class. Once again, however, even as class harmony results from the merging of all classes into a single class, the Whigs would achieve this end through the leadership of the middle class. The *London and Westminster Review*, for example, argued that "the motto of a Radical politician should be, Government by means of the middle for the working classes" (quoted in *Examiner* 7 Apr. 1839: 193). In this way, both parties paradoxically envisioned an end to class conflict being achieved when one class—the aristocracy or middle class—gains social dominance, and both depicted the classes vying for political control as acting on behalf of a working class that they insist cannot act for itself, let alone for the nation as a whole.

In their claims that they could better govern the nation, however, the parties depicted the opposition as no more capable of acting disinterestedly than the Chartists. Whereas in relation to Chartism they employed a dichotomous model of the propertied versus the poor, in this contest for power within Parliament the Whigs and Tories employed the tripartite model in which each claimed it would govern disinterestedly and blamed the Chartists' contention that their interests were not represented in Parliament on the fact that the opposition acted in the interest of a class. The *Morning Post*, for example, contended that Chartism had arisen because the "mass of the working people . . . have seen through the fraud intended to be practised upon them" by the "greedy manufacturing capitalists" who sought repeal of the Corn Laws not, as they claimed, for the sake of the poor but to protect their own "selfish" interests (14 Jan. 1839: 4); elsewhere it insisted that the opposition press incited the working classes to "insurrectionary violence" to "benefit a certain class of manufacturers" but that the "interests of millions of the labouring people are bound up with the interests of the owners of land" (20 Dec. 1839: 2). Correspondingly, the *Morning Chronicle* alleged that Chartism had arisen because "landowners," who "benefit" personally from the Corn Laws, are "utterly regardless of all but their own selfish advantage" and that the Tories were promoting the "sinister interest of a class" over the "well-being of a nation" (27 Nov. 1838: 2, 25 Nov. 1841: 2; see also 3 Jan. 1840: 2).

〜

Chartist discourse exploited these allegations of self-interest by employing the tripartite model of class to depict the parties as "factions" acting for interested classes rather than virtually representing the nation as a whole.[6] At the Manchester demonstration of September 24, 1838, the radical MP John Fielden challenged the principle of virtual representation, contending that "virtual representation was no representation at all, because [the Chartists] had no control over the individuals who were returned."[7] A *Northern Star* editorial similarly rejected the related idea that the House of Commons is a "miniature of public opinion," arguing instead that MPs represent "orders" that are "opposed to the interest of the people" (1 Sept. 1838: 4). As the Chartist petition itself put it, "The few have governed for the interest of the few; while the interest of the many has been sottishly neglected" (*Northern Star* 16 June 1838: 3).[8]

While the Chartists employed the tripartite model in order to depict the Whigs and Tories as factions protecting their own interests, when asserting the consequent need for the working classes to protect their own interests, they privileged a dichotomous model in which society is "divided" into "two classes," the "classes of non-elective influence and elective power" (*Northern Star* 13 Oct. 1838: 4). Thus a typical editorial in the *Northern Star* began with the tripartite model, distinguishing between the moneyed and landed interests, but then went on to merge them and produce a dichotomous opposition between the "represented classes" and the "unrepresented class" (28 July 1838: 3). In this context, they did not distinguish between aristocracy and middle class, instead collapsing them into variants of a single class that possesses the franchise (*Northern Star* 8 Sept. 1838: 8, William Lovett as reported in 22 Sept. 1838: 3). In keeping with the radical tradition that critiqued the aristocracy as "old corruption" (Stedman Jones 121), Chartist discourse in effect denied the emergence of a new middle class and depicted it merely as an expansion of the aristocracy. To this end, the Chartist press deployed a range of terms—*aristocracy* and *millocracy*, "landlords and the fundlords," "landed aristocracy" and "steam aristocracy"—portraying the landed and commercial interests as "rival aristocracies" that are ultimately "one flesh" (*Northern Star* 14 May 1842: 1, 16 Mar. 1839: 3, 7 Apr. 1838: 3).[9]

Consequently, a key element of Chartist discourse was the further reframing of the parliamentary language of interests in terms of the language of class by portraying the Whigs and Tories as acting for class interests in order to promote "class legislation—the representation of exclusive interests in the House of Commons" (*Charter* 28 Apr. 1839: 209).[10] The term "class legislation," which appeared with great frequency in Chartist discourse, links the older language of interests to the new language of class through which, in the post–Reform Bill era, parliamentary discourse depicted the contention for power between the Tories and Whigs.[11] While the language of interests had a long history, this application of it in terms of class—as manifested in the dichotomy of the "represented classes" and the "unrepresented class" cited above—was new. The Whigs and Tories had referred to the commercial or industrial interests on the one hand and the landed or agricultural interests on the other. However, the Chartists insisted that particular economic interests did not matter so much as the fact that both the Whigs and Tories had a political interest in the continued disenfranchisement of the working classes. Thus, as we have seen, the Chartists rejected the attempts of both the Whigs and Tories to appeal to their economic interest by seeking to unite with them in support of repeal, respectively, of the Corn Laws and the New Poor Law. The parliamentary parties supported repeal in each instance, the Chartists contended, not because they intended to act for the people but to gain the upper hand over the opposition. This meant that the only way to ensure that changes in the law would serve the interests of the people was for the people to have their own representatives in Parliament (e.g., *Northern Star* 2 Feb. 1839: 4, 9 Mar. 1839: 4). As Feargus O'Connor put it, "Universal Suffrage" is "the only remedy for all [our] grievances" (*Northern Star* 11 Aug. 1838: 7).[12]

Just as the parliamentary parties claimed to act on behalf of all classes even as they privileged a particular class that would create a classless future, so the Chartists envisioned the "people" both as a privileged class—those currently disenfranchised—and as the nation as a whole.[13] Like parliamentary discourse, Chartist discourse contended that the "interests" of the working classes "are identified with the general interests of the whole" and that once the people gained possession of the franchise, they would not enact class legislation but would act for "the good of all" (*Charter* 5 May 1839: 230; *Northern Star* 17 Feb. 1838: 5; see also *Northern Star* 16 June 1838: 3). While aristocratic discourse envisioned a hierarchy without "class" and middle-class discourse the displacement of aristocracy and absorption of the working classes, Chartist discourse envisioned the elimination of class through the eventual congruence between the people and the nation. As the *Northern Star* argued, whereas "all agitations till the present one have been for class distinction, . . . our principles tend to destroy all class distinction" (7 Sept. 1839: 4). The utopian dimension of this argument comes across clearly in the *Star*'s claim that "laws, made by all, would be respected by all" and that "Universal Suffrage would, at once, change the whole character of society from a state of watchfulness, doubt, and suspicion, to that of brotherly love, reciprocal interest, and universal confidence" (17 Feb. 1838: 5). From the Chartist perspective, universal suffrage would ensure protection not only of the interests of those currently excluded from the franchise but also those of the nation as a whole.

೧

In response to the Chartist claims that the parliamentary parties enacted class legislation and that the working classes must therefore act for themselves, parliamentary discourse constructed the disenfranchised lower classes as incapable of acting as a class that protects its own interests or of virtually representing other classes and acting disinterestedly. This discourse underwrote its claims of disinterestedness and virtual representation by contending that property ownership alone enables one to act rationally on behalf of the nation as a whole. The *Scotsman* editorial cited above argued that it "would be absurd to deny that the man who has accumulated a hundred pounds—whether in money, land, goods, or household furniture—has a greater stake in the well-being of society than the wayfarer or 'landless resolute,' who relies solely on the day's labour for the day's subsistence" (quoted in *Morning Chronicle* 5 Sept. 1838: 3). The *Times* similarly justified the property qualification by claiming that "money" is "the legitimately presumptive symbol of good education" (5 Nov. 1841: 4; see also *Examiner* 9 Dec. 1838: 769), while editorials opposing universal suffrage routinely linked "poverty and ignorance."[14] This argument left open the possibility—on occasion affirmed by the Whig press—that as the lower classes become more prosperous and better educated they might be granted the franchise, but the *Times*, arguing that "manual labour . . . is the species of labour which is most unfavourable to mental cultivation and acquirement of any kind" while the "proprietary classes have the largest amount of both," implied that the incapacity for exercising social agency is inherent in being a member of the working class (20 June 1839: 5).

The elite press depicted the Chartists as lacking the "free agency" to protect their own interests by repeatedly depicting them as "dupes" acting in response to manipulation by others who, by this logic, become the real agents determining working-class behavior (*Times* 12 Apr. 1839: 4).[15] The *Morning Chronicle* insisted that because "the lower orders of the people" have not manifested an "increased morality or . . . ripened wisdom" that would "furnish . . . proof of advanced qualification for power," they are "more exposed than any other class in the community to be tainted by corruption, and converted to the vicious ends of faction" (13 Apr. 1839: 4). It thus elsewhere suggested that "spouters at meetings of the working classes" were able to exploit the "astonishing ignorance and credulity on the part of the hearers" (1 Sept. 1838: 2). By the circular logic of these editorials, the fact that workers believed or approved Chartist "demagogues" became evidence of their ignorance and gullibility and reinforced the argument that they lacked sufficient rationality and independence to act responsibly in the political arena.

Parliamentary discourse reinforced the depiction of the Chartists as incapable of acting for themselves by insisting that Chartism ultimately was the result of actions by the parliamentary parties rather than the working classes themselves. A characteristic editorial would begin by lamenting the dangers of Chartism but would then devote most of its criticism to its real target, the political opposition, which it blamed for fomenting these dangers (e.g., *Examiner* 10 Nov. 1839: 705; *Morning Post* 28 Sept. 1838: 2). Whig papers insisted that Tory legislation, in particular the Corn Laws, led working people to embrace Chartism, while the Tory press charged that the Whig New Poor Law had produced the Chartist crisis. The *Morning Post* repeatedly suggested that the Whigs were responsible for Chartism because their campaign for the Reform Bill had led the lower classes to believe that they had a right to the franchise and that it was legitimate to create social unrest in order to gain it.[16] The Whig press countered by contending that Chartism was the consequence of "long years of Tory misrule" prior to passage of the Reform Bill and of Tory resistance that had undermined the process of reform subsequent to its passage (*Morning Chronicle* 8 Nov. 1839: 2, 25 Mar. 1839: 2; see also 15 Sept. 1838: 2).[17] In these arguments, the tripartite model of parliamentary discourse served ultimately to locate social agency in the enfranchised elites and to reduce working-class behavior to an effect of their actions.[18]

While these allegations might suggest that the people acted on their own initiative in response to the failure of the elites to govern properly, elsewhere the press depicted the parliamentary parties as the real agents motivating and even directing Chartist behavior. The *Morning Chronicle*, for example, claimed that the Tories were "encouraging [the Radicals] in their most extravagant demands" in order to "depriv[e] the Whigs of their support" and that "the first Chartist movements towards violence originate[d] . . . in Tory *agency* and Tory stimulus" (*Morning Chronicle* 11 Sept. 1838: 2, 12 Nov. 1839: 2; emphasis added).[19] The Tory press similarly alleged that the Whigs were deliberately "driv[ing] the labouring population into insurrectionary violence upon the pretext of injury derived from the existing Corn Laws" (*Morning Post* 20 Dec. 1839: 2). Both sides charged that the opposition had "allied" itself with the Chartists and were using them to achieve its own ends.[20] The papers even went so far as to claim that the opposition was funding Chartism, an allegation that simultaneously made the parties the ultimate agency behind the movement and depicted the Chartists as acting for personal gain rather than for the working classes.[21]

Parliamentary discourse further contended that the incapacity for acting rationally meant not only that members of the working classes could not act disinterestedly but also that they could not act cohesively as a class. Allegations that the Chartist leadership were demagogues who manipulated the working classes implied that they could not speak for them and were not acting in their interests.[22] By designating them demagogues (the Greek word means merely leader of the people, but since the seventeenth century it had acquired pejorative connotations) the elite press suggested that the leadership did not belong to or speak for the people. The *Morning Chronicle* claimed that the Chartist leaders were a "faction isolated from the population, . . . that the great body of the people do not sympathise with them," and that, as these leaders come from "other classes," the "working classes do not speak with their own voice" (7 Jan. 1839: 2, 19 Mar. 1839: 4).[23] The *Times* similarly maintained that the Chartist leadership acted "*not* for the good of the people," but rather to "raise *themselves* into notoriety, and to thrust *themselves* into importance and Parliament" (29 Dec. 1842: 4).[24] Correspondingly, parliamentary discourse insisted that the rank and file did not have the same aims as the leadership. The *Examiner*, for instance, claimed that it was "convinced that the feelings and objects of the working people engaged in the present agitation have little real correspondence with the language" of the Chartist leadership (2 Dec. 1838: 755), while the *Morning Post* insisted that coordinated action did not reflect "unanimity of will" but was rather evidence that the participants were merely "so many professional *claqueurs*" who have been "drilled for the exercise they are to go through" (28 Sept. 1838: 2).

In addition to depicting the Chartist movement as split between an elite leadership and a gullible rank and file, parliamentary discourse insisted that the Chartists did not represent the working class but were merely a faction of the working classes, which did not on the whole support the movement. The press cast doubt on popular support for the movement by routinely insisting that the crowds at Chartist demonstrations were much smaller than anticipated or claimed by Chartist leaders and crowing with delight when a demonstration was, in their view, a "complete failure."[25] On occasions when the numbers were undeniably high, it suggested that the majority of those present were not committed to the movement but were "mere spectators," either taking advantage of the occasion for a bit of a holiday or being bullied into participating by the Chartist leadership.[26]

In either case, the point was that, contrary to appearances, Chartist activities did not demonstrate the capacity of the working classes to act on their own behalf.

Chartist discourse generally ignored the suggestion that the working classes could not act as a class while vigorously rejecting the underlying contention that they did not possess the rational capacity to act in a disinterested manner. To begin with, Chartists challenged the equation between poverty and ignorance by suggesting that ignorance is as common among the upper classes as the lower (*Northern Star* 20 Oct. 1838: 4). Indeed Chartist orators often mocked claims for the intelligence of the governing elite, pointing out that for generations Parliament had been controlled by an aristocracy that was illiterate and insisting that if poverty is conducive to ignorance, wealth is no guarantee of knowledge or wisdom (e.g., *Northern Star* 18 Aug. 1838: 8). They contended, furthermore, that the working classes were as intelligent and well informed as the ruling elites, the *Northern Star* even going so far as to insist that the lower classes possess "superior intelligence, induced by an active acquaintance with the real business of life" (7 Apr. 1838: 3; see also Hetherington's speech reported in Sept. 22, 1838: 2–3). The *Charter*, in an extensive response to these claims, similarly contended that the people have a "practical knowledge of their situation" that is more than sufficient to enable them to act rationally in selecting their representatives (5 May 1839: 230).

~

When we turn from the social agents defined by parliamentary and Chartist discourse to the forms of social action they envision, we find both embracing the constitutionalist assumption that action takes the form of legislating but disagreeing about the legitimacy of the repertoire of moral- and physical-force strategies through which the Chartists sought to persuade Parliament to establish universal suffrage. While Chartist discourse insisted that these tactics were fundamentally moral and constitutional—indeed the sole means of acting to produce a just social order—parliamentary discourse construed the entire range of strategies as fundamentally violent and unconstitutional, thus the opposite of disinterested social action.

The elite press contended that in spite of the claim that they sought constitutional reform, the Chartists really sought revolutionary changes that would destroy the British constitution, that, as we have seen, "'revolution,' not 'reform,' is the object in view" (*Morning Chronicle* 23 Apr. 1841: 2). The *Times* accordingly demanded that the government suppress the "democratic revolutionists" who were "assault[ing] the constitution" (12 Apr. 1839: 4; see also 25 Sept. 1838:

3), and the *Morning Post*, which similarly deplored the Chartists' "revolutionary violence" and "revolutionary sentiments," described the movement as a confederacy "organised for the avowed purpose of destroying every vestige of the British Constitution" (18 Oct. 1838: 2, 15 Sept. 1838: 2, 28 Sept. 1838: 2).[27] Even as Chartism explicitly sought to establish working-class agency within the constitutional framework by seeking the franchise and parliamentary representation, the elite press construed its extraparliamentary efforts—demonstrations, boycotts, strikes, and so on—as evidence that it was acting outside of, and therefore could not be included within, that framework. Indeed, by engaging in activities that it construed as illegal and unconstitutional, it argued, the Chartists had manifested their "absolute unfitness for the franchise" (*Examiner* 17 Sept. 1842: 593).[28]

Parliamentary discourse consequently treated even moral-force activities as, at bottom, forms of physical force or revolutionary violence. Press reports on what were generally peaceful demonstrations frequently depicted Chartist oratory as "violent," "inflammatory," or "incendiary," a choice of words that conflates speech that is impassioned or vehement with speech that urges its audience to violence.[29] As if to imply the true physical-force intent behind the moral-force thrust of these speeches, the *Examiner* italicized the small handful of sentences in which speakers raised the possibility of employing physical force, thus making them stand out in its dense full-page reports of Chartist demonstrations.[30] Similarly, the press repeatedly referred to nighttime gatherings as "torchlight meetings," thus raising the specter of arson and evoking memories of the era of Captain Swing, even though, as Malcolm Chase notes, the Chartists met at night in part because they worked during the day (*Chartism* 39).[31] Not surprisingly, it published numerous stories of arming and drilling and seldom let pass a police report of the confiscation of pikes and knives.

In order to suggest that such activity was not the result of individuals uniting in a concerted fashion, the press depicted them as an irrational mob whose behavior could lead only to "anarchy" (*Times* 27 Apr. 1839: 5). The *Times* claimed that a Chartist "look[s] upon the exercise of the franchise as a matter on which he may gratify his pleasure, or caprice, or love of power—not to speak of love of *gain*" and so is "not fit to have the right to vote" (5 Sept. 1842: 4; see also 22 Sept. 1842: 4). The press in turn linked this pursuit of self-interest and self-gratification to acting on the basis of feeling rather than rational decision making, as when the *Morning Post* alleged that the Chartists manifested an extreme form of self-interest and sought only to gratify their "basest passions."[32] In such depictions, the violence through which the Chartists would obtain the franchise gets transferred to universal suffrage itself, as when the *Times* contended that enactment of the

Charter would "transfer all power to the weakest heads and the blindest and most reckless passions—utterly to overthrow the church and state" (20 June 1839: 5).[33] Following this argument to its logical conclusion, the press depicted the Chartists as pursuing their desires to the detriment not only of others but of themselves, with the result that Chartism was "perishing of its own violence" (*Examiner* 10 Nov. 1839: 705).

⁓

Whereas parliamentary discourse portrayed moral force as merely a disguise for physical force and revolution, Chartist discourse portrayed its repertoire of supplemental strategies, including physical force, as working in the service of moral-force reform. In accord with the constitutional histories commonplace in political debates of the era, the Chartists contended that in demanding universal suffrage they were seeking not to overthrow the constitution but to restore it.[34] Invoking the myth of the Norman yoke, they claimed that "the people's" right to the franchise was "formerly part of the Constitution" that had been gradually stripped away and that their aim was to see "the Constitution restored to its original purity."[35] In a characteristic move, the *Charter* inverted the claims of parliamentary discourse by describing these encroachments on universal suffrage as an "unconstitutional . . . usurpation" on the part of the parliamentary parties themselves (28 Apr. 1839: 213).

The Chartists similarly developed and legitimated their repertoire of contention, notably the right to petition the government, the right of assembly, and the right to bear arms in self-defense, as constitutionally sanctioned forms of social action.[36] As Charles Tilly has shown, the rights to assemble and petition had become so well established by the time of the Reform Bill agitation that the government generally acknowledged them (12–14, 60–61, 308–10), but the same could not be said for the right to bear arms, which the elite press depicted as preparation for revolutionary insurrection. The Chartists insisted, however, that they would take up arms only in self-defense, whether it be defense from a government attack on one of their mass meetings or defense of the constitutional right of parliamentary representation itself. In this respect, they could construe their entire repertoire of contention as constitutional and thus moral, even though it sometimes involved the use, or at least the threat, of physical force.

Turning the tables on the parliamentary elite, the Chartists depicted their tactics as moral actions taken in defense of their constitutional rights against a regime that used physical force to keep an unconstitutional government in power. Implicit in the claim that they were defending their constitutional right to the franchise was the notion that the government that denied them this right was

itself unconstitutional and that the Chartists were the true defenders of the constitution (e.g., *Northern Star* 13 Oct. 1838: 4). The *Northern Star* headline "Moral
Influence, When Inculcated by Edicts and Enforced by the Bayonet, Compared
with Moral Influence When Inculcated by Reason and Enforced by Argument"
characteristically transformed the government's supposed moral force into
physical force while claiming that the Chartists are the true advocates of moral
force (3 Nov. 1838: 4). Neatly completing the process of inversion, the *Northern
Star* elsewhere asserted that the Chartists would respond to the authorities' use
of "physical force" by "persist[ing]" with "moral or passive resistance" (11 May
1839: 4).

Most significantly, Chartist discourse made physical force moral by treating
it as something that never actually happens, an unrealized potentiality held in
check while moral force acts. The mass demonstration itself employed this strategy, as an editorial describing the Kersal Moor meeting as a "moral demonstration
of physical strength" indicates (*Northern Star* 1 June 1839: 4). While the meetings
themselves were peaceful, constitutional, and moral, the gathering of a massive
crowd simultaneously *demonstrated* the potential for physical force. We can see
this conception of physical force as a potentiality that acts without being activated
in a *Northern Star* editorial that both advises its readers that they will be "irresistible, if they do not damage their own cause by *premature* violence" and encourages them to arm in self-defense (11 May 1839: 4; emphasis added).

As this passage indicates, in order to imagine moral force as effective, Chartist
discourse expressed a willingness to employ physical force but at the same time
postponed it to the future, hence the slogan "peaceably if we can, and forcibly
if we must" (e.g., *Northern Star* Apr. 6, 1839: 6). Feargus O'Connor's speeches
carefully blurred the line between moral and physical force by claiming that the
Chartists would be compelled to use force in the future if Parliament did not act
in the present. For example, at the August 11, 1838, demonstration at Birmingham,
he asserted that "there was not a man among them who was not satisfied to trust
the moral power of the nation, even to downbending, even to submission" rather
than "rush into maddening conflict" and that "moral power was that principle
of the human mind which taught man how to reason, and when to bear, and
when to forbear" but went on to insist that "he was not to be understood to imply
that he was content to live a slave, rather than die a freeman": "when the moral
strength was expended . . . then . . . if wrong should come from any party, cursed
be that virtuous man who refused to meet force by force" (*Northern Star* 11 Aug.
1838: 6; see also 22 Sept. 1838, 2–3, 19 Jan. 1839: 4). Similarly, the *Northern Star*
contended that the "moral organ has the constitutional right . . . to call in the aid

of physical force" when moral force has failed and elsewhere argued that if the working classes are denied the Charter, "brute force must be called to the aid of moral weakness" (3 Nov. 1838: 4, 9 Feb. 1839: 4).[37] In sum, these rhetorical strategies sought to make moral force effective by raising the specter of physical force, even as they sought to moralize physical force by indefinitely deferring its use.[38]

As we have seen, however, both moral and physical force failed to persuade Parliament to adopt the Charter. As early as 1839, *The Political Pilgrim's Progress* portrayed the character Moral-force as a coward incapable of confronting, let alone persuading the Chartists' enemy, Political Apollyon, who, in a reversal of elite-press discourse that portrayed the lower classes as unreasoning and violent, is filled with destructive rage. Consequently, Radical cannot enter the City of Reform until he employs physical force to kill Political Apollyon. As Doubleday anticipated, moral force proved insufficient to persuade Parliament to endorse universal suffrage, but whereas Radical readily defeats Political Apollyon, the Newport uprising made it clear that the government would prevail in any armed confrontation. Until the failure of the strike wave of 1842, however, moralized physical force remained the principal strategy through which the Chartists hoped to exercise social agency.

In the chapters that follow in part 1, I discuss three historical novels—Pierce Egan the Younger's *Wat Tyler*, Harrison Ainsworth's *Guy Fawkes*, and Charles Dickens's *Barnaby Rudge*—each of which was published (or completed serial publication) in 1841 and depicts an attempted uprising against the established government. While only *Wat Tyler* directly alludes to Chartism, all three novels employ contemporary discourses that envision social agency in terms of moral versus physical force while also seeking to envision alternative social agents and forms of social action.

By 1840, Dickens and Ainsworth, who met and became friends in the early 1830s, were among Britain's literary elite. Ainsworth, who was a few years Dickens's senior and the first to achieve success, introduced Dickens into London's literary circles; when Dickens resigned from the editorship of *Bentley's Magazine*, he handed it over to Ainsworth. Although his father was well known for his *Life in London* (1822), Pierce Egan does not appear to have moved in the same circles, and there is no evidence that he crossed paths with Dickens or Ainsworth. Yet Egan's literary career was as long and, in terms of productivity, as successful as theirs. While it is difficult to know who bought their books, we can conclude from the venues in which they published that while the works of Dickens and Ainsworth were consumed primarily by the more prosperous upper classes, Egan found his audience among the lower classes, who were the primary purchasers of novels in the cheap serial, or "penny dreadful," format.

We have little direct evidence about the political sympathies of these authors, but what we do know corresponds with the milieu of their audience. Egan had radical sympathies and went on to become a regular contributor to the radical publications *Reynolds's Miscellany* and the *London Journal*. Ainsworth, who came from a Whig non-Conformist background, seems to have had liberal sympathies, and Dickens, who worked as a reporter for the *Morning Chronicle* from 1834 to 1836, had similar leanings. Dickens and Ainsworth, whose *Barnaby Rudge* and *Guy Fawkes* adopted the Whig position on religious toleration in response to the Tory "No Popery" campaign, employ versions of Whig parliamentary discourse blaming the use of physical force on the failure of the aristocracy to govern justly, while Egan, who chose to depict an established radical hero, draws more heavily on Chartist discourse arguing for the rights of the people. Yet Egan's depiction of a Chartist uprising also employs parliamentary discourse representing the people as not sufficiently rational to exercise social agency, while Dickens takes up Chartist proposals for an alliance with the middle classes. Ainsworth too takes up the Whig discourse of toleration but envisions the achievement of toleration through the Chartist rhetoric of moralized physical force. Through such dialogic intersections of Chartist and parliamentary discourse these novels imagined new possibilities for social reform.

CHAPTER 3

Egalitarian Chivalry and Popular Agency in *Wat Tyler*

Toward the end of 1840, just a little over a year after the first large demonstrations on behalf of the Charter and the presentation of the first Chartist petition, Pierce Egan's "historical romance" *Wat Tyler* began serial publication, with complete book publication following in 1841.[1] The novel was popular enough to be reprinted several times over the next decade, its publication and popularity coinciding with the heyday of Chartism.[2] Unlike the other two novels discussed in part 1, *Wat Tyler* has direct connections to Chartism, for the figure of Wat Tyler was a mainstay of radical discourse, and Egan's depiction of Tyler's 1381 uprising not only draws on the discourse of Chartism but also evokes direct parallels with it.

By 1840 Wat Tyler was a well-established figure in radical discourse, owing mainly to Robert Southey's *Wat Tyler: A Dramatic Poem* (1817). Prior to the publication of Southey's play, literary and historical texts had consistently portrayed Tyler as a traitorous villain.[3] During the French Revolution, however, Tyler became a reference point for both defenders and opponents of radicalism. Following the earlier tradition, for example, the *Times* attacked the French National Assembly for its willingness to follow Wat Tyler in "level[ing] all distinctions,"[4] while Thomas Paine, in a brief note to the second part of *The Rights of Man* (1792) that purportedly inspired Southey's play, defended him as "an intrepid disinterested man" and a plebian hero (112). Similarly, James Northcote's *Sir William Walworth Lord Mayor of London, Killing Wat Tyler in Smithfield, 1381* (1787), originally exhibited just before the revolution and then engraved (1796) and widely exhibited during the course of it, presents Walworth as the heroic slayer of the traitor Tyler, while his rival Henry Fuseli's *Wat Tyler and the Tax-gatherer* (engraved by William Blake 1798) uses a similar visual structure to depict Tyler heroically slaying the tax collector who has molested his daughter.[5] Although Southey wrote his play depicting a heroic Wat Tyler fighting a corrupt aristocracy in 1794, it did not appear in print until 1817, when radical printers published it to embarrass the now conservative poet laureate, who had recently published articles opposing extension of the franchise.[6] The play thereafter became a staple of the radical canon, with advertisements for it appearing regularly in the *Northern Star* and other Chartist papers, while Wat Tyler himself became a member of the Chartist pantheon and his rebellion an important historical precedent for Chartist tactics.[7]

Although it never explicitly mentions the Chartists, *Wat Tyler* certainly deserves a place in the canon of Chartist fiction.[8] Drawing on the fact that Tyler and his followers sought "charters" granting them rights, Egan's Tyler makes six demands, a number that corresponds to the six points of the People's Charter (3.12.841).[9] Evoking the radicals' disappointment that, after having sought working-class support for passage of the Reform Bill, the middle classes refused to help them win universal suffrage, the narrator suggests that for a time prior to the death of the Black Prince the people had anticipated *"reform* in the [nation's] *legislation"* (3.11.794; emphasis added). Moreover, like the Chartists, who knew that such petitions were often ignored and so insisted that the Charter would be their final petition (D. Thompson 57–58; Chase, *Chartism* 2–3, 19), Tyler responds to King Richard's demand that they petition rather than rebel: "We sent petition after petition — every country town, village, or castlewick in the kingdom; to what effect? — they were spurned and unheeded! We found petitioning a weak manner of proceeding, and therefore we now *demand* redress" (3.14.861; see also 3.10.795).[10] Earlier, in what looks very much like one of the major Chartist demonstrations, Tyler addresses a crowd of one hundred thousand men from a platform, laying out for them "the code of laws or *charter* which he intended to demand the King's sanction to" (3.12.835; emphasis added). Although Tyler's demand for "an entire enfranchisement of the peasantry" in its fourteenth-century context refers to emancipation from serfdom, in 1841 the evocation of the electoral franchise would have been inevitable (3.10.794). Most significantly, Egan imputes to Tyler the fundamental Chartist assumption that legislative representation is the only means through which the people can be assured of a just social order by having him argue that earning more than a "bare subsistence" requires changing "present laws" (3.14.862) and that "the people" (elsewhere he calls them "the sovereign people") are "the true source of all power" and deserve legislative representation (3.12.839, 3.14.864).

While Egan followed Southey in depicting a heroic and chivalrous Wat Tyler, he innovated by adding to the history of his rebellion of 1381 a substantial prehistory, which takes place in 1336–1341 during the period of Wat Tyler's youth and occupies the first nine-tenths of the novel (787 of 874 pages in the first edition). The novel is divided into three books, the first of which centers on Wat Tyler's rescue of the woman he has grown up with and loves, Violet Evesham, from the son of Sir John Maltravers. Although Violet loves Wat, the question of whether they will marry appears to hinge on the discovery of her parentage, and the corresponding plotline involves the complicated story of her foster father, Halbert (who unbeknownst even to himself is her real father), and his brother, Ethelbert, to whom he bears a close resemblance; of their wives, Ghita and Editha, who are also nearly identical in appearance; and the plots perpetrated against them by members of the Maltravers family and their henchman, Grif of the Bloody Hand. These questions about parentage lead in turn to the possibility that Violet might instead marry Sir Walter Manny, who assists Wat in rescuing her from her oppressors. Book 2 and the first half of book 3 develop alternating plotlines, one tracing Wat's success as a follower of Sir Walter during the Hundred Years' War and the other centering on Violet's attempt to discover her parentage and the younger Maltravers's continued attempts to seduce her. No sooner do these narratives conclude with the revelation that Violet is not noble, thus clearing the way for her marriage to Wat and an apparent happy ending, than things begin to fall apart. The second half of book 3 swiftly covers the years from the marriage in 1341 to the time of the rebellion, in 1381, during which the chivalrous Normans (King Edward, Sir Walter, John Chandos, etc.) all die and the ministers of the teenaged King Richard II allow or encourage the oppression of the Saxons. The concluding chapters recapitulate the standard accounts of the Peasant Rebellion, which ends when the mayor of London fatally wounds Tyler.[11]

In inventing the narrative of Tyler's youth—no history had ever suggested that Tyler played a role in the Hundred Years' War and indeed none had suggested he was even alive in 1336–1341—Egan was providing a backstory to underwrite Southey's depiction of Tyler as a chivalrous hero, but he was also rewriting the national narrative of Scott's *Ivanhoe* (1820) and the myth of the Norman yoke that it invokes.[12] Like *Waverley* (1814), which in many ways is its model, *Ivanhoe* depicts a conflict between two cultures, transferring the opposition between England and Scotland in the eighteenth century to the opposition between the Normans and Saxons in the middle ages. *Waverley*, of course, follows the pattern of the national tale in imagining the resolution of this conflict through the marital union of an English male (Waverley himself) and a Scottish woman (Rose Bradwardine). *Ivanhoe* varies this pattern somewhat by envisioning a resolution through the marriage of a Saxon, Lady Rowena, to Ivanhoe, who is also a Saxon but is affiliated with Richard I and the Normans. In *Wat Tyler*, as in *Ivanhoe*, rogue Normans abduct and assault Saxon women and are defeated in a pitched battle by Saxon men, and the union of Saxons and chivalrous Normans is signaled by the marriage of two Saxons, Tyler, who like Ivanhoe is affiliated with the Normans and has adopted their manners, and Violet Evesham.

However, *Wat Tyler* revises *Ivanhoe* by altering the standard narrative, followed by Scott, in which the Norman yoke is imposed following the eleventh-century Norman conquest and delaying its imposition until the fourteenth century during the interval between Wat's participation in the Hundred Years' War and the uprising in 1381. On the one hand, following Scott and the standard narrative, Egan depicts Normans as oppressors of the Saxons, who in turn hate them. On the other hand, he depicts Wat Tyler and his fellow Saxons as freemen who through their alliance with a separate group of chivalrous Normans establish the principles of the British constitution. As in *Ivanhoe*, marriages signal the resolution of ethnic conflict and establishment of a single nation, a "merry England" (3.10.802), but, in contrast to Scott's novel, Egan's proceeds to depict the decay of that idyll followed by the imposition of the Norman yoke.

The part of *Wat Tyler* set in 1336–1341 depicts the establishment of a British constitution in which all citizens are fully enfranchised. This narrative represents Saxon men as social agents first through their capacity to liberate women subjected to archaic Normans who continue to adhere to the kinship ideal and then through an egalitarian chivalry in which one's status is earned, not merely inherited from one's parents. The companionate marriages that conclude this part of the novel reproduce the homosocial bond that unites Normans and Saxons as English citizens and signal the full achievement of social agency by the Saxons. Over the next forty years, however, the earlier conflict between opposing ethnic cultures becomes a conflict between classes, the corrupt aristocracy disenfranchising the people.

Consequently, the novel depicts the Peasant Rebellion as an attempt not to gain but to restore the constitutional rights of the people, who have been disenfranchised in the interval between 1341 and 1381. The novel moralizes physical force by depicting Tyler as chivalrously defending his family and fellow citizens and aiming, as he says, to effect a "moral revolution" (3.11.817). However, it depicts his followers as irrational and lacking the social agency to proceed after his death. The conclusion tentatively answers the question of how moralized physical force might be a form of agency—the same question confronted by the Chartists after the failures of 1839—by suggesting that the people must recognize themselves as social agents with the power to effect social change.

⌒

The 1336–1341 narrative depicts the establishment of the British constitution by representing the British—both Normans and Saxons—as adherents of a modern form of chivalry who displace an archaic remnant of the conquering Norman nobility. Although the novel employs the discourse of the Norman yoke in its depiction of its most thoroughly Saxon character, Leowulf, who "prided himself on having no cross of Norman blood in his veins; nothing but the pure Saxon blood, and possessed the same unalloyed hatred to the Normans which his forefathers had borne towards them" (1.11.111), Wat Tyler and the majority of his fellow Saxons manifest little enmity toward the Normans.[13] Similarly, the novel confines Norman oppression of the Saxons to the family and followers of Sir John Maltravers, who was notoriously implicated in the assassination of Edward II.

Consequently, the novel does not depict the Maltravers family as members of a ruling elite who reduce all Saxons to an enslaved class in servile bondage but as sexual predators who confine and bind women. The novel contains a remarkable number of narratives of the abduction and attempted molestation of women, at least nine, involving six different victims, including both Violet Evesham's mother, Ghita, and her aunt, Editha, who are held in bondage by the elder Maltravers and his cousin, respectively.[14] The plot centers on the attempts of the younger John Maltravers to obtain Violet in marriage, to which end he abducts her on three different occasions and on one threatens her with rape. Maltravers in turn employs the brigand Grif of the Bloody Hand, who, we learn early in the novel, has taken revenge on a village that defied him by having his men hang the males on gibbets and then "with brutal violence, ravish . . . their wives and daughters" (1.8.64–65). Yet while they employ Grif and use coercion themselves, the fact that the Maltraverses also feel compelled to persuade women to consent to marriage suggests that such brutal subjection is becoming archaic.

In this depiction of the Maltraverses, the novel draws on radical critiques of corrupt aristocrats who pursue kinship alliances to further their selfish interests, but this pursuit does not become class oppression because they are motivated only by libidinous desire, not by desire to gain status or economic advantage, and thus do not, like Grif, use subjection of women as a means of subjugating their menfolk. At the same time, however, the fact that they seek to marry these women—and only threaten rape in order to achieve that aim—indicates their desire to bind the women to them. The curious way that one family (Maltravers, his father, and his father's cousin) seek to force marriage on another family (Violet, her mother, and her aunt) suggests that the lust that apparently drives each man is mediated by the pursuit of a form of kinship union in which one family binds another to it. The novel further emphasizes how the kinship model violates the companionate ideal by depicting the women that the Maltraverses seek to marry as either already married or in love with another man. By contrast, it links the kinship ideal to indiscriminate lust by depicting the elder Maltravers as a bigamist who is already married when he attempts to marry Ghita.

The novel makes sexual bondage represent a residual or archaic state in which the Saxons have not yet fully achieved social agency, rather than a generalized subjection of the Saxons under the Norman yoke, not only by isolating the Maltraverses as the oppressors but also by confining subjection to Saxon women.[15] In this portion of the novel there appear to be no serfs, and the inhabitants of Brenchley all appear to be freemen engaged in commerce or a trade (Tyler's name was taken to indicate that he was a tiler). Whereas in the episode discussed above Grif suppresses the men along with the women, Wat and his friends successfully rescue Violet and defend Brenchley from a similar attack. The distinction between free males and subjected females is also apparent in the structure of book 2, in which the hero and heroine, Wat and Violet, become the protagonists in alternating narrative threads, one in which Wat fights alongside English nobility in the Hundred Years' War and becomes fully enfranchised when he is offered a knighthood and the other in which Maltravers continues his efforts to seduce Violet.

The novel figures the fact that Saxon men along with honorable Normans possess social agency through their mutual adherence to the companionate ideal, in opposition to the exercise of promiscuous kinship marriage by the Maltraverses. As we have seen, the companionate model of marriage involves the complementary ideals of the free choice of one's marriage partner and the formation of a partnership of equals. In contrast to the polygamous promiscuity of the kinship ideal that corresponds to the self-interested acquisition of the wife as property, the companionate ideal is monogamous, uniting individuals on the basis of their interior qualities rather than their property. Although the Maltraverses manage to abduct Saxon women and threaten to sexually assault them, the women's commitment to the companionate ideal enables them to avoid the physical transgression of rape and thereby complete subjection and loss of agency. Indeed, both Violet and Editha are prepared to commit suicide rather than submit to sexual assault.[16] Moreover, these characters are so committed to the monogamous companionate ideal that they are incapable of falling in love a second time. Violet is attracted to Sir Walter, who has fallen in love with her, but because she has first loved Wat she declares that she can never love another, even if Wat dies. Sir Walter in turn swears that he will never marry, and in order to explain the fact that the historical Walter *did* marry, Egan resorts to a narrative in which he must marry a woman who has fallen so desperately in love with him (of course, *she* can never marry any other) that he has to marry her to prevent her from pining to death.[17] Although Violet affirms the companionate ideal, she worries that her parents—who are unknown to her but may be of "noble birth"—might, in correspondence with the Maltraverses' assaults on her, adhere to the kinship ideal and object to her marrying Wat (1.17.222; see also 1.9.84–86). When she does finally discover her parents, however, it turns out that they are not nobility but commoners who espouse the companionate ideal, and this discovery finally clears the way for their marriage.

Corresponding to the companionate ideal, the honorable Normans and the Saxons espouse an egalitarian chivalry promoting nobility that one earns through one's own action, not through birth. The novel distinguishes this form of nobility as modern in contrast to the assumption of privilege by the archaic Normans by suggesting that "the laws of chivalry are conducted upon a different plan to what they have been" (2.3.352). This "plan" ascribes chivalrous behavior not to being born of a noble family but to possessing the character to act in a chivalrous and noble manner. Thus Sir Walter and Sir Lewis Beauchamp on separate occasions lecture the callow young noble Rupert that his birth does not make him better than a "peasant" (1.13.134, 2.3.351). Although this society does retain distinctions of rank, its chivalry is egalitarian in that it allows for social mobility because any man can prove himself noble through honorable actions.

In accord with these principles, the novel depicts Wat Tyler as innately chivalrous and noble. Violet's uncle, Ethelbert Evesham, recognizes his "nobility" early on (1.7.45, 1.11.119), and Wat manifests the whole panoply of chivalric ideals—honor, courtesy, justice, and mercy—well before he encounters the chivalrous Normans. Upon his first appearance in the novel he wrestles with and kills a wolf, an incident that serves as a metonym for the bravery and strength he will exhibit in leading the fight against the marauders who will soon attack his village and in turn serves as a proleptic anticipation of the leadership role he will play in the rebellion.

In accord with this chivalric ideal, the modern Normans deem Wat noble on the basis of his heroic actions. John Chandos declares in response to one such incident, "By the bright star of chivalry, you have done nobly!" (2.3.336; see also 342), and Sir Walter Manny, himself famous as a flower of chivalry, praises Wat for his "knack of doing everything which helps to make a squire, a true, honourable, high, and chivalric knight" (3.1.584). Insisting on "the difference in real value . . . between a man who can boast of nobility of nature alone for his position in society, and he who prides himself upon nobility of birth for his station," Sir Walter decides to make Wat his squire because his "deeds" have shown him worthy of "nobility of station" (2.5.450). King Edward himself affirms this egalitarian social mobility when he points out that "some of the proudest nobles round my throne have sprung from families not less humble than" Tyler's and then offers Wat a knighthood that will grant him "the power of ennobling [his] family" (3.5.686). In conformity with the historical record, Egan has Tyler decline the knighthood, but the offer itself establishes the equality of the freeborn Saxon with the Norman nobility.

Under egalitarian chivalry the ethnic opposition between Norman and Saxon disappears, and they become united during the Hundred Years' War as Englishmen who oppose the French. In what becomes one of the principal narrative elements in book 2, Tyler manifests his chivalry, not by rescuing a Saxon woman from a Norman as he does in book 1, but by freeing a Flemish woman (Rubacelle) from a Saxon soldier (Bulfric). Tyler's actions in this episode are dictated by the code of chivalry that he shares with Sir Walter rather than a Saxon identity shared with Bulfric. Likewise, the nobility become English in opposition not only to their French antagonists but also to the elder Maltravers, who had reputedly conspired to kill Edward I (the murder itself was reportedly committed by the Maltraverses' servant William Ogle, a.k.a. Grif of the Bloody Hand), and the younger Maltravers, who remains in England oppressing women rather than joining Edward II and his fellow Englishmen in the fight against France.

The novel represents this union between Saxons and Normans by establishing a homosocial bond between Wat and Sir Walter.[18] Wat and Sir Walter are doubles not only in sharing the same ideals and name—the novel treats Wat as a nickname for Walter (1.7.46)—but also in their mutual love of Violet Evesham. The persistence of the kinship ideal that leads Violet briefly to consider accepting Sir Walter's affections on the basis of his social status threatens to make them sexual rivals and to reintroduce class division. However, precisely because they are both noble and chivalrous, they do not become rivals, and each instead insists on deferring to the other in their quest for her hand in marriage. The novel displaces this rivalry from Sir Walter to Maltravers, whose adherence to the kinship ideal leads him to privilege his own interests over those of England. In turn, Violet's utter rejection of Maltravers corresponds to the fact that she ultimately chooses to marry Wat on the basis of her prior affection rather than Sir Walter on the basis of his status.

This marriage between free commoners—duplicated in the marriage of Wat's friend Michael and his beloved, Flora—in turn institutes an egalitarian "merry

England" in which the British constitution guarantees that Saxons are fully enfranchised citizens (3.10.802). Accordingly, the deaths of the Maltraverses and
Grif of the Bloody Hand in the conclusion of the 1336–1441 narrative signal the
end of distinctions of rank and of the kinship model. In this respect, Wat's refusal
of knighthood accords not only with the historical record but also with the need
to affirm the ideal of a single people without social distinctions.

Whereas national narratives typically conclude with such a union that ends
conflicts and projects an idyllic future, *Wat Tyler* depicts this idyll as a lost past,
for in the last tenth of the novel egalitarian chivalry disappears and oppression
in the form of serfdom takes its place. In accord with this narrative of decline,
death enters Edenic merry England. In the earlier part of the novel, there is little
indication of disease or poverty, but now both are pervasive. The plagues of 1350,
1361, and 1369 carry off Wat's and Violet's parents as well as all of their children
(not to mention Michael's mother, Flora's parents, and all of her kin). With the
concurrent passing of the chivalrous John Chandos, Sir Walter Manny, Edward
III, and Edward the Black Prince, a new aristocracy emerges that enforces distinctions of status and reintroduces peasant bondage. No longer finding Brenchley
idyllic ("its charms were fled" [3.10.790]), Wat and Violet move from its timeless
space to Deptford and the pages of history (nothing prior to Tyler's emergence as
a leader at Deptford is present in the historical record).

The expulsion from this Eden takes the form of a fall into class division. Only
at this stage of the narrative does the narrator begin using the term *the people* —
much favored by dichotomous Chartist class discourse — to distinguish commoners from the aristocracy.[19] Furthermore, their oppressors are no longer an archaic
remnant of Norman nobility but the entire aristocracy. Employing the discourse
of radicalism, the novel depicts the court of the teenaged Richard II under the
rule of John of Gaunt as a corrupt aristocracy that is, as Rupert asserts, "shame-
fully perverted from what it ought to be," its nobles having become "vultures . . .
fattening on the gifts of the king—gifts which are not his to bestow, but trusts
placed in his hands for the benefit of the people at large" that now "are squan-
dered and wasted in riot and debauchery" (3.11.827, 3.10.799; see also 3.12.836).

This class structure takes the form of the Norman "yoke," which disenfranchises all commoners and subjects them to servile bondage (3.11.803). Whereas
the earlier narrative depicts Saxons as freemen, the narrator now reports that the
"people . . . were still in a horrible state of vassalage" (3.10.794). Recapitulating
the novel's trajectory of freedom gained and lost, Egan includes from the historical record the episode in which Sir Simon Burley apprehends and claims as his
"bondsman" a serf who had previously won his freedom (3.10.797).[20] This act

reverses the social mobility marking the egalitarian chivalry that we saw in the narrative of Wat Tyler's rise and the offer of knighthood, replacing it with a fixed hierarchy in which the lower classes have no power to change the social order.

The novel makes the imposition of bondage the disenfranchisement of an entire class, not just of individuals, by depicting its extension from women to men. Just as the entire aristocracy, not merely the Maltraverses, are now oppressors, so too all English freemen are now in bondage. Merging what in all other versions of the history are separate episodes, Egan depicts Tyler discussing with fellow villagers the reenslavement of Burley's bondsman at the moment that a tax collector molests his daughter when he attempts to determine whether she is required to pay the poll tax levied on all individuals above the age of fifteen by looking to see if she has pubic hair.[21] In representing multiple instances of the molestation of women in the earlier part of the novel, Egan was no doubt guided by the idea of making them proleptically anticipate this widely circulated albeit apocryphal episode. However, by making the rebellion a response not only to the insult to his daughter but also to the imposition of servile bondage, he suggests that Saxon men now have been reduced to the state of Saxon women who lack social agency.

The depiction of the Saxons as English freemen who have been disenfranchised enables Egan to represent Tyler as moralizing physical force by making his rebellion a "moral revolution" that aims to restore the constitution through "enfranchisement of the peasantry" (3.11.817, 3.10.794). Invoking a popular constitutionalism that distinguishes the ruling elite from the state and its monarch (see Vernon, *Politics* 320–21), Tyler assures King Richard that the "peasantry support the state" and that "the indignation of the people is not directed against [him] personally, but against the ministers" who have abrogated their rights (3.14.863, 862). Like the Chartists who inverted the charge that they were revolutionaries by asserting that it is the state that has acted unconstitutionally, he claims that it is Richard who deserves to be accused of treason: "You call me rebel; you call those who have risen, because they can no longer bear the wrongs heaped upon them, rebels; but, King of England, which most deserves the title, thou or we? . . . You rebel against every law imposed on you, and we bear your injustice, your exactions, your injuries, your oppressions, until we can bear no longer—until we must rise up to assert the rights which are ours" (3.14.861).

Tyler similarly employs Chartist discourse treating physical force as a potentiality that need not be realized in order to make moral force effective (see above, chap. 2). While the historical record of the rebellion reports numerous acts of violence, Tyler claims that "it is not [their] intention . . . to commit one excess, one act of violence" (3.11.817). Expanding the speech Tyler makes to King Richard at Smithfield from a mere few lines in the historical records into three pages of dialogue, Egan transforms him into a Feargus O'Connor–like orator who seeks to effect change through moral force and would resort to violence only when that fails. Just as the *Northern Star* had claimed that the Chartists would be "irresistible if they do not damage their own cause by premature violence," so Tyler responds to the violence of his followers by endeavoring to "convince them how much injury they were doing their cause" (3.14.856).

The depiction of Tyler's nobility during the Hundred Years' War further establishes that his use of violence is not barbarous and self-serving but the chivalrous defense of the people. When he asks his followers "whether you will longer submit to have the sanctity of your homes violated with impunity—your daughters subjected to insult it makes honest men shudder to think upon" (3.10.798), he is invoking the definition of chivalry that Sir Walter Manny had delineated when he insisted that a knight goes to war "from no desire to excel in the slaughter of his fellow creatures, but rather that the victory may be decided in favour of those he has left behind, . . . who look to his exertions as well as to the efforts of others, to defend them from oppressive conquerors, to *preserve their homes*, and protect their *rights and liberties*" (1.13.139; emphasis added). Making explicit the linkage between defense of the domestic female sphere and the domain of male rights, Sir Walter concludes that "he who has a happy fireside, with smiling faces round it, and would keep it sacred . . . has ever reason and *right*, when [his country] is in jeopardy, to arm himself and go forth to do battle in its behalf" (1.13.139; emphasis added). Thus not only is chivalry fundamentally egalitarian, but it establishes constitutional rights and legitimates the use of force in their defense.

However, Tyler follows the code of chivalry not so much in defending the rights of the people as in restraining their violence against the ruling elite.[22] On one occasion, he prevents a thief who has joined the rebellion for the opportunity of plunder from molesting the daughter of Sir Simon Burley, and on another, when his men in disobedience to his orders apprehend and demand kisses from the Countess of Kent (the mother of King Richard), he both gives them a tongue-lashing and apologizes to the countess. Although the novel does not omit the many instances of attacks on members of the ruling elite and professional classes recorded in the historical records, it works to minimize them and to shift responsibility away from Tyler. The killing of the tax collector—presumably a justifiable defense of his daughter's virtue—was an integral part of the Tyler legend, but otherwise he is not responsible for any deaths and, on the contrary, spends a great deal of his time "persuading, exhorting, and *preventing* [the people] committing desperate deeds" (3.13.843). Moreover, whereas Froissart makes Tyler responsible for the summary execution of many of the people killed during the uprising, Egan not only constructs the narrative so as to absolve him from such responsibility but also insists that Wat tried to "save" them, concluding that "it is almost incredible the number of lives and houses marked for demolition which Wat Tyler saved" (3.13.848; see also 843).[23] Thus we have the spectacle—at times to unintentionally comical effect—of the leader of a rebellion who devotes most of his energy to neutralizing the actions of his followers. Instead of chivalrously defending the people from the state, he ends up seeking to protect the state—or at least its ruling elite—from the people.

As these examples demonstrate, Egan makes Tyler chivalrous in part by distinguishing him from his irrational and violent followers. Shifting from Chartist discourse to parliamentary discourse depicting the lower classes as incapable of exercising social agency, the narrator contends that the uprising might have succeeded even after the death of Wat Tyler "*if* the insurgents had acted upon more mature plans, and proceeded with judgment instead of following mad impulses, and suffering themselves to be led by blind passions" (3.14.868). The insurgents obey Tyler's injunctions against looting the homes they destroy, not because they seek to act disinterestedly or chivalrously, but because they are too "maddened by wine and excitement" to understand their rational self-interest (3.13.845). Consequently, when they vent their anger by destroying property and executing their enemies, they take no care for their own safety, with the self-destructive consequence that many fall "victim to their over exertion" and "perish . . . from the effects of drink and delirium" (3.13.845).

The rebellion fails, the novel suggests, because the people have not yet become social agents capable of reforming the social order. Because they do not have the rational capacity to organize themselves, the people are "paralysed by the fall of their leader" (the killing of Wat Tyler), and the rebellion collapses (3.14.868). While the history of Tyler's rebellion might be used to legitimate Chartism, the fact that it failed raises questions about whether moralized physical force is an effective form of social agency. Egan's depiction of the split between Tyler and the people suggests, however, that the failure did not result from employing this form of agency but because the people had not yet become united as a social agent. In 1841, the rejection of the 1838 Chartist petition and the suppression of the Newport uprising might similarly be explained not as a failure of moralized physical force but as a shortcoming of the people.

By suggesting that the rebellion could have succeeded "if the insurgents had acted upon more mature plans" (3.14.868), Egan draws on Chartist rhetoric that projects a future in which the people have obtained social agency by coming to understand the nature of moralized physical force. This rhetoric is typified by Feargus O'Connor's contention that "there would be no change for the better until the masses were set in motion—till they were *made acquainted* with their own *strength*" (*Northern Star* 11 Aug. 1838: 6; emphasis added). The fact that O'Connor makes this assertion in the context of his contention that if moral force fails, they must resort to physical force makes clear that what he means by becoming acquainted with their strength is the recognition by all of the people that if they join the Chartist movement, they will overwhelmingly outnumber the ruling elite and their physical force will be so irresistible that, paradoxically, it would not be necessary to employ it in order to enforce their demands. In the concluding chapter of *Wat Tyler*, the narrator draws on this rhetoric when he suggests that "it would be easy" to write a "long appendage" in which the rebellion succeeds once "the people . . . know . . . rightly how to use" their "strength in great numbers" as a means of realizing the "power and strength they possess . . . in themselves" (3.14.868, 867).

As if to hold open this possibility of writing an alternative history in which the rebellion succeeds, Egan revises the conclusion of Tyler's history. The narrator's description of Tyler suffering a "deadly blow" and his friends carrying away "the body" accord with the historical accounts, which assert that he was killed during the meeting with King Richard (3.14.864, 866). However, after making the suggestion that he might add an appendage depicting the success of the rebellion, Egan goes on to invent a scene in which Tyler survives the attack and appears to be on the road to recovery but insists on being taken to his native village, a journey that ultimately leads to a peaceful death surrounded by his family. In effecting a Christlike death and resurrection—the period during which he survives paralleling the period before Christ's ascension into heaven—Egan suggests that the rebellion does not end at the moment when Tyler is struck down by the mayor of London and that he lives on as an inspiration for the Chartists four and a half centuries later.

Tellingly, this concluding incident does not envision the people acting to reform society, but the survival of their leader. At its beginning, Tyler suggests that the rebellion can only succeed if the people as a whole acquire social agency: "The time has come when there must be a change, a great and glorious change— and *the people must work it themselves*" (3.10.799; emphasis added). Significantly, however, Egan does not dramatize the people learning their strength and so beginning to "work it themselves" and can only envision this possibility in a narrative intrusion suggesting that he might have done so. He thus leaves the acquisition of social agency unimagined, a history still to be written.

CHAPTER 4

Unconsummated Marriage and the "Uncommitted" Gunpowder Plot in *Guy Fawkes*

In January of 1840, about half a year before *Wat Tyler* began its serial run, Harrison Ainsworth's *Guy Fawkes* began serial publication in *Bentley's Magazine*, where it immediately followed his immensely popular *Jack Sheppard*.[1] Like *Wat Tyler*, Ainsworth's novel depicts a disenfranchised people—in this case Roman Catholics—employing moralized physical force in order to gain the franchise and full citizenship. Like Egan, Ainsworth explores this form of social agency by transforming a figure who had traditionally been treated as one of the villains of British history into a man of moral integrity. Whereas Egan framed the Peasant Rebellion in terms of Chartist discourse, however, Ainsworth employs parliamentary discourse that enables him to envision a tolerant Whig middle class that incorporates Catholics into the nation, even as it denies citizenship to the working classes.

Parliamentary discourse of the 1830s exploited Catholicism, as it did Chartism, as a means of setting forth the Tory aristocracy's and Whig middle class's respective claims that they could best govern the nation. The Whigs had pushed through the Catholic Relief Act of 1829 against Tory opposition, and the question of whether Catholics should be enfranchised continued to be subject to debate throughout the following decade. In response to the Whigs' return to power in 1835, the Tories sought to win support from dissenters who had supported Whig reform by appealing to their prejudices against Catholics (Cahill 66; see also Paz, *Popular Anti-Catholicism* 200). The Whig press responded by portraying the Tories as bigots mounting a "no-Popery" campaign "play[ing] upon the love and attachment which the people of Great Britain have to their religious faith" in order to pursue "political" objectives.[2] Of course, the Whigs' advocacy of reli-

gious tolerance was no less politically calculated than the anti-Catholicism of the
Tories.

The resulting parliamentary discourse drew upon and promoted depictions
of the Gunpowder Plot focused on the question of whether Catholics were loyal
citizens or sought to overturn the constitution by making England a Catholic
state. As James Sharpe has shown, Catholic emancipation, which began in the
late eighteenth century, coincided with a change in representations of the Gunpowder Plot that shifted responsibility from the Catholic Church and Catholics
in general toward a handful of conspirators, the effect of which was to suggest that
most Catholics, unlike the conspirators, were loyal citizens (115–16, 138). In line
with their advocacy of tolerance, the Whigs embraced this revisionary history,
while Tory discourse maintained that Catholics' divided loyalties—to Rome as
well as to England—had not diminished since the era of the Gunpowder Plot.

The first important revision of the history of the plot was set forth by John
Lingard, a Roman Catholic priest who, though not a Whig apologist, had connections with Whig circles in part because of their sympathy for emancipation. In
his *History of England*, which began appearing to considerable acclaim in 1819,
Lingard employed a two-pronged approach to Catholics' role in the plot. On the
one hand, he suggested that the plot was justified because the Catholics had been
deprived of their rights by an "inexorable" monarch who had "extinguished the
last ray of hope" for justice (9.37). On the other hand, he sought to demonstrate
that the majority of Roman Catholics nonetheless remained loyal citizens and
did not support the plot, reinforcing his argument for their loyalty by contending
that Rome and the church had no hand in it and that the Jesuits who advised the
conspirators even sought to prevent it.[3] Moreover, he constructed his narrative
so as to suggest that even after the conspirators formulated the plot to blow up
Parliament, they saw the plan as a measure of last resort and continued to work
for a negotiated settlement. When, a few years later, the barrister and legal scholar
David Jardine evaluated the legal evidence in the second volume of his edition
of *State Trials* (1835), which Lingard in turn cited in the revised edition of his
history consulted by Ainsworth, he concluded that in its main outlines Lingard's
account was correct (xi). While acknowledging that, from a legal point of view,
the conspirators were clearly guilty, he nonetheless concurred that their "political
situation," in which they were deprived of "the common rights and liberties of
Englishmen," provided "sufficient motives to insurrection" (7, 185; see also 7–17,
22–25). Like Lingard, he concluded that the "general body of Catholics" were
loyal citizens who were not aware and would not have approved of the plot (2;
see also 25, 187–88).

While views of the Gunpowder Plot changed in tandem with increasing toleration of Catholics, anti-Catholicism remained very much alive in the 1830s.
In this context, the Church of England clergyman Thomas Lathbury, who published a series of anti-Catholic polemics in the late 1830s, sought in *Guy Fawkes;
or, A Complete History of the Gunpowder Plot* (1839) to defend the Church of
England from "Popery" by countering "recent" work by "Roman Catholic writers," undoubtedly a reference to Lingard (iv, 44). Accordingly, he attacked both
sides of Lingard's and Jardine's arguments. On the one hand, he dismissed the
argument that Catholics were justified in seeking to remedy their situation by
contending that they never "suffered under the execution" of the recusancy laws
(44). On the other, he portrayed Catholics as a threat to the constitution because
their loyalty was to Rome, not to England, by insisting that the Catholic Church
had repeatedly plotted to overthrow the Protestant state and that the pope himself
"approved of the deed" (44; see also iv, 96). Indeed, Lathbury's stated reason for
producing this new history of the plot was to make his readers aware of the continued threat to England posed by the Roman Church (iii–iv).

In choosing to write about Guy Fawkes and making a plea for "TOLERATION"
in his preface (xi), Ainsworth was aligning himself with the Whig response to
the Tory "No Popery" campaign. Early in his narrative, he invokes Whig accusations that the Tories were exploiting a popular desire to find an object of "hate,"
"Papists" now replacing former enemies such as the Welsh, the Scots, or the
Spaniards (1.1.1.12).[4] Following Lingard, whom he cites in his preface (vii–x), he
depicts Catholics as oppressed citizens who see "no hope of better days" and are
entitled to act in defense of their rights, and he then asks: "Is it to be wondered
at that the Papists should repine, — or that some among their number, when all
other means failed, should seek redress by darker measures?" (1.1.1.13, 15). He also
follows Lingard in depicting the plot as a conspiracy led by a very small group that
was not supported by "the whole body of Catholics" (1.1.3.45). On the contrary, he
insists, the "mass of the Catholics had no share" in the various plots against the
state and even when suffering the "bitterest persecution . . . remained constant in
their fidelity to the crown" (1.1.3.44).

While Ainsworth embraces the general idea that the plot was conceived and
carried out by a small group isolated from the majority of Catholics and was opposed by the church, he departs from the tendency in the nineteenth century
to make Guy Fawkes the primary villain and thus the face of the conspiracy. As
Sharpe points out, the movement toward toleration of Catholics seems to have
led participants in November Fifth commemorations to begin displaying effigies

of Guy Fawkes in place of the formerly popular effigies of the pope. This change shifts responsibility for the plot away from the church and the Catholic majority and toward the band of conspirators and, more particularly, the man who was designated to light the fuse (115–16, 138).[5] Although the choice of Fawkes as protagonist reflects this general trend, the novel makes Robert Catesby the mastermind of the plot and its principal villain. From the beginning, therefore, Ainsworth distinguishes between the two men, contrasting Catesby's "mixed" motives with Fawkes's single-minded dedication to the cause (1.1.3.45) and aligning Fawkes with the "secular priests" who "would have been well-contented with toleration for their religion," while associating Catesby with the Jesuits, who "desire the utter subversion of the existing government,—temporal as well as ecclesiastical" (1.1.3.46).

By shifting responsibility to Catesby, Ainsworth aligns his account of the plot with the middle-class critique of aristocracy that exploits religion in order to preserve its social power and status. The novel depicts the Protestant aristocrat Salisbury and the Catholic aristocrat Catesby as mirror images, the former seeking to consolidate state power by exploiting religious prejudice and the latter as seeking to overturn the state. It envisions through Humphrey Chetham the rise of a Whig middle class that does not yet possess the capacity to displace the corrupt aristocracy and restore the rights of Catholics.[6] Drawing on Chartist discourse, Ainsworth instead constructs a marriage plot in which the Catholic Viviana Radcliffe, also a member of the upper classes, rejects both Catesby and Chetham in favor of Guy Fawkes and depicts their unconsummated marriage as a moralizing physical force by transforming the Gunpowder Plot into an act "uncommitted."

❦

Like other Victorian novels, *Guy Fawkes* internalizes to England the national narrative that imagines the resolution of conflict between nations through a marriage plot uniting representatives of each culture. The opposition between Catholic Ireland and Protestant England in a novel like *The Wild Irish Girl* becomes in *Guy Fawkes* the conflict between recusant Catholics and the Protestant state. Accordingly, the novel depicts the courtship of the Catholic Viviana Radcliffe by the Protestant Humphrey Chetham. Moreover, in keeping with the shift from culture to class in the Victorian novel, Viviana belongs to the aristocracy, while Humphrey is a merchant belonging to the rising middle class.[7] Thus the novel's marriage plot projects the possibility of a union in which, in accord with the companionate ideal, the partners come to love and respect one another precisely through the articulation of their disagreements, hence enabling them to unite in spite of class and religious difference. In this respect, Chetham's courtship of Viviana Radcliffe accords with the Whig discourse of toleration that would accord citizenship and equal rights to Catholics.

In keeping with the rise-of-the-middle-class narrative, Chetham would displace his aristocratic rival, the Catholic Robert Catesby, who adheres to the kinship model of courtship. Catesby treats class and religion not as qualities of self that he shares with Viviana and that might form the basis of companionship but rather as forms of political allegiance that would provide the basis of a kinship alliance. Accordingly, he insists that Viviana will not marry a man of Chetham's "degree" or "faith," not because these differences make them personally incompatible, but because they do not provide the basis for a kinship alliance (2.1.18.49; see also 1.1.5.89). In keeping with the kinship model, Catesby and his supporters invoke patriarchal authority, as when, for example, Father Oldcorne claims to "represent her father" in forbidding her to marry Chetham and in attempting to make her marry Catesby (1.1.5.90, 2.1.19.61). However, the novel undercuts these claims by making her father's role indirect—it never depicts him forbidding her to marry—and by shifting paternal authority to the suspect Jesuit, Oldcorne, whom Viviana, in accord with convention, addresses as "father." She insists, moreover, that while her father might have forbidden her to marry Chetham, he would "never" have forced her to marry Catesby (2.1.19.62). In keeping with this depiction of kinship alliances, Ainsworth makes this attempt to compel Viviana to submit to a "forced marriage" quite literal when Catesby engages Oldcorne to make her go through with the ceremony and resorts to a thinly veiled threat of rape when he warns her that "the time will come when you may desire to have the ceremony repeated" (2.1.19.57, 64).

Precisely because of their apparent similarity in rank, Catesby courts Viviana not for the unique qualities that distinguish her but for the sake of his own personal interests. He seeks to restore his family fortunes both by obtaining her property—he asserts that he will make the "mistress [of Ordsall Hall] mine, her estates mine," thus equating her with her property (1.1.15.286)—and by making her father an ally in the plot that will bring his family back into power. Viviana accordingly "doubt[s] the *disinterestedness* of his love" (1.1.13.233; emphasis added). The novel further reinforces the depiction of kinship unions as transgressing the companionate ideal, which as we have seen in *Wat Tyler* emphasizes monogamy, by depicting Catesby as conspiring to commit bigamy, the revelation of which ultimately saves Viviana from the marriage.

Catesby's courtship of Viviana parallels his use of the Gunpowder Plot for his own personal ends rather than for the sake of his fellow Catholics. Just as Catesby courts Viviana in order to promote his own self-interests, he promotes the Gunpowder Plot in order to "retriev[e] his own condition" and restore his fortune (1.1.3.41). The intertwining of the marriage and national plots is apparent from the beginning in Catesby's belief that his success would be assured if he "could but link Radcliffe [her father] to our cause, or win the hand of his fair daughter [Viviana], and so bind him to me" as well as in Father Garnet's linkage of the plot and marriage when he insists that Radcliffe "*shall* join the plot, and [Viviana] *shall* wed Catesby" (1.1.3.40, 1.1.11.208).

The novel thus links the use of force in marriage and the use of physical force in the Gunpowder Plot to the imposition of religion, as opposed to religious tolerance, thus depicting the plotters as paradoxically promoting the very intolerance under which Catholics suffer. Catesby seeks to employ physical force not merely to "redress . . . the wrongs of his church" and end the oppression of Catholics but also to foment an "insurrection" that will overturn the constitution by restoring Catholicism as the state religion (1.1.3.41–42, 45). As in depictions of Chartist oratory in parliamentary discourse, he addresses a "long and inflammatory harangue" expatiating with "great eloquence and fervour on the wrongs of the Catholic party" and calls not merely for the parliamentary franchise but for a complete reordering of the state: "The Parliament-house being the place where all the mischief done us has been contrived by our adversaries, it is fitting that it should be the place of their chastisement" (1.1.13.243, 245). Consequently, the Gunpowder Plot would merely invert the existing situation, in which the Protestant aristocracy disenfranchises Catholics, with another in which a Catholic aristocracy disenfranchises Protestants.

In parallel with the Catholic aristocracy as represented by Catesby, Ainsworth, in accord with Whig discourse, depicts a Protestant aristocracy that, as in the Tory "No Popery" campaign, claims to defend the Protestant constitution but in fact oppresses Catholics to further its own political aims. Following Lingard, Ainsworth suggests that the conspirators resorted to violence only because King James was exploiting the recusancy laws for his own "profit" (viii, 1.1.1.14).[8] While James benefits from the fines he levies on recusants, Salisbury goes even further by allowing the plot, which he has discovered early on and "could at any time have crushed," to go forward "for his own purposes" (3.2.14.83, 3.3.7.245; see also 2.2.9.284, 3.2.12.32). If the Gunpowder Plot is primarily a means for the Catholic aristocracy to restore its fortunes, so too the Protestant state serves the ends of a corrupt aristocracy that has gained its power and wealth at the expense of Catholics.

Because the conflict is not between aristocratic Catholics and middle-class Catholics but between Catholic and Protestant aristocrats, it cannot be resolved by uniting Viviana with Chetham, and the novel instead seeks a resolution by uniting her with Guy Fawkes. While the companionate courtship of Viviana by Chetham looks forward to a reformed society dominated by a tolerant middle class, the novel does not realize the possibility that Chetham can effect that reform. Instead it is Guy Fawkes who, insisting that his role is to "act, not talk" (1.1.13.243), possesses the capacity to act so as to enfranchise Catholics. Unlike Chetham, Fawkes is willing to employ physical force to back up his moral-force claims even as his union with Viviana enables him to moralize physical force.

Just as Catesby's attempts to force Viviana to marry are both a means of forwarding the plot through kinship alliance and a parallel to its use of force, so Viviana marries Fawkes as a means of forestalling the plot, and her marriage itself becomes an analogue for moralizing physical force. She marries Fawkes in the hope that she can "save" him by preventing him from carrying out the plot and repeatedly attempts to foil it (2.2.10.303). Furthermore, just as she contrives to keep their marriage unconsummated by making "the moment of [their] union . . . the moment of [their] separation" (3.3.9.274), so, upon learning that the plot has failed, she rejoices that the "dreadful crime with which [she] feared [her] husband's soul would have been loaded is *now uncommitted*" (3.3.2.127; emphasis added). By depicting a union that, although unconsummated, remains a marriage, the novel suggests that the Gunpowder Plot, though uncommitted, ultimately enfranchises Catholics.

Although, in keeping with the companionate ideal, Guy and Viviana fall in love, the monogamy imperative means that they do not consummate it. Guy worries that marrying Viviana will make him unfaithful to "Heaven, to which [he] was first espoused" (3.2.11.18) and elsewhere proclaims that he is "wedded to the great cause" (2.1.20.77; see also 2.2.10.302). In accord with the companionate principle that one cannot fall in love a second time, Viviana, whose first love is Humphrey Chetham, contrives that "the moment the ceremony is over" she and Guy will part and "shall never meet again in this world," their union "an espousal with the dead" in which she will "mourn [him] as a widow" (3.2.11.16). If her intention of not consummating the marriage is not already obvious, she makes it abundantly clear in her assurance to Chetham that he should not be "jealous" of her love of Guy because it is "a higher and a holier passion . . . affection mixed with admiration, and purified of all its grossness" (2.2.5.184). At the beginning of the narrative, when she is in love with Chetham but cannot marry him, Viviana intends to honor the monogamy imperative by entering a convent. The unconsummated marriage to Fawkes both honors that imperative and enables her to act to make possible such a union in the future.

Similarly, Viviana seeks both to prevent the execution of the plot and to advance it as an act uncommitted. In its very grammatical construction—the "crime
. . . is now uncommitted"—her statement suggests that the failed plot is an action, though reversed, rather than a nonaction. On the one hand, she attempts to
persuade Guy that the plot is evil, manages to prevent her father from joining it,
intervenes herself to derail it, and, when Guy declares his love, wishes that she
could "prevent" him from acting and so "save" him (2.2.10.303). Similarly, after
the plot fails, she repeatedly seeks to "bring him to repentance" so as to save his
soul (3.3.2.129, 3.3.9.274, 3.3.11.291, 3.3.14.323). On the other hand, however, she
claims that she "should never have loved" Fawkes if he "had not been a conspirator" (3.3.9.273) and, once they are married, offers him her fortune, "even in the
furtherance of his design against the state, which, though I cannot approve it,
seems good to him" (3.2.11.17). After her initial arrest, she declares her loyalty to
the Crown in accord with her commitment to the constitution but nonetheless
refuses to betray the conspirators, and later she admits that her failure to reveal the
plot makes her "as guilty as if [she] had been its contriver" (2.2.7.220–21, 3.3.2.128).
Just as, in Lingard's account, the conspirators held the plot in abeyance while
pursuing more peaceful means of achieving their aims (9.36) and just as the
Chartists treated physical force as an unrealized potentiality held in check while
moral force acts, so Viviana seeks to achieve the aims of the plot by allowing it to
go forward even as she hopes that it will remain uncommitted.

Viviana falls in love with Guy because he alone has the potential to make the
plot moral. He claims that the plot is the only means to achieve justice, but he
ultimately persists in it for a different reason: he has sworn an oath declaring that
he will not "desist from the execution thereof" unless the other conspirators give
him leave to do so (title page). By focusing on the oath—he quotes it on the title
page and has the conspirators swear to it on three occasions (1.1.3.43, 1.1.13.242,
3.2.11.24)—Ainsworth transforms Fawkes's perseverance in the plan to commit
an atrocity into a sign of his sincerity and integrity.[9] In contradistinction to the
rhetoric suggesting that Catholics are loyal to Rome rather than England, which
dictated that in order to exercise the rights granted by Catholic Emancipation
they must take an oath declaring their loyalty to the English constitution, Ainsworth makes Fawkes's refusal to break his oath a sign not of disloyalty but of the
purity of his motives.[10]

Fawkes can persist in the plot while remaining moral—and once again manifest his integrity—because a series of proleptic visions make him increasingly
aware that it will remain uncommitted. The novel begins with a proleptic vision
of the failure of the plot by the Catholic prophetess Elizabeth Orton (1.1.2.29–30)

and similar predictions by Dr. Dee and Saint Winifred follow (1.1.8.162, 1.1.12.223). There are many other omens that it will miscarry, including the sight of the heads of traitors on London Bridge (2.2.1.97), the mysterious tolling of a bell when the conspirators are at work on the tunnel underneath Parliament (2.2.4.174), and the prorogation of Parliament until November, a month that is "unlucky" for Fawkes (3.2.11.4; see also 2.2.11.306). Unlike the normal use of dramatic prolepsis, which forewarns the reader of a possible outcome, these visions announce something the reader already knows; by reinforcing from the beginning the fact that Fawkes will not commit the crime, these forewarnings further encourage us to see him as a man of integrity. Thus, even as he feels compelled to persist with the plot himself, he seeks to save others from association with it, assisting Viviana in preventing her father from becoming involved and resisting the involvement of Viviana herself.

The action of the last third of the novel consequently focuses not on the plot but on Fawkes's repentance for his crime. Rather than make November Fifth the climax of the novel, Ainsworth locates the exposure of the plot and the arrest of Fawkes just before the end of the second of its three parts. The resulting anticlimax enables him to subvert the forward momentum toward the planned explosion and to shift the emphasis to the process of Fawkes's repentance.[11] In keeping with his persistence in the plot as a matter of justice and honor, Fawkes declines to repent his role in it but ultimately, at the moment of Viviana's death, accedes to her pleas and acknowledges his "error" (3.3.11.292, 3.3.14.323–24; see also 3.3.5.188). In this way he insists on the integrity of his motives and at the same time makes the confession that absolves him from the crime he intended to commit.

While the union of Viviana and Chetham cannot resolve the conflict between Catholics and Protestants, the unconsummated union of Viviana and Fawkes holds open a future in which, in accord with the companionate ideal, Catholic and Protestant might marry. On two occasions, Fawkes encourages a union between Viviana and Chetham (2.2.4.162–63, 2.2.10.288–89), and Viviana herself more than once suggests that she would be "happier" married to Chetham than to Fawkes (2.2.8.228, 243). These passages suggest that in marrying Fawkes she forgoes the happiness associated with the companionate ideal because it is not available so long as Catholics are disenfranchised.

Yet by keeping open the possibility that Viviana might have married Chetham, the novel projects a future in which a tolerant (Whig) middle class displaces an aristocratic culture that oppresses Catholics. Catesby, Fawkes, Viviana, Garnett, and the other conspirators die, and the only character for whom the novel

imagines a future is Chetham. Near the end of the narrative, when Chetham declares—in allegiance to the companionate ideal—that he will "never love again,"
Viviana suggests that he find a substitute for marriage in devoting himself "to
the *business* of life," advice that he takes quite literally by "sedulously" following
"his mercantile pursuits" and becoming the "wealthiest merchant" in Manchester (3.3.10.282, 283–84; emphasis added). By employing his wealth to found a
school and a library, moreover, he becomes, although unmarried and childless,
a "father to the fatherless and the destitute" (3.3.10.284; see also preface x). In the
nineteenth century, the narrative implies, these progeny have become the Whig
middle class who manifest the belief in "toleration" espoused by Viviana shortly
before her death when she envisions a future in which "all the believers in the
True God will be enabled to worship him in peace, though at different altars"
(3.3.7.231). In accord with Whig discourse, the novel's conclusion suggests that
privileging the agency of the middle class—making it the governing party—will
unite not only Catholics and Protestants but also upper and lower classes.

CHAPTER 5

Class Alliance and Self-Culture
in *Barnaby Rudge*

Barnaby Rudge joins both *Wat Tyler* and *Guy Fawkes* in depicting a popular uprising at the moment when the first phase of Chartism was coming to a close and the second phase was getting under way and, like the latter, adopts the Whig critique of the "intolerance" of the Tories' "No Popery" campaigns (3).[1] *Barnaby Rudge* differs from *Wat Tyler* and *Guy Fawkes*, however, in that it does not depict the men who employ physical force as having been deprived of their rights. Indeed, whereas Ainsworth depicts Catholics using force in an attempt to restore their rights, Dickens represents Protestants using force in order to maintain the oppression of Catholics, while the novel's heroic protagonists, Edward Chester and Joe Willett, fight against, not with, the insurgents.

While *Barnaby Rudge*, like *Guy Fawkes*, does not depict Chartism, it does represent the past in terms of contemporary parliamentary discourse depicting the competition between the aristocracy and middle class for the right to govern the nation. Dickens chose the topic of the Gordon Riots nearly two years before the emergence of Chartism, almost certainly in response to the revival in 1835 of the Protestant Association (in its earlier incarnation the fomenter of the Gordon Riots) and the "No Popery" campaigns through which the Tories sought to regain control of Parliament, but when he wrote the novel in 1841, the similarities between 1780 and 1839—notably thousands of protestors marching through London to present a petition to Parliament and then subsequently rioting—would have been unmistakable. However, this does not mean that Dickens sought to represent the Chartists in his depiction of the rioters.[2] Rather, he portrayed the rioters in terms of Whig discourse by depicting a Tory aristocracy that foments anti-Catholic feeling among the lower classes in order to promote its own interests. In other words, Dickens responded not directly to Chartism but rather to the parliamentary discourse that developed in response to it, with the Whigs arguing that the Tories, who had exploited anti-Catholicism for political purposes, were now exploiting and indeed allying themselves with the Chartists to the same end.[3]

Accordingly, the novel's fictional plot employs parliamentary discourse depicting the aristocracy and middle class as possessing the capacity to exercise social agency on behalf of the lower classes, who do not have the capacity to act responsibly. In accord with Whig discourse contending that the aristocracy uses its political power to promote its own interests rather than those of the nation as a whole, the novel depicts the antipapist rioters as allied with and acting under the direction of Sir John Chester, who leads them to believe that they are united by a shared English Protestantism, whereas his real interest is in preserving his class status, which divides him from them. As in Whig discourse, which at this time was proposing an alliance between the Chartists and the middle class (Chase, *Chartism* 173–178, 193–201), the novel's conclusion depicts Chester's son Edward, who rejects his genteel status and enters the rising middle class, offering an alliance with the lower classes that will provide them with social agency.

Parliamentary discourse manifests itself primarily in the novel's national marriage plot, which centers on the union of a Catholic woman, Emma Haredale, and a Protestant male, Edward Chester.[4] In order to prevent this marriage and so preserve his status by marrying his son to a wealthy heiress, Sir John stirs up religious conflict, both between the two families and between English citizens. To this end, he forms an alliance with Sim Tappertit and the United Bulldogs by appealing to a shared English Protestantism in which both he and they presumably share an interest. As Sir John's motivations reveal, however, the barrier to the marriage of Edward and Emma is not religion but class. Consequently, the companionate marriage with which the novel concludes does not involve the suppression of Catholicism in favor of Protestantism—Emma converting in order to become united with Edward—but rather Edward converting from gentleman to member of the rising middle class. In turn, this marriage, together with the marriage of their doubles, Joe Willett and Dolly Varden, mediates a homosocial bond uniting the middle class and lower classes and displacing the self-serving aristocracy.

In its depiction of working-class agency as alliance with the middle classes, *Barnaby Rudge* does not, like *Wat Tyler* and *Guy Fawkes*, employ Chartist discourse depicting moralized physical force as a form of social agency but rather depicts moralized physical force as a form of nonagency. The novel represents the dominant aristocracy, in particular Sir John, as exercising social agency by preventing the lower classes from developing the rationality necessary to become social agents and thereby manipulating them into serving its own interests. Because the aim of the Gordon Riots—in contrast to the aims, if not the means, of the Peasant Rebellion and the Gunpowder Plot—is unjust, the riots can be moral only in the negative sense that the rioters' antipathy toward Catholics has been fomented by a governing class that exploits their incapacity for rational judgment, a situation manifested in its most extreme form in the mentally debilitated Barnaby Rudge, who gets caught up in a cause that he cannot understand. The novel instead envisions the lower classes allying with the middle class, which, unlike the aristocracy, does not seek to maintain its position by co-opting the lower classes but unites with them in the common project of self-culture that develops the capacity for reason necessary for exercising social agency responsibly. Thus, at the novel's conclusion, even Barnaby Rudge is becoming "more rational" (82.687).

⌒

Barnaby Rudge depicts John Chester as an aristocrat whose actions always aim ultimately to protect his genteel status, which means having a source of income—if not rent from an estate, then funds in the bank—ensuring that he does not have to work to support himself. In accord with middle-class discourse depicting an unproductive and idle aristocracy, the novel depicts him as a fop and "idler" who first attempts to maintain his status through kinship alliance and, when that fails, obtains a seat in Parliament—for a close borough, of course—and through it a knighthood (15.128). Just as he keeps his distance from Gordon and the Protestant Association while secretly fomenting the "No Popery" cause for his own purposes, so he becomes a member of the governing elite in Parliament, which makes a show of rejecting the Protestant petition but creates the Protestant mob by supporting "bad criminal laws, bad prison regulations, and the worst conceivable police" and then fails to prevent the conflict from evolving into a full-blown uprising (49.407, 52.435).

The novel's national narrative centers on Sir John's attempt to maintain his status by matching his son with a wealthy heiress, which in turn leads him to conspire against his son's intention to marry Emma Haredale. In accord with the view of marriage as a "contract between two families" in which parents choose their children's marriage partners for "economic or social or political consolidation or aggrandizement of the family" (Stone 182), he insists that "marriage is a civil contract; people marry to better their worldly condition and improve appearances; it is an affair of house and furniture, of liveries, servants, equipage, and so forth" (32.268). As "a younger son's younger son" who would not receive an inheritance, he had contracted to receive a "fortune" in exchange for providing the granddaughter of a butcher entry into "the politest and best circles" of society. Having exhausted this fortune, he now expects his son to marry wealth in order to "provide for" him and "preserv[e] . . . that gentility . . . which our family have so long sustained" (15.133–34, 134, 32.270).

In order to form kinship matches in an era in which the competing companionate ideal has begun to prevail, Sir John appeals to religion and foments religious conflict. He must overcome the problem that, in accord with the companionate model, the butcher's daughter has fallen in love with another man, the Catholic Geoffrey Haredale. Consequently, he not only offers the usual exchange of his status for her money but also claims an underlying religious affiliation in order to persuade her father that she should not marry a Catholic.[5] Similarly, he invokes the "religious point of view" as the reason his son should not marry Emma Haredale, even as he reveals that his main concern is not religion but status when he admits that he would allow his son to marry a Catholic if she were "amazingly rich" (15.136). While this appeal to religion does not persuade Edward precisely because it reveals its roots in class interest, Sir John is able to persuade Geoffrey Haredale to join him in opposing the marriage by avoiding the issue of class and appealing only to his religious antipathies. Haredale in turn fails to recall that the antipathy between their families arose not from the difference of religion per se but from his sexual rivalry with Sir John, who used religion to thwart his companionate union.

Just as he exploits religion in an attempt to force his son into a kinship union, Sir John foments the antipapist riots both to preserve his status and, implicitly, to preserve the political power of the governing aristocracy. Not surprisingly, he self-consciously adopts the role of Salisbury, the secretary of state who, as we have seen, was suspected of allowing the Gunpowder Plot to proceed "for his own purposes."[6] Indeed, nearly all of Sir John's actions—particularly the attack on Haredale's home, which serves as cover for the kidnapping of Emma—can be traced back to his desire to prevent the marriage of Edward and Emma in order to promote a kinship match and, more generally, to consolidate the power of his class.

To this end, the novel constructs chains of social agency with Sir John as primary agent at one end and various proxies who merely enact his commands at the other.[7] In one of these chains, he makes Gordon's secretary, Gashford, his "fit agent" whom he "set on" to do his "work" (81.677). Gashford in turn acts both through George Gordon and through the supposed leaders of the riots. He ventriloquizes Gordon's speeches, which explains why the latter can be surprised at his own boldness (35.290), and originates the plan for the procession to Parliament that leads to a violent confrontation that Gordon did not intend to take place. He also selects Barnaby, Hugh, and Dennis as leaders during the riots and directs their actions, whispering to Hugh the command to leap into the lobby of Parliament when the other men are beginning to panic (49.411), goading Hugh and Dennis to attack Catholic chapels, complaining that they are not putting enough "meaning into [their] work" (52.435), and urging them to utterly destroy Haredale's home. To ensure that Gashford does not stray from his purposes, Sir John forms another chain, in which he makes one of these men, Maypole Hugh, a second proxy, whom he "set[s] . . . on" both to thwart the Edward/Emma romance and to foment the riots (23.198–99). He thus not only uses Gashford to direct the actions of Barnaby, Hugh, and Dennis and, through them, the lower classes, but also uses Hugh to ensure that Gashford acts according to his plan.

By using these proxies Sir John and Gashford conceal their agency and thus their pursuit of self-interest. Although Gashford tells Dennis that "Lord George has thought of [him] as an excellent leader," it is Gashford himself who has chosen him (37.313); similarly, while he repeatedly intervenes to make sure that Dennis and the others act according to plan, he insists that Dennis is the "perfect master of [his] own actions" (53.439). Sir John likewise denies that he has "set [Hugh] on" to accost Dolly Varden (23.198), and when, later, Hugh intimates that he has carried out Sir John's commands maintains that he has not given him any orders: "When you say I ordered you, my good fellow, you imply that I directed you to do something for me—something I wanted done—*something for my own ends and purposes*—you see? Now I am sure I needn't enlarge upon the extreme absurdity of such an idea, however unintentional" (40.334; emphasis added). In accord with Haredale's observation that "men of [Sir John's] capacity plot in secrecy and safety, and leave exposed posts to the duller wits" (43.360), he does Gashford one better by keeping his distance from Gordon's Protestant Association and so ensuring that he can deny his role in the antipapist campaign. Similarly, although both men remain behind the scenes during the riots so that their role will not be visible, Gashford risks exposure by visiting the Boot Inn and the Green Lanes to give directions to his lackeys, while Sir John maintains an even greater distance from events by working exclusively from his private apartment.

Consequently, the elites are able to persuade members of the lower classes that Catholics, not the aristocracy, are the source of their oppression. Although the novel alludes to Gordon's speeches, it does not represent him or anyone else articulating a reasoned case for the antipapist cause, and the rioters have at best a confused notion of why they have joined it. Barnaby "believe[s] with his whole heart and soul that he [is] engaged in a just cause," but he is incapable of understanding what it is about (49.412). Hugh, who has such a confused notion of the cause that he confuses "no popery" with "no property," joins not because he believes it is just but because Sir John orders him to do so (38.316). Meanwhile, Dennis the hangman characteristically understands the cause in terms of his self-interest, opposing the "papists" because they prefer "boil[ing] and roast[ing]" to the "sound, Protestant, constitutional, English work" of hanging (37.312, 311). Appropriately, the rioting mob, like Barnaby's raven, merely mimics the "no popery" cry without understanding what it means.

In keeping with this depiction, the novel links agency with the rational ability to calculate one's self-interest and the relative lack of agency with the absence of rational calculation. Sir John's insistence on genteel poise—the novel repeatedly depicts him as calm and imperturbable—arises from his determination to subordinate emotion to cool calculation (e.g., 12.108, 24.203). While Gashford calculates his self-interest and thus has the rational capacity to manipulate "poor crazy Lord" Gordon (82.683), he is also driven by passionate hatreds, which make him susceptible to manipulation by Sir John. In turn, both Sir John and Gashford can manipulate the lower classes, who are almost completely incapable of rational calculation. Dickens's original intention of making the leaders of the riots a trio of escapees from Bedlam survives in repeated depictions of the rioters as "madmen" and in the comment that "if Bedlam gates had been flung wide open, there would not have issued forth such maniacs as the frenzy of that night had made" (55.461–62; see also 67.557).[8] Far from acting in a rational manner to achieve a specific aim that would improve their condition, the rioters are driven by "spontaneous" feelings: "The great mass never reasoned or thought at all, but were stimulated by their own headlong passions, by poverty, by ignorance, by the love of mischief, and the hope of plunder" (53.438).

At the same time, however, the novel suggests that this irrationality is not intrinsic to the lower classes but has been "fostered" by the governing elite (49.407). Sir John brings Hugh under his power in part by offering him drink, and Hugh obligingly declares that given enough drink he will "do murder" (23.196). Gashford likewise plies Hugh and Dennis with liquor in order to bring them to a fever pitch during the riots (50.417–18). Not coincidentally, Dickens chooses as the culminating scene of the riots the attack on the premises of Langdale the vintner, during which the rioters reach such a degree of "maniac rage" that they drink themselves to death (68.569).

In this respect, whereas *Wat Tyler* suggests that physical force might have succeeded if the people understood their strength, *Barnaby Rudge* implies that it is doomed to failure precisely because the people do not understand that the riots are not a means of achieving reform but of maintaining the power of the governing elite. Persuaded by the aristocracy that they are acting in their own interests, the rioters attack Catholics they have been led to see as the other, but ultimately their violence rebounds upon themselves, and they die in the fires they have set, transformed into "the dust and ashes of the flames they had kindled" (68.571).

While Egan and Ainsworth employ Chartist discourse in which physical force can be an element of social agency, Dickens depicts the use of physical force as ultimately serving the interest of the governing elite and so seeks to envision an alternative form of agency. Whereas *Wat Tyler* and *Guy Fawkes* construct heroic figures who seek to moralize physical force while advancing the aims of those who employ it, the heroes of *Barnaby Rudge*, Edward Chester and Joe Willett, oppose the aims of the mob and therefore have no reason to moralize its violence. At the same time, however, they do not join the governing elite in attempting to suppress the riots but, acting of their own accord, merely rescue the victims of the rioters' violence. Dickens thus imagines social agency through the history that brings about the sudden reappearance of Edward and Joe, each having spent the previous five years in the New World.

The novel envisions this alternative form of agency through a national marriage plot involving two pairs of rivals, Edward Chester and Gashford, who pursue Emma Haredale, and Joe Willett and Sim Tappertit, who court Dolly Varden. Gashford and Tappertit seek to affiliate themselves with the aristocracy by attempting to enhance their social status through kinship marriage. By contrast, the companionate unions—of Edward and Emma, Joe and Dolly—with which the novel concludes signal the triumph of the middle-class ideal of self-culture and mediate an alliance between the middle class and working class that does not, like the aristocrat–working-class alliance, involve domination of the latter by the former but rather enables members of the working classes to become rational social agents. In place of the alliance between Sir John and Sim Tappertit, through which the novel represents aristocrats as agents who manipulate and subordinate their working-class allies, the novel depicts the companionate union of Edward Chester and Joe Willett.

Sim, like Sir John, ultimately does not seek social reform but rather foments the riots in order to make possible a kinship alliance that will serve his own interests.[9] The Prentice Knights' chief grievance is not that their masters mistreat them in the workplace but that they do not allow them to marry their daughters, which would enable them to become their successors through marriage rather than through their own efforts in learning their trade. The only complaint made by Mark Gilbert, an applicant for admission to the Prentice Knights, is that his master pulled his ears for looking at his daughter, and although Sim claims that Gabriel Varden is "tyrannical," he never cites any specific abuses (59.496). What hinders both men is not an imperious master but the fact that they regard court-ship as a negotiation with their master rather than as a matter of winning the affection of his daughter. Thus Mark Gilbert admits that he "cannot say that [his master's] daughter loves him" (8.74), and the fact that Sim does not proscribe Gabriel Varden but his rival, Joe Willett, reveals that the real barrier to his court-ship of Dolly is that she loves another man.

Sim allies himself with Sir John by offering to help thwart the romance be-tween Edward and Emma in the hope that he will in turn help him interfere with the romance between Joe and Dolly. Like Sir John, Sim has no real interest in the anti-Catholic cause but seems to have transformed the Prentice Knights into the United Bulldogs for the express purpose of using the riots as a cover for the abduction of Emma and Dolly. Accordingly, he envisions "the altered state of society" that will emerge when the Protestant Association is "victorious" not as establishing a new social or political order but as enabling him to take possession of Dolly Varden in marriage (39.331).

Like Sim, with whom he conspires to abduct Emma and Dolly, Gashford seeks to enhance his status by allying himself with Sir John. Whereas Sim joins the Protestant cause and allies with Sir John to prevent one marriage in order to promote his own, Gashford joins in the plot to prevent the marriage of Edward and Emma as a means of affiliating himself with Sir John and gaining acceptance as a member of the Protestant nation. The fact that he is willing to achieve this status at the expense of his former coreligionists manifests itself in the way that his support for kinship alliances involves the forceful imposition of a marriage partner on an unwilling woman. Gashford had previously made an advantageous match with the daughter of his "benefactor" by "robb[ing] her of her virtue" and then compounded the element of coercion by physically abusing her once they were married (43.362). Similarly, his aim in abducting Emma Haredale is not to make a kinship match but, in an inversion of the kinship ideal, to make her unmarriageable by "dishonouring" her—sexually assaulting her or creating the suspicion that she has had sexual congress—and leaving her unmarried (81.678).

In opposition to Sir John, who foments religious discord in order to promote kinship alliances that sustain the aristocracy, his son Edward embraces the com-panionate ideal that resolves religious conflict by uniting Catholic and Protestant. As previous discussions have suggested, the gendering of such unions—typically the man is English and Protestant and the woman Celtic and Catholic—implies that these resolutions involve the subordination of the latter to the former. As I discuss in the introduction, however, authors of national narratives could envision the resolution of conflict through marriage precisely because their novels depicted it as a companionate union between individuals who, though different from one another in gender and religion, are equal partners in marriage.[10]

The union between Edward and Emma therefore does not involve a Catholic woman adopting the Protestant religion of her husband but rather the aristocratic male forgoing his genteel status and entering the tolerant middle class. Just as Lord Gordon persuades members of the lower classes that Protestantism provides the basis of their shared political interests as Englishmen, so Sir John equates being "undutiful" with being "irreligious" and seeks to make familial loyalty a matter of religious piety by threatening his son with a "curse" that would exclude him from the family, and the nation. His agency—the power of his curse—consists in the ability to advance his class interests by creating the illusion that they are equals who share a single religious identity. When, however, Edward responds to his father by declaring his belief that no "man on earth" has the "power to call [a curse] down upon his fellow—least of all, upon his own child," he manifests the rational capacity to recognize that this power rests not on religion but on class privilege (32.270–71).

Consequently, he shifts his attention from religion to class and rejects the gentility that has prevented him from pursuing self-culture. Sir John has raised his son in "luxury and idleness," giving him a gentleman's education that teaches him to disdain "those means, by which men *raise* themselves to riches and distinction" and refusing, by the same token, to give him "the means of devoting [his] abilities and energies . . . to some worthy pursuit" (15.132, 133; emphasis added). When Edward breaks with his father, he seeks instead to make his own way in the world by going to the West Indies, where he is not "too proud to be employed" working on a friend's estate (78.651). In short, he rejects the idle aristocracy and becomes an industrious member of the rising middle class. As opposed to aristocratic agency that seeks to ensure its status and power by subordinating its working-class allies, middle-class agency takes the form of self-culture and self-making that can be adopted by the lower classes.

By making the trajectories of Edward Chester and Joe Willett symmetrical, the novel envisions a shift of social agency from an aristocracy that co-opts the lower classes to a middle class that, as in companionate marriage, unites with them as equal partners. Edward and Joe court the quasi sisters Emma and Dolly (they were raised together in the Varden household), come into conflict with their fathers over the question of who controls decisions about marriage, and ultimately break with them, the latter episodes occurring in successive chapters that mark the conclusion of the first half of the novel.[11] When they reappear many chapters later, they have become allies who unite to rescue victims of the riots.

In this respect, the novel suggests, like Whig discourse, that the lower classes should abandon their alliance with the aristocracy (Sim Tappertit and Sir John) and instead join with the middle classes (Joe Willett and Edward Chester). The Whig press not only accused the Tories of allying with the Chartists but also suggested that it would be in the interest of the working classes to support the Whig campaign to repeal the Corn Laws. Indeed, even as Dickens was working on *Barnaby Rudge*, the *Morning Chronicle* was suggesting that the Chartists were having second thoughts about their alliance with the Tories and were now beginning to support the campaign for repeal, while some Whig politicians, as noted above, were explicitly proposing an alliance between the Chartists and the middle class.[12]

The novel depicts Joe Willett as such a working-class ally through its representation of the courtship plots that position his rivalry with Sim Tappertit in parallel with Edward's courtship of Emma and Gashford's attempt to dishonor her. Whereas Sim and Gashford seek to advance their status through alliance with Sir John, Joe not only assists Edward in resisting his father's attempts to interfere with his courtship of Emma but also rebels against his own father, who supports Sir John's claim to dictate who his son will marry when he declares that there will be "no love making . . . unbeknown to parents" (29.242). Yet, just as Edward recognizes that his father's curse has no power over him, so Joe can defy John Willett's attempt to put him "upon his patrole" (29.242). Indeed, putting him on *parole* (his word of honor) instead sends him on *patrol* as a soldier who aims not to fight for "king and country" but to work for "bread and meat" and so make his own way in the world (31.260).

Edward's and Joe's subsequent courtships of Emma and Dolly mediate a homosocial bond in which they ally against the social order that seeks to prevent them from forming companionate unions. Whereas the alliance of the lower classes with the aristocracy leads to attacks on Catholics, Edward and Joe unite first to rescue the Catholics Haredale and Langdale from the rioters and then to rescue Emma and Dolly from their rivals. Thus, even as their courtship of Emma and Dolly mediates their relationship, leading them to become allies, only by becoming allies can they complete the process of courtship and form marital unions.

This homosocial alliance takes the form of mutual self-making, with Joe announcing that he intends to join Edward as his employee in the West Indies. In accord with the companionate model in which the partners are equal but different, Joe will be subordinate to Edward as his employee but will nonetheless be his equal in that he can similarly cultivate himself and rise into the middle class. Moreover, by conveying the knowledge that Edward had previously been employed on a friend's estate through the speech in which Joe informs his father he intends to work for Edward, the novel suggests that, like Edward, he will eventually rise to the status of employer himself (78.651). The novel thus implies that instead of seeking to enhance his status by allying with Sir John and attempting to marry Varden's daughter, Sim should have sought to rise into the middle class through diligent labor as Gabriel Varden's apprentice. Whereas Edward and Joe are willing to accept a decline in their fortunes that enables them to rise into a middle class that is "superior" to the aristocracy, Sim's attempt to rise through his alliance with the aristocracy leads only to decline, from locksmith's apprentice to shoeblack.

While these symmetries in the marriage plots draw on Whig discourse contending that the lower classes should join with the middle classes, the novel's depiction of the fate of its major characters raises questions about the degree to which it succeeds in portraying self-culture as a form of social agency. The summing up of characters' fates in the concluding chapter omits all mention of Joe's plan to go to the West Indies and instead depicts him as having assumed his father's role as proprietor of the Maypole. On the one hand, this new status corresponds with the idea that he will rise into the middle class. On the other hand, the conclusion gives no indication that he has earned this position through his labors; on the contrary, he finances the restoration of the Maypole through the traditional kinship-marriage mechanism of the dowry and eventually, in spite of having abandoned the possibility, inherits it from his father. Perhaps even more surprisingly, the conclusion gives the reader only the barest glimpse of what is in store for Edward, the fact that he and Emma "came back to England" appearing only as a brief aside in the narrator's three-paragraph account of the fate of Barnaby Rudge. The fact that the narrative gives no indication of what Edward does once he returns to England suggests that the work of self-culture has come to an end.

While this disappearance of industrious self-culture suggests that self-making can only take place outside of England, Dickens must have been aware that the New World to which Edward and Joe emigrate was under the dominion of English law and so reproduced the old social structures that thwart self-culture. Edward finds work on an estate that presumably would have used slave labor, and Joe ends up fighting a war to maintain British rule over the American colonies. While it seems unlikely that Dickens meant to undermine his vision of self-culture as the basis of a middle- and working-class alliance, the conclusion of his novel suggests that he cannot yet imagine an England in which it can be realized.

PART II

"The Land! The Land! The Land!"

Land Ownership as Political Reform, 1842–1848

Agricultural Reform, Young England's Allotments, and the Chartist Land Plan

On October 19, 1844, the *Northern Star* reprinted without comment a report from the *Times* under the title "Young England in Yorkshire! The Land-Allotment System" (7; see *Times* 14 Oct. 1844: 3). Why would the leading Chartist newspaper show interest in the activities of the group of romantic Tories that had recently been denominated Young England? The answer lies in the fact that Feargus O'Connor was at this time promoting—often under the headline "The Land! The Land! The Land!"—his own land scheme as a new means of achieving the goals of Chartism. Both projects reflect the fact that throughout the 1840s agricultural land was the locus of a wide variety of projects for reform.

Even as the Reform Bill of 1832 redefined the property qualification so that it no longer meant landownership, land remained politically powerful, both practically and imaginatively.[1] As Walter Gerard puts it in Disraeli's *Sybil*, "they [the ruling classes] have got the land and the land governs the people" (3.5.211). Underlying the notion of the electoral franchise as the principal and most legitimate form of social agency was the long-standing claim that landowners were disinterested because landownership kept them out of the marketplace and made them independent. Although it granted the franchise based on other forms of property than landownership, the Reform Bill of 1832 retained in the property qualification the principle that only those who owned property have sufficient interest in the national welfare to choose or serve as its governors. Consequently, even after 1832 the long-standing association between land and the franchise could be recognized in political movements ranging from radical agrarianism to Young England.[2]

However, projects for land reform both reinforced the conception of social agency in terms of the franchise and posed alternatives to it. On the one hand, these representations continued to conceive social agency in terms of the franchise that had traditionally been based on landownership. On the other hand, landownership could become not only a means of gaining the franchise but also a form of agency in itself. Although Feargus O'Connor insisted that the goal of the Chartist Land Plan was to obtain the franchise, the idea that acquiring their own land would give Chartists the right to vote played almost no role in the public discourse about the plan. Rather, the Land Plan was a supplemental form of agency intended to help obtain the franchise and was capable therefore of becoming a primary form of agency in its own right.

∽

The redefinition of the property qualification by the Reform Bill of 1832 did not all at once break the linkage between the franchise and landownership. The Reform Bill retained the principle that electors must be property owners; even the provision that gave the vote to tenants paying fifty pounds per annum was intended to enhance the political power of the landowners from whom they leased their property. Although England was becoming more urban and industrial, the economy remained predominately agricultural, and the landowning aristocracy thus continued to dominate in Parliament, where it persisted in maintaining the Corn Laws that protected the economic interest of landowners.

In this context, the traditional symbolic power of landownership remained intact, continuing to play an important role in the discourse of social agency. The idea that land made its owners disinterested citizens who sought to serve the nation as a whole was key to the claim for aristocratic governance in the debates over whether Parliament should be controlled by the aristocracy or the middle class. Aristocratic discourse, drawing on rhetoric that dated to the eighteenth century, contended that landowners had a "real and substantial stake in the country" because it gave them "independence and a sense of responsibility," so they could serve the "best interests of the nation as a whole" (Dickinson, *Liberty* 170). In this context social agency is defined in terms of landownership, the owners of the land acting for the nation as a whole. Consequently, those wishing to claim social agency must either become landowners or challenge the linkage of social agency to the land.

In allotment schemes, like the one being celebrated by Young England in the passage quoted in the *Northern Star*, a landowner rented out parcels of land to wage earners so that they could supplement their income through small-scale farming. Whether the motives of those who promoted allotments were altruistic or self-serving, the system by its nature located agency in the landowners, who act on behalf of the poor. In this respect, the movement manifested the commonplace of aristocratic discourse that landowners act for the nation as a whole by promoting the idea that they have a responsibility to the poor, especially to their tenants. To be sure, some proponents of allotments depicted the scheme as a means of making the working classes independent (Burchardt 5, 72, 127); however, their aim was not to make them autonomous social agents but merely to make them less dependent on poor relief or, at best, less dependent on the wages from their principal form of employment. As Feargus O'Connor pointed out, because the plots of land were too small to provide anything more than a supplement to wage earning, allotment holders inevitably remained dependent on the landowners who rented the allotments to them.

Landowners embraced the allotment movement, first in the late eighteenth century and then more wholeheartedly in the 1830s, not merely to assist the working poor but also to defuse social unrest (Burchardt 4). The movement thus gained considerable momentum in the early 1840s, at which time some proponents argued that the system would discourage the poor from supporting the Chartist movement (Burchardt 199–201). Not coincidentally, the question of government support for allotments came before Parliament in the spring of 1843, following the wave of strikes and riots in the industrial midlands of August 1842.

Young England's association with the movement culminated in the October 11, 1844, dinner celebrating the allotment scheme at Cottingley Bridge, established by Margaret and Walker Ferrand, relations of Busfeild Ferrand, a Tory critic of industry who was the principal parliamentary advocate of allotments. Ferrand was one of several MPs associated with the informal group of Tories who gathered around Disraeli beginning in 1842 and came to be known as Young England. On March 30, 1843, Ferrand introduced an allotment bill in Parliament and on April 11, after the bill failed, prevailed on the House to appoint a select committee on the question. Serving on the committee with Ferrand was Lord John Manners, a leading member of Young England who had already persuaded his father to establish an allotment project on his family's Belvoir estate. The resulting report reflected a broad consensus on the value of allotments but contended that they would best be promoted by individual landowners, not Parliament.

In his speech at the Cottingley Bridge dinner, Disraeli depicted allotment schemes as realizing Young England's ideal of ending class conflict by restoring the traditional role of the aristocracy within a finely graded hierarchy: "England should be once more a nation, and not a mere collection of classes who seem to think they have nothing in common. . . . We are anxious to do our duty. . . . If that principle of duty had not been lost sight of for the last 50 years, you would not have heard of the classes into which England was divided" (*Times* 14 Oct. 1844: 3). His contention that the current ruling elite had not performed the "duty" of attending to the needs of the nation makes clear that he was not envisioning a classless society but one in which classes are linked together by a system of responsibility and deference in which landed proprietors act on behalf of the lower classes. Thus the reforms promoted by Young England would reestablish the "ancient hereditary sentiments of loyalty and good faith and mutual trust." Disraeli had little interest in allotments per se—there is no evidence of his support for them apart from this speech—but they did provide a way to envision his conception of a revived aristocracy. While his only direct reference to allotments in his condition-of-England novels serves to demonstrate that Lord Marney fails to do his duty as a landed proprietor, landed estates are at the center of both *Sybil*'s and *Coningsby*'s attempts to envision an alternative social order (*Sybil* 2.1.73).

c~

Founded in 1838, the Royal Agricultural Society of England began to articulate an alternative conception of social agency based on landownership. While Young England was advocating allotment schemes in terms of the aristocratic discourse defining the relations of responsibility and deference that undergird finely graded hierarchy, the RASE was employing the middle-class discourse of entrepreneurial industry by contending that agricultural productivity could be increased through "the methods which had transformed manufacturing industry . . . in particular the application of 'capital' and 'science'" (Goddard 12; see also 13–16, 22). In keeping with the conception of a finely graded hierarchy, the Tories contended that the Corn Laws protected landowners, who in turn were protectors of the poor (Roberts, *Paternalism* 249–50).[3] The founders of the RASE sought to avoid controversy over the Corn Laws by adopting a policy dictating that it would not involve itself with politics. Nonetheless, several of its chief supporters were Whig advocates of free trade, and the society's focus on agricultural improvement led it to espouse the position that the interests of agriculture could be better served through the application of entrepreneurial and scientific principles than through protectionism (Goddard 13, 21). Like Young England, then, the RASE sought to reform landed property by revising the aristocratic discourse of class and social agency.

Moreover, just as parliamentary discourse had earlier confined social agency to the Tories and Whigs, so too the advocates of allotments and of agricultural improvement both conceived of themselves as social agents whose actions would determine the response of the lower classes. Thus, whereas Young England sought to respond to social unrest through allotments that would help workers supplement their income, supporters of the RASE sought to lower the price of food by increasing agricultural productivity. Neither envisioned the possibility that the working classes could themselves use the land as a means of acting in or transforming the social domain.

⌒

While, as we will see, Feargus O'Connor's Land Plan was in some respects a variation on the allotments schemes, he conceived it as a means of obtaining social agency for the working classes. On April 15, 1843—four days after the House of Commons established the Select Committee on allotments—O'Connor announced in the *Northern Star* that he would publish a series of letters explaining his own scheme for land reform (15 Apr. 1843: 1).[4] That July he published the details of his plan in the widely disseminated pamphlet *A Practical Work on the Management of Small Farms* (it went through seven editions in the next four years), and that September the Chartist convention adopted the plan as the central plank of its platform (Chase, *Chartism* 248–49). In a column in the *Northern Star* entitled "The Land! The Land! The Land!," published two weeks after it reprinted the report on the Ferrand allotment dinner, O'Connor retorted that while it was a good sign that Young England was advocating allotments, his own scheme would better serve the interests of the lower classes.[5] In 1845, the Chartist convention established the Chartist Co-operative Land Society, and over the next two years thousands of working people signed up for the plan. Legal barriers and an unfeasible system of financing led to its collapse and failure by the end of the decade, but during the mid–1840s the Land Plan, like the combination of moral and physical force before it, became the principal means through which the movement pursued social agency.

While the Chartist movement made a claim for the agency of those who do not own land, the Land Plan, like its precedents in radical agrarianism, instead sought to claim the franchise by constituting the disenfranchised as landowners. Thomas Spence, who initiated the radical agrarian movement, insisted that social agency was rooted in landownership rather than the franchise. He endorsed the principle that landownership gives one a stake in the nation but argued that the land had been usurped from the people by the aristocracy and must be restored to them. In the 1790s, when the London Corresponding Society and other groups were advocating universal suffrage, Spence published a series of tracts in which he set forth his basic argument that "political rights alone, however extensive, could never prevent the rich from dominating the poor," for which reason he advocated placing "the source of all real power—the land—into the hands of all citizens; men, women and children alike."[6] In the prefatory dialogue to *The Meridian Sun of Liberty* (1796), in which he debates an advocate of universal suffrage, he went so far as to argue that those who have abandoned their claim to a right in the land cannot claim a right to citizenship: "Nobody ought to have right of suffrage or representation in a society wherein they have no [landed] property," and so no one has "a right to vote or interfere in the affairs of the government of a country who [has] no right to the soil" (2). For Spence, then, social agency lay fundamentally in ownership of the land, and the franchise was simply a vehicle through which it was exercised.

As Malcolm Chase has demonstrated, Spencean agrarianism continued to influence the radical tradition throughout the early nineteenth century, and many Chartists considered themselves Spenceans or were influenced by Spence's ideas (*People's Farm* 1–7, chap. 5). In the 1830s, working-class radicals developed a wide range of land plans, many of them blending Spencianism with Robert Owen's cooperative projects, and most insisting upon the principle that the land must be returned to the people (Chase, *People's Farm* 153–73). The Spencean and Owenite movements of the 1830s in turn influenced the thinking of many Chartists, among them Thomas Wheeler—who was editor of the *Northern Star* when the plan was first set forth, was responsible for much of the writing on the plan that appeared under O'Connor's name, served as secretary to the National Land Company, and praised the plan in his novel *Sunshine and Shadow*—and George Julian Harney, his successor at the *Star*.[7]

O'Connor's plan drew on both the allotment movement and the radical tradition, even as he sought to distinguish it from both. The *Northern Star* launched its land campaign in a pair of articles commenting on James Garth Marshall's allotment scheme (which preceded the Ferrand scheme) and Robert Owen's Harmony Hall estate.[8] The first article praised the good intentions of Marshall's scheme but criticized it as merely "an *ekeing-out* [sic] of the slender means of the under-paid operative." The second praised Owen's estate for seeking to enable laborers to become self-sufficient rather than merely supplementing their income but distanced the Chartist plan from the "socialism" associated with Spence, Owen, and Fourier so as to defuse anxieties about the abolition of private property as well as Owen's heterodox opposition to marriage and Christianity.[9] Thus, while O'Connor's plan differed from allotment schemes and resembled cooperative projects in that it did not involve the poor renting from wealthy landowners but rather collectively purchasing land, it also differed from socialist plans and resembled allotment schemes in that it called for settling individual families on their own plot of land. However, by providing two acres of land—as opposed to the fraction of an acre provided by the typical allotment scheme—it aimed to make a family financially self-sufficient, which in turn would promote the radical aim of reclaiming the land that had been "stolen" from the people and the Spencean principle that the "land is the thing that produces everything upon which you live" (*Northern Star* 22 Nov. 1845: 1; see also 8 Nov. 1845: 1, 17 May 1845: 1).

By positioning his plan in this way, O'Connor addressed the moral- versus physical-force dilemma that had haunted Chartism since its inception. As we have seen, Parliament's rejection of the petitions of 1838 and 1842 made it clear that the moral force of rational arguments from principles of justice was inadequate as a means of gaining the franchise, and the failure of the Newport uprising of 1838, as well as the government response to the strike wave of 1842, had shown that physical force was unlikely to succeed. Moreover, the use of moral force backed by the threat of physical force in such supplemental forms of agency as demonstrations, boycotts, or strikes had also failed to bring about acceptance of the Charter (e.g., *Northern Star* 21 Mar. 1846: 1). In this context, O'Connor described the Land Plan as a new form of moral force—the *"moral means* of achieving" enactment of the Charter (*Northern Star* 15 Apr. 1843: 1)—and insisted that it would be much more successful than "political agitation" (1 Nov. 1845: 1). Accordingly, he argued that the Land Plan, like other forms of moral force, would persuade the governing elite to grant the justice of the Chartist cause, that no "other inducement . . . will be sufficiently strong to produce such a public feeling as will bring into moral action such an amount of mind in favour of both changes [restoring the land and granting the franchise to the people], as neither minister or party would dare to resist" (*Small Farms* 11).

In this regard, O'Connor portrayed the Land Plan, like moral force, not as a form of agency in itself, but as a means of obtaining social agency in the form of parliamentary representation. He repeatedly insisted that he was not abandoning the demand for the franchise but merely devising a new supplemental form of agency in order to obtain it. If he had to choose, he declared, he would favor the Charter over the Land Plan, and he argued, accordingly, that the Land Plan would not achieve its goal until the Charter was made law (*Northern Star* 1 Nov. 1845: 1, 22 Apr. 1843: 1).[10] If the Land Plan were an end in itself, then one would want to make it available to all of the working classes, but because it was merely a means to an end, O'Connor contended, settling "a very small minority of the people" on allotments would soon lead to passage of the People's Charter (*Northern Star* 1 Nov. 1845: 1). Whereas Spence had argued that one must own land in order to exercise the franchise, O'Connor maintained that the people could not ultimately reclaim all of the land from which they had been dispossessed unless they gained the franchise, concluding that "without political power the system never could be made so general as to be of national benefit" (*Small Farms* 11).

Precisely because of its purported ability to bring about adoption of the Charter, however, the Land Plan constituted an alternative to the franchise as a form of social agency. O'Connor frequently appealed to the idea that the plan would make workers independent social agents, hence the importance of supplying larger plots of land than those provided by the allotment system, which, as we have seen, he depicted as merely supplementing the wages of the "under-paid operative" (*Northern Star* 14 Jan. 1843: 4; see also 13 May 1843: 1, 8 Nov. 1845: 1). By contrast, his plan would provide sufficient acreage to enable workers to become completely self-sufficient. In *A Practical Work on the Management of Small Farms* and his many editorial letters in the *Northern Star*, he elaborated the argument that this self-sufficiency would establish the "natural" rate of wages as opposed to the "artificial" wages of the marketplace (*Small Farms* 28, 142–43, 149; *Northern Star* 13 May 1843: 1, 30 Aug. 30, 1845: 1).[11] The "natural" wage established by what a laborer could produce on his farm would set the standard for the "artificial" market for wage labor with the result that participants in the plan would know what their labor was worth and would refuse to work for less as wage laborers. Furthermore, by "removing [the allotment holders] as competitors from the artificial labour market" (*Small Farms* 143), the plan would reduce the supply of labor and thus act to transform the marketplace itself. The laborer thus becomes an agent who controls his relation to the labor market, "free" to enter it but never forced to accept "slavery" (i.e., a wage that is beneath what he can earn on his own farm; see *Northern Star* 13 May 1843: 1, 8 Nov. 1845: 1).

The Chartist Land Plan both looked back to established conceptions of social agency and opened up the possibility of alternatives to it. Insofar as it was a means of promoting the Charter, it reflected the conception that defined social agency in terms of the franchise and legislation. However, insofar as the plan sought to establish new social institutions through which workers could act, it became the basis for imagining alternative ways of conceiving agency. Strikingly, O'Connor's *Small Farms* concluded by declaring that his aim was "to destroy [his] own and all other demagogues' trade, by enabling the people to do for themselves that which they now rely upon political traffickers to do for them" (149). In this respect, the emphasis in the Land Plan on making workers autonomous meant making workers independent agents who need not rely upon the Chartist leadership or the Chartist movement; it meant as well that it was possible to conceive of social agency in social as well as political terms.

⁓

In the next three chapters, I discuss how novels by Benjamin Disraeli, Robert Smith Surtees, and Thomas Martin Wheeler envision social agency in relation to these projects for land reform. Like the novels discussed in part 1, these novels adapt national narratives developed in the historical novel by shifting the locus of conflict from nations or cultures to social classes. Rather than representing contemporary conflict in terms of analogous conflicts in the past, however, they depict the history of the present. Disraeli's *Coningsby* (1844) and *Sybil* (1845) employ the standard conventions of the historical novel—depiction of historical characters and events as well as the evocation of a historical milieu—but bring the history they portray up to the present moment, with *Coningsby* beginning in the year of the First Reform Bill and concluding with the Tory victory in the elections of 1841 and *Sybil* starting in 1837 with the onset of the Chartist movement and moving forward to the Manchester strike wave of 1842. While it does not employ the conventions of the historical novel, Surtees's *Hillingdon Hall* (1843–1844), like Disraeli's novels, depicts contemporary politics, notably the Corn Law controversy and Young England, and features a parliamentary election (once again, presumably, the election of 1841). Wheeler's quasi-allegorical *Sunshine and Shadow* (1849–1850) does not attempt to portray the texture of the historical milieu, nor does it make the many contemporary political figures to which it alludes novelistic characters, but it does depict its protagonist partaking in historical events—the narrator describes it as a "History of Chartism" (192)— that, like Disraeli's novels, bring the narrative up to the present moment.

Disraeli, who at the time was a Tory MP, wrote his novels to disseminate his version of the revived aristocracy envisioned by Young England. Consequently, even as he employs aristocratic discourse contending that landed proprietors can best govern the nation, he also draws on the middle-class critique of the aristocracy in order to establish the necessity of its reform. Surtees was also a Tory and had, like most landowners, favored the Corn Laws, but he would eventually follow the Royal Society, to which he dedicated *Hillingdon Hall*, in coming to the conclusion that improving agricultural production was more important than protectionism. Like Disraeli, he satirizes the aristocracy in part by displacing the object of critique from the Tories to the Whig oligarchy, but rather than advocate a reformed Tory party, he extends his satire to Young England and envisions a rural squirearchy imbued with the entrepreneurial ethos. As a lecturer and journalist, Wheeler belonged to the intellectual leadership of the Chartist movement, and he was deeply involved in both the development of the Land Plan and the presentation in April 1848 of the third and, as it turned out, final Chartist petition, which once again raised questions about the use of moral versus physical force. Written after the rejection of the third petition and at the time that the incipient collapse of the Land Plan was becoming apparent, *Sunshine and Shadow* attempts to find in these previous efforts principles for imagining new forms of popular agency and so looks forward to the "social turn" that is the subject of part 3.

The Landed Estate, Finely Graded Hierarchy, and the Member of Parliament in *Coningsby* and *Sybil*

Disraeli's *Coningsby; or, The New Generation* (1844) and *Sybil; or, The Two Nations* (1845) resemble novels like *Barnaby Rudge* that ascribe social problems to a self-interested aristocracy, but they differ from them in the way they conceive social reform. Whereas Dickens's novel employs middle-class discourse that treats self-interest as intrinsic to an inherited-landowning class, Disraeli's novels ascribe it to the shift of aristocracy from a harmonious social structure organized as a finely graded hierarchy to a structure of conflicting classes. Social reform therefore takes the form of restoring a hierarchical social structure in which reformed aristocrats are the principal social agents.

In keeping with their aim of imagining the reform of the aristocracy, *Coningsby* and *Sybil* revise the middle-class and Chartist reform narratives that define social reform and social agency as the displacement of the aristocratic ruling elite by the middle class or working class, respectively. The plots of these novels instead enact the transfer of forms of agency developed by the middle class and working class to their aristocratic hero. Each novel consequently concludes with members of the opposing class ceding authority to a reformed aristocrat.

Although these novels represent finely graded hierarchy through the medieval landed estate, they do not define social agency as the noblesse oblige of a chivalrous landowner toward his tenants but instead use this figure as a model for the relation between a reformed Parliament and the nation. Each novel concludes with the hero uniting an inherited estate with his wife's estate so as to constitute himself as the possessor of political power, a member of Parliament. Although these novels, like many contemporary social critiques, ascribe England's social ills to a Parliament that acts for the interests of particular factions—political parties acting as proxies for the conflicting classes of post-hierarchical England—and thus seek alternatives to it, they do not ultimately depict the land as providing an alternative form of social agency but rather as underwriting the agency of the reformed aristocracy.

~

Coningsby and *Sybil* devote considerable space to satire on an aristocracy that regards parliamentary power as a means of advancing its self-interest and fails in its duty to serve the nation as a whole. Whereas contemporary antiaristocratic discourse tends to depict it as idle, effete, and moribund, however, the focus of these novels is on the machinations through which party operatives and society hostesses as well as baronets, marquesses, and dukes attempt to gain a Tory majority in Parliament with the aim of enhancing their wealth and status. The principal ambition that drives Lord Monmouth throughout *Coningsby* is to obtain a dukedom, for which end he collects a dozen seats in Parliament: "After all," he concludes, "what is the end of all parties and all politics? To gain your object" (8.3.428). If his counterpart in *Sybil*, Lord Marney, is less ambitious—he merely aspires to high office—he surpasses Monmouth in abdication of responsibility; whereas the latter merely neglects his tenants, Marney regards them as a nuisance and actively seeks to drive them away.

Like the novels discussed in part 1, these novels link the aristocratic pursuit of self-interest and, more particularly, of political power, to the embrace of the kinship model of marriage. In order to envision the reform of the aristocracy, Disraeli confines this pursuit of self-interest, and attendant allegiance to the kinship ideal, to the older generation (hence the subtitle of *Coningsby*). Monmouth thus simultaneously demands that Coningsby stand for a seat in Parliament to aid him in obtaining a dukedom and suggests that he make a "considerable [marital] alliance" so as to further his own fortunes (8.3.428). Similarly, when, in *Sybil*, Egremont stands for a seat for the sake of his family, his brother, Lord Marney, insists that he pay off the campaign debts, for which Marney as head of the family is responsible, by marrying an heiress. Moreover, both Monmouth and Marney not only affirm the kinship model of marriage but also violate the companionate ideal. Monmouth, who in the course of the novel has a child by an actress, marries and separates from Princess Lucretia, and dies in the company of courtesans, is a serial polygamist who, according to London gossip, "never could live with a woman more than two years" (8.1.412).[1] Although Marney is comparatively unexceptional as a husband, he too has transgressed the companionate ideal by winning his wife away from her first love, none other than his own brother, Egremont.

However, these novels do not define self-interest as the consequence of belonging to a heritable-landowning class but rather as the displacement of the traditional hierarchical aristocracy by self-interested Tories who are merely the Whig
oligarchy in disguise. Disraeli's elaborate historical explanation of how the "Venetian constitution" accounts for the present state of the aristocracy ultimately
serves the purpose of distinguishing the modern aristocracy constituted within
tripartite or dichotomous models of class from an aristocracy constituted within a
finely graded hierarchy.[2] Whereas the former acts to preserve its interests against
what it construes as the self-interested claims of the middle and working classes,
the latter, Disraeli contends, disinterestedly preserves the social order through a
set of reciprocal social relations, acting for the nation as a whole as the landlord
acts for the benefit of his tenants. Rather than critique the opposing middle and
lower classes, therefore, these novels instead seek to dissolve them into a variety of
social roles within a hierarchical structure in which each individual is respected
by but subordinate to the aristocracy. Although each novel represents class conflict and thus features claims of agency on the part of middle and working classes,
each implicitly seeks to confine agency within the aristocracy. This explains why,
in spite of its satire on the aristocracy, the majority of the principal characters
in each novel belong to the aristocracy, which even in its present corrupt state,
remains the primary locus of social agency.

The conflict between aristocracy and middle class in *Coningsby* would appear to
confirm the assumption of post–Reform Bill political discourse that improving
the condition of England is a matter of determining whether the aristocracy or the
middle class can best govern "the people." However, the novel empties this conflict of economic and social content by transforming it into sexual rivalry arising
from the violation of the companionate ideal — associated with the middle class —
by an aristocratic kinship marriage. The industrialist Millbank's hatred of aristocracy in general and enmity against Monmouth in particular do not arise from
opposing economic interests but from sexual rivalry, for Monmouth's younger
son (the father of Coningsby) has used his social status to win away Millbank's
first love. It remains to the "new generation" to replace the kinship with the companionate ideal. By marrying Millbank's daughter, Edith, Coningsby transforms
the sexual rivalry that leads to class conflict into a companionate parliamentary
coterie comprising Millbank's son as well as fellow Etonians.

In order to effect this transformation, the novel makes the primary locus of
conflict not the sexual and class rivalry between the aristocrat Monmouth and the
entrepreneur Millbank but, as its subtitle — *The New Generation* — indicates, the

generational conflict between the old Tory, Monmouth, and his grandson, Coningsby, the leader of a Young England–like coterie that will reinstate the founding
principles of the Tory party. We see a repetition of the opposition between kinship
and companionate ideals when Coningsby confronts the dilemma that his grandfather's demand that he stand for the Darlford constituency would mean not
only using parliamentary power for personal gain (in violation of his "principle"
of using it for the national good) but also supplanting Millbank, the father of his
close friend and of the woman he loves. Although he initially regards the cost of
his refusal to accede to this demand, which leads his grandfather to disinherit
him, to be the loss of both his political ambitions and his marriage prospects, his
disinheritance, as his mentor Sidonia points out, "free[s]" him from the "paralys-
ing influence" of Tory aristocratic "culture" so that he can "work . . . for his own
bread" on the basis of his "health, youth, good looks, great abilities, considerable
knowledge, . . . fine courage . . . lofty spirit, and . . . experience" (9.3.471, 9.6.489,
9.3.470). Rather than opposing himself to the industrialist Millbank family, he
thus adopts the entrepreneurial ideal of self-making.

Working for his own bread, however, means becoming not a self-made entrepreneur who tests himself in the marketplace but a self-made aristocrat who
pursues self-culture by rejecting the traditional Oxbridge curriculum in favor
of studying constitutional history and, through this pursuit, defining a place for
his "new generation" in a renewed aristocracy. He thus decides to forgo seeking
"University honours" and "chalk[s] out for himself that range of reading" through
which he constructs the history of the Venetian constitution that leads him to
break with the Tory party and eventually with his grandfather (5.1.278, 280). In
accord with the principles of self-culture, Coningsby constitutes his authority in
terms of the integrity of his interior self rather than his inherited status, his refusal
to compromise his "convictions" concerning matters of public policy affirming
the integrity of his character (8.3.429; see also 425).

The integrity of the self-made man guarantees that he acts for the nation
rather than for personal interest. Coningsby ceases to regard politics as a "struggle
whether the country was to be governed by Whig nobles or Tory nobles" and
instead aims to "maintain the realm and secure the happiness of the people"
(2.7.131, 8.3.430). The extent of his disinterestedness is emphasized by the fact that
he becomes "an almost unconscious candidate" for a seat of Parliament, when,
having refused to seek office himself, he is instead nominated by the elder Millbank and learns of his nomination while glancing through a newspaper at dinner
(9.6.487).

Coningsby's break with the aristocracy does not, like Edward Chester's in

Barnaby Rudge, involve entering the middle class; rather, members of the middle class recognize his difference from the old aristocracy and consequently acknowledge his social authority. Whereas Monmouth demands that he stand for Darlford in order to serve his own personal interests, Millbank nominates him for the very same seat because of the integrity that he manifests in refusing his grandfather. By resigning his own seat and nominating Coningsby to stand for it, the elder Millbank implicitly acknowledges that the young aristocrat is better suited to governing the nation, and nominates him, at least putatively, not because of his kinship (even though he will be marrying his daughter) but because of the "high principles, great talents, and good heart" exhibited in his willingness, after he is disinherited, to "work . . . for his bread" (9.6.493, 489). Although in the first part of the novel Millbank serves as one of his mentors—he learns from and is "influenced" by "one of the most eminent manufacturers, and . . . the greatest capitalist in the kingdom" (5.1.277–78)—he eventually shifts from tutee to tutor, persuading the younger Oswald Millbank that his father is mistaken about the nature of the aristocracy, when properly constituted, and in turn changing the views of the elder Millbank himself.

Coningsby's "new generation," however, is not defined as an aristocratic social class—it includes, after all, an industrialist with no claim to gentility—but as a political coterie. Through his embrace of the companionate ideal, he forges a set of homosocial bonds through which, as Mary Poovey has observed, he constitutes a new generation and a political movement.[3] Apart from the fact that he is struck by her beauty, the novel does not account for his falling so deeply in love with Edith Millbank, who rarely utters a word and never establishes any kind of presence in the narrative. In this respect, the novel fails to conform to the companionate norm, in which love follows from conversations through which lovers mutually come to admire and respect one another. Coningsby's love makes sense, however, when we recognize that it is mediated by and serves to cement his prior friendship with her brother, with whom, as with his other Etonian "companions," he frequently converses and discovers a "deep communion" (7.8.406).[4]

Because, as I will discuss below, Disraeli insists that the English constitution makes equality consistent with hierarchy, the unions that conclude his novels combine the companionate model of marital equality with hierarchy. The mediation of Coningsby's relation to the younger Oswald through Edith confirms an existing relationship of leader and disciple. Already at Eton, where Coningsby had been "their leader alike in sport and study," Oswald Millbank develops a "passionate admiration and affection for Coningsby" and willingly assumes a role subordinate to him (1.8.68, 1.9.72; see also 7.2.379). Consequently, when, in the conclusion of the novel, his like-minded friends—Millbank, Sydney, Buckhurst, Lyle, and Vere—stand for Parliament, Coningsby is able to trace in their election addresses "the influence of his own mind" (9.6.485). Significantly, the narrative reaches its climax when the elder Millbank awards his own seat in Parliament to Coningsby, assigning another to his son. Rather than an alliance between aristocracy and middle class, which would keep the tripartite class structure intact, the marriage of Coningsby and Edith Millbank constitutes a hierarchy, with the hero as the leader of a coterie that in turn acts for the nation.

∾

Whereas *Coningsby* seeks to reframe the debate about whether the aristocracy or middle class can best govern the people and therefore should control Parliament, *Sybil* contests the Chartist claim that the people can act for themselves. Like *Coningsby*, nonetheless, it locates agency in the aristocracy. Significantly, it does not blame the industrial middle class for the plight of the poor. Indeed, Trafford, like Millbank, is an enlightened industrialist, while, by contrast, Lord Marney abuses his tenants, driving them into industrial labor. Like *Coningsby*, *Sybil* seeks to resolve class conflict, this time between aristocracy and the working class, but it does not displace it into a generational conflict within the aristocracy. On the contrary, the plot of the later novel moves from a fraternal conflict within the aristocracy—between the hero, Charles Egremont, and his brother, Lord Marney—to sexual rivalry between the aristocrat Egremont and Stephen Morley, his working-class rival for the love of Sybil. Although the novel seeks to demonstrate that the "rich and the poor" ought not be divided from one another, this plot structure, which aims to imagine the resolution of class conflict while denying the working-class claim of social agency, depicts a much more intense class rivalry than we find in the earlier novel. Whereas *Coningsby* resolves the conflict between aristocracy and middle class by transforming the tripartite class structure into a finely graded hierarchy and according members of the middle class a role within the ruling coterie, *Sybil* represents a working class that ultimately relinquishes its claims for a role in governance and accepts the benign rule of a single aristocrat.

Sybil carries over from *Coningsby* the critique of the existing aristocracy that self-servingly privileges kinship over companionate marriage and, correlatively, employs political power for personal rather than national or communal ends. The Marney family obtained its lands (Marney Abbey) through the dissolution of the monasteries, became part of the Whig oligarchy, and then, as a matter of political expediency, joined the Tories. Lord Marney has, like Coningsby's father, used his status as heir to gain his wife, the first love of his brother, Egremont, and compounds the transgression when he insists that his brother marry for money and political gain. Marney also represents the failure of the aristocracy as currently constituted to take responsibility for the welfare of its tenants, which has led to the division of England into "two nations . . . THE RICH AND THE POOR" (2.5.96). At the beginning of the narrative, Egremont himself has imbibed the reigning aristocratic assumption that a "manly career" consists of aiming "to do nothing, and get something," and he runs for a seat in Parliament in order to assist his kin rather than the nation (1.5.54). However, his lack of interest in the woman his brother proposes he marry—together with his interest in Sybil—leads him to question not only the kinship ideal of using his parliamentary office to benefit his family but also his brother's attitude toward the working poor.

Whereas *Coningsby* had focused on the resolution of social problems through the displacement of an older aristocracy committed to the kinship ideal by a newer one modeled on the companionate ideal, *Sybil* focuses on the displacement of Chartists by a "new generation" of "aristocracy" who are the "natural leaders of the People" (4.15.334). Walter Gerard, the father of the novel's heroine, and Stephen Morley, who is in love with her, are the novel's Chartist leaders. Like the elder Millbank, Walter Gerard seeks political power in opposition to an aristocracy that has abdicated its social responsibilities. In this case, however, the younger man, Stephen Morley, is not, like the younger Millbank, the mediator, or even the true object, of the hero's quest for companionship but rather his homosocial rival. Whereas the marriage of Coningsby and Edith Millbank mediates the formation of the alliance between Coningsby and her brother, Oswald, the marriage of Sybil Gerard and Charles Egremont involves the supplanting of his rival, Stephen Morley. By winning the love of the "daughter of the people," Egremont establishes his claim that the reformed aristocracy are the "natural leaders of the People" (4.15.336).

The novel differentiates between the reformed aristocrat, who is a disinterested leader of the people, and the Chartist, who is incapable of serving as their leader, through the different ways that Egremont's and Morley's love of Sybil inspires their commitment to the cause of the people. Both claim to be inspired by her, Morley declaring that "it is [her] image that has stimulated [his] ambition, developed [his] powers, sustained [him] in the hour of humiliation, and secured [him] that material prosperity which [he] can now command" (5.4.366), and Egremont avowing that from the first moment he saw Sybil her "spirit ruled [his] being and softened every spring of [his] affections" with the consequence that her "picture consecrates [his] hearth and [her] approval has been the spur of [his] career" (4.15.335). However, whereas love of Sybil inspires Egremont to self-reform that transforms his inner being (his "affections"), it leads Morley to espouse a cause with which he has "little sympathy" (5.4.366). In effect, the desire to obtain Sybil enables Egremont to understand his proper relation to the people, whereas it leads Morley to establish a false relation to them.

The novel thus constructs Morley as a specious "leader of the people"—a demagogue—in order to constitute Egremont as their "natural leader." Like the elite-press representations of the Chartist leadership, *Sybil* represents Morley as a demagogue who embraces the cause in order to pursue a personal agenda— obtaining the love of Sybil—rather than to serve the ostensible objects of that cause, the people. By contrast, once Sybil accepts Egremont's claim that he is the natural leader of the people, she reads in his speech "the voice of a noble, who without being a demagogue, had upheld the popular cause" (5.1.350).

This speech makes apparent the degree to which Egremont forecloses popular agency, for in it he expresses the desire to obtain "the results of the charter without the intervention of its machinery" (5.1.341). Egremont makes the claim that the new generation of aristocracy are the natural leaders of the people in response to Sybil's claim that the people now have the power to act. Echoing Chartist discourse such as Feargus O'Connor's assertion that "there would be no change for the better until the masses were set in motion—till they were *made acquainted* with their own strength" (*Northern Star* 11 Aug. 1838: 6; emphasis added), Sybil has argued that "the People" will be able to act now that they "have learnt their strength," but Egremont insists that "the People never can be strong" and thus that others must act for them (4.15.334).

Whereas the Chartists regarded physical force as necessary to make moral force effective, *Sybil* reinforces the lack of Chartist agency by employing the elite-press representation of moral force disguising physical force and physical force compromising moral force. This representation reproduces the Chartist dilemma in which the working class either lacks agency (moral force has no real force) or employs a form of agency that violates the constitution (physical force as revolution). Thus Walter Gerard possesses moral integrity—he is no demagogue—but advocates physical force, while Stephen Morley promotes moral force but is insincere and unscrupulous.

The very disinterestedness that makes Walter Gerard a sincere spokesman for the people leads him to the use of physical force and ultimately to failure. The fact that he has the oratorical power to move the people by appealing to their "passions" and cannot express himself in writing suggests that he speaks authentically from his inner self (4.4.266). As we have seen, however, elite-press coverage of Chartism linked the appeal to the passions to irrationality and violence. Even the enlightened manufacturer Trafford, who has rewarded Gerard's intelligence and integrity with the position of factory inspector, worries that his opinions are "violent" (3.8.229). It is not a contradiction therefore that the man of integrity—who might be expected to advocate moral force—becomes the novel's advocate of physical force. Rather, the novel reinforces the inevitability of his resorting to physical force precisely by showing how he attempts to find alternatives to it but always falls back on it in the end. In the debates about what measures to take after Parliament rejects the Chartist petition, for example, he begins by playing a moderating role, advocating a national strike, but eventually concludes that an armed uprising is more likely to achieve their aims.[5]

Stephen Morley's advocacy of moral force produces a similarly self-defeating double bind. Whereas Gerard appeals to the passions, Morley, who understands "principles," has the capacity for rational analysis that makes him an effective journalist, but rational analysis only leads to abstraction that has no appeal for the people. The Wodgate miners, for example, respond to his proposal that they establish a socialist cooperative by complaining that he "speak[s] like a book" (3.1.183). Moreover, the novel treats his use of intellectual abstraction as a sign of a split between his interior self and the principles he publicly advocates, for although he presents himself as a moral-force Chartist, he does so to promote a socialist agenda of revolutionary change.

The self-defeating contradiction between moral and physical force manifests itself in the assault on Mowbray Castle, in which Walter Gerard, the advocate of physical force, employs moral suasion to deflect an attack on Trafford's mill, and the moral-force advocate Morley uses the attack on the castle as a cover for his search for documents proving that it belongs to the Gerards. By having both men die during this episode, the novel literalizes their lack of agency, just as it dramatizes the passing of the old aristocracy through the death of Lord Marney. The ultimately self-defeating and self-destructive nature of any attempt of the people to act for themselves becomes apparent when, in parallel with similar scenes in *Wat Tyler* and *Barnaby Rudge*, the rioters die in the fires they have set during their attack on the castle.

Set against this representation, the novel depicts Egremont the reformed aristocrat as assuming the position of social agent vacated by the Chartist leadership, in particular his rival Stephen Morley. Like *Coningsby*, *Sybil* imagines a process in which the hero first learns from and then becomes the instructor of members of the opposing class. During their first encounter, Gerard and Morley teach Egremont about the condition of the people. Subsequently, Egremont begins to assume the place of Morley not only by becoming a rival for the love of Sybil but also by emulating the autodidact newspaper editor when he begins reading up on the condition of the working classes and poses as a journalist. Whereas Morley studies socialism and attempts to persuade members of the working class to act for themselves by establishing cooperatives, however, Egremont reads parliamentary blue books and attempts to persuade members of Parliament to act for the poor. As in *Coningsby*, in which Edith Millbank becomes the means through which the hero moves from being instructed by Millbank senior to being the leader who instructs the younger Millbank, Egremont begins as the student of Gerard and Morley but then becomes the instructor of Sybil, whom he disabuses of the belief that the interests of the rich are inalterably opposed to those of the working poor.[6] Just as Millbank eventually cedes his seat and authority to Coningsby, Sybil shifts her loyalty from the Chartists to Egremont.

Both *Coningsby* and *Sybil* depict members of opposing classes vying for control of a landed estate that is linked to the possession of political power and, more particularly, parliamentary representation. In the former, Lord Monmouth and the elder Millbank seek to purchase Hellingsley and gain control of its borough seat. In the latter, Walter Gerard sets out to regain the estate usurped from his family by the Mowbrays while simultaneously promoting the Chartist campaign to gain the franchise, from which, of course, he is excluded because he does not meet the property qualification. These novels represent a process in which the representatives of the middle classes and working classes wrest control of the estate from an unreformed aristocrat and then cede it to a reformed aristocrat, reform involving, as we have seen, a shift from the tripartite and dichotomous models of class to finely graded hierarchy.

In *Coningsby* the fate of Hellingsley reframes the relationship between the rising middle class and the reformed aristocracy. Monmouth seeks to purchase Hellingsley in order to replace the dozen parliamentary seats he had accumulated in his quest to obtain a dukedom but then lost with the passage of the Reform Bill. However, in keeping with the narrative of the rise of the middle class, the more energetic Millbank manages to purchase it, together with its borough seat, for himself. In order to revise that class narrative and imagine the reform of the aristocracy, the novel then effects a double move that detaches Coningsby from the old aristocracy and, via the middle class, positions him as leader of the new. First Monmouth disinherits him—depriving him of the estate and baronetcy he had purchased for him—and then Millbank cedes political authority to him by nominating him for his seat in Parliament and bequeathing Hellingsley to him. In the meantime the estate his grandfather had intended for him has been purified of its associations with the old aristocracy by passing through the hands of his half sister, allowing him to inherit it not as the heir of the old aristocracy but as leader of a reforming Young England. The effect of this transfer of the estate is to dissociate it from the tripartite model of class that leads to contention between Monmouth and Millbank and to reinsert it within the hierarchical model in which Coningsby takes his place.

Sybil effects a similar but more complex refashioning, imagining reformed aristocratic agency in relation to Chartist attempts to gain social agency through both the franchise and landownership. As in *Coningsby*, an opposing class, in this case the working class, seeks political power but ultimately cedes it to the aristocracy. Walter Gerard simultaneously campaigns to gain the franchise for the working classes and to reclaim the landed estate that would, although he never alludes to it, give him the right to vote, not to mention control of one or more seats in Parliament. Instead of depicting the restoration of the estate to the Gerards as enabling Walter to participate in governing the nation, however, the novel ties it to Stephen Morley's designs to establish a socialist community. Whereas the younger Oswald Millbank persuades his father to cede power to Coningsby, Walter Gerard and Stephen Morley never abandon their quest for political power. With their deaths, however, the estate passes to Sybil who, of course, cannot exercise the franchise, and she, like Millbank, cedes authority to the reformed aristocrat.

Whereas the Millbanks as landowners can readily cede authority to the aristocracy precisely because their wealth guarantees that they retain political power, *Sybil* needs to imagine a process whereby Walter Gerard and Stephen Morley do not gain political power, even as they regain the land that has been taken from them. Thus the novel literalizes the claim of the agrarian radicals that the land has been usurped from the people in the Gerards' quest to reclaim their family estate from the usurping Mowbray family. Just as using physical force to obtain the franchise demonstrates the lower classes' "unfitness for the franchise," so the attack on Mowbray Castle delegitimizes what is otherwise a legitimate claim to the property (*Examiner* 17 Sept. 1842: 593). Reclaiming the lands that have been taken from them paradoxically comes to resemble socialist schemes for the seizure of private property.

The novel thus represents the aim of Chartism as the abolition of private property and its replacement by socialist cooperatives. To this end, Disraeli ignores O'Connor's attempts to distinguish the Chartist Land Plan from Owenite and other socialist schemes emphasizing communal ownership and living arrangements.[7] Accordingly, Stephen Morley seeks to restore the land to the people — and thus to establish popular agency—by making landownership collective rather than individual. Walter Gerard has promised him that when he regains his rights to the Mowbray estate, he will provide land on which Morley, who has clearly been influenced by Charles Fourier and Robert Owen, plans to establish a utopian community that would place fifty families under one roof in order to realize his ideal of "community" as "co-operation" rather than mere aggregation (3.1.183, 2.5.94).[8] By casting Morley as the leader of the attack on Mowbray Castle, however, the novel implies that this abolition of private property will produce not social harmony but anarchy.

Sybil revises the meaning of returning the land to the people by shifting the moment of usurpation from the Norman Conquest—the moment when the people became dispossessed according to the radical narrative of the imposition of the Norman yoke—to the dissolution of the monasteries. The novel conflates the Mowbrays—the literal usurpers of the Gerard estate—with the Marneys, who obtained Marney Abbey and their status through the dissolution. Indeed, the fact that the first scene depicting the Gerards takes place in the ruins of Marney Abbey and the last abbot, whose tomb they see there, was their ancestor initially suggests that Marney Abbey is the estate that had been usurped from their family; only later does it emerge that the disputed estate is Mowbray Castle. Moreover, Lord Marney repeats the act of usurpation committed by his ancestors when he attempts to "expel" the people from the land by destroying the cottages on his estate (2.3.81). This explains why Sybil asks her father not to restore the land to the people but to "bring back the people to the land" (2.8.114). Apparently unaware of the significance of the distinction, she anticipates the novel's argument that the land does not belong to the people but the people to the land and the ruling elite.

Indeed, the Gerards, who never themselves endorse Morley's socialist views and what he regards as an orientation to the future rather than the past (3.9.237–38), imagine the restoration of the rights of the people in terms of the medieval monastery. Whereas Morley asks for a portion of the estate to establish a socialist cooperative, Sybil asks for land on which she can "raise a holy house for pious women" (2.8.115), and while Morley reads Fourier and Owen, Walter Gerard has apparently been reading Cobbett's *History of the Protestant Reformation* (1824), which shifts the usurpation of the land from the Norman Conquest to the dissolution of the monasteries.[9] In his first encounter with Egremont, he explains that because the monks "could possess no private property" and held the land "in common," the monastery was a "deathless landlord," governing the land for the sake of its tenants and making it a "refuge for all who needed succour, counsel, and protection" (2.5.92). Consequently, as "long as the monks existed, the people, when aggrieved had property on their side" (2.5.93).

In this context bringing the people back to the land means replacing the dichotomous model of class, in which classes vie for power, with a hierarchical model in which classes are united. In the middle ages, Walter Gerard contends, "the country was not divided into two classes, masters and slaves" (2.5.91), but with the dissolution of the monasteries the free "subject has degenerated again into a serf" (6.13.497). As Patrick Brantlinger and others have pointed out, the novel ultimately discredits Stephen Morley's depiction of England as divided into "two nations . . . THE RICH AND THE POOR" (Brantlinger 102; *Sybil* 2.5.96). What it denies, however, is not the existence of wealth and poverty—these it regards as the very real consequences of a corrupt social system—but the idea that the aristocracy and working classes are inevitably opposed to one another. By granting agency to the working classes, Chartism would only intensify conflict with the upper classes, just as the Reform Bill, in granting the franchise to the middle class, put it into opposition to the aristocracy. The novel seeks to portray monastic hierarchy, by contrast, as establishing a set of reciprocal social relations that unite rather than divide the ruling elite and the working poor.

The novels make this claim that hierarchy unites rather than divides by defining social equality in terms of social reciprocity within a hierarchical structure. In the conclusion of *Vindication of the English Constitution* (1835), Disraeli had distinguished the modern kind of equality associated with "Gallic" socialism from English equality that is hierarchical:

> The basis of English society is Equality. But here let us distinguish: there are two kinds of equality; there is the equality that levels and destroys, and the equality that elevates and creates. It is this last, this sublime, this celestial equality, that animates the laws of England. The principle of the first equality, base, terrestrial, Gallic, and grovelling, is that no one should be privileged; the principle of English equality is that every one should be privileged. (204)

In *Sybil*, where one observer claims that Egremont's speech opposing the aims of Chartism is the "most really democratic" he has ever read (5.1.341), Egremont reiterates Disraeli's argument in the *Vindication*: "The future principle of English politics will not be a levelling principle; not a principle adverse to privileges, but favourable to their extension. It will seek to ensure equality, not by levelling the Few but by elevating the Many" (5.2.354). As the *Vindication* goes on to explain, this distinction between forms of equality rests on the claim that because no citizen is barred by birth ("caste") from rising in social status, England is hierarchical in structure (a "nation of classes") but egalitarian in principle:

> As Equality is the basis, so Gradation is the superstructure; and the English na-
> tion is essentially a nation of classes, but not of castes. Hence that admirable or-
> der, which is the characteristic of our society; for in England every man knows
> or finds his place; the law has supplied every man with a position, and nature
> has a liberal charter to amend the arrangement of the law. Our *equality* is the
> safety valve of tumultuous spirits; our *gradation* the security of the humble and
> the meek. (205; emphasis added)[10]

As the final clause indicates, Disraeli regards this hierarchy of stations as providing a set of reciprocal relations that protects rather than oppresses those at the bottom of the hierarchy. Elevating the many does not mean according them social
agency but situating them in reciprocal relation to an aristocracy modeled on the
medieval monastery.

This view of hierarchy as ultimately egalitarian explains how the novel uses
the marriage of Egremont and Sybil to represent the union of the classes. Some
critics have suggested that the conclusion of *Sybil* muddles what would appear to
be a figure of union between the aristocracy and working classes because Sybil is
discovered to be the heir of the Mowbray estate and thus presumably a member
of the aristocracy.[11] What these commentators are recognizing is that the novel
does not follow the convention of national tales that employ the marriage plot
to imagine the union of opposing cultures or, in this case, classes. Because *Sybil*
does not seek to imagine the union of aristocracy and working classes so much as a
shift from dichotomous to hierarchical social structure, it represents this marriage
in terms of Egremont's vision of a society that "ensure[s] equality, not by levelling
the Few but by elevating the Many." Consequently, while it borrows middle-class
discourse that privileges the companionate ideal, Disraeli's depiction of the companionate union both affirms equality between marriage partners and retains the
hierarchical relation between husband and wife.

⌒

Not surprisingly, both novels depict men who attempt to effect social reform by
modeling their estates on the medieval monasteries. At St. Geneviève, the Roman
Catholic Eustace Lyle seeks to restore monastic social relations by establishing
an alms-giving ceremony that enables "the people constantly and visibly to comprehend that Property is their protector and their friend" (*Coningsby* 3.4.170).
Henry Sydney similarly seeks to "elevate the character of the people" by reviving
medieval customs at Beaumanoir (9.1.460). In *Sybil*, the industrialist Trafford,

who not coincidentally is a younger son of a genteel Roman Catholic family from which he has imbibed "a correct conception of the relations which should subsist between the employer and employed," has built a quasi-gothic factory, designed a model village (with a "gothic church") to house his workers, and situated his own "baronial" home in close proximity to it so as to maintain direct relations with them (3.8.224, 226).[12]

Yet even as the novels evoke the neomedieval experiments of Young England as a means of imagining social reform, they distance their heroes from them. While they depict as admirable the attempts by the Catholics Eustace Lyle and Mr. Trafford to restore the monastic model, neither Coningsby nor Egremont, both staunchly Anglican, gives any indication of following their lead. Disraeli goes Dickens and Ainsworth one better not only by advocating religious toleration but also by expressing admiration for Catholicism, yet he nonetheless envisions the reformed aristocracy that will govern England as thoroughly Protestant.[13] While the novels' heroes seek to restore the conception of social order manifested by the monasteries, they do not aim to revive monastic institutions but merely take them as models for a reformed social order.

In advocating allotment schemes, the principal members of Young England — who, in spite of Anglo-Catholic influences, were Anglican — sought to establish a modern version of the unifying hierarchical structure of the feudal or monastic estate. In accord with the principle that social agency in such a system is the domain of the governing elite, the allotment system does not, like the Chartist Land Plan, seek to make laborers financially independent but to mitigate their dependent position by enabling them to supplement their income. John Manners, a major advocate of allotments, even went so far as to contend that reestablishing feudal relationships was an alternative to "giving the people political power" (Whibley 1:137). From this point of view, the Chartist Land Plan would reinforce class division by defining social agency in terms of class, while allotments would establish reciprocal relations that promote social harmony by erasing class difference. As we have seen, Disraeli thus contended that allotments schemes, which manifested an attempt by the aristocracy to reform itself by returning to the "principle of duty," would make "England . . . once more a nation, and not a mere collection of classes who seem to think they have nothing in common" (*Times* 14 Oct. 1844: 3; see also Burchardt 127).

Yet just as the heroes of the novels never seek to adopt monastic or feudal principles, neither explicitly embraces the allotment movement. *Sybil* endorses allotments indirectly by satirizing Lord Marney's disparagement of allotments and potato grounds as another sign of his failure to accept his responsibilities to his tenants (2.1.73, 2.12.144). Nevertheless, allotments are conspicuous by their absence in the novels, and the only character who embraces the system is the medievalizing Roman Catholic industrialist Trafford (6.10.467). Like the medieval abbot, therefore, the advocate of allotments remains rooted in the past, an analogue for rather than a version of the modern reformer.

The conclusions of the novels emphasize instead the acquisition and merging of landed estates as the means of establishing the hero as a leader in the House of Commons. As we have seen, Coningsby combines the estate he inherits from his grandfather with the estate acquired by his middle-class father-in-law, while Egremont similarly combines the estate he inherits from his brother with the estate recently restored to his working-class wife. In keeping with their commitment to the reinstatement of hierarchy, both novels espouse the restoration of sovereignty to the monarch and the House of Lords.[14] However, just as the heroes do not attempt to revive the past by reproducing feudal estates, they do not cede authority to the queen or the peerage. Instead of representing the House of Commons ceding power to the monarch and Lords, the novels represent members of the middle and working classes ceding power to aristocratic members of the House of Commons.

Rather than imagining the reform of England through the creation of neomedieval estates, the novels use these estates as figures for reform of the House of Commons that reverse the consequences of the Reform Bill. As we have seen, the Reform Bill debates established a discourse of class conflict—the aristocracy versus the middle class and upper classes versus lower classes—as the dominant mode of social explanation during the following decade. This discourse depicted classes as social agents acting through Parliament, the aristocracy and middle classes vying for control of the House of Commons and the working classes seeking entrée into it. Disraeli's novels seek to imagine a new reform of Parliament that would reverse this process and reunify the nation by replacing these triadic and dichotomous models of class with finely graded hierarchy. The relationship between abbot or lord and his estate comes to stand for the relationship between the MP and the nation.

In 1842, after Peel refused to offer him a post in the new Tory government, Disraeli began to form the alliances that became Young England and then proceeded to challenge Peel whenever the prime minister could be construed to depart from Tory principles, notably on the protection of the landed interest (Weintraub 208). He followed these first challenges by writing Coningsby, which appeared in May of 1844, and then almost immediately commencing Sybil, which he was working on when he gave his speech at the Ferrand allotment dinner that autumn and which appeared the following May. Both novels satirize Peel, in one case depicting him giving self-contradictory but flattering responses to deputations representing the landed and manufacturing interests (*Sybil* 6.1.411–14). Around the time of the publication of *Sybil*, which makes no allusion to Young England, two key members of Young England failed to back his attack on Peel's bill providing funding for the seminary at Maynooth. While Young England would soon cease to act in concert, Disraeli, whose speeches on these issues had distinguished him from the rest of Parliament, would emerge as a leader of the Tory party.

It is not insignificant, then, that in the conclusion of *Sybil*, the author steps out from behind the mask of the narrator and assumes the identity of the author of *Coningsby*, who in turn appears on the title page as "B. Disraeli, M. P." Moreover, whereas *Coningsby* imagines the formation of the Young England party as a means of reforming the aristocracy and in turn the nation, *Sybil* focuses on a single man who, after undergoing a process of reform, becomes the nation's principal social agent. In this context, the function of those passages advocating the restoration of royal sovereignty is to mediate between the figure of the feudal lord and the future prime minister that these novels seek to write into being.

CHAPTER 8

Agricultural Improvement and the Squirearchy in *Hillingdon Hall*

In February 1843, a little over a year before *Coningsby* appeared, Robert Smith Surtees commenced serial publication in the *New Sporting Magazine* of *Hillingdon Hall, or the Cockney Squire: A Tale of Country Life*, his third novel featuring the Cockney grocer and foxhunting enthusiast John Jorrocks. Serialization ended abruptly with the June 1844 installment, and when the complete novel, with an additional fifteen chapters, appeared a few months later—from Colburn, the publisher of Disraeli's novels—Surtees had added an allusion to Young England in one of the early chapters, an election campaign that turns on the Corn Laws, and a concluding speech in which the newly elected Jorrocks announces his intention to support Peel rather than Young England.[1]

Surtees (1803–1864) had much in common with Disraeli (1804–1881). Both began writing to earn an income—Disraeli in 1826 and Surtees in 1831—but by the 1840s their fiction writing had become avocational, Disraeli because he was in Parliament and Surtees because he had inherited the family estate at Hamsterley. *Hillingdon Hall*, like *Coningsby* and *Sybil*, satirizes the Whig aristocracy, and in it Surtees, as would Disraeli in Parliament, opposes repeal of the Corn Laws. Finally, just as Disraeli failed in his first attempt to run for Parliament, Surtees was, in 1837, an unsuccessful candidate in his first and only campaign for a parliamentary seat.

Yet the differences between the two novelists are apparent from the fact that Surtees refused several subsequent offers to run for Parliament, while Disraeli not only persisted in running for Parliament but indeed had considerable political ambitions. Whereas *Coningsby* and *Sybil* appeared under the authorship of

"B. Disraeli, M. P." and served as publicity for his campaign for party leadership, Surtees jealously guarded his anonymity, with *Hillingdon Hall* appearing under the name of the "Author of 'Handley Cross' &c." Disraeli, writing in the service of his political ambitions, adopted the characteristically earnest authorial voice of the reformer. By contrast, Surtees, relieved of the necessity of earning a living after inheriting Hamsterley Hall, adopted the persona of the amateur who seeks merely to entertain.

Nonetheless, as its commentary on agricultural improvement and the Corn Laws, its election plot, and an allusion to Chartism ("the new charter") indicate, *Hillingdon Hall*, for all of the comedy and satire that, after all, it shares with *Coningsby*, seeks to intervene in contemporary debates about social agency (3.36.93). Like the two preceding Jorrocks novels, *Hillingdon Hall* consists of a series of humorous episodes depicting the London native's encounters with rural culture. Unlike its predecessors, however, it has a loosely organized plot, the central thread of which involves the electoral campaign conducted by the Duke of Donkeyton, a Whig lord whose son, the Marquis of Bray, gets maneuvered by the Anti–Corn Law League into supporting repeal and loses the election to Jorrocks, who has taken up the cause of protection on behalf of his farming tenants.[2] One could thus make the case that Surtees invented the scenario in which his rich Cockney grocer retires and purchases a country estate in order to satirize those among the Whig aristocracy, in particular members of the recently established Royal Agricultural Society of England, who advocated free trade and repeal of the Corn Laws.

Like Disraeli, Surtees envisions social agency in terms of landed property and a finely graded hierarchy that displaces the agency of the Whig oligarchy, but he differs in his depiction both of the land itself and of the nature of the hierarchy. As we have seen, Disraeli envisions a hierarchy in which the reformed aristocrat establishes a set of reciprocal relations of responsibility and deference between himself and his "peasantry" (*Coningsby* 3.5.173).[3] By contrast, Surtees depicts a hierarchy that occupies a much narrower range, comprising the country squire as landed proprietor and yeoman farmers as his tenants, both of which share an interest in protecting the value of the land. Whereas Disraeli's novels treat the landed estate as a figure for the nation governed by a reformed aristocrat, *Hillingdon Hall* remains resolutely, albeit comically, focused on the ins and outs of working the land. Disraeli would reform the nation by reforming Parliament, but Surtees would do so by reforming agriculture. Finally, while Coningsby and Egremont embrace middle-class self-culture as a means of reforming the aristocracy, the role of the squire is to provide capital necessary to the reform of agriculture.

~

Like the unreformed aristocrats in Disraeli's novels, the Duke of Donkeyton promotes his self-interest by adhering to the kinship ideal in relation to both marriage and parliamentary politics. Employing a satirically inverted version of the national narrative with its parallel courtship and political plots, the novel depicts the Duke's attempts to maintain his family's status being undermined by the romantic entanglements that result from his attempt to court voters for the county's parliamentary seat. The dinner for electors that introduces the Duke into the novel initiates the novel's two main plotlines, its marriage plot and its political plot. His invitation to the widow of the late parson of Hillingdon, Mrs. Flathers, and her daughter, Emma, sets in motion a courtship plot in which his son, the Marquis, becomes entangled with a commoner, and his invitation to Jorrocks, the Cockney grocer become squire of Hillingdon Hall, introduces an election narrative in which the Marquis ends up supporting repeal of the Corn Laws and losing the election to the Whig grocer become Tory squire.

In accord with the kinship ideal, the Duke conceives the county's parliamentary seat as family property. The convergence of property and kinship manifests itself in the Duke's claims that the seat is "ours" and that it is a "birth-right" that passes from father to son (3.41.169, 177). Accordingly, when they announce the Marquis's candidacy, the Duke and his attorney justify their avoidance of specific political positions by invoking the kinship ideal, declaring that the Marquis's "public conduct will be governed" by those "principles" that "have been maintained by [his] family throughout many succeeding generations" (3.41.168; see also 172).

Consequently, the Duke conceives the election campaign as condescending to the "commonalty" rather than uniting with voters who share his political interests (1.9.99). By hosting dinners for county families who possess the franchise and subscribing to "two organs, two churches, [and] three races," he assumes the role of private benefactor who directs the electors to vote for his son in deference to his family (3.41.171). Correspondingly, he not only avoids stating specific principles but also detests the idea of a "personal canvass" that would require the Marquis to appear on the public hustings and there attempt to persuade voters that he will protect their interests. Whereas assuming the role of host and public benefactor enables the Duke to maintain his status as social superior, the canvass would put his son in the position of equality with commoners. Not surprisingly, he believes that his party went "too far" in passing the Reform Bill, which had increased the number of electors with the consequence that elections were more likely to be contested, and suggests that it should instead have "abolished" the personal canvass (3.41.176, 170; see also 3.44.231).

The Duke's attempts to conduct the election by establishing relations of deference with the "commonalty" lead directly to and parallel his son's romantic entanglement with a "commoner." The Duke has been accustomed to inviting the late Rev. Flather, a rare "Whig Parson," to the dinners he hosts for county electors. However, he fails to recognize that, just as the Reform Bill has put electors on a more equal footing with his son, so too the companionate marriage ideal has displaced the kinship model of marriage. In accord with the companionate model, the widowed Mrs. Flather answers the question of "why her daughter and she should be invited now that there were neither politics nor guidance to get in the way of return" by concluding that it must be because the "Duke and Duchess of Donkeyton had determined on perpetuating their line" through a marriage of the Marquis and her daughter (1.9.109, 110). Although she in fact seeks to marry for wealth and status, Emma Flather invokes the companionate ideal, declaring in accord with its monogamy imperative "that a person is never *really* in love but once" and lamenting that the Marquis should not be able to "marry who he pleases" (2.30.289, 3.37.109). The Duke, however, is firmly committed to the kinship model of marriage and, in accord with his declaration that the county seat is his son's birthright, insists that a marriage between his son and a "commoner" is "impossible" (3.35.80; see also 3.34.56, 64).

Unlike Coningsby, who rebels against the older generation and marries against his grandfather's wishes, the Marquis adheres to the kinship ideal. In the opening chapters of the novel, Surtees sets up the expectation that the Marquis will eventually reject the "cold, calculating, and cunning" Emma Flather and form a companionate union with her rival, the "warmhearted, but shy and reserved" Eliza Trotter (1.2.13). However, the Marquis not only accepts his father's determination that he not "marry anything below a Duke's daughter" but also, in keeping with the promiscuity associated with the kinship ideal, "look[s] upon everything below a nobleman's daughter as fair game" (1.11.171, 176). The Duke does not object to his son's promiscuity and merely seeks to safeguard him by recommending "Lord Chesterfield's Letters to his Son"—the favorite reading of Sir John Chester—"with the passage recommending young men to attach themselves to married women, underlined in red ink, and marked in the margin" (3.35.78). Whereas Disraeli envisions Coningsby making an alliance that reforms England by displacing the promiscuous Marquess of Monmouth, Surtees depicts the Marquis of Bray as merely reproducing the existing social order.

In place of a companionate marital union between the Marquis and Emma Flather that would undermine his family's status, the Duke seeks to substitute a kinship alliance between Jorrocks and a bull named "the Marquis," which will help sustain his family's status by securing the "fifteen or sixteen votes" in the squire's control (1.9.100). In keeping with his notions of agricultural innovation, Jorrocks seeks a prize breeding bull, and the Duke's offer of the bull literalizes Sir Robert Peel's facetious suggestion, quoted in the epigraph of the chapter, that he intends to buy "the best bull [he] can find" and to offer his "tenants and their cows . . . free access to the animal" (2.22.103). The hint that not only the cows but also the tenants might mate with the animal accords with the comic homosocial triangulation in which Jorrocks's "love" for the "Marquis" is intended to create a political bond between the Duke and the Cockney squire (3.45.246; see also 3.44.234).

However, the Duke fails to establish this alliance and thus loses the parliamentary seat because he sees it in terms of the kinship ideal as maintaining the status of his family, not, in terms of contemporary politics, as protecting his interests as a landowner. In order to persuade the Anti–Corn Law League's rival Whig candidate to withdraw, the Duke instructs his son to support repeal of the Corn Laws, a position that, as the local farmers put it, is at odds with the fact that the "bulk of [his] income was derived from the land" (3.43.213). Although contemporary political discourse associated the Corn Laws with the Tories, many Whigs, like Donkeyton, were themselves landowners and opposed repeal, precisely because the laws served their economic interests. Consequently, the Anti–Corn Law League often found itself at odds with the Whig party. In 1841 at Walsall, for example, it set up a rival to the incumbent Whig, who did not favor repeal, with the result that the Whig vote was split. In *Hillingdon Hall*, the farmers set up Jorrocks as a Tory rival to the Marquis, and, as at Walsall, what had once been a safe Whig seat is turned into a Tory one.

The Duke's failure to protect his interests as a landowner implies that the Whig aristocracy has become disconnected from the land, a disconnection manifested in the Duke's agricultural practices and conception of agricultural improvement. The Duke speaks the language of agricultural reform and knows from the scientific literature that farmers should "apply their land to proper purposes" and not "force it to grow crops that it has no taste for" (1.12.195). Nonetheless, he regards agricultural science as a means of "triumph[ing] over nature" and so "plant[s] potatoes in autumn" and insists on making Cheshire cheese, even though his pasturage is not suited for it (2.22.132). It is no surprise, therefore, that, in spite of his claim that "scientific farming" is "the only thing to make money of," his dairy operates at a loss (1.12.199, 2.22.126).

The Duke regards agricultural improvement, like the seat in Parliament, as a means of enhancing and displaying his status rather than protecting and enhancing the value of his land. He makes Cheshire cheese not because it is suitable for his land but because producing it enhances his status among his guests (see 2.22.127). Rather than entrust his "model farm" to energetic and industrious scientific farmers, he employs men who "loiter" about looking "far too white and puffy to work" (2.22.126). Instead of serving as a standard for modern agriculture, Strawberry Hill, as he sentimentally names his model farm, is yet another means of enhancing his status and his estate. Like other members of the aristocracy who exploit their estates for self-serving purposes, the Duke has theories and "notions about the management of property" that "generally end . . . in beggaring the tenants and impoverishing his estates" (1.12.198–99).

∽

The satire on Donkeyton's farming together with his being inveigled to support the repeal of the Corn Laws makes it clear that Surtees's criticisms are aimed not only at the "theoretical" follies of the RASE, but also at the free-trade views of several of its leading Whig supporters. The first president of the RASE, John Spencer, third Earl Spencer, was a Whig free trader who had publicly declared his support for repeal of the Corn Laws, while other Whig members were even more vocal in their calls for repeal.[4] Thus, just as the farmers in *Hillingdon Hall* cannot understand how the Duke could support repeal of the Corn Laws when the "bulk of [his] income was derived from the land," many members of the RASE condemned Spencer and the free traders for betraying the agricultural interest (Goddard 16).

As we have seen, however, Spencer and the RASE contended that the landed interest need not rely on protection and could be better served by the improvement of agricultural production through the "methods which had transformed the manufacturing industry . . . in particular the application of 'capital' and 'science'" (Goddard 12; see also 13–16). Unlike the Duke, Spencer was no mere theoretical farmer and made important contributions to agricultural improvement, which accounts for the fact that in this respect Donkeyton is based not on Spencer but on Hugh Percy, third Duke of Northumberland.[5] Whereas the Anti–Corn Law League was content to anticipate that repeal would lower the price of grain by increasing the supply of imported grain, the RASE sought to increase the supply of domestic grain through agricultural improvement. As James Smith of Deanston, whose innovations were a major influence on the RASE in its early years, contended, the increase in production resulting from improvements such as his system of draining would "overthrow . . . the bugbear corn laws without a political struggle" (20; see also Goddard 19).

Although it satirizes the disconnection between Donkeyton's position as a landowner and his support of free trade, the novel, which is dedicated to the RASE, in other respects supports the movement for agricultural reform that the society advocated. As its brief preface explains, the novel's satire is not intended to "discourage improvement, but to repress the wild schemes of theoretical men, who attend farmers' meetings for the pleasure of hearing themselves talk, and do more harm than good by the promulgation of their visionary views." Indeed, although Surtees joined the Northumberland Society for the Protection of Agriculture while he was writing *Hillingdon Hall*, his support for the Corn Laws seems to have been soft, for he abandoned protectionism once they were repealed. By 1850 he was taking up the position earlier advocated by Spencer, advising farmers that they should give up hope that protection would be restored and urging them instead to make agriculture profitable by adopting the kinds of improvements advocated by the RASE (Gash 144).

In keeping with this view, the novel contends that what farmers need is not more knowledge about agricultural science but capital investment. In his longest aside, the narrator, echoing the preface, insists that he is not against "agricultural improvement" and contends that it is "want of capital" rather than ignorance of science that prevents it: "So long as people look upon [farming] as an exception to other trades, *and requiring no capital to set up with*, so long we fear will be the want of energy and taste for improvement" (1.15.251; emphasis added). While the novel lampoons the foibles of farmers, along with those of most of its other characters, it nonetheless depicts them as fully cognizant of this need. Jorrocks, who like the Duke has a merely theoretical knowledge of farming, takes up the view that farmers are ignorant about agricultural reform, complaining that his tenants are "a long way behind the hintelligence o' the day" (1.7.76; see also 1.13.216, 1.14.234). Yet, as his tenant Johnny Wopstraw explains, farmers have long known that draining is "the foundation of all agricultural improvement" (1.7.77). The problem is not lack of knowledge but lack of capital. As another farmer puts it, draining is "nothing new—my grandfather drained—I'd have had all the wet off my farm before now, if I had had the money" (1.17.304). Moreover, as Mark Heavytail, his most prosperous tenant, points out, because farming tenants do not have a long-term investment in the land, capital investment must come from the landowner (1.6.70).

Indeed, whereas the Duke's ideas about agricultural improvement are linked to his conception of the land as a means of sustaining his social status, Jorrocks's are linked to his view of the land as an investment. If the Duke seeks to create a picturesque farm and produce that does not suit his land but will impress his guests, Jorrocks's entrepreneurial notion of improvement takes the form of contriving inventions, including a formula in which the former grocer confuses the clay used in the manufacture of draining tiles with "clayed sugar" (brown sugar) and a steam-driven "machine that will cut and grind your corn and plough the land at the same time" (1.15.266, 1.17.300; see also 1.16.283–84). Appropriately, he repeatedly praises James Smith of Deanston, the industrialist mill owner who developed the drainage system that had become the standard throughout Britain and made him a hero to the RASE. This perspective takes comic form when he appears to consider Smith of Deanston a descendent of Adam Smith (1.16.279), his exaggeration of James Smith's achievement in making two blades grow where one grew before into four, eight, ten, and then sixteen blades, echoing Adam Smith's depiction of the quasi-miraculous power of the division of labor to increase production (1.13.217, 1.14.230, 235, 237, 1.15.247).[6] Moreover, the resemblance between this sequence and the geometric increase in population that Malthus had contended would outpace the arithmetic increase in production takes up the RASE's claims for the social value of agricultural improvement.

What Jorrocks fails to recognize is that increasing agricultural production, like any enterprise, requires not only an initial outlay but continuous capital investment. Instead, he assumes that purchasing land is like putting money in "the funds" and receiving a regular return of 3 percent. When, on his first round of visits to his tenants, Mark Heavytail asks for repairs to his kitchen and water pump, a new bier (cow house) and dairy, and improved field drainage, Jorrocks learns that "landed property is not quite so manageable as money in the funds" (1.7.81). In retiring to the country, he had expected to escape the variable returns of capital investment, but he discovers that investing in land is even more unpredictable: "Money i' the funds may pay small interest; but . . . funds pay punctual, and the gates never want repairin'" (3.32.17). Soon thereafter he concludes that because "farming, which he thought was a sure fortune," instead seems to be "attended with no end of trouble," he will "shut up shop" and return to London (3.32.25). When he is invited to run for Parliament, he objects that he would have to abandon country life and return to London, but, as this passage indicates, the invitation instead provides him with the opportunity to escape it.

While the election of Jorrocks would seem to represent a shift of social agency from the Whig aristocracy to the Whig grocer turned Tory squire who understands the landed interest even as he brings to it the energies of the middle class, Jorrocks's shortcomings suggest that the novel ultimately rejects the assumption that social agency is a matter of which party or class controls Parliament. Jorrocks's understanding of parliamentary politics is shaky at best, as manifested by his embrace of the designation of "Conservative[s]" as "Tory men with vig [Whig] measures," an epithet that Disraeli had intended as a condemnation of Peel's administration (3.47.295).[7] Although he promises that he will "keep a watchful eye on" the "interest" of the farmers, his plan to make the wily James Pigg the manager of his property and to "establish a model farm, like the Duke of Donkeyton's" suggests that he does not yet recognize the extent of his ignorance about farming (3.47.295). He will undoubtedly benefit the farmers primarily through his absence.

The novel ultimately depicts social agency not as a matter of whether the Whigs or the Tories, or the aristocracy or the middle class, controls Parliament but rather as the agricultural reform undertaken by a traditional squire who resides at the apex of a finely graded hierarchy consisting of squire, yeoman farmers, and farm labor. *Hillingdon Hall* features two such squires, both of whom are exempt from the satiric treatment it metes out to nearly every other character. The novel begins with a nostalgic description of Jorrocks's predecessor, Westbury, as "one of the last of the old-fashioned race of country gentlemen who lived all the year round on their estates" (1.1.6). This ideal is manifested in particular by another squire, an "old-fashioned English gentleman" who is "at home everywhere, from the palace of the Sovereign to the cottage of the labourer" and is "looked up to and respected by all" (2.29.242–43). This squire appropriately depicts the meeting of the St. Boswell Agricultural Society, which, of course, is dedicated to agricultural improvement and over which he presides, as a model for a social order in which "a number of persons whose interests were identical, were assembled in social intercourse — the enterprising farmer and the honest industrious labourer" (2.29.248). Unlike the Duke, who disdains the idea that he shares the same interests as the voters he considers beneath him, the squire can assume the position of "patriarch of the district" who is "looked up to and respected by all," even as he treats their "interests" as "identical" (1.1.7).

The squirearchy is distinct from the finely graded hierarchy of Disraeli's novels precisely because of the nature of the relationships between squire, farmer, and laborer. Disraeli's model estates, as manifested in the quasi-medieval estates of Coningsby's friends — Henry Sydney's Beaumanoir and Eustace Lyle's St. Geneviève — consist not so much of a finely graded hierarchy as of the titled owner of a vast estate and his peasantry. As David Roberts has pointed out, "The vast estates and exalted titles of dukes and earls often brought a loftiness and remoteness that did not burden the gentry. The squire's estate proved more personal and intimate" (*Social Conscience* 48). In the Disraelian models, the peasants remain an anonymous mass who do not interact with the lords except in rituals of deference. By contrast, the agricultural meeting in *Hillingdon Hall* serves as a forum in which squire and farmer confer on agricultural reform.

Hillingdon Hall differs from *Coningsby* precisely by taking literally Tory claims about the importance of the land and landownership to the nation. As we have seen, Disraeli's novels ultimately treat the landed estate as a figure for agency, the member of Parliament standing in relation to the nation as the lord does to his estate. In *Hillingdon Hall* by contrast the squire is first and foremost a farmer, not an MP. Moreover, the novel's constant references to guano and manure, plowing and draining, while often comic, nonetheless emphasize the physical aspect of the land.

In the victory speech that concludes the novel, Jorrocks distances himself from Disraeli, informing those who have elected him that although "Young England, at one time, had favour in his eyes, . . . they lost it by steeple-chasin'—above all, by Conin'sby ridin' a steeple-chase in Hautumn" and that he intends instead to "support" Sir Robert Peel, whose economic reforms have "restored" the country to "hunexampled prosperity" (3.47.294, 295). This characteristically Jorrocksian reasoning, which comically echoes criticisms that Disraeli did not know firsthand the milieu he depicted in *Coningsby*, suggests that Young England understands the natural rhythms of rural England no better than does the Whig Duke of Donkeyton.[8] By contrast, Peel, an early supporter of the RASE, had enacted measures designed to provide capital investments in drainage (Gash 144). If Parliament is to play a role, the novel seems to say, it is in providing the capital necessary for agricultural improvement and then giving way to an alliance of enlightened squires who invest in their property and industrious farmers who improve the land.

Yet the novel's narrative of reform does not ultimately merge the roles of the traditional and the Cockney squire. Jorrocks might be regarded as bringing the entrepreneurial spirit of the rising middle class to the improvement of agriculture and then undergoing a process of reform through which he comes to understand the landed interest and converts from Whig to Tory. However, this process of conversion does not appear to enlighten him about the importance of capital investment in agriculture. Similarly, although the squire who occupies the chair at the St. Boswell Agricultural Society meeting embraces agricultural reform, the novel does not show us how a traditional squire like Jorrocks's predecessor, Westbury, might be reformed into an enlightened agricultural improver. Indeed, while the novel expresses admiration for these squires, they ultimately play a minor role in a narrative whose conclusion leaves the county, and the country, in the hands of a befuddled MP.

CHAPTER 9

The Land Plan, Class Dichotomy, and Working-Class Agency in *Sunshine and Shadow*

Four years after the appearance of *Sybil*, Thomas Martin Wheeler's *Sunshine and Shadow: A Tale of the Nineteenth Century* began serial publication in the *Northern Star*.[1] Wheeler, a longtime Chartist activist, had been awarded one of the Land Plan allotments at O'Connorville, and it was there that he wrote *Sunshine and Shadow*. While Disraeli appeared on the title pages of his novels as "B. Disraeli, M. P.," the weekly numbers of *Sunshine and Shadow* designate Wheeler "Late Secretary to the National Charter Association and National Land Company" (72). As we have seen, Disraeli's novels seek to persuade a readership of enfranchised citizens that the nation will be best served by a Parliament controlled by a reformed aristocracy with Disraeli, MP, at its head. *Sybil* in particular makes the claim that this Parliament will solve the problem of Chartist social unrest by taking responsibility for the condition of the lower classes. By contrast, when Wheeler designates himself "late secretary" to the Land Plan, he lays claim to a position of authority within the Chartist movement, but his novel does not envision that he, or the hero who serves as his proxy, will lead the movement for reform. Written in 1848, when, as the novel itself would acknowledge, the "tide of popular support" for the Land Plan had begun to recede and the final attempt to present the Chartist petition had turned into a debacle, his novel instead seeks to sustain his readers' confidence that the only way to address the condition of the working classes is to obtain parliamentary representation for them (34.177–78).[2]

While it makes no explicit allusions to Disraeli's novels, *Sunshine and Shadow* does appear to echo—and radically revise—the national narratives of *Coningsby* and *Sybil*.[3] Just as Coningsby is "the favourite" and "hero" of Eton (1.9.71, 72), Walter North is the "leader" of "every frolic and school-boy enterprise" at College House Academy (2.75), and the bond formed between Walter North and Arthur Morton closely resembles the friendship of Coningsby and Millbank at Eton.[4] Both novels depict idyllic schooldays giving way to conflict, but whereas Coningsby and Millbank remain friends and the conflict is displaced to the older generation, in *Sunshine and Shadow* a permanent rift arises between North and Morton. When North seeks to gain parliamentary power in order to obtain a peerage, he comes to resemble not Coningsby but his grandfather Monmouth, while Morton, having become a Chartist, in turn comes to resemble the hero of *Sybil* when, in an inversion of the moment when the aristocratic Egremont persuades the Chartist Sybil that the aristocracy are the "natural leaders of the people," he convinces North's sister, who is married to a baronet, that the "redemption of the working classes must spring from themselves alone" (*Sybil* 4.15.334; *Sunshine and Shadow* 13.108).

Whereas the Disraelian national narrative depicts the marriage of an aristocratic hero uniting social classes and thus resolving class conflict by establishing a finely graded hierarchy, Walter North's marriage produces disunion and class dichotomy, the schoolboy friends and social equals set on opposite trajectories with the one becoming a peer of the realm and the other an impoverished Chartist. Like Disraeli's heroes, North unites his landed property with his wife's, but he does not do so, like Coningsby and Egremont, in order to provide for the nation as a whole but, like Monmouth, to serve his own interests. Consequently, Morton becomes a Chartist and unites not with the upper classes but with a fellow Chartist, Mary Graham. He takes part in advancing the Land Plan, which does not seek to combine estates for the sake of a single individual but subdivides the land among members of the working class as a means of obtaining the franchise for his entire class.

Sunshine and Shadow thus depicts as romance the national narrative in which marriage consolidates the power of the upper classes and excludes the lower classes, rejecting it in favor of the historical narrative in which the lower classes exercise social agency. As the narrator explains in the novel's final paragraph, "We might have made our tale more interesting to many, by drawing more largely from the regions of *romance*, but our object was to combine a *History* of Chartism, with the details of our story" (37.192; emphasis added). The novel accordingly gives North and Morton, once they leave school, separate narrative trajectories, Walter North following the romance script of the rise of the middle class and Arthur Morton enacting the entire history of Chartism.

This narrative structure explains how the novel treats the Chartist Land Plan and the ways in which landownership provides possibilities of social agency. *Sun-*

shine and Shadow seeks to sustain working-class agency in the face of the failure of the 1848 petition and the imminent collapse of the Land Plan. As we have seen, O'Connor depicted the Land Plan both as a substitute for obtaining the franchise and a means acquiring it, a view with which Wheeler would have been very familiar, for he was the unnamed coauthor of the pamphlet in which O'Connor laid out the plan.[5] The novel's structure and its depiction of the Land Plan suggest that insofar as it is a substitute for the franchise, the plan involves a retreat into the pastoral domain of romance but that its failure as the result of being subject to historical contingency means that it can succeed if it remains focused on securing social agency for the working classes. Wheeler himself remained committed to the campaign for universal male suffrage for the rest of his life, but his novel opens the possibility that it too is a historically contingent form of social agency.

⌒

The opening of *Sunshine and Shadow* depicts an idyllic era during which the schoolmates Walter North and Arthur Morton are social equals who develop a "brother[ly]" bond that becomes the basis of the "most perfect friendship" (2.74, 75). The narrator gives us few details about Morton's family, but there is no indication that he is in any way inferior in social status to North. Indeed, Morton is the ward of an uncle who is, apparently, a prosperous wool merchant, while North's parents had been servants prior to his father's rise to public-house owner and successful wine merchant. The idyllic nature of the relationship between the schoolmates is confirmed when Morton visits the Norths during vacations and the friendship becomes "attached" to "the ideal of home and comfort, of female loveliness and domestic peace" (2.75).

However, differences in family circumstances, already evident while they are at school, eventually break the bond between them. Morton is an orphan and only child whose guardian pays little attention to him, while North, an eldest son, possesses both parents and siblings. In spite of the idyllic, even nostalgic tone that marks the narrator's description of the boys, these differences are already manifest during their school days. Made "self-confident" by the prospect of inheriting the family business, North becomes the "undisputed leader" of the school and offers his "patronage" to the younger Morton (2.75). The resulting "friendship" is asymmetrical, "often thoughtless and exacting on the part of [North], but ever self-sacrificing and trusting on the part of [Morton]" (2.75). The novel reinforces these inequalities within the apparently egalitarian friendship by opening with a description of the boys leaving school, thus implying that the era of idyllic friendship is receding into the past from the very beginning.

Precisely because North has a family to support him, he fails to develop an interiority that would sustain his "companionship" with Morton (2.74). As we have seen, the nineteenth-century novel depicts companionship developing through the encounter of interiorities, mediated by conversation. While just such interactions mark Morton's encounters with North's sister, the novel never depicts the male friends in conversation. Although North belongs to the commercial middle class, the fact that his family is already prosperous and he will inherit his father's business means that he does not need to develop the middle-class virtue of self-culture. Consequently, he has little interest in study, learns little at school, and remains "destitute of any high principles, and deficient in intellectual attainments" (6.84). Wheeler makes North a flat character not because he is incapable of making him round or lacks knowledge of the upper classes but because North has no interiority: his life is a "vacuity" (36.188).[6]

North's failure to develop an interior life makes him incapable not only of conversation and true companionship but also of forming memories that will sustain friendship over time. At the moment of their parting, Morton anticipates the division that will arise between himself and North by expressing a fear of being forgotten: "After three years' companionship, during which time I have looked up to you as an elder brother, I feel that I am about to be thrust alone into the world; you have parents, brother, and sister to love you, but I have only an uncle to look to, and he is so immersed in business that I fear I shall almost be forgotten" (2.74). While he here ascribes amnesia to his uncle (correctly, as it turns out), the fact that he is expressing this anxiety to North indicates that he also fears being forgotten by his friend. Indeed, in spite of North's assurance that that he "will never be forgotten" and "many protestations of kindness and mutual remembrance," within a few years North has "forgotten the very existence of his quondam friend" (2.74, 4.78).

In terms of the novel's national narrative, this process in which one friend forgets the other allegorizes the betrayal of the working classes by the middle classes after the passage of the Reform Bill. The novel opens in 1831, when the campaign for the Reform Bill was at its peak. In accord with Chartist discourse, in waging this campaign, the middle classes had sought and gained working-class support for the Reform Bill but then had failed to follow through by supporting the enfranchisement of the working classes. As Morton explains, "Prior to the passing of the Reform Bill" the middle class and "working men" were "equally disenfranchised; but when, by aid of the energy of the workingmen, they achieved that measure, the chain of the labour slave was riveted still firmer," while the "employer was politically free." Moreover, "the ladder by which the middle class had risen was thrown down as useless, and they had ever since endeavoured . . .

to ally themselves to the upper class, and to build up a wall of separation between them and the working men" (13.107). Similarly, the middle-class North becomes divided from his friend, who is now thrust into the working class, and seeks to rise into the aristocracy. In this respect, there is little distinction between the aristocracy and the middle class; rather, the novel employs the dichotomous model of class, defined in terms of possession of the franchise.

However, the novel seeks to invert the upper-class conception of social agency by suggesting that although North gains status and political power, his lack of interiority means he has no agency. His incapacity to form memories corresponds with an inability to envision a future. After all his successes, he discovers not only that his "past" is "one vast blank" but also that he has "no hopes for the future" (36.188). He cannot act because he does not possess an interiority capable of formulating a future aim as the basis of independent action. Even his "rise" is not the result of middle-class self-making, for the aspirations that lead him to acquire a seat in Parliament and a patent of nobility do not come from within but from the prescribed script of the rise-of-the-middle-class narrative.

Accordingly, North rises not through adhering to the middle-class ideal of self-culture but by adhering to the aristocratic kinship ideal — hence his desire to become a peer of the realm. He consequently constructs a middle-class version of kinship marriage, in which, rather than seeking "genuine love," he "look[s] on marriage as he did on any other portion of his business — with the keen eye of a trade"; consequently, he forces his sister into marriage with a baronet, whose "name and connexions, [would] be of service" to him in his own "matrimonial *spec*" (22.134, 6.83, 7.87, 6.85; emphasis added). The lack of interiority that causes him to forget his school companion also makes him incapable of forming a companionate marital union and appreciating the domestic so that just a few months after his marriage, "home cease[s] to have charms in his eye" (32.169). Thus he not only treats marriage as "legalised prostitution" but also, in accord with the promiscuity trope that we have seen in Disraeli, literally resorts to patronizing prostitutes (7.87).

In characteristic fashion, the novel links the aristocratic preference for kinship marriage to the exercise of political power for personal advantage rather than for the sake of the nation as a whole. North joins the Anti–Corn Law League and becomes a "tool of the Whig faction" not for the sake of the nation or even of the middle class but in order to achieve a seat in Parliament and a "patent of nobility" (21.131; see also 32.168). He secures his election "in good measure" through the influence of the Earl of Altringham and subsequently cements the alliance that provides his entrée into the aristocracy by marrying the earl's granddaughter. As

Morton concludes when describing the rise of the middle class after the passage of the Reform Bill, "selfishness is [his] ruling principle" (13.107).

Whereas the fact that North has family makes it unnecessary to develop his interiority, Arthur Morton's childhood as a solitary orphan leads him to develop a rich interior life. Precisely because he finds himself "alone in the midst of a crowd" (4.80; see also 5.82), he develops the "habit of self-dependence" on which he must rely when, during his early adulthood, his uncle marries and informs him that he must henceforth "depend on his own exertions for his support" (2.74, 4.80). These circumstances lead him to turn inward and develop a "cultivated intellect" and then to become a lover of literature and the "best scholar" in the school (6.84, 3.77).

Morton's fully developed interiority provides him with the capacity of memory that sustains his relationships after he leaves school. In contrast to North, who immediately forgets his friend, Morton never forgets North, whose "image" is "never . . . entirely absent" from his mind (4.78). Indeed, when he finds himself without friends or family after leaving school, the memory of North and his family sustains him, "the recollections of the past, and friendship suppl[ying] to him the place of parents and kin" (4.78). Thus, in one of the novel's characteristic paradoxes, "unkindness and neglect" in the present lead him to recall the happiness he had formerly experienced at North's home (2.75).

Memories of the past help Morton deal with the difficulties of the present by providing him with the means of imagining that the divisions of the present will give way to unity in the future. The narrator thus concludes that although Morton is tried by "adversity," he is "less to be pitied than" North, who has "no hopes for the future" (36.188). Indeed, hope is the hallmark of Morton's character. He has "aspirations" for a "future career" (4.79), "longs to have some definite object to do" (40.80), "yearns for something, of the very nature of which he [is] yet unaware" (40.80), and persists in "hopes and anticipations of profitable employment, and vague dreams of future greatness" (5.82). Whereas North merely follows the scripted and predictable path of the rise of the middle class, the uncertainties that Morton anticipates indicate that his future is open, that society can be changed.

Accordingly, Morton, in spite of belonging to the disenfranchised classes, possesses social agency. "Hope" with a capital *H* even leads him to travel by chance to Birmingham, where he discovers the Chartist movement, which gives "form, proportion, and colour to the shadow of his imagination" and enables him to envision his youthful "dreams" becoming "realities" (8.91, 92). Not surprisingly, Morton becomes a "prominent actor" in the Chartist movement, taking part in nearly all of its major initiatives (10.95). In turn, it is by acting that Morton and the Chartists sustain hope for the future. As the narrator puts it in addressing the "man of the Future": "The present transition phase of society is already passing away, and the bright future appears in dim perspective" (6.84). Chartism, the narrator suggests in his concluding paragraph, "whilst working for the present . . . holds the future in its grasp" (37.192). Whereas North has no capacity to envision the future and thus no basis for autonomous action, Chartism as "the offspring of imagination" enables Morton to become a social agent (18.124).

This interiority paradoxically transforms his self-dependent "isolation" into the capacity to form social relationships and aligns him with the companionate ideal. Morton's deep interiority and resulting capacity for memory and "recollection" (2.75) enable him to develop companionate bonds. While North plays the role of "benefactor," Morton comes to "love" his friend, this love becoming in turn the basis for a communal orientation, "love for Walter beg[etting] love for all human kind" (2.75). The memory of this homosocial bond, which was what "first love is to many in more mature years," mediates his adult affection for North's sister, Julia, which is "unmixed with aught of selfish wishes" (2.75, 12.104; see also 18.122, 123). Accordingly, Julia, who has inherited "the whole intellect of the family," has a well-developed interior life and the capacity for memory (3.77). Oppressed by a kinship marriage and having "no hope for future happiness," she is sustained by the "pleasant recollection" of Arthur, whom she considers "a hero of romance," and even as she lies on her deathbed, the "power of memory" temporarily revives her (14.111, 15.113, 13.106, 17.121). In accord with the companionate ideal, they fall in love in the course of a series of conversations in which "his sentiments [become] her sentiments,—his feelings her feelings" (13.108). When, after Julia's death, Morton courts Mary Graham, a fellow Chartist who is "possessed of a strong mind," their developing relationship similarly involves sharing "feelings" and "ideas" (28.155, 153).

This commitment to the companionate ideal corresponds with Morton's desire to gain political power not for "self" but for "mankind" (37.192). He loves the "land of his birth" (10.98, 35.142), and "patriotism" leads him and his wife to "dream of serving their country," not merely by advancing the cause of the working class, but also by seeking the "regeneration of their country" (37.191, 9.93). While the companionate ideal of selfless love characterizes their relationship to the nation as a whole, the ideals of Chartism correspondingly mediate romance, with Arthur and Julia falling in love while discussing the "wrongs endured by the people" (13.106) and Arthur and Mary falling in love while serving on a Chartist committee. Explicitly linking the personal and the political, the narrator explains

Arthur's transgressive romance with a married woman by insisting that the "feelings" of "chivalrous devotion, and disinterested purity" aroused by Chartism "are the true essence of love" (18.124).

Moreover, the novel's national narrative links the marriage plot to the political plot by associating marriage with romance and amnesia, and the political with history and hope for the future. As we have seen, the narrator concludes the novel by explaining that he has not drawn "more largely from the regions of romance," because he has sought to combine a "History of Chartism, with the details of [his] story" (37.192). Yet while the narrator implies that romance without history is delusive because it leads to amnesia and despair, he does not dismiss romance. Indeed, hope for the future can only be sustained through the memory of romance.

The novel makes the narrative of the life of Walter North a romance by depicting his steady, uninterrupted rise as taking place outside of history. While he benefits from the circumstance that his father has been successful, once he is set on the path to success, historical circumstances never get in his way. In spite of the fact that the novel records key events in the history of Chartism as well as the dates on which they take place, no historical event figures in the story of Walter North. Indeed, there is no indication that his business suffers during the economic downturns that have such devastating effects on Arthur Morton.

By contrast, the Morton narrative is episodic, marked by both advances and setbacks, as he struggles against and seeks to shape historical circumstances. The novel not only depicts him as contending with financial challenges, in particular difficulty in finding work, but also links these challenges to the historical economic depressions of 1842 and 1846. These events in turn lead him to engage in political activities aimed at changing social conditions, and he participates in the main episodes in the history of Chartism from 1838 to 1848, including the first Chartist convention, the Bull Ring Riots, the Manchester strike wave of 1842, promotion of the Land Plan, and the Kennington Common meeting of April 10, 1848.

Appropriately, at the only two points when the Morton and North narratives intersect after they leave school, history fails to disrupt romance, but romance impinges on history. When Morton, out of work and angry at the death of his son, assaults North, making him "victim to his necessities," it would seem that for once economic contingency is, at least indirectly, coming to bear on North (33.174; see also 31.166). However, the next chapter, which makes no reference to this episode, details North's ultimate success in being named Lord Maxwell, thus implying that he suffers only a temporary injury that does not alter his fortunes.

By contrast, North's rise dramatically alters the course of Morton's life when the former forces his sister to marry Sir Jasper Baldwin, thus thwarting the budding love affair between Julia and Arthur. Although North himself is not constrained by historical contingency, his success has historical effects, the rise of the middle class coming at the expense of the possibility of "romance" for the working class.

Morton's marriage to Mary Graham appears, at least at first, to offer the romantic possibility of escaping history and entering the domestic idyll. In accord with the discourse of separate spheres, and in contradistinction to her role as a Chartist, Mary is a mistress of "the secrets of domestic economy" who "devote[s] her whole time to the comforts and attentions of home," which becomes "a pleasant retreat from the cares of business—a spot where strife and unkindness can never enter— a heaven where all is peace and love" (28.155, 29.156). However, this entry into the romantic domain of the domestic entails the transformation of Mary from Chartist activist "possessed of a strong mind" into a "retiring nature—more fitted to adorn home than shine in public" (28.155). The discourse of separate spheres thus dictates the gendered division of labor through which Arthur can be a historical actor while Mary maintains the domestic space to which he will return upon achievement of his political goals.[7]

As it turns out, however, domesticity also removes Arthur from the domain of public action that alone can sustain the home. Initially, domestic contentment leads Morton to experience an amnesia—similar to North's forgetting of his "brother"—in which "politics were almost forgotten" and he occupies himself by "compos[ing] tales of love and romance" (29.157, 30.160). But when history again impinges in the form of the recession of 1846, he discovers that in order to save romance and the domestic he must forgo it and leave his "pleasant cottage" (30.160). Just as having a family makes North selfish, so having a family keeps Morton, who realizes that if he had "been alone in the world he could have battled with poverty," from acting in the public domain (30.161). In order to be "a better citizen," he can "no longer [be] so affectionate an husband"; consequently, he loses his "love of home" and flies "with avidity to the excitement of politics" (34.176).

However, the novel does not dismiss romance or the possibility of occupying the domestic idyll but rather insists that to inhabit it while injustice remains is to evade the demands of the social. As Martha Vicinus has suggested, the novel's open-endedness derives from its assumption that although "revolutionary forces" will eventually "triumph . . . change had not yet come and did not appear imminent" (133). The novel accordingly concludes with Morton in exile, separated from Mary but longing to return to her. In contrast to the "home-breathing tales of Dickens" which, especially before 1850, tend to conclude by installing their heroes in a domestic idyll, *Sunshine and Shadow* defers this conclusion to the future by depicting Arthur and Mary as retaining a "hope" that "they shall again meet in happiness" (29.157, 37.192). Being a historical actor requires one to hope for, but also to defer, romance. Hence, Morton's narrative is characterized by shifts between memory and forgetting, echoed in the repeated allusions to the novel's title, memory offering the "sunshine of unity and hope," forgetting the shadow of despair (10.96).

⁓

When Walter North purchases an estate and then combines it with his wife's estate in order to gain political power (22.134–35), he resembles the heroes of *Coningsby* and *Sybil*, who join their own estates with those of their wives as a means of establishing their authority as members of Parliament. In keeping with Morton's assertion that the upper classes are self-interested and the working classes must act for themselves, however, the novel depicts North not as seeking power in order to serve the people or the nation as Disraeli's heroes do but instead as amassing property in order to advance his own interests.

The Land Plan, by contrast, does not involve the joining of estates, but the reverse, the redistribution of land to the people in accord with the concept of "jubilee," to which Morton and his wife look forward at the conclusion of the novel (37.192). As Malcolm Chase has pointed out, the radical agrarian tradition of the early nineteenth century invoked the Old Testament practice of jubilee—in which every fifty years slaves were to be set free and lands that had been sold were to revert to their former owners—as an agrarian law providing for the periodic redistribution of property in order to counteract the accumulation of property by the wealthy (see *People's Farm* 55). In advancing the Land Plan, Chase points out, the Chartists almost inevitably adopted this conception, with the *Northern Star* celebrating the opening of O'Connorville, the first of the Land Plan estates, as a "Chartist Jubilee."[8] Like Spence and the radical agrarians, the Chartists also associated jubilee with contemporary millennialism that linked the religious "belief in a future (and typically imminent) thousand-year age of peace and righteousness associated with the Second Coming of Christ" to visions of political renewal or transformation (OED; see Chase, *People's Farm* 54–56). Accordingly, O'Connor declared that the opening of the estate indicated that the "day of judgment is at hand," Ernest Jones, in an article entitled "Chartist Jubilee," reported that in arriving at O'Connorville he had "come from the land of slavery, to the land of liberty . . . the promised land," and the editorial author, in "Labour's Jubilee," deemed it "The People's Paradise" (22 Aug. 46: 2, 1, 4).

The divided aims of the Land Plan—as both a means of obtaining the franchise and as socioeconomic reform that displaces the quest for the franchise—manifest themselves in *Sunshine and Shadow*'s division between romance and history.[9] On the one hand, the Land Plan followed the Spencean millennialist tradition that envisions the jubilee as the end of history, as arrival at the promised land. In this respect, O'Connor's claim that the plan would enable workers to escape the contingencies of the labor market and earn a "natural" wage invokes a pastoral ideal associated with the restoration of Eden. In allotting a plot of land to each family (in contradistinction to contemporary agrarian programs employing a collective model of organization), he similarly drew on related contemporary discourses that opposed the domestic to the marketplace. On the other hand, as we have seen, O'Connor consistently maintained that his plan was a means of obtaining the franchise, not an end in itself, that "without political power [i.e., the franchise] the system never could be made so general as to be of national benefit" (*Small Farms* 11). From this point of view, withdrawing from the marketplace is not a means of escaping it but of putting pressure on it, the "natural" wage forcing changes in the "artificial" wage. Thus, while the Land Plan as domestic idyll accords with romance, the plan's role in the ongoing effort to achieve the franchise, and ultimately social reform, belongs to history.

As might be expected, given that Wheeler apparently wrote much of *A Practical Work on the Management of Small Farms*, *Sunshine and Shadow* represents the plan in similar terms. On the one hand, it depicts the plan in terms of romance as an escape from historical contingency. Borrowing the distinction between the "natural" and "artificial state[s] of society," Morton concludes that the land will "free" workers from the marketplace (35.182). Even after its failure, Morton and his wife anticipate a "national jubilee" (37.192) that invokes the plan's intention to restore to its "rightful owners," the people, "national property" that has been concentrated in the hands of the few by the "law of Primogeniture" (34.177, 176, 177). This aspect of the Land Plan manifests itself in another Chartist story, "The Charter and the Land," which appeared in 1847, at the time of the plan's greatest popularity. The story's hero, William Wright, does not see the Land Plan as a means of gaining the franchise but, on the contrary, deems the Chartist movement as having been the "means" to the "end" of gaining an allotment of land (191). In accord with the tradition of jubilee, this brief narrative invokes the millennialist tradition of exile and return, depicting Wright's family as "emancipated slaves" who enter the "Holy Land" of O'Connorville (193). Thus, once he is enfranchised as a voting citizen in the vestry of O'Connorville, the campaign for *parliamentary* representation drops out of sight.

Yet *Sunshine and Shadow* ultimately depicts the Land Plan from the perspective of 1849, when its fortunes had begun to wane, as part of a historical process rather than a means of escaping from history. Although the narrator describes the allotments as "happy retreats" and "verdant oases" built on "principles" that have "stood the test of time" (35.182, 34.178), these principles do not protect them from contingencies such as bad weather, industrial laborers' ignorance about farming, and, perhaps most significantly, the attitudes and assumptions of the urban marketplace that the laborers bring with them (34.178, 35.182).

The structure of the narrative itself enacts this impingement of history on the plan. Chapter 34 begins with Morton watching with satisfaction the development of the National Land Company but shifts to the events of 1848 and the failed attempt to present the Chartist Petition on April 10, 1848. Chapter 35, after beginning with a continuation of the latter, returns to the subject of the Land Plan by depicting Morton's tour of the estates. Although the events of 1848 have no direct bearing on the fortunes of the Land Plan, this narrative sequence implies, as the narrator suggests, that the "events of February, 1848, in France, and April in England, threw into obscurity the minor interest of the Company" (34.177). The plan failed, he implies, because it was overwhelmed by historical events.

Rather than escaping history and abandoning the franchise, the narrator, like O'Connor, envisions a future in which the "Walter Norths of the House of Commons are superseded by the men of the people" (21.132). Moreover, the plan belongs to the history of supplemental forms of agency through which the movement has sought to obtain the Charter. As an alternative to "eloquence," the plan is a successor to the earlier moral- as well as physical-force forms of agency (34.176).

Writing at a moment when the future of Chartism was unclear, Wheeler depicts the Land Plan not as creating the promised land but as part of a historical process that will eventually lead to the promised land. Although the plan has failed, it has effected a "revolution in public opinion" that will ultimately lead to "Success" (34.177, 178). Accordingly, although Wheeler was writing the novel at his allotment cottage in O'Connorville, he does not depict Morton as obtaining a Land Plan allotment but merely as touring the estates and then going into exile, becoming a wanderer in the desert who looks forward to the jubilee that will bring him to the promised land. Indeed, a mere three years later, Wheeler was offering his allotment for sale (Chase, *Chartism* 353).

Although he implies that forms of social agency may be historically contingent, Wheeler did not abandon his belief in the franchise as a fundamental form of social agency. As the movement splintered into a variety of factions, Wheeler remained steadfast in support of the Charter, sustaining the remnants of the organization until his death in 1862.[10] As we will see in the following chapter, however, after 1848 many other Chartists concluded that they must shift their focus not only away from land but also away from the franchise.

PART III

The Social Turn

*From Chartism to Cooperation and
Trade Unionism, 1848–1855*

Christian Socialism and Cooperative Association

Following the failure of the petition presented on April 10, 1848, Chartist discourse frequently signaled a shift of agency from the domain of the political to the social. As we have seen, the Land Plan had already introduced this possibility insofar as it not only sought to pursue the political goal of obtaining the franchise but also aimed to establish an alternative economic, or social, domain. Not coincidentally, at this time trade unions came to the fore, and the first successful national union, the Amalgamated Society of Engineers, was formed in 1850. Simultaneously, a group of young professionals committed to social reform also sought, though for different reasons, to promote a shift from the Chartist program of political reform toward social reform and what they would eventually call Christian Socialism. In the early 1850s, the Christian Socialists worked with Chartists and the ASE to establish cooperative associations as a form of social agency that, depending on their particular points of view, either supplemented or supplanted the Charter or conventional union strategies such as the strike and negotiation.

After the disappointments of April 10, the Chartist consensus about the primacy of the franchise as a form of agency began to break down, leading to debates about whether priority should be given to "political" or "social" reform. Although O'Connor had insisted that even as his Land Plan moved in the direction of socioeconomic reform, it would not become universal until the goals of the Charter were achieved, after April 10 he welcomed the "social turn" toward questions of labor (Chase, *Chartism* 332; see also 336). Even as George Julian Harney, who edited the *Northern Star* from 1846 to 1850 and then edited his own papers, and Ernest Jones, who took over leadership of the National Charter Association when

O'Connor's health began to fail, upheld the long-standing Chartist argument that comprehensive social reform could not be achieved without first obtaining political power, they acknowledged that they must change the motto of the movement from "The Charter and nothing less" to "The Charter and something more" (Chase, *Chartism* 336–37).[1] Writing in his new paper, the *Red Republican*, Harney conceded that "Chartism in 1850 . . . is a different thing from Chartism in 1840" because the "leaders of the English Proletarians . . . have progressed from the idea of simple *political reform* to the idea of *Social Revolution*" (22 June 1850: 2). Most important, perhaps, the leadership could no longer muster widespread support for the Charter, and the NCA lost control of the discourse as one group after another sought to promote alternative means of achieving its aims.

Underlying the discussions of a possible shift from the political to the social was the emergence of a movement that had come to be known as socialism. In 1848, the term *socialism* did not yet designate a form of government or even the control of the means of production but referred rather to the establishment of cooperatives of production and consumption. Newspapers first began to use the term *socialism* in 1838–1839 to designate Robert Owen's project for establishing "villages of cooperation" and, accordingly, employed it as a synonym for "Owenism." In the early 1840s, by which time Owen's villages had proved failures, the term appeared only infrequently, but it came into widespread use again in 1848 to designate the projects of Charles Fourier and Louis Blanc, the latter of which the provisional government of France adopted following the February revolution.[2]

By 1848, the form and purpose of cooperatives had changed from the initial conception of Owen and Fourier, in which they were only subordinate elements of larger utopian schemes that were self-sufficient and thus separate from the capitalist economy, to self-contained operations intended to transform the existing socioeconomic sphere. The utopian aim of establishing a community operating separately from mainstream society is evident from the projects Owen and Fourier either created or inspired, including the Owenite Harmony Hall in England and New Harmony, Indiana, and the Fourierist experiments at Rambouillet and Brook Farm. These schemes would establish a new set of social relations within an autonomous community but would not directly affect existing social relations. The indebtedness of O'Connor's Land Plan to these projects is evident in the attempt to establish independent communities—the first being O'Connorville—but O'Connor did not see them as isolated from the mainstream; on the contrary, as we have seen, he contended that by withdrawing labor from the marketplace his communities would intervene in the mainstream marketplace.

As opposed to these utopian schemes, which were devised by the sons of

wealthy businessmen, laborers involved in the development of trade unions began to devise forms of cooperation with the more pragmatic aim of responding to
specific economic conditions within the marketplace. In the 1830s striking workers, many influenced by Owenism, began to set up schemes of cooperative production (Cole 24), and in the 1840s the cooperative store movement began with
the renowned Rochdale Society of Equitable Pioneers. In France, Louis Blanc in
his *L'Organisation du travail* (1839) established a set of principles that promoted
the establishment of cooperative workshops as the means through which laborers
could establish social agency. As opposed to the large-scale autonomous communities envisioned by Owen and Fourier, these new cooperative schemes involved
relatively small groups of men setting up a workshop or store in competition with
existing commercial enterprises. Rather than attempting to provide an alternative
to the status quo, they sought to act on it.

Indeed, the dominant form of working-class agency that emerged after 1848
was not the cooperative association but the trade union. Although some members
regarded cooperatives as a means of gaining complete control over industrial production, the unions never fully committed to this strategy and continued to turn
to them primarily as a temporary means of providing employment during labor
actions. Although in 1851 the Christian Socialists persuaded the ASE to support
cooperatives and two workshops were set up with their assistance, these ventures
failed by 1854, and the union thereafter focused on other strategies (Jeffreys 33–34,
42–44). While they might use cooperatives as part of their repertoire of strategies,
workers turned to the trade unions themselves as the principal agents of social
change. Rather than seeking political power so that they could legislate the conditions of labor, trade unions sought direct control of working conditions through
negotiations with employers.

That many Chartists were willing to shift their focus from the political to the
social after 1848 should not be surprising, for the movement included working-
class leaders of all types, including Owenites and trade union activists, and these
two groups themselves had overlapping memberships. Many of the earliest references to socialism in the elite press pair it with Chartism, and thus it is no
coincidence that it first appears with frequency in 1839, just as the movement was
getting under way.[3] With the failure of Owen's projects in the late 1830s, Owenites
became active in Chartism and embraced the Land Plan, and when Chartism
in turn began to falter, the Owenite tradition made them receptive to socialist
experiments, in particular the French models proposed in 1848. Similarly, the
ranks of Chartism included many trade unionists, who had pioneered the cooperative workshop and store and adopted methods of organization developed

by the Chartists. Not coincidentally, just as Chartism was ceasing to command widespread popular support, trade unionism developed into a national movement with the founding of the ASE.

❧

When, in 1848, a group of clergy, attorneys, and other professional men began their campaign to "Christianise Socialism," it was the conception of socialism deriving from the writing and experiments of Owen, Fourier, Blanc, and English trade unions to which they referred. Although their purpose was quite different from that of the Chartists, socialists, and trade unionists, they also sought to promote a shift from the political to the social.[4] Their initial aim, as manifested in their short-lived series of pamphlets, *Politics for the People*, was merely to persuade workingmen that they should abandon the political aim of obtaining the franchise. However, in 1850 they embraced "socialism" and began working with Chartists and trade unions to promote social reform and, in particular, the formation of cooperative associations.

In this respect, the Christian Socialists broke new ground in their willingness to envision members of the working class as social agents, but even as they articulated an egalitarian ideal through which they sought to unite themselves with workingmen in projects for cooperation, they asserted a principle by which the clerical elite guided workingmen in a process of cultivation that would make them capable of exercising social agency.[5] Unlike previous reforming authors who addressed themselves to members of the upper classes from whom they demanded reform, the Christian Socialists sought to address and eventually to engage in dialogue with members of the working classes. From the beginning, however, they debated whether to address themselves primarily to the workers or members of the ruling elite, John Ludlow favoring a publication addressed to the working classes and Frederick Denison Maurice a new series of "'Tracts for the Times,' addressed to the higher orders" (Kingsley, *Letters* 1.156). Significantly, the group ultimately split over whether to effect reform by giving priority to promoting socialism—focusing on the cooperative associations that were a mechanism of working-class agency—or to promoting a Christianity that would initiate a process of self-transformation as the basis of broad social reform. In effect, they were to disagree about whether to privilege working-class cooperation or clerical guidance.

This dual conception was most fully manifested in the thinking of the group's leader, Maurice, whose theology envisions human individuals as brothers of Christ the Son, who acts in accord with the will of his divine Father (see Christensen 24, 94). Thus, in his article "Fraternity," in the first issue of *Politics*, Mau-

rice suggests that insofar as Christ became man, he united humanity in an egalitarian brotherhood: "We pretend to think that an Everlasting Father has revealed
Himself to men in an elder Brother, one with him and us, who died for all" (1.3).
At the same time, Christ is an "elder Brother" because he is one with the Father
and acts in accord with his will. The egalitarian aspect of this conception leads
Maurice to reject a paternalism that, in "treating [the poor] merely as poor," seeks
to help them on the assumption that they are, and will remain, inferior to the
elite. Yet even as he insists that the poor are not innately inferior, he contends that
corrupt social institutions have lowered them and that it is therefore the duty of
the clergy to "raise the poor into men" (*Dialogue between Somebody* 10; see also
1.6). In a lecture given on the occasion of the opening of a tailors' cooperative in
Southampton, he similarly suggests that "reform" does not mean the creation of
new institutions but "putting into its proper and original shape that which has got
out of shape" (*Reformation* 4; see also *Dialogue between Somebody* 8).

Maurice and his fellow Christian Socialists thus depicted the tripartite class
structure not only as the source of social conflict but also as the site of social injustice that violates the principle of egalitarian brotherhood. In naming their pamphlets *Politics for the People*, they invoked the dual meaning of the term *people*
in radical discourse as both a class—within a dichotomous model that opposes
the people to the enfranchised elite—and the nation as a whole. Thus, while the
Christian Socialists' aim of addressing the series to the working class, and in particular to the Chartists, suggests that its title refers to the disenfranchised, Ludlow
claims, in an article entitled "The 'People,'" that it indicates not a social "class"
but the "English nation." In so doing, he seeks to delineate an authorial identity
that is not defined in terms of the elite professional class to which he and his
fellow authors belong but an Englishness that joins them to the working class as
"part of the People" (2.17). In his article on fraternity, Maurice similarly declares
that he and his fellow authors can "address" working-class readers because they
have "cast off alliances" and abandoned pre-existing class and political positions
(1.4).

However, the conception of a society in which the egalitarian ideal has been
corrupted leads the Christian Socialists to invoke a dichotomous distinction between the cultivated and uncultivated in place of the tripartite model of class.
In a series of articles on the franchise published in *Politics*, Ludlow supports
universal suffrage in principle but employs the long-standing parliamentary press
argument that the working class in its current state cannot be accorded social
agency because it does not have sufficient interest in the nation as a whole and
does not have the education to act rationally. In what would become a constant

refrain in Christian Socialist publications, he suggests that their defiance of the ban on the April 10 assembly, their "monster meetings," their lack of education, and even their poverty, demonstrate that they are not "fit" or "worthy" to exercise the franchise responsibly (*Politics for the People* 1.10–11, 2.31, 3.43, 6.84, 7.104).[6]

Whereas questions about social agency conceived in terms of the tripartite model of class had focused on the question of whether the aristocracy or the middle class could best govern England, the Christian Socialists used a dichotomous model in which the people are divided between the cultivated and the yet to be cultivated. John Conington's poem "The Rightful Governor," published in *Politics*, rejects in turn the claims of the three classes of the tripartite model of contemporary political discourse—the aristocracy, entrepreneurs, and Chartist working class—to the title of governor and instead awards it to the intellectual elite:

> The man whose thoughtful mind
> In action's school has learnt to read
> The lessons of mankind—
> Not bound by need or tie of class
> To fawn on rich or poor. (4.60)

It bears repeating in this context that, as indicated above, the Christian Socialists were professionals who staked their claim to authority not on their social position but on their intellectual ability and cultivation. Conington was, not coincidentally, a classicist and an Oxford fellow.

This emphasis on cultivation meant that, for the Christian Socialists, social agency involved not only reforming social structures but also reforming the self or self-cultivation under the guidance of a clerical elite—in short, religious conversion. For Maurice in particular, the solution to social problems was not the construction of new forms of social agency but the recovery of the principle of brotherhood established by Christ. Unlike Carlyle, who had implied that the ruling elite needed to undergo a reconversion to Christian principles, the Christian Socialists focused on the conversion of the lower classes, hence their aim, as Maurice put it in a letter of 1850, of "Christianis[ing] Socialism" (*Life* 2.36).[7] They should teach workingmen, he contends, that they cannot "act as brothers, merely because [they] call [them]selves so" and "are working for mutual profits" in cooperatives, but instead they must establish their brotherhood on the "deeper ground" of Christianity (*Dialogue between A. and B.* 9–10).

Just as Disraeli and Young England envisioned a reformed aristocracy, the Christian Socialists sought to define a clergy that merits this status as cultural elite by differentiating the reformed clergy from existing church authorities. Both Maurice and Kingsley angered fellow clergymen by suggesting that working-men had lost faith in the Church because they regarded it as colluding with a ruling elite that has abandoned brotherhood and adopted the principle of "self-ish rivalry" and "Mammon worship" (Maurice, *Dialogue between Somebody* 7, *Dialogue between A. and B.* 8; see also Kingsley, *Politics for the People* 4.58–59). When fellow clergymen were incensed by Kingsley's criticism of the clergy in his "Letters to the Chartists" in *Politics*, Maurice defended him by insisting that "every paper which has any circulation among the Chartists regards the clergy as preachers of mere slavery out of the Bible" (*Life* 1.476). However, rather than conclude that the clerical elite do not merit social agency, they call for "an Eng-lish theological reformation" and insist that "reform in the clergy"—the reformed clergy implicitly being the Christian Socialists—alone could guide workingmen in the process of self-cultivation (Maurice, *Life* 1.459, *Dialogue between A. and B.* 5; see also *Dialogue between Somebody* 6–7, and *Dialogue between A. and B.* 8).

Although Maurice was the dominant voice and, in keeping with the role of leader accorded him by the younger men in the group, at times suppressed views of some of its members, other members of the group, notably John Ludlow, did not entirely share this view of social agency. Indeed, one could say that the group ultimately split apart over the question of whether social agency most fundamen-tally involved pastoral instruction and conversion or the practical institution of the fraternal principle of cooperation. Maurice tended to oppose the various schemes of social reform that his fellow Christian Socialists devised, and his ar-ticles repeatedly focus instead on education. Consequently, he turns cooperation into a metaphor for moral behavior (in opposition to competition) rather than a material set of social institutions through which human actions can be con-ducted. While acknowledging the complexity of the negotiations over the direc-tion of the movement that Maurice and Ludlow engaged in, it would be fair to say that while Maurice ultimately regarded the restoration of Christian principles as the solution to social problems, Ludlow was fully committed to establishing a version of socialism that was Christian. Accordingly, even as Ludlow vigorously promoted workingmen's cooperatives, Maurice was already redirecting his ener-gies toward the establishment of his Working Men's College.

⌒

These tensions in the Christian Socialist conception of social agency manifested themselves in the group's efforts to put its theory into practice by forming a broth-erhood with workingmen. The first number of *Politics for the People* invited the "Workmen of England" to write about their experiences and contribute to the discussions it sought to foster (1.2). In the article "Fraternity," which immediately followed this invitation, Maurice envisions developing a dialogue in which they would "try to understand one another, and bring in their different lights as to the way of attaining" their shared goals (1.4); while he desires "a conflict of opinions," this process, by enabling them "to hold converse with our readers of all classes, as fellow-men and fellow-workmen," would enable them together to "realize the true Fraternity of which this age has dreamed" (1.4, 5). As if to put this principle into practice, Maurice frequently composed his contributions in the form of a dialogue among men from different walks of life, and some other contributors followed suit.

At the same time, *Politics for the People* repeatedly seeks to set the people straight about the shortcomings of Chartism. The majority of the articles were written by Ludlow, Maurice, and Kingsley (in that order), and almost all the rest were written by members of the cultural elite to whom they were connected through their university education and their role as professionals.[8] The invitation for working-class contributions to *Politics* met with very little response, and apart from a couple of letters, the series did not publish any writing by workingmen. Similarly, Maurice's dialogues in the Socratic tradition generally conclude with a Maurician figure settling the debate by stepping in and instructing his interlocutors.[9]

Although the contributions from workingmen did not for the most part materialize, some dialogue between the Christian Socialist publications and the radical press did occur. (One reason that few workingmen submitted material to *Politics* must have been that there was little opportunity to do so, given that it lasted for a mere three months.) On June 4, 1848, for example, *Lloyd's Weekly* published a letter under the headline "Libellers of the People" (signed "Radical"), which criticizes Maurice's article "Fraternity" for advocating brotherhood but then arguing against the franchise and for producing a "*libel* on the people" by depicting them as unworthy of the suffrage (5).

After *Politics for the People* ceased publication, Kingsley and Ludlow sought to establish direct dialogue with members of the working class. Kingsley had been stung by criticisms in the short-lived radical paper the *Commonwealth* and wrote to the Chartist poet Thomas Cooper—whose People's Charter Union (a rival to O'Connor's National Charter Association) promoted a policy of peace and legality—in the hope that as "brother-poets, as well as brother men," they might "fraternise" (*Letters* 1.183). Although he did not have much direct involvement with Christian Socialism, Cooper did respond to Kingsley and later enthused in his newspaper, the *Plain Speaker*, over the establishment of the first cooperative associations (16 Feb. 1850: 98–99). Ludlow's encounter with Cooper's cousin Walter (also a prominent Chartist) was ultimately more fruitful. Through him Ludlow established contacts with a number of working-class leaders and intellectuals—among them Walter Cooper himself as well as Lloyd Jones, Joseph Millbank, and Thomas Shorter—and initiated dialogue with them at a series of meetings at the Cranbourne Coffee Tavern.

While the attempts at egalitarian dialogue were important and, as an innovation, one could even say remarkable, the Cranbourne Tavern meetings and other forms of dialogue were marked by the impulse on the part of Maurice and company to assume the role of clerical guides. Accounts of the meetings indicate that decisions about what subjects to discuss involved mutual participation but that Maurice—whom his young friends had taken to calling "the Master" or "the Prophet"—was the ultimate arbiter. Moreover, as in his dialogues, he concluded each session by summing up the discussion, a role that privileged his views over those of his interlocutors.

Nonetheless, the meetings did accord agency to workingmen not only by involving them in dialogues about how best to respond to social problems but also by involving them in the process of shaping a concrete form of social agency, the cooperative association. Although *Politics for the People* was mainly reactive in its opposition to Chartism, Ludlow, at least, aimed from the beginning to engage with the "socialism" that emerged after 1848. The immediate spur to the establishment of the production cooperatives came in December 1849 in response to Henry Mayhew's articles in the *Morning Chronicle* exposing the abuses of the sweated tailor and seamstress trades. The professional men embraced the principle of cooperation as consonant with Christian brotherhood, but it was the workingmen who had direct experience with the operation of cooperatives, for, as discussed above, trade unionists had been involved since the 1830s in setting up small, localized production and consumption cooperatives. Lloyd Jones, an Owenite and moral-force Chartist who was one of the leading participants in the dialogues, had run a cooperative flour mill in the late 1840s and had, under the influence not only of Owen but also of Blanc, promoted cooperation in the radical press.[10] It seems likely, therefore, that in moving from theory to practice, the role of Jones, Cooper, and other workingmen was crucial.[11]

⌒

While Maurice was circumscribing dialogue by assuming the role of "master," some radicals refused to accept the displacement of the political by the social and challenged the Christian Socialist project. As we have seen, George Harney and Ernest Jones (no relation to Lloyd Jones) recognized and accepted the need for social as well as political reform, but they continued to insist that the former could not occur without the latter. In his *Notes to the People*, Jones engaged in dialogue with the Christian Socialists, critiquing their program, publishing responses by Edward Vansittart Neale (who had joined the Christian Socialists after the founding of the first association) and then replying to them in turn, and responding as well to articles by Kingsley.[12]

Jones endorsed the idea of cooperation in principle, but contended that its ultimate success required political power; as he put it in response to Kingsley, "the Charter is the leverage" to make cooperation possible (623). Furthermore, he insisted that cooperation as practiced by the Christian Socialists "perpetuat[es] the evils which it professes to remove" (27). He argued that, contrary to their theoretical opposition of cooperation to self-interested competition, the Christian Socialists' piecemeal approach would only exacerbate competition (30). Linking the problem of competition in particular to the need to raise capital for cooperatives in a competitive marketplace, he pointed out that the Christian Socialist project was dependent upon capital provided by professional men, in effect making it a paternalist scheme (584). In keeping with Blanc's proposals, in which the state provided capital for establishing cooperative workshops, he argued that workingmen could exert complete control over cooperatives only if they possessed political power (584).

In the following chapters, I examine how novels by Charles Kingsley and Elizabeth Gaskell engage with the Christian Socialist conception of social agency in terms of dialogue and cooperative association. Kingsley was, of course, one of the founders, along with Maurice and Ludlow, of the Christian Socialist movement, while Gaskell closely followed their activities and corresponded regularly with members of the group.[13] In April of 1849, Kingsley, who had a year earlier, on April 10, 1848, drawn up placards addressed to workingmen, published a review of Gaskell's *Mary Barton* in which he imagined a similar address to the ruling elite: "Had we wit and wisdom enough, we would placard its sheets on every wall, and have them read aloud from every pulpit, till a nation, calling itself Christian, began to *act* upon the awful facts contained in it" (429; emphasis added). The admiration was mutual, and in a letter that may recall this stirring affirmation, Gaskell declared Kingsley her "hero" (*Letters* 90).[14] Yet while Gaskell and Kingsley both sought to address the need for social reform and, in particular, for Christian brotherhood and cooperation, each envisioned a distinct form of social agency.

Gaskell's *Mary Barton: A Tale of Manchester Life*, which depicts the Chartist trade unionist John Barton going up to London to present the first Chartist petition, appeared in October 1848, just months after the presentation of the third and final Chartist petition. Indeed, in the weeks leading up to April 10, Gaskell had written her publisher, Chapman and Hall, who had accepted the novel in late 1847, urging immediate publication: "I can not help fancying that the tenor of my tale is such as to excite attention at the present time of struggle on the part of work people to obtain what they esteem their rights" (*Letters* 54). Before the novel appeared that autumn, she added a preface that alludes to the revolutions on the continent and suggests that her novel not only depicts events of the past but also speaks to the present.

By the time *Mary Barton* appeared, Kingsley's *Yeast* was midway through its July through December serial run in *Fraser's Magazine*. Like Gaskell, who lived in Manchester and was involved in district visiting in working-class neighborhoods, Kingsley, rector of the rural parish of Eversley, drew on his personal experience in depicting the encounter between his protagonist, a young gentleman, and the rural working class. As he explains in a gloss on the title, he regarded his novel "from beginning to end, as in name so in nature, Yeast—an honest sample of the questions which, good or bad, are fermenting in the minds of the young of this day, and are rapidly leavening the minds of the rising generation" (*Fraser's Magazine* 38.12 [1848]: 690). Making its first appearance weeks after April 10, *Yeast*, like Kingsley's other writings of the time, responded to Chartism prior to his direct engagement with the urban working class and the development of Christian Socialism.

Whereas Gaskell, living in the industrial midlands, had years of experience working with the urban poor, Kingsley only began to encounter the urban poor after April 10. A year after *Mary Barton* took as its protagonist a young seamstress, Henry Mayhew's *Morning Chronicle* reports on the sweated garment trade (the first, published on December 4, 1849, describes the plight of seamstresses and was followed later that month by two reports on tailors) stirred Kingsley, Ludlow, and company into action, first in writing polemics and then almost simultaneously in establishing cooperative associations. Kingsley's *Cheap Clothes and Nasty*, which announced the first Christian Socialist cooperative, the Working Tailors' Association, appeared in January 1850, and he almost immediately began work on a new novel, *Alton Locke, Tailor and Poet*, which would appear that August. Just as *Mary Barton* depicted a seamstress and her Chartist father, Kingsley's novel took as its protagonist a character who works in the garment trade and becomes a Chartist, but rather than imagine a reconciliation between workers and industrialists, it would depict the founding of cooperative associations. The following spring, he published the first book edition of *Yeast* (now subtitled *A Problem*), with a revised conclusion; whereas the earlier version depicts the hero partnering with another gentleman, the new ending depicts the gentleman protagonist uniting with his working-class mentor. However, this marked the beginning of the end of Kingsley's major contributions to the Christian Socialist project. In 1851 he gave lectures on cooperation, and he continued to write for the *Christian Socialist* until it ceased in June 1852, but his literary interests soon shifted, and his next novel, *Hypatia* (1852), turned from social to church reform.

This shift coincided with the emergence in 1852 of divisions among the Christian Socialists, just as the movement appeared to be at the height of its success. That year, they obtained passage of the Industrial and Provident Societies Act, which provided legal protections for cooperative associations, and they held a national conference on cooperation. Yet a variety of difficulties plagued the movement. Ludlow, Hughes, and Neale sought to support the Amalgamated Society of Engineers during the 1852 lockout and successfully persuaded the union to adopt cooperation as one of its key strategies, but Kingsley accepted Maurice's position that they should remain neutral.[15] The underlying disagreement about principles led to a growing rift between Maurice and Ludlow and the demise of their journal the *Christian Socialist* (by this time entitled the *Journal of Association*) in June of that year. The following year, the cooperatives, most of which were losing money, began to fail, and the report of the 1853 conference manifested the growing discouragement of participants (Raven 314). Not insignificantly, this was the last time Maurice made a public appearance at an event related to the cooperatives. The following year, he became embroiled in the religious controversy that led to his being deprived of his professorship at Kings' College, London, and from that time forward his efforts were dedicated to working-class education, in particular the Working Men's College, which opened in 1854.

Gaskell met Maurice and others in his circle during the spring following the publication of *Mary Barton* and from that time forward closely followed their activities. She corresponded with members of the group and read their pamphlets as well as the *Christian Socialist*, which was launched in November of 1850 and republished two of her early stories. About the time of the founding of the Working Men's College, she began writing *North and South*, which commenced its serial run in *Household Words* in September 1854 and ran until the following January. This novel's reflection on the Christian Socialist project is evident from the opening chapters, in which the event that sets the plot in motion is the religious crisis of the heroine's clergyman father, who later offers lectures to workingmen — and so recalls Maurice's contemporary career — to its conclusion, in which a mill owner and the working-class protagonist collaborate in the founding of a cooperative dining facility for laborers. *North and South,* however, departs from Christian Socialism in its treatment both of cooperatives and of Christian brotherhood. Whereas Kingsley was responding primarily to conditions in the small-scale sweated tailoring trade in London, Gaskell was concerned with the textile mills of the north. Consequently, both of her novels recognize the growing importance of trade unionism and the inevitability that trade unions would play a significant role in the shaping of working-class agency.

While these novels do not explicitly allude to one another, they respond to the changing terrain of contemporary discourse about social agency following April 10, 1848. Both Kingsley's and Gaskell's later novel reconsiders and revises the earlier one. Kingsley makes a workingman rather than a gentleman his protagonist and envisions cooperation between the ruling elite and workingmen as the formation of a Christian brotherhood, while Gaskell revises her representation of both mill owners and workingmen and replaces a resolution based on reconciliation with one based on the recognition that engaging in dialogue does not mean reaching agreement, that one's "friend" could also be one's "enemy."

CHAPTER 11

Clergy and Working-Class Cooperation in *Yeast* and *Alton Locke*

Charles Kingsley's writings, in particular *Alton Locke*, borrow Disraeli's national narrative of the fall into class division, but rather than imagining the resolution of class conflict through the reform of the aristocracy, he depicts its achievement through the reform of the clergy. Furthermore, rather than depicting a shift from a conflictual dichotomous model of class to a finely graded hierarchy in which the aristocracy takes responsibility for and becomes united with the people, Kingsley envisions an egalitarian brotherhood of clergy and workingmen and thus also depicts reform of the working class. In this respect, he differs from Disraeli in locating social agency in both the elite and the lower classes. At the same time, however, he depicts workingmen as not yet "fit" to exercise social agency and reintroduces a hierarchical relation in which the cultivated elite guides them in the process of self-cultivation that will realize the ideal of egalitarian brotherhood.

Kingsley's engagement with the condition-of-England question focused from the start on social agency, more particularly on the urgency of "doing something." On the eve of April 10, he went to London, where he sought out Frederick Denison Maurice, who sent him to John Ludlow with a letter of introduction indicating that his young friend was "possessed with the idea of *doing something* by handbills" (Martin 81; emphasis added). After spending the night of April 10 writing copy for his placard, he reported excitedly, "I am helping in a glorious work. . . . I feel we may *do something*" (*Letters* 1.155; emphasis added). Apart from expressing sympathy for the poor, however, the only thing the placard aimed to do was to discourage the Chartists from the pursuit of their fundamental goal of obtaining the franchise. However, Kingsley did not stop there but, as we have seen in the preceding chapter, joined with the Christian Socialists in a series of experiments in social action, the most notable of which were cooperative workshops.

Although Kingsley's initial writings concurred in the opposition to Chartism articulated by Ludlow and Maurice, he differed from them in addressing himself to Chartists and workingmen. Maurice, who advocated publishing a series of tracts addressed to the "higher orders," or more specifically "the religious people and clergy, pointing out to them the necessity of their meeting the questions of the day," for the most part sought to impress upon the upper classes a sense of their duty to the poor (Kingsley, *Letters* 1.156; Maurice, *Life* 1.461; see also Kingsley, *Letters* 1.157). Even Ludlow, whose idea it was to launch a newspaper "addressed specially to the working classes," tended to address a generalized "people" equivalent with the nation rather than the working classes specifically (Christensen 73). In this respect, they followed in the footsteps of their predecessors among the cultural elite—Carlyle, Dickens, Disraeli, Barrett Browning, and so on—while Kingsley's addresses to workingmen anticipate the shift that would occur when, in his second social-problem novel, he took as his hero not a "gentleman" but a Chartist tailor.

In these early writings, we can see Kingsley moving toward the dialogue with workingmen that was eventually realized in the weekly meetings between the Christian Socialists and Chartist leaders. The April 10 placard asserts "brother[ly]" solidarity between the "working clergy" and "intelligent and well-read" workmen but undercuts the implications of equality by claiming that the clergy "know what [workingmen's] rights are, better than [they] know [them]selves" (*Letters* 1.156). The first of the three "Letter[s] to the Chartists," much in the manner of the placard, asserts that men who associate themselves with writers of questionable morals are not fit to exercise the franchise (*Politics for the People* 2.29). The second letter, however, redirects the moral critique toward the clergy, blaming "us parsons" for failing to teach the Chartists that the Bible is the "true poor man's book" and instead using it "to keep the poor in order." Turning the critique directly on himself, he concludes: "I have been as bad as any one, but I am sick of it" (4.58). Unlike Maurice, he is not addressing this critique to the clergy in an attempt to spur them to self-reflection and self-reform but attempting to distinguish himself from other clergy so as to win the trust of Chartist readers.

The distinct shift in tone and rhetorical strategy between the first and second letters reflects the Christian Socialists' emerging determination to engage in direct dialogue with workingmen. As we have seen, on June 4, 1848, *Lloyd's Weekly* published a letter criticizing the authors of *Politics* as "Libellers of the People."[1] Although *Lloyd's* was actually rather kind to Kingsley, a commentary in the *Com-*

monwealth stung him so deeply that he wrote to the Chartist poet Thomas Cooper on June 19 to "see if among the nobler spirits of the working classes, [he] could not make one friend who would understand [him]" and expressing the hope that they might "fraternise" as "brother-poets, as well as brother men."[2] In this letter, Kingsley moves toward imagining reform as a process involving dialogue between the elite and workingmen. While his emphasis is on asking the workingman to listen to him, he recognizes, as in the second "Letter to the Chartists," that Chartist distrust of the clergy was legitimate—he explicitly raises the possibility that Cooper might mistrust a clergyman—and also expresses the desire to gain "insight" into the "life and thoughts" of workingmen so that he can "live more completely for them" (*Letters* 1.183–84). This desire to be accepted by the Chartists and to fuse them with the clergy manifested itself dramatically when, at one of the first meetings with workingmen, he famously declared, "I am a p-p-parson and a ch-ch-chartist" (Ludlow 149).

〜

Yeast; or, The Thoughts, Sayings, and Doings of Lancelot Smith, Gentleman, which began appearing in *Fraser's Magazine* in July 1848—the month *Politics for the People* ceased publication and just three months after April 10—revises the Disraelian national narrative ascribing the fall into class division to the dissolution of the monasteries.[3] The Lavington family, like the Egremonts, are heirs to the nobility established through the dissolution and are thus responsible for the fact that the "Whitford folks have been getting poorer, and wickeder, ever since that time" (11.546).[4] Moreover, they have been "cursed" for "turn[ing] . . . out" the nuns and "tak[ing] the lands for [their] own" and will not escape the curse until they help "the poor in the spirit of the nuns of Whitford" (11.546), a reversal to be achieved—in keeping with the baptismal topos to which Kingsley would return in later writings—through reversing the flow of the "Nun-pool" so that it "washes" the village of Ashy "clean" (13.704).[5]

Yet even as this historical narrative critiques the aristocracy for neglecting the poor, the novel's national marriage plot shifts the critique to the clergy by constructing a sexual rivalry between the novel's hero, Lancelot Smith, and the local vicar over the Lavingtons' daughter, Argemone. Although Squire Lavington is a "do-nothing," he does not disdain the poor in the manner of Disraeli's Monmouth or Marney (5.288). The novel displaces adherence to the kinship ideal of marriage onto his wife, who lacks authority to enforce it. Instead, it is the vicar who attempts to enforce the ideal, not by seeking to marry Argemone to an aristocrat of higher standing than Lancelot (whose father was in trade), but by seeking to hold her to her intention of becoming a nun. When Argemone begins to waver because of her growing affection for Lancelot, the vicar clearly perceives him as a sexual rival, concluding that "either the lover or the father-confessor must speedily resign office" (8.450) and then subsequently deciding "that he must either oust Lancelot at once, or submit to be ousted by him" (9.460). The sexual rivalry further manifests itself when Lancelot in turn becomes jealous upon seeing Argemone "listening in absorbed reverence" to the vicar (5.288). Employing the trope of the secret Jesuit, Kingsley makes the vicar a villain who unscrupulously contrives to bring about Lancelot's financial ruin so as to make him ineligible to marry Argemone.[6]

Alongside this depiction of the vicar, the novel depicts the church itself as failing to address the needs of the nation. Lancelot and the Lavington gamekeeper, Paul Tregarva, criticize the clergy of the Church of England for being out of touch with the poor and consequently failing to address their needs (11.537; see also 9.456). As Tregarva complains, the vicar's theological interests are not meaningful to the poor, who "don't understand him, nor he them" (3.199). The novel implicitly links these failures to the clergy's inability to appeal to young gentlemen like Lancelot, who has consequently become alienated from the church; on the contrary, the vicar responds to his request for guidance by offering him "spiritual lies" and rejecting the kinds of spiritual ideas that would address his doubts (3.203). The novel thus ascribes the apathy of the idle and aimless young gentleman, interested mainly in hunting and fishing, to the failure of the clergy. The church fails the poor not only because it cannot understand them but also because it fails to imbue the upper classes with a sense of purpose and social responsibility.

Although this critique of the clergy would seem to imply, as Maurice had suggested, the need for a "theological reformation," a reform of the church, the novel does not depict reform of the clergy but instead the "conversion" of its lay hero. This process of conversion is further complicated by the fact that it is not clear what Lancelot is converted to. In the concluding chapters, he takes up art, is instructed that he should instead take up politics, and finally sets off on a spiritual quest. The latter, of course, accords not only with the idea of religious conversion but also with the idea of establishing a new church and clergy. Yet in spite of its many autobiographical elements, the novel never suggests that Lancelot, like Kingsley, will become a priest.

As in *Coningsby* the companionate marriage plot constructs a homosocial coterie that will undertake the project of reform. In a letter outlining his plans for a continuation of the novel—written before he completed the final chapters—Kingsley envisions the characteristic national marriage plot that heals social division, Lancelot and Argemone becoming "an ideal pair of pioneers toward the society of the future" (*Letters* 1.220).[7] Furthermore, this third and final part of the novel was to follow a middle section, entitled "The Artists," in which "the Art of a people" would provide "a good path in which to form the mind of [the] hero, the man of the coming age" (*Letters* 1.219). In the novel as published, however, the Lancelot/Argemone marriage becomes the basis for a homosocial bond between Lancelot and his cousin, Luke, that in turn forms the basis of the coterie of "artists of the people" who will attempt to reform the "social problems which are convuls-ing more and more all Christendom" (12.695, 700). The marriage does not lift the family curse but rather falls victim to it when Argemone contracts a fever and dies. A series of parallels between Luke and Argemone indicate that Lancelot's relationship with Luke will take the place of his marriage to Argemone. Just as the vicar attempts to persuade Argemone to become a celibate nun, he has led Luke to the celibate Roman Catholic priesthood, and no sooner does Lancelot receive a letter from Argemone declaring her love than the narrator informs us that he is becoming very close to his cousin. Just as Coningsby's relationship to Millbank forges a bond among a group of Eton classmates, Lancelot's relationship with Luke forms the basis of a group of artists, the third being the Cockney painter Paul Mellot.

The novel seeks to distinguish the agency of this coterie from that in *Coningsby* not only by making its members artists rather than politicians but also by reject-ing what it regards as the paternalism of "Young Englandism" (3.196). As the role played by Catholicism in Disraeli's novels indicates, several members of Young England were Catholic or drawn to Anglo-Catholicism, and Kingsley's portrait of the vicar may allude to the Reverend Philip Faber, an Anglican priest who strongly influenced members of the Young England circle and purportedly served as the original of the Reverend Aubrey St. Lys in *Sybil*. At the beginning of the novel, Argemone is being courted by Lord Vieuxbois, who has come under the influence of the Tractarians and is modeled, as an explicit allusion to *Coningsby* makes clear, on Disraeli's Eustace Lyle, a Roman Catholic who seeks to restore a feudal ideal of social deference (11.538). In keeping with the Young England ideal of finely graded hierarchy, Vieuxbois insists that the poor cannot educate themselves but must be educated by the clergy and gentry (5.291). By contrast, Argemone eventually recognizes that her own views of social reform have been paternalistic. Her desire to become a nun and serve the poor has not arisen from "genuine love of the poor, but from 'a sense of duty'" as well as a "lust for singular-ity and self-glorification" (8.451); on her deathbed she confesses that even as she sought to aid the poor, she maintained her distinction from them, "wanton[ing] in down and perfume, while they, by whose labour my luxuries were bought, were pining among [the] scents" of "filth and misery" (13.704, 703). Accordingly, Paul Tregarva criticizes Vieuxbois, who sees no reason that the "people should wish to rise in life" (5.291), for failing to recognize that the people do not want him to reach down to them but rather to "be raised . . . up to" his level (11.538).

Yet *Yeast* itself inscribes a hierarchical relation between the coterie of artists and the working class. Although Paul Tregarva is a poet who seeks to employ art as a form of social agency (his satire on the squirearchy gets him fired), Lancelot does not include him in the coterie of artists, an exclusion reinforced by the distinction between Tregarva's role as a writer and the coterie's commitment to painting, which Lancelot takes up in place of an earlier career as a writer. Moreover, in his description of his projected narrative, "The Artists," Kingsley portrays Tregarva as "the type of English Art-hating Puritanism" who will only become convinced of the "divine mission of Art" when Lancelot completes his grand synthesis of all the major genres of painting (*Letters* 1.219–20). Thus, in his summary of the fates of the various characters, the narrator reports that a man like Paul will become socially isolated ("a solitary trapper, wandering moonstruck and alone" in America [14.711]) and thus be unable to participate in the process of reform.

The novel's use of the companionate marriage that posits both equality and gender difference suggests, as do Kingsley's "Letter[s] to the Chartists," that the working classes share with women an incapacity for the rational thought necessary for social agency. While Lancelot's romance with Argemone mediates his homosocial bond with Luke, it also serves to structure his relationship with Paul. In the letter describing his plans for the novel, Kingsley depicts men and women as equal but possessing different mental capacities, with Argemone serving as Lancelot's "*complementum*," meaning that "she must be educating her head through her heart, he his heart through his head" (*Letters* 1.220). This explains the contradictory depiction of Argemone and Paul both as rational actors and incapable of rational action. Argemone is an intellectual woman who resists "giv[ing] up [her] will to any man" and has longed for "woman's enfranchisement" (8.452), and Paul is a well-read autodidact who, although he has questioned the Chartists' lack of religious faith, becomes a "Chartist lecturer" campaigning for the franchise (14.711). Consequently, each initially assumes the role of Lancelot's instructor, seeking to convert him from religious skepticism and the related failure to assume social responsibilities. Yet the novel depicts Argemone as recognizing not only that Lancelot is the first "man who was her own equal in intellect and knowledge" but also "how real was" the "sexual inferiority" of women (8.447). Thus, Lancelot (like Coningsby and Egremont) soon shifts from instructed to instructor, Argemone's "new pupil . . . rapidly becoming her teacher" (8.447). Once she persuades Lancelot to abandon his skepticism, he leads her away from her High Church faith toward his Broad Church one. Similarly, Paul teaches Lancelot about the plight of the poor, but in retrospect Lancelot casts Paul as the student who is "begin[ning] to understand what [he] was driving at" (12.695).

The reversal of the educator and the educated echoes a similar reversal in the process of spiritual conversion that will enable Lancelot to take up reform. As Allan Hartley has noted, *Yeast* depicts a series of religious conversions, the most significant of which, he argues, is the retrospectively narrated conversion of Paul Tregarva, which not only anticipates but implicitly shapes Lancelot's own conversion (chap. 3, esp. 51). Yet the conclusion of the novel implies that although Paul has the agency to lead Lancelot toward conversion, Lancelot alone possesses the agency to enact reform. Likewise, the narrative structure that situates Paul's account of his conversion in the middle of the novel, long after Lancelot's conversion is under way, gives priority to Lancelot's agency.

This problem of priority—and in consequence the ultimate location of social agency—is reflected in the novel's ambiguous treatment of the question of whether reform begins with the people or the priests. In the final chapters of the novel, a mysterious prophet—a mélange of Carlyle and Maurice—tells Lancelot that "the people, rather than the priest" are "to blame" for the failure of their contemporaries to follow divine teachings: "As they [the people] are, so will he [the priest] be in every age and country."[8] The state of the priesthood, he goes on to say, is merely an "index" of the people's "spiritual state" (14.708). Rather than suggesting that a reformed clergy, in place of a reformed aristocracy, would take responsibility for the state of the nation, in particular of the "people," the prophet appears to blame the failures of the clergy on the failures of the people. On the one hand, this formulation would appear to shift social agency to the people. Just as Paul Tregarva's conversion precedes and prompts Lancelot's, it would seem that the people must act first and only then can the church be reformed. On the other hand, the language of blame or responsibility ("you have to blame for that the people") is not the same as the language of agency. The ambiguity of the phrasing produces a circular logic. If there is no adequate priesthood, then how will the people be converted so as to produce such a priesthood? If neither priest nor people can act unless the other acts first, then action is impossible.

Kingsley's attempt to resolve the contradiction between the novel's critique of Disraelian paternalism and its reinscription of it in the relationship between Lancelot and Paul helps to explain both how the ending of the 1848 version differs from the plot outlined in his letter and how he further revised the novel in

1851. The ending as published in 1848 forecloses not only the planned conclusion of the marriage plot but also the planned narrative of "The Artists," for the discussions about art are interrupted by the prophet, who instructs Lancelot that he is "meant for better things than art" and insists that his true vocation is to be a "politician" (12.699, 700). However, the prophet does not guide him toward the political domain but, quite literally, to the church, when he leads him through the wicket door of Saint Paul's and charges him with restoring the church to life. Significantly, this resolution, which gestures toward envisioning reform of the church as the ultimate means of reforming the social order, involves only Lancelot and thus abandons the coterie of artists.

In keeping with the changed perspective manifested in *Alton Locke*, and perhaps as a result of Kingsley's dialogue with workingmen, the revised conclusion of the 1851 edition of *Yeast* further shifts social agency away from the elite coterie of artists by having Lancelot unite himself instead with Paul Tregarva, the workingman. Whereas in the 1848 version Smith sets out alone on his quest to discover "the idea which shall reform the age" (14.709), in the 1851 edition Luke declines to join him, and Lancelot invites Paul in his stead. Making explicit that this partnership is a substitute for the companionate marriage that was originally to have joined Lancelot and Argemone in a project of reform, they pledge themselves to a "sacred bond . . . the utter friendship of two equal manful hearts," and Paul, adopting the passage from Ruth often used in marriage services, promises that "where thou goest, I will go" (15.300, 299). Reform is no longer the visionary project of a coterie of artists but a practical project involving an alliance of the ruling elite and workingmen.

Although the allusion to Ruth invokes the companionate ideal in which husband and wife are equal but complementary, the novel accords the working-class male a potential rationality that its plot denies to the genteel woman. Whereas Kingsley's letter depicts a gender difference rooted in nature, the novel suggests that the difference between Paul and Lancelot—between working class and gentleman—is a matter of culture. The cultural elite guide the people not because they are naturally superior but simply because they are already cultivated. Even as Lancelot acknowledges that he has learned more from Paul than Paul has learned from him, they nonetheless agree to form a relationship in which Lancelot is the "master" and Paul the "servant." However, this relation is only temporary, for Paul projects a future "when [he will be] as learned and as well-bred" as Lancelot and will "not refuse to call [him]self . . . equal" (1851 15.299).

Kingsley's conception of self-culture corresponds with this representation of working-class agency. Lancelot had responded to Vieuxbois's resistance to people "ris[ing] in life" by contending that "if man living in civilised society has one right which he can demand it is this, that the State, which exists by his labour, shall enable him to develope, or, at least, not hinder his developing, his whole faculties to their very uttermost, however lofty that may be" (1848 5.290, 291). On the one hand, the concept of self-culture implies an agent capable of self-development, but on the other hand, it implies a self that, because it is not yet cultivated, cannot yet act rationally. Thus Lancelot's comment gives a role to an elite—authorized by "the State"—that will guide this process of self-culture and enable working people to develop their rational faculties.

∼

Questions about self-culture are, as we will see in his remarks on its "moral," at the heart of *Alton Locke*, which depicts Chartism as seeking not to gain the right to vote but rather the right to education. Yet while it supports working-class education, it also represents individual self-culture as the self-serving attempt to rise above one's equals. The novel's representation of the sexual rivalry between Alton and his clergyman cousin, George, both of whom seek to use their education to win the hand of Lillian Winnstay, thus links self-culture to class conflict. Like the 1851 version of *Yeast*, which undoubtedly was influenced by it, *Alton Locke* seeks to resolve this conflict between the working class and a clergy defined as genteel by invoking the companionate marriage ideal as a model of "cooperation" and "brotherhood" between a reformed working class and a reformed clerical elite.

However, even as it represents a self-serving clergy, the novel envisions a clerical elite that guides the process of working-class self-culture so that it will serve the people and the nation rather than the individual. The novel depicts George Locke as unrepentantly self-aggrandizing throughout, while Alton undergoes a process of conversion and self-reform under the guidance of Lady Ellerton (the former Eleanor Staunton), who furthermore seeks to transform sexual rivalry and class conflict into brotherhood by mediating a union between workingmen and the clergy. However, in its national marriage plot, the novel displaces the reform of the clergy onto Lady Ellerton herself. In the discussion that follows, I examine how these resolutions construct the novel's vision of social agency.

We can see *Alton Locke* as attempting to envision a process of reform in which the self-culture that leads Paul Tregarva, in the 1848 version of *Yeast*, to become a Chartist lecturer and from there to decline to a solitary backwoodsman, serving instead, in the 1851 version, as the basis for his partnership with Lancelot Smith. Indeed, Kingsley was clearly reworking material from his first novel, employing a similar plot with parallel sets of relations among characters as a means of exploring the questions it raised about what it means for members of the working class to "rise." In both novels the protagonist's rival in love is a clergyman, his love object is one of a pair of closely related genteel women (the sisters of *Yeast* becoming cousins in *Alton Locke*), his cousin plays a major role (shifting from companion to rival), the working-class protagonist is a poet, a prophetic figure sends the protagonist on a quest for knowledge, a central character whose initials are A.L. contracts a fever that ultimately proves fatal, and the marriage resolution toward which the narrative seems to be pointing fails to materialize, a homosocial bond between men taking its place. *Alton Locke* revises in particular the central triad of male protagonist, cousin/rival, and female protagonist. Most significantly, the working-man, Alton Locke, replaces both the gentleman, Lancelot Smith, as the novel's protagonist and (as indicated by their initials and their death from fever) the chief love interest, Argemone Lavington, with both substitutions tending to refocus questions of agency on the working class. Furthermore, the protagonist's sexual rival conflates the cousin with the vicar in keeping with the novel's conception of class conflict as arising from the attempt of one "brother" to rise above the other. Finally, the novel's courtship plot complicates and ultimately circumscribes the possibilities of working-class agency.

Like the national narratives of the novels I discuss in preceding chapters, *Alton Locke* portrays class conflict as sexual rivalry between men of opposing classes; rather than locating the source of the rivalry in class difference, however, it defines class, and thus class conflict, as the attempt of one "brother" to rise above the other. This explains why Kingsley claimed that the "moral" of his novel is "that the working man who tries to get on, to desert his class and rise above it, enters into a lie, and leaves God's path for his own—with consequences" (*Letters* 1.247). Although the phrasing here implies a conflict arising within an already existing class system, his novel portrays conflict as the result of the emergence of class division itself. The fever dream that Alton experiences near the end of the novel allegorizes this emergence as a fall into class from an Edenic state in which all men are "brothers" who are "equal" and "free," with "every man [receiving] an equal plot of ground," until one individual takes advantage of his physical strength to rise above the others (36.345, 344). Whereas Disraeli had depicted a fall from finely graded hierarchy into tripartite class, Kingsley depicts a fall from Edenic brotherhood—of Cain and Abel—into a dichotomous class structure.[9]

George Locke is the first to betray his class by attempting to rise, this rise in turn motivating Alton's own desire to rise. Alton and George are the sons of brothers who began with the same opportunities—they work in the same grocer's shop—but are divided when one becomes a financial success and the other fails. Whereas George's father had "steadily risen in life," following the kinship model by marrying his master's widow in order to become "the owner of a first-rate gro-cery" and seeking to "convert" George the "tradesman's son into a gentleman" by sending him to Cambridge, Alton's father, pursuing the entrepreneurial ideal, fails at business, dies, and leaves his family in poverty (2.20). When Alton "betrays" his fellow laborers by excising the political content of his poetry, he is merely re-peating the betrayal of George, whose courtship of Lillian causes him to call his cousin a "traitor" (35.327).

Yet, as the reference to the "working man" makes clear, Kingsley is referring in the letter quoted above not to George but to Alton, who attempts to rise above the working class by stripping his poetry of its social critiques in order to be ac-cepted by the genteel Lillian and her family. In contrast with the novel's explicit characterization of Alton as hero and George as villain, the parallels between the cousins make George, as Rosemary Bodenheimer suggests, Alton's "sinister double" (*Politics of Story* 146), whose actions reveal the dangers of Alton's pursuit of self-culture.

The novel distinguishes between education as a means of developing one's faculties—rising through merit—and education as the acquisition of cultural privilege through the means of political power.[10] As Alton's fever dream suggests, George wins out not because he is intellectually superior to or more meritorious than Alton but simply because he is physically stronger (Alton, it might be noted, is weaker, at least in part, because of living in poverty). In this dream, a group of men contend that because they "are stronger than [their] *brethren*, and can till more ground than they," they should receive "a greater portion of land, to each according to his power" (36.344; emphasis added). The result of employing their "might" to "swallow . . . up the heritage of the weak" is a dichotomous class struc-ture in which "a few grew rich, and many poor" (36.345).

The novel's marriage plot follows the same pattern, George claiming that he has won Lillian Winnstay, who has been courted by both cousins, because he is "strong" and Alton is "weak" and making it clear, when their rivalry comes out in the open, that he will use his status to "drive over" his rival (35.327, 24.227). This plot enacts Ludlow's claim that the Chartists' attempts to use physical force on April 10 were doomed to be defeated by the superior strength of the ruling elite: "The Chartists chose to stake their cause upon a display of physical force, and by a display of physical force they were overwhelmed" (*Politics for the People* 1.11; see *Alton Locke* 34.323). Thus it is on April 10 that Alton, upon learning that George has won Lillian's consent to marriage, attempts to strike his cousin, who, pos-sessing greater physical strength, "carelessly" brushes the blow aside and knocks Alton to the ground (35.327).

As the latter instance indicates, the novel links the pursuit of self-culture as a means of gaining power to the kinship model of courtship. George judges all actions and relationships—not least his Cambridge education—in terms of whether "it pays" to engage in them. He becomes a clergyman not because he is concerned with spiritual matters or because he wishes to serve society but because it is a means to "get on" (24.222) and cultivates a relationship with Lord Lyndale, whose ideas about social reform he mocks, only because Lyndale can help him obtain a clerical appointment. In keeping with the kinship ideal of marriage, he is quick to conclude that it might "pay" to know the Winnstays and courts Lillian not for her own sake but as a means of enhancing his status (6.74). Accordingly, the novel depicts his desire as mere lust—he calls her a "tit-bit" while "smacking his lips like an ogre over his prey" (24.227)—and in accord with the kinship ideal, he treats her merely as "property" (35.326). Most significantly, in a classic case of Girardian mediation of desire, George only begins to pursue Lillian after Alton is smitten with her, his courtship serving to consolidate his power when he wins out over his cousin.[11]

While Alton believes his desire is not tainted in this fashion, his courtship of Lillian, like his other actions, reveals that he too, though less consciously, adheres to the kinship ideal. George's insistence that Alton's initial encounter with Lillian is a "dodge" to "hook" a "dean and two beauties," for example, has the effect of revealing what Alton denies to himself (6.74, 73). Similarly, Alton's professedly "pure" admiration for Lillian's "beauty," rather than her interiority, becomes indistinguishable from George's erotic attraction to her, while Lillian's ultimate decision to accept George's marriage proposal confirms that she does lack interior depth and that in pursuing her, Alton has strayed from his ideals.

Although Alton begins his pursuit of self-culture in accord with the ideal of developing one's innate faculties and using learning to serve others, the inequalities that ensue from George's prior rise transform this pursuit into a similarly self-serving betrayal of his brother workingmen. While Alton's assertion that he has the same "right" as "aristocrats" to court Lillian in itself makes a claim for all men of his class, in his betrayal of that class it becomes indistinguishable from George's social climbing (7.77). Just as George employs his knowledge of culture as a means of gaining Lillian and thus raising his status, so Alton agrees to omit "certain passages of a strong political tendency" (18.179), in particular the (presumably Chartist) "political and social nostrums" (18.180) he considers "the very pith and marrow of the poems," merely "for the sake of popularity, money, patronage," in short, for "seeing more of Lillian" (18.182). Using language that Kingsley echoes in his letter on the moral of his novel, Alton eventually comes to "feel the awful sacredness of [his] calling, as a champion of the poor, and the base cowardice of *deserting* them for any *selfish* love of rest"; in short, he "had *betrayed* [his] suffering brothers" (24.229; emphasis added).

Accordingly, the novel portrays Chartists as seeking not the right to vote but the right to education that by its nature fails in the aim of improving the conditions of the working class and serves only as a means of elevating individuals above their fellow laborers. When Alton claims he has the "right" to court women of the upper classes, he echoes his fellow Chartist Crossthwaite's claim that Alton has "a right to aspire to a college education" so that he can "become what Nature intended [him] to become" (4.48; see also 10.110). Extending the narrative of the fall into class difference, Crossthwaite contends that the universities "were bequeathed by the people's friends in old times, just to educate poor scholars like you and me" but have been appropriated by the upper classes, and he approves the argument of the Chartist newspaper editor and orator O'Flynn, who argues that intelligence rather than social status "constitute[s] man's only right to education" (4.49, 48).[12] Significantly, Alton claims that this discussion of education—not as one might expect the horrendous conditions of the tailor shop in which he has labored—first led him to believe "that society had not given [him his] rights" (4.50).

Whereas education ought to transform Chartists into rational citizens, Crossthwaite abandons moral-force persuasion and comes to the conclusion that only physical force will succeed (see 32.301). When he first invites Alton to a Chartist meeting, Alton is struck by the "fluency and eloquence" of the speakers and reassured that the Charter has nothing to do with conspiracy, revolt, and bloodshed. Yet although Crossthwaite scoffs at the idea that Chartism involves "revolt and bloodshed," he does not rule out the use of "ulterior measures" if moral force should fail (10.107). As with George, the pursuit of education for the purpose of gaining power reduces culture to sheer force. Consequently, when Alton employs his rational power of persuasion in a speech to agricultural labors, his arguments unintentionally instigate a riot. This episode recurs to the problem that the Chartists had struggled with from the beginning, that moral force tends to be inextricably linked to physical force. Indeed, Thomas Cooper—the poet to whom Kingsley had written in 1848 and the chief model for Alton Locke—had claimed in the preface to his epic poem, *Purgatory of Suicides* (1845), that the speech that led to his conviction for sedition did not, as the government claimed, aim to incite the rioting that followed but merely urged his listeners to pursue the "legal and constitutional course" of "ceas[ing] labour" until the Charter was made law (vii).[13] It therefore seems inevitable that just as the persuasive speeches made Alton a Chartist "from that night," Crossthwaite's account, later on, of how the government dismissed the tailors' petition concerning the practices of government contractors leads him to embrace physical force and become "a rebel and a conspirator . . . from that moment" (10.110, 32.303).

The novel's solution to the problem that self-culture leads to the betrayal of one's class and to physical force is to posit a process in which workingmen remain agents of their own self-culture yet are guided by a clerical elite. Alton describes his mentors as "guides," and his specific depiction of a mentor as "shepherd" implies a conception of the guide as pastor (20.192, 2.30). As the frequent allusions suggest, Kingsley here draws on a conception that Carlyle had frequently invoked in works such as *Chartism* (1840) and *Past and Present* (1843). In *Chartism*, for example, Carlyle writes that "the poor labourer," as an "ever-toiling inferior, . . . would fain (though as yet he knows it not) find for himself a superior that should lovingly and wisely govern," that, in short, he longs for the "guidance and government, which he cannot give himself" (3.134; see also 6.155). Similarly, in *Past and Present*, he repeatedly implores the ruling elite to take on the role of guides so as to obtain "noble loyalty in return for noble guidance" (4.4.270). However, whereas Carlyle tends to portray the worker as requiring rational and orderly guidance because he is fundamentally irrational ("Your world-hosts are all in mutiny, in confusion, destitution; on the eve of fiery wreck and madness!" [4.4.270; see also 1.5.31, 3.8.177]), Kingsley imagines a process in which the guide helps the worker develop an innate capacity for rationality.[14]

Even as *Alton Locke* envisions these guides as pastors, it depicts the clergy as incapable of providing guidance. George Locke remains self-serving to the end, dying from a fever contracted from the coat that he buys—in accord with the principles of "buy-cheap-and-sell-dear commercialism" (39.372)—from a sweated tailor shop. Even those genteel clergy who do seek to provide guidance are, in Maurice's terms, effectively atheists because they do not adhere to the true gospel of brotherhood dictating that all men possess an innate capacity for self-culture and rationality.[15] Instead of seeking to help men develop from within, they seek to repress and discipline them. No sooner does Dean Winnstay acknowledge Alton's poetic abilities than he insists that Alton achieve "far stricter mental discipline" and begins cajoling him to suppress the political content of his poetry (15.164). The prison chaplain, who censors Alton's political writing and "delug[es]" him with Christian tracts that seek to "keep up the present system" (30.286–87), enacts the Chartist complaint that Kingsley had endorsed in his second "Letter to the Chartists" when he wrote that some clergy treat the Bible as a "mere special constable's handbook . . . a mere book to keep the people in order" (*Politics for the People* 4.58).

The Chartist bookseller Sandy Mackaye would seem to offer better guidance. In retrospect, Alton claims that it was not from the physical-force Chartist Crossthwaite that his "mind received the first lessons in self development. For *guides* did come to me in good time" (2.30; emphasis added). The first of these guides is Sandy Mackaye, who throws open the resources of his bookshop and becomes Alton's "tutor" (6.62). By becoming a bookstore owner and making reading and pursuit of knowledge a lifelong activity, Mackaye has sought to realize the ideal of pursuing self-culture for its own sake. Like Crossthwaite, he promotes the egalitarian ideal of self-culture ("Who'll teach a man anything except himsel'" [3.35]), but he is also aware of the danger that it can become self-serving. When he discovers that Alton's first poem is an allegory of individual desire depicting a Byronic "pious sea-rover" who encounters a "troop of naked island beauties," Mackaye instructs him in the poetics of service to the people, insisting that he should be a "cockney or people's poet" who "writes aboot London town," not an author of exotic fantasies (8.84, 85, 88, 86; see also 94). It is no coincidence, then, that when Locke insists that he should be able to court an aristocratic woman, Mackaye counters that marriage will lead him away from the "Cause" merely to "please yersel'" and praises "Roman times, when folks didna care for themselves, but for the nation, and a man counted wife and bairns and money as dross and dung" (7.78–79).

Yet although Mackaye has all but rejected Chartism and maintains a moral-force stance, he ultimately is "no shepherd" because the Chartist self-culture he promotes is secular and he offers "nothing positive" (20.192, 193). As Kingsley puts it in his letter about the novel, "The cream and pith of working intellect is almost exclusively self-educated and therefore, alas! Infidel" (*Letters* 1.248). The rationality of Mackaye's tutelage is positive insofar as it "emancipate[s]" Locke from the "modern Puritanism" of his mother, which with its predestinarian view that one cannot change one's fate forecloses the possibility of social agency, but this same rational skepticism cannot produce a faith to take its place (3.40). Just as Crossthwaite's self-culture leads not to moral force but to physical force, so Mackaye's leads not to reform but to impasse: "Mackaye had nothing positive, after all, to advise or propound. . . . He grew daily more and more cynical, more and more hopeless about the prospect of his class and of all humanity" (20.193). Mackaye's secularism ultimately limits his tuition to enabling Alton to see the injustice of contemporary society and the way it makes action impossible, but for the same reason, it cannot envision action that produces reform because, having abandoned Christianity, he cannot guide Alton toward the ideal of brotherhood. In spite of his disdain for the romantic poet, Mackaye's skepticism makes him, in the terms of his hero, Carlyle, another Byron railing against the times rather than a Goethe offering a new gospel.

That Mackaye's guidance is thus indistinguishable from that of the unre-formed clergy is emphasized by the fact that he too seeks to discipline rather than merely guide Alton's education. Insisting on "self-restraint and method" (2.34), he bans "desultory reading" and "soul-destroying trash" like Byron (3.35). He extends the privilege of reading in his shop on the condition that Alton learn Latin and offers rent-free accommodations on the condition that he minds "the scholastic methods and priorities" and reads only what Mackaye approves (6.62).

When Sandy Mackaye dies on April 10, Chartist guidance dies with him, and Lady Ellerton takes over his role with the specific purpose of Christianizing Chartism. The novel reinforces the transference of this role from Sandy to Lady Ellerton by having the latter, like Mackaye, frequently echo the writings of Car-lyle. However, just as Kingsley and company sought to Christianize socialism, Lady Ellerton Christianizes Carlyle, whose writings, while dismissing the specific forms of Christian faith, employ its vocabulary in order to articulate the idea of a divine providence ensuring that justice will ultimately prevail. Lady Ellerton's Carlylean teachings restore the Christian content of this vocabulary, as we can see when she makes Jesus Christ a Carlylean "hero" (37.360; see also 37.356). She similarly transforms Chartist doctrines, founding their claims not on "abstract rights" but on divine teaching (37.361). Whereas the clergy treat the Bible as a "book to keep the people in order," she claims that it is the true "charter" declar-ing freedom and equality (37.362).

While Lady Ellerton's guidance leads to the conversion of workingmen by Christianizing Chartism, she does not attempt to convert the clergy to egalitar-ian, or brotherly, Christianity, but instead undergoes that conversion herself. She initially shares with the clergy the assumption that agency is confined to the elite and performs the "vast duties and responsibilities of [her] station" only for "self" by assuming the role of "a philanthropist, a philosopher, a feudal queen" in or-der to gain the "praise of dependent hundreds" (39.374). Her conversion occurs when she recognizes that these philanthropic activities aim only at "keeping the poor in their degradation, by making it just not intolerable to them" and begins to "suspect that those below might be more nearly [her] equals than [she] had yet fancied" (39.375, 374).

Through the figure of her husband, Lord Ellerton, the novel suggests that aristocratic philanthropy will always fail because it is intrinsically hierarchical. It distinguishes Ellerton from Disraeli's Young England paternalists, who combine two estates in order to consolidate parliamentary power, by depicting him as selling "one [estate] in order to be able to do justice to the other" and taking up all of the current land reforms, including agricultural improvement, allotments, and Owenite association. Yet his reforms come to nothing when he dies, and his property passes to an heir who has no interest in his projects. Reform must take the form of conversion in which the aristocrat fully embraces the brotherhood of the "bon sans-culotte" Jesus (37.360).

Alton's own conversion involves a similar shift in point of view that is figured through the marriage-plot convention in which the protagonist courts one woman in accord with the kinship ideal but then turns to another in accord with the companionate ideal.[16] In accord with this convention, Alton fails to recognize, and even suppresses his awareness of, the superiority of Lady Ellerton and attributes to Lillian all of Lady Ellerton's expressions of interest in his welfare (among them inserting into one of his books a slip of paper with useful advice, repaying the debt that has put him in thrall to his cousin, setting his verses to music, and paying his attorney fees when he goes on trial). From the beginning, he has been attracted by her speech and intellect but has suppressed this attraction in favor of the superficial beauty of Lillian. When, during their first encounter at the Dulwich Gallery, he hears a "woman's voice," he turns around and sees "not . . . the speaker," Eleanor Staunton (later Lady Ellerton), but Lillian, he ignores the woman who attempts to engage him in conversation and instead fixates on "an apparition the most beautiful [he] had ever yet beheld" (6.71). On the two subsequent occasions when he glimpses his true relation to the women, he immediately suppresses it. On one occasion a smile from Lillian sends him into an "extacy" that erases his momentary recognition of the "shallow[ness]" and "empti[ness] of Lillian's eyes and face . . . compared with the strength and intellectual richness" of Lady Ellerton's (23.217, 216). Similarly, her disdain for Lady Ellerton's attempts to provide for the people "shakes" his "estimate" of Lillian, but his "bliss" upon receiving her invitation to a tea at which he will be lionized again sweeps aside the revelation (25.235). Alton's recognition that it is Lady Ellerton who has appreciated him and whom he should appreciate thus signals his abandonment of the desire to rise and conversion to the companionate ideal. In accord with this ideal, Lady Ellerton and Alton interact with one another on the basis of their inner selves, not their status, which means that, in accord with novelistic conventions, they engage in spirited conversation, and their disagreements, far from resulting in discord, signal mutual respect.

However, Lady Ellerton rejects the marriage ending that this convention calls for and substitutes in its stead cooperative association between workingmen and clergymen. Whereas the purpose of cooperatives was to give workingmen control of production and thus economic power, however, she makes them a figure for sibling union. She declares that, insofar as they are merely economic arrangements, cooperatives are subject to the same dangers of self-interest as other forms of commerce ("the innate selfishness and rivalry of human nature") and they can only succeed if they are Christianized, a process that transforms them from working people uniting with one another into working people joining with their Christian guides. Lady Ellerton forms her own cooperative in which she would "teach" working women "to live as sisters, by living with them as their sister [her] self" (39.376) and proposes a similar union of clergy and workingmen: "Will your working brothers co-operate with these men? . . . Do you think, to take one instance, the men of your own trade would heartily join a handful of these men in an experiment of associate labour, even though there should be a clergyman or two among them?" (40.381). By envisioning gender-segregated cooperatives, Lady Ellerton emphasizes a relation of equality akin to that between siblings (elsewhere, Alton describes "association" as "the embodiment of brotherhood and love" [32.301]) and thus attempts to avoid producing a gender-reversed version of the marriage plot of *Sybil*, in which the male aristocrat retains a hierarchical relation to his working-class wife.

By displacing the conversion of the clergy onto Lady Ellerton, Kingsley seeks to solve the problem of whether the people or priests should lead reform—the "like people, like priest" dilemma that we have seen in *Yeast*. Although Lady Ellerton's conversion precedes and enables her to effect Alton's, his precedes and presumably will in turn prompt the conversion of the clergy. Moreover, although it occurs earlier in time, she narrates the history of her conversion when her instruction of Alton is at an advanced stage, so that in narrative terms they are contemporaneous. Most important, her narrative gives priority to Alton when she concedes that it was his "capabilities" that initiated the process of her awakening and conversion (39.374).

In this respect, Kingsley seeks to avoid the problem of paternalist guidance by revising Disraeli once more, substituting for Egremont and his claim that the aristocracy are the "natural leaders of the people" a vision of Christ as the "true demagogue" (*Sybil* 4.15.334; *Alton Locke* 37.356).[17] As discussed above, Maurice's theology conceives clergy and workingmen as brothers guided by their brother Christ, who is at the same time one with his father. This conception solves the problem of providing guidance without treating the other as inferior by making the guide divine, but it raises the question of how Christ's guidance can manifest itself. If such guidance is through his earthly representatives, the clergy, then the problem of one group of men claiming greater reason than another once again emerges. If it is through his own word—the Bible—then the problem of Chartist self-culture similarly manifests itself.

◦∾

For all of its efforts to imagine egalitarian guidance, *Alton Locke* tends to privilege the cultural elite, as we can see in its treatment of one of the key elements of the Christian Socialist experiment, its commitment to egalitarian dialogue. Drawing on the history of the meetings between Chartists and the Maurice circle, the novel depicts Lady Ellerton as seeking to mediate dialogue between clergy and laborers: there are clergy, she insists, who "do not want to be dictators to the working men. They know that they have a message to the artisan, but they know, too, that the artisan has a message to them" (40.380). As suggested above, Lady Ellerton depicts cooperative associations as substitutes for her companionate relationship with Alton and, in accord with the companionate ideal, envisions clergy and workingmen engaging in dialogue in which each partner recognizes the rationality of the other.

At the same time, however, she insists that workingmen are not yet capable of rational action and so are not yet "fit for those privileges which [they] so frantically demand" (37.365). Although she has come to believe that "those below might be more nearly [her] equals than [she] had yet fancied," she is unable to represent herself as the "slave of those whom [she] was trying to rescue" without depicting herself also as their "teacher" and "minister" (39.374, 376). In the concluding chapters of the novel—in which her conversion is complete while Alton's is still in progress—Lady Ellerton herself assumes the role of cultivated elite in relation to the not yet cultivated workingman, becoming the dominant speaker and ultimately deciding Alton's future for him. In spite of insisting that the clergy do not want to be "dictators" and that they wish to exchange "messages," therefore, she charges the clergy with responsibility for "enabling the artisan to govern himself" (40.381).

This contradictory attitude to dialogue manifests itself as well in the form of the novel's first-person retrospective narrative. As Patrick Brantlinger has noted, the novel gives equal weight to points of view that contradict one another (137–39; see also Bodenheimer, *Politics of Story* 137; Gallagher, *Industrial Reformation* 91–95). While he contends that this practice results from Kingsley's desire to reconcile contradictory ideas, I would explain it as an attempt to embody the ideal of dialogue that treats opposing discourses as rational and coherent, even though they contradict one another. For these opposing ideas are never reconciled; they simply confront one another from within the opposed perspectives of Chartists and clergy. While the novel's narrative history represents Chartist discourse as rational, however, Alton's retrospective narration undermines Chartism by adopting Kingsley's Christian Socialist perspective.

Not surprisingly, the novel sets forth many of Kingsley's and the Christian Socialists' views as articulated elsewhere in their writings, yet it also presents as rational and cogent Crossthwaite's arguments that persuade Alton to embrace Chartism (10.103–9), Alton's speech to agricultural laborers (28.267–68), and his summary of Chartist arguments prior to the events of April 10 (32.296–301). The narrative even confirms Chartist suspicions that government-backed *agents provocateurs* had attempted to lure them into the use of physical force (chap. 33). When he speaks to the laborers, for example, Alton eschews emotional appeals and seeks to

> show them how all their misery sprung (as I then fancied) from being unrepresented—how the laws were made by the rich for the poor, and not by all for all—how the taxes bit deep into the necessaries of the labourer, and only nibbled at the luxuries of the rich—how the criminal code exclusively attacked the crimes to which the poor were prone, while it dared not interfere with the subtler iniquities of the high-born and wealthy—how poor-rates . . . were a confession on the part of society that the labourer was not fully remunerated. I tried to make them see that their interest, as much as common justice, demanded that they should have a voice in the councils of the nation, such as would truly proclaim their wants, their rights, their wrongs; and I have seen no *reason* since then to unsay my words. (28.267; emphasis added)

Alton's aim is not to move the audience but to make it "see," and even as retrospective narrator, he regards his speech as reasonable. Unlike so many other contemporary representations, the novel does not depict Chartist orators as demagogues (in the pejorative sense) manipulating an irrational mob. Employing the trope that privileges orality over print, the novel instead presents these discourses as true within their own terms, as opposed to the false discourse of both the Chartist press—represented by O'Flynn's *Weekly Warhoop*—and "the venal Mammonite press," for which Crossthwaite blames misrepresentations of Chartism as a treasonous movement (10.107).

However, in spite of his comment that he sees no reason to "unsay his words," Alton's retrospective narration (note the parenthetic "as I then fancied" at the beginning of the passage) represents Chartism as irrational and thus legitimates the need for guidance in order to make workingmen "fit" to act as citizens. Perhaps the most salient example of Alton the narrator adopting the point of view of the implied clerical author occurs when, upon hearing Lady Ellerton's narrative of conversion and self-reform, he addresses an audience of workingmen that apparently includes Alton the character:

> Oh, my brothers, my brothers! little you know how many a noble soul, among those ranks which you consider only as your foes, is yearning to love, to help, to live and die for you, did they but know the way! Is it their fault, if God has placed them where they are? Is it their fault, if they refuse to part with their wealth, before they are sure that such a sacrifice would really be a mercy to you? Show yourselves worthy of association. Show that you can do justly, love mercy, and walk humbly with your God, as brothers before one Father, subjects of one crucified King—and see then whether the spirit of self-sacrifice is dead among the rich! (39.376)

While the character articulates the case for Chartism, the retrospective narrator explains that he was wrong to hold the very views that, as we have seen, the novel presents as rational. Similarly, in the chapter mentioned above, the prospective narrative depicts Crossthwaite's rational arguments as persuading Alton to become a Chartist, but the retrospective narration that follows dismisses these arguments by treating Chartism as misguided: "About the supposed omnipotence of the Charter, I have found out my mistake. I believe no more in 'Morison's-Pill-remedies,' as Thomas Carlyle calls them" (10.111; see 110–11).[18]

A similar division between Sandy Mackaye's radical past and his opinions about Chartism during the period when the novel's events take place embeds this critique of Chartism within Chartism itself. Although Mackaye is often identified with Carlyle, it is important to note that Carlyle was never, like Mackaye, a radical Chartist, but the identification is possible because the novel confines his radicalism to a period well before the beginning of the narrative, the era of the early nineteenth-century radicalism of John Cartwright (1740–1824), Robert Burns (1759–1796), Sir Francis Burdett (1770–1844), Henry "Orator" Hunt (1773–1835), and William Cobbett (1763–1835).[19] However, in spite of the fact that during the time of the principal narrative (about 1843–1848) he is supposed to be a Chartist, the novel never depicts him participating in any Chartist meetings or activities. By the time of his death on April 10, he is insisting that physical force is doomed to failure, criticizing the petition for its fake signatures, and generally recanting his belief in Chartism as a movement, if not as a set of ideals. Most important, he often cites the views of Thomas Carlyle, whose *Chartism*, echoed by *Past and*

Present, contends that although the movement is significant as a symptom of social problems, it is wrongheaded as a means of ameliorating them. Thus it appears that precisely at the moment when Chartism was beginning, Sandy Mackaye was moving away from it.

If the death of Sandy Mackaye marks the death of the possibility of Chartist guidance, the death of Alton Locke might be considered the death of the Chartist character, Alton the narrator having taken his place. Such a reading might suggest that a reborn working class—Alton's conversion follows his death and "rebirth" from fever—will lead the process of social reform. Yet it might also suggest that Alton has merged with and disappeared into the character of the implied clerical author. For although the narrative does not depict a clergyman reforming himself, the novel's implied author is a member of the reformed coterie identified by Lady Ellerton: "a rapidly-increasing class among the clergy, who [are] willing to help [workingmen] to the uttermost . . . towards the attainment of social reform" (40.378). Lady Ellerton's related claim that there has been a "miraculous, ever-increasing improvement in the clergy," which is contradicted by every example in the novel, can only make sense with reference to the implied author and his circle (40.377).

This implied author does not attempt merely to Christianize Chartism or socialism, as the Christian Socialists set out to do, but to replace Chartism with Christianity. In order to join with the clergy, Lady Ellerton tells Alton, the Chartists must "waive for a time merely political reform," yet Chartism was in its essence all about political reform; consequently, as she goes on to say, the "Charter . . . must die to itself before it lives to God" (40.378). Just as Alton becomes Kingsley, Chartism is reborn as Christian Socialism, a set of principles that more or less transform socialism into Christianity. As we have seen in the case of Alton Locke defending the aristocracy, instead of engaging in dialogue with Chartists, the implied clerical author puts into the mouth of the workingman words he never would have spoken.

CHAPTER 12

Reforming Trade Unionism in
Mary Barton and *North and South*

Whereas Kingsley's novels construct national narratives uniting the working classes with the clergy, Elizabeth Gaskell's national narratives imagine the union of the working classes with industrial entrepreneurs. *Mary Barton*, which probably influenced the conception of agency in *Alton Locke*, depicts reform as the religious conversion of entrepreneurs and workingmen that replaces dichotomous conflict with cooperative Christian brotherhood. *North and South* revises both *Mary Barton* and *Alton Locke* by making the creation of a cooperative the means of moving beyond class discourse to "personal intercourse" that does not expect to eliminate conflict but rather achieves reform through a process in which entrepreneurs and working classes educate each other about their differences. In imagining a reformed trade unionism, Gaskell partially solves the problem of maintaining the social agency of the working class even as she ultimately, like Kingsley, privileges the elite.

~

Gaskell began writing *Mary Barton* in late 1845, at a moment when the future of Chartism was uncertain and well before the events of 1848 that led to the founding of Christian Socialism. Following the failure of the 1842 petition, the movement reached its "nadir" (Chase, *Chartism* 241), and as we have seen, O'Connor sought to revive its fortunes by shifting its emphasis from the Charter to the Land Plan. During this period, by contrast, trade union activity was increasing, and, as many Chartists were involved in unions and vice versa, it is not surprising that Gaskell represents John Barton as involved in both. Furthermore, the novel's depiction of Barton's involvement in the presentation of the Chartist petition and his subsequent turn to union activities invokes the events of 1842 when the rejection of the Chartist petition by Parliament was succeeded by a wave of strikes throughout Manchester and the industrial midlands.[1]

The marriage that concludes *Mary Barton* does not follow the typical pattern of the national marriage plot, which may explain why the critical literature tends to regard the social and romance plots as in tension with one another.[2] Critics have pointed in particular to the fact that for much of the second half of the novel John Barton and his social concerns are displaced by Mary Barton and her quest to exonerate the man she loves, Jem Wilson, from the charge of murder. Yet, as in other national narratives, the romance plot does not displace but rather allegorizes the social plot.

Gaskell emphasizes the parallels between the romance and social plots through the juxtaposition of analogous scenes. The parallel between Harry's attempt to seduce Mary and the masters' treatment of workers manifests itself when in successive paragraphs the narrative moves from a description of Harry's "unflinching resistance to claims urged" by the union to his use of "threats" to "beset" Mary after she has decided she will no longer see him (15.224).[3] Correspondingly, the novel juxtaposes Jem's "solemn . . . oath" to "save Mary" with John Barton's and his fellow trade unionists' "fierce terrible oath" to kill Harry Carson (14.216, 16.241). Moreover, the novel employs similar juxtapositions to reinforce the central plot device, in which Jem Wilson is suspected of the murder committed by John Barton, the assumption being that Jem acts out of jealousy, whereas in fact Barton acts from political motives. Jem's violent encounter with Harry Carson, in the latter part of chapter 15, is sandwiched between scenes involving the masters and the union that lead to the murder: the masters' decision to lower wages that results in the union's decision to strike, in the first half of chapter 15, and the scenes depicting the meeting between masters and men at which Carson draws the caricature and the subsequent union meeting at which the men decide to kill him, in chapter 16. These parallels in the novel's narrative of conflict find their correspondence in its resolution, when, as Rosemarie Bodenheimer points out, the romance plot concludes with Mary in Jem's arms and the social plot with John Barton dying in Carson's embrace ("Private Grief" 213).

What makes the allegory of the social plot less visible than in a novel such as *Sybil* or *North and South* is that the courtship plot does not lead to a marriage between classes. As Katie Trumpener notes, national tales moved from depicting marriages that recognize "cultural distinctiveness and . . . the possibility of transcultural unions, toward a more separatist position" with the result that "culminating acts of union become fraught with unresolved tensions, leading to . . . marriage crises, and even . . . to national divorce" (146). Whereas in Disraeli's novel Egremont's attraction to Sybil leads to his growing sympathy with and understanding of the working class and their marriage represents his assumption of the role of responsible aristocrat, Harry Carson's attraction to Mary Barton, like his attitude toward the working class, takes the form of objectification and thus of attempted seduction. In keeping with the conventions of the marriage plot, a courtship conducted in accord with the kinship model gives way to marriage in accord with the companionate ideal, but whereas Disraeli's novels represent this shift through an enlightened aristocrat displacing an elder relation, in *Mary Barton* the self-made workingman displaces the heir of an industrial entrepreneur.

While Mary's quest to prove Jem's innocence dominates the latter half of the novel, the murder plot implies that the real source of conflict is social rather than sexual. Although most of the characters assume that the motive for killing Harry Carson is sexual jealousy, the plot of the novel demonstrates that it is social, the murderer being Mary's father the trade unionist, not her lover, Jem Wilson. Gaskell goes out of her way to emphasize this point by revealing that John Barton had no knowledge of Carson's designs on his daughter and that therefore his motive does not stem from the concerns of the romance narrative. The fact that, as one character indicates, Barton would have intervened if he had known that Carson had designs on his daughter both emphasizes the parallels between the romance and social plots and demonstrates that what drives Barton is not the personal and private but the public and social.[4] Moreover, while the fact that Gaskell gives credence to the masters' claim that they cannot control the rate of wages makes their treatment of their employees morally ambiguous, Harry Carson's treatment of Mary Barton manifests no such moral ambiguity. This treatment in turn corresponds to his disdain for the union delegation. When John Barton and Jem Wilson come into conflict with Harry Carson, however, their behavior in each case takes a different form corresponding to their distinctive characters as workingmen.

The novel makes the rivalry between Jem Wilson and Harry Carson romantic rather than social by locating Jem outside of the dichotomous model of class conflict.[5] Jem does not, like Barton and his father, work in a textile mill but in a foundry, where his talent for invention nets him £200–£300—an enormous sum for a workingman—and enables him to begin the rise from poverty to a level of affluence that separates him from the working poor and makes him, in Margaret Jennings's view, "a gentleman" (12.189). While John Barton frequently complains about the division between the rich and poor, Jem never voices such concerns or shows any interest in Chartism or the union. By differentiating Carson, who gains his status and wealth through birth, from Jem, who possesses the energetic character of the self-made man, the novel transforms the latter into a workingman who does not act as a member of the working class.

Accordingly, Jem regards his rivalry with Carson as entirely romantic and having nothing to do with class. Mary's aunt Esther depicts her own seduction, by "one above me far" and the threatened seduction of Mary by "one above her in station" as instances of class exploitation (14.209, 213). Nonetheless, Jem, who deems Harry superior only "in externals," invokes the egalitarian principle enunciated in Burns's "a man's a man for a' that" and urges Harry to treat Mary as an equal by making an honorable offer of marriage (15.226). Furthermore, while the homosocial rivalry between Jem and Harry is reminiscent of the rivalry between Stephen Morley and Egremont in *Sybil*, the violent impulses Jem initially feels upon learning of Carson's attentions to Mary do not arise from class resentment but from a "frenzy of jealousy"; indeed they are initially directed not at Carson but at Mary and then ultimately at himself (14.215). Whereas Stephen Morley lies in wait for Egremont and attacks him from behind, Jem suppresses his jealousy and, deciding to act as Mary's "brother" rather than a rival lover, confronts Harry directly and only strikes in self-defense (14.217).

In contrast to Jem, John Barton, who constantly struggles to provide for his family and lives in continuous antagonism with the masters, conceives society in terms of the dichotomous model of class. In the era prior to the beginning of the narrative, he loses his job when his employer, Mr. Hunter, goes bankrupt. He has found a new job, but when his hours are reduced, he gives it up in order to join the Chartist delegation in London, only to find upon his return that employers refuse to hire a man who is "a Chartist delegate, and a leading member of a Trades' Union" and that, in any case, jobs are becoming scarce because of the deepening economic recession (10.158). While Jem, the son of his friend George Wilson, is becoming successful, Barton's son, Tom, has died because of the poverty that results when Hunter's mill fails, even as the Hunters continue to enjoy luxuries. Consequently, Barton, like Stephen Morley, frequently invokes the dichotomous model of a society divided between the rich and the poor and complains that the masters have unjustly appropriated to themselves the fruits of the labor of working people.[6]

To this end, the novel displaces the sexual rivalry between Jem Wilson and Harry Carson onto the class antagonism between John Barton and the mill owners. Barton's antagonism toward Harry Carson thus derives, as discussed above, not from the romantic relationship with his daughter, of which he is ignorant, but, as he explains on his deathbed, from the death of his son (35.440; see also 1.45). Although this motive might seem to be just as personal as the threat to his daughter, Barton conceives it as a response not to an individual transgression against a member of his family but to social injustice deriving from a corrupt social system. This is why he insists that he does not act for himself—he even refuses financial assistance from the union—and is willing to die for the general good in a "fight" against the masters (16.241). Correspondingly, the men select Harry Carson as their victim not because they take personal offense at the caricature but because they seek, as Barton later explains, to "intimidate a class of men" for the sake of the community (35.435).

Harry Carson shares with John Barton this view of a dichotomous social structure, but whereas Barton considers it the artificial consequence of unjust social relations, Carson assumes he deserves his place in society by virtue of his privileged status as the son of a wealthy man. His caricature of the union delegation manifests his tendency to see them merely as a class, not as fellow human beings, and when he first sees Jem, he does not recognize the successful member of the labor elite but sees only a caricature of the workingman, a "grimy mechanic, in dirty fustian clothes" (15.227). Whereas Jem is provoked to thoughts of violence solely by jealousy, Carson's desire to strike Jem arises directly from his contemplation of the class distinction between himself and the "mechanic," which for him amounts to comparing "Hyperion to a Satyr" (15.227). Even his attack on Jem—he strikes him with a cane—gives his violence a class form.

The novel depicts Carson's violence as arising from a conception of class division as a distinction not merely between wealth and poverty or upper and lower classes but also between rational and irrational, human and subhuman. He can countenance seducing Mary Barton because he is attracted only by her physical beauty, not by her interiority. The belief that he and Carson are equals leads Jem to set aside his emotions and to attempt to use rational persuasion to urge Harry to be "fair and honourable" to Mary, but Harry's caricatured view of Jem leads him to resist engaging in dialogue and to resort to physical attack (15.228). Similarly, the fact that his caricature of the union delegation dehumanizes a group of men that he regards, as his allusion to *Henry IV, Part I* makes clear, as "food for powder" is of a piece with his and his father's roles as leaders of "the *violent* party among the masters" who refuse to negotiate with the union (16.234; emphasis added; see also 15.224). As the narrator indicates, this attitude extends to other masters who fail to see the men as equals, "as brethren and friends" or as "reasonable men" with whom they can negotiate (16.232).

Accordingly, the novel suggests that workingmen like John Barton resort to violence because they have been dehumanized by the ruling elite. The novel carefully traces John Barton's violence to the deaths of his wife and son and these in turn to callous industrialists. We have already seen that his son died as a result of the failure of his previous employer, even though that employer did not suffer from the failure. The death of his wife subsequently leaves him without "one of the ties which bound him down to the gentle humanities of earth," and he becomes a "changed man" (3.58). When he is once again out of work, he turns to opium to stave off the pangs of hunger, and his addiction together with his growing depression leads to "monomania" and "diseased thoughts" (15.218, 219; see also 10.161–62). Even after they become deadlocked in their negotiations with the masters, the men are initially content to follow the resolutions and measures suggested by a union official from London, and it is only when Barton sees the caricature making a "jest" of men who merely sought relief from want that he expresses the desire "to avenge" himself on the masters (16.238, 239).

Generalizing from Barton, the novel indicts the ruling elite for making the working class irrational and violent. Just as his son's death makes Barton desire vengeance, the recession of 1839–1841 leads to "vindictive feelings" among the workingmen, and just as Barton becomes depressed and his thoughts diseased, so the people become "worn, listless, diseased" (8.126, 10.157). When the narrator generalizes from Barton to the "uneducated" people by comparing them to a Frankenstein's "monster" who is "ungifted with a soul," she extends the analogy by comparing herself and her readers to the monster's creator and asking why we have "made [the people] what they are" (15.219–20). Thus, when one of the masters claims that the workingmen are "more like wild beasts than human beings," he fails to recognize that the men's actions are not a consequence of their nature but of the masters' refusal to see them as "brethren and friends" (16.232).

In keeping with this conception, the novel treats trade unions not as a form of social agency but as an irrational, albeit understandable, response to dehumanization.[7] Accepting the axiom from political economy that strikes are not rational because wages are determined solely by the law of supply and demand, Gaskell's narrator depicts the basic union strategy of work stoppages as "insane, and without ground of reason," the response of men driven mad with "want and need" (16.232).[8] She further contends that while trade unions possess a "power" that can "obtain a blessing" only if it "work[s] under the direction of a high and intelligent will" that is "incapable of being misled by passion, or excitement," the "will of the operatives had not been guided to the calmness of wisdom" (15.223). On the contrary, as in elite-press representations of Chartism, they are vulnerable to the "burst of eloquence" and petty bribery of a demagogue like the "gentleman from London" who has been sent to advise them during the strike (16.237, 236).

Consequently, the novel does not treat trade union actions as rational strategies for achieving working people's goals but as the violent actions of men driven by anger and a desire for revenge. Barton joins the union not as an effective means of asserting his rights but as a response to his wife's death. His son's death leads to his desire for "vengeance . . . against the employers," but the irrationality of this desire for vengeance manifests itself when his growing anger leads him to assault not his employer but his own daughter (3.61). Similarly, as in *Wat Tyler* and *Barnaby Rudge*, in which the irrational violence of the insurgents ends up leading to the death of fellow rioters, so the "insane" belief in strikes is the "cause" of the union's "violence" against strike breakers who are, after all, fellow members of the working class (16.232). Even when Barton seeks to redirect this violence and "fight the masters," he regards their plan to kill Carson as a way to "avenge us" rather than a means of achieving their goals (16.241, 239). While, as we have seen, he later suggests that the plan was intended to "intimidate" the masters so that they would accede to the union's demands, once the killing takes place, the union's activities fade from view (35.435).[9] Just as the 1842 Manchester strike wave failed to win any concessions from the masters, the strike apparently does not result in any concrete gains for the workers.

Even as it portrays trade unionism as irrational physical force rather than a form of social agency, so the novel portrays moral-force Chartism as an extremely limited and circumscribed form of agency. It transforms the moral-force strategy of using reason to make a case for the rights of the people into merely "imploring Parliament to hear witnesses who could testify to the unparalleled destitution of the manufacturing districts." Its Chartists consequently believe that the "government" could not know—indeed had even denied "the existence" of—the "misery" of the people and that once their misery was "revealed in all its depths . . . then some remedy would be found" (8.127). Moral force works here as an appeal to a ruling elite to sympathize with the poor and do their duty. Rather than conceiving workers as citizens who share the same capacity to provide remedies as the ruling elite, it depicts them as inferiors who appeal to the elite to act on their behalf.

The novel reinforces this representation of Chartism as lacking social agency through the complete and remarkable omission of its primary goal, the citizen's right to representation in Parliament. Far from leaving the remedy to Parliament, the Charter, with its demands for universal male suffrage and other reforms of parliamentary representation, was itself a remedy. Whereas Gaskell repeats the contemporary platitude that the interests of masters and men are identical, the Chartist petition argued that, as currently constituted, Parliament represented only "the interests of the few" who could vote—that is, the upper classes—and

that it would act on behalf of the lower classes only if those classes were represented there (*Hansard* ser. 3, 62.1377). In 1842, the Chartists did ask to present witnesses who would testify to the condition of the people, but this was, as the Whig
leadership insisted, primarily a way to press their demand for the Charter.[10] The
novel further bolsters this view of the incapacity of working people to produce rational argument by depicting Barton's neighbors as substituting for the demands
of the Charter a range of incoherent and short-sighted solutions that include
breaking machines, shortening work hours, allowing child labor, promoting the
use of cotton rather than linen, and free trade (8.128–30). These Chartists are not
capable even of determining what is in their own interest.

From this point of view, working-class agency is always secondary to the social
agency of the ruling elite. In accord with the narrator's description of the Chartists
as seeking "remedies" from Parliament (8.127), John Barton, upon hearing the
various solutions proposed by his neighbors, replies that the best he can do is bear
witness to the people's "distress" on the supposition that when the members of
Parliament hear of it "they'll surely do somewhat wiser for us than we can guess
at now" (8.130). Even his contention that their demand for higher wages really
amounts to a request "for a bit o' bedding, and some warm clothing to the poor
wife as lies in labour on th' damp flags; and for victuals for the childer, whose little
voices are getting too faint and weak to cry aloud wi' hunger" tends to transform
their wages from something they have earned into a charitable gift from the prosperous (16.238).

In accord with this conception, the novel depicts a shift from moral-force
Chartism to physical-force trade unionism arising from the refusal of Parliament
to hear the Chartist witnesses and the masters' refusal of the union's demands.
When Parliament "refuse[s] to listen to the working-men," they turn from the
moral force of bearing witness to the physical force of trade unionism (9.141).
When, in turn, the masters say no to their demands, they resort to murder (16.239).
In other words, the working classes resort to an illegitimate form of social agency;
from this point of view, legitimate agency must consist of the elite acting hu-
manely so that the people are not driven to irrational violence.

In accord with Carlyle's *Past and Present*, the novel envisions the reformed
industrialist or captain of industry rather than a reformed Parliament as the locus
of social agency. *Past and Present* dismisses the Chartist aim of gaining parliamentary representation as misguided because Parliament is an institution in which
men talk instead of acting, and it instead envisions reform as the conversion of industrial "bucaniers" into "captains of industry" (3.10.192, 4.4.269). Just as Carlyle
indicts the middle class for professing to be Christians but instead following the

"Gospel of Mammonism" (3.2.147), so John Barton has concluded that neither masters nor men live in accord with the Bible (35.440–41). This claim leads the elder Carson to read his Bible, which, indeed, has been "little . . . used" and, having imbibed its spirit, to undergo a conversion leading him to forgive John Barton and to express the hope that "the Spirit of Christ" will henceforth regulate the relationship between masters and men (35.438, 37.460). This location of social agency in the reformed masters rather than the men is evident from the fact that it is Carson alone who is responsible for "the improvements now in practice in the system of employment in Manchester" (37.460).

In one important respect the novel limits the agency of the masters by depicting the conversion of Carson not as leading him to institute remedies that alleviate the conditions of poverty but as recognizing the humanity of the poor. Once again acceding to the principles of political economy, it depicts Carson as insisting that because industrialists "cannot regulate the demand for labour" (37.456), they do not have the "power" to "remedy the evils the men complain of" (37.458). Job Legh responds that what matters is not the remedies but the effort to find them, which will demonstrate that the masters sympathize with the poor so that "even if they could find no help, and at the end of all could only say, 'Poor fellows, our hearts are sore for ye; we've done all we could, and can't find a cure,'—we'd bear up like men through bad times" (37.458). Accordingly, the reformed Carson seeks to create a "perfect understanding, and complete confidence and love . . . between masters and men" (37.460). As the narrator's commentary on the strike indicates, this would not mean changing their living conditions but, on the contrary, making "known" to workers the circumstances that have forced the masters to reduce wages and that make going on strike an action "without ground of reason" (15.221, 16.232). This conception suggests that a change in attitude—more particularly a change in the nature of how masters interact with their men—would prevent men like John Barton from becoming morose and violent. Yet while the attitudes of the Hunters and the Carsons do contribute to his antipathy toward the rich, it is not how they are thinking but the very material circumstance of hunger that leads to his desperation.

The novel's depiction of workers bearing witness to the conditions of their poverty and employers explaining the conditions under which they provide employment envisions a relationship in which each considers the other rational and understandable, but it does not necessarily imagine an egalitarian relationship. The act of bearing witness is not the same as an act of rational persuasion. In this respect, Gaskell portrays the working poor as eliciting sympathy but not as setting forth arguments about the injustice of their situation. Similarly, when the narrator suggests that in explaining their situation the masters would be "treating the workmen as brethren and friends" as well as "reasonable men," she conceives them as treating them as equal (16.232), but when she depicts Carson as wishing to have laborers "bound to their employers by the ties of respect and affection, not by mere money bargains alone" she depicts a relationship more in line with Disraeli's finely graded hierarchy (37.460).[11] Although such acts of sympathy are premised on the recognition of similarity between self and other, they simultaneously construct a fundamentally hierarchical relation in which the sympathizer is social agent and the other a passive recipient of sympathy.[12]

Yet because she imagines that a reformed attitude toward the working class would prevent it from becoming irrational, Gaskell does suggest the possibility of a working class that possesses rational agency that extends beyond merely seeking sympathy. As Catherine Gallagher has noted, no sooner does the narrator describe how the elite have "made" the people into Frankenstein monsters "ungifted with a soul" than she concludes that, in becoming a "wild and visionary" Chartist, John Barton "shows a soul" (Gallagher, *Industrial Reformation* 74–75; *Mary Barton* 15.220). Instead of depriving him of his humanity, conditions drive him to imagine that he can act to improve his situation. Indeed, Barton's discourses on the condition of the people are, though passionate, quite rational. His contention that "our labour's our capital," for example, derives from Adam Smith, whose theory of political economy virtually defines the rational for the ruling elite (6.104). While she attributes Barton's view of society as unjustly divided into rich and poor to his "widely-erring judgement," she elsewhere represents him as rationally invoking biblical teaching (15.219; see also 1.45, 9.142). In this context, we see him seeking not the "charity" of a superior but his "rights" as a fellow citizen (10.159). Significantly, in these speeches he is not bearing witness to the ruling elite but addressing his fellow workmen about their grievances.

However, the novel presents a rather ambiguous depiction of what it would mean to have an educated working class. In accord with its view that the people do not understand why strikes do not work, the autodidact Job Legh manifests no antipathy to the rich and distrusts the trade union. Although he cares deeply about friends and family, his interest in scientific study puts his intelligence in the service of a personal hobby rather than the needs of the people. His hobby, moreover, is a drain on the family finances, and his granddaughter must seek employment to ensure that they can make ends meet.

The novel's national marriage plot provides an alternative to the culture of letters in the more general concept of self-making. Jem Wilson is on the same path taken by the elder Carson, who began as a workingman and who preaches the

Smilesean gospel of self-help when he contends that "facts have proved and are daily proving how much better it is for every man to be independent of help, and self-reliant" (37.457). Whereas Carson's own son has merely inherited his status, Jem Wilson has achieved his status as "gentleman" through his own efforts. Although the novel does not inform us about his education, he clearly has followed a path of self-culture that has led to his success as an inventor. Indeed, this depiction suggests that self-culture has more to do with self-making than with scholarly achievement. These efforts have earned him not only a financial reward but also the respect of his employer, who believes in his innocence and helps him find a new post in Toronto. The way for Mary Barton to become a lady is not to marry Harry Carson but to marry the self-made man, and the way for the workingman to achieve social agency is not to demand political rights or negotiate economic terms but to pursue self-culture. Yet what this means is that Jem's, like Job's, self-culture enables him not so much to negotiate better relations with his employers as to rise out of the working class.

This version of working-class self-culture accords with the novel's conclusion, in which the principal characters emigrate to Canada. In his seminal discussion of the novel, Raymond Williams contends "that there could be no more devastating conclusion" than Jem's decision to emigrate to Canada, for it does not provide a "solution within the actual situation" of industrial Britain (*Culture* 91). While subsequent criticism has produced a number of cogent responses to this criticism, Williams's point that Jem Wilson and Mary Barton cannot thrive within the social structure of industrial Manchester remains valid. The fact that self-culture leads him out of the working class indicates that, even before he decides to emigrate, Jem has already come up against the structures of class, nowhere more clearly than in his encounter with Harry Carson. While an individual member of the working class can exercise agency in the form of self-culture, working-class collectivities—the Chartists and trade unions—do not achieve social agency.

⌁

Gaskell portrays her novel—a cultural production aimed at the cultivated elite—as succeeding in doing what it depicts the Chartists setting out but failing to accomplish. In the preface to the novel, she states that she wants to give "utterance to the agony" of the people with the hope that she will spur a "public effort . . . in the way of legislation, or private effort in the way of merciful deeds, or helpless love in the way of widow's mites" (37–38). Although her novel does suggest certain remedies—the conversion of masters to captains of industry as well as working-class self-help—her main purpose, as she describes it, is to invoke in her readers the "sympathy" she herself feels for the working people of Manchester (37). In other words, like her novel's Chartists, who seek to bear witness to their condition while leaving it up to Parliament to act, the implied author of *Mary Barton* does not seek to employ reason in order to persuade her audience but rather to describe the conditions of the people in the hope that her readers will sympathize with them and act to provide remedies for their condition.[13]

However, many contemporary reviewers of the anonymously published *Mary Barton* constructed a different implied author, who, engaging in the contemporary political debates about whether the aristocracy or middle class can best govern the nation, employs the aristocratic critique of the middle class. In this political context, they take her assertion that she hopes to inspire "a public effort . . . in the way of legislation" to mean that she hopes that an aristocratic Parliament will intervene in the business of industry. The *British Quarterly Review* recognized that the novel's representation of the strike draws on the Manchester strike wave of 1842, in which the "supporters of the corn laws"—by implication Tory landowners or aristocracy—sought to "direct the angry feelings of the workpeople against their employers" (Easson, *Critical Heritage* 109). The reviewer thus aligns the implied author with the Tory press that had in 1842 insisted that the Anti–Corn Law League was conspiring to provoke workers into anger against their employers so as to pressure Parliament to repeal the Corn Laws.[14]

For this reason, even though the novel does not represent the aristocracy, reviewers could regard it as employing the aristocratic version of the tripartite model of class in which the aristocracy of the south intervenes in order to protect the northern working class from the industrial middle class. Passing over the passages in which the narrator affirms the nostrums of political economy, they focus, not surprisingly, on the plot depicting the masters as coldhearted villains. The *Manchester Guardian* complained that the novel favors the perspective of "the gentry and landed aristocracy" (Easson, *Critical Heritage* 125; see also 126), and William Rathbone Greg, a Manchester manufacturer and acquaintance of Gaskell, maintained that the author sympathizes with aristocratic defenders of the Corn Laws who, "protected by privilege of parliament," seek to cast opprobrium on the ranks of the middle class (Easson, *Critical Heritage* 170; see also 109).

These reviews challenge the depiction not only of the masters but also of the men. The *British Quarterly Review* claimed that the novel's depiction of the attitudes of working people may accurately reflect the situation in 1842 but insisted that in 1848 there was an "improved state of feeling . . . on the part of the working classes . . . towards the masters" (Easson, *Critical Heritage* 106; see also 169, 181). It further contended that the working class does possess agency and mocked Gaskell's claim to speak for a "dumb people" by quipping that workingmen "always seemed to us by no means chary of expressing what they think and feel" (Easson, *Critical Heritage* 106; see also *Mary Barton* 38). As against the novel's desire to prompt the elite to act on behalf of the working classes, Greg apparently accords the working class social agency by contending that neither "parliament" nor "employer[s]" can improve their situation (Easson, *Critical Heritage* 177–78) and that they alone "can raise their own condition" (176). But he almost immediately withdraws it by depicting the workers as irrational and lacking the "power of *will*" to act (179). His aim in according them agency, it becomes clear, is merely to challenge the novel's advocacy of legislative intervention and of entrepreneurs undergoing ethical conversion.

⌒

As previous commentators have observed, in writing *North and South* Gaskell sought to respond to these criticisms of *Mary Barton*.[15] While the focus has been on how the later novel substitutes a virtuous industrialist for the villainous one of the earlier novel, however, the revisions are much more extensive, for Gaskell alters her representation not only of the entrepreneurial class but also of the working class. Moreover, *North and South* responds to the allegation that the implied author of *Mary Barton* had adopted the perspective of aristocratic discourse by dramatizing the aristocratic, or genteel, point of view and the operations of class discourse as the perspective of the novel's characters, not its author. Finally, whereas *Mary Barton*, like *Yeast* and *Alton Locke*, had followed Carlyle in envisioning reform as religious conversion, *North and South* critiques the correlative Kingsleyan conception of cultivation of the working class by a clerical elite in favor of a model of direct encounters between the working class and entrepreneurs. Accordingly, rather than employing the cooperative as a figure for a bond between clergy and working people, it depicts it as the occasion for envisioning a new kind of trade unionism through which entrepreneurs and working people seek common ground.

As we have seen, Gaskell closely followed the development of Christian Socialism and corresponded regularly with several of its leading figures.[16] At one point she even made the playful suggestion that her attempts to be "a true Christian" had led some people to call her a "socialist and communist" (*Letters* 108), a comment she seems to recall when Adam Bell teasingly proposes that Margaret Hale is becoming "a democrat, a red republican, a member of the Peace Society, a socialist" (2.15.330).[17] However, when she began writing *North and South* four years later, she would have known that the cooperatives were beginning to fail and that Maurice was at that moment turning his attention to the education of the working class.[18] While Gaskell undoubtedly approved the new scheme, especially given that her clergyman husband was himself a prominent and successful lecturer for working people, *North and South* nonetheless depicts the clerical elite and classical culture as having little to offer by way of changing the nature of relations between the classes.

Gaskell had firsthand knowledge of the efforts of clergy to remedy the conditions of the working classes. Her husband, the Reverend William Gaskell, not only gave lectures but also played a prominent role as secretary of the Manchester Domestic Mission, and it was through the Gaskells' involvement with the mission that Elizabeth gained the intimate knowledge that set *Mary Barton*'s depictions of the conditions of working-class life apart from those in contemporary novels. Like many similar projects, the founders of the mission regarded themselves as taking responsibility for helping the lower classes by cultivating in them a rational appreciation for prudence, thrift, and sobriety. However, as John Seed has shown, the missionaries' encounters with members of the working poor, especially during times of economic crisis, eventually led this clerical elite to recognize that poverty was a matter not merely of irrational behavior but also of structural economic conditions (16–20). Consequently, they began to criticize forms of interaction in which the elite assumes the position of the rational agent who cultivates rationality in the working class and to promote egalitarian "intercourse" between the classes (Seed 22–23).

When, in the concluding chapters of *North and South*, John Thornton explains that he wants to "cultivate some intercourse with the hands beyond the mere 'cash nexus'" (2.26.431), he is invoking not only Carlyle but also the Reverend William Gaskell, who, as Elizabeth Gaskell herself explained, sought to replace top-down education with the cultivation of "individual intercourse" that recognizes the particularity of the participants (*Letters* 193). In the novel, however, it is not the clergyman but his daughter who first engages in such intercourse. Moreover, the Reverend Hale advocates not dialogue but explanation on the older model of inculcation of rationality in the working classes. *North and South* attempts to avoid the reintroduction of such a hierarchical relation by substituting the entrepreneur, Thornton, for the clergyman. Whereas Kingsley had envisioned the reform of the clergy and Maurice in his story "Recollections and Confessions of William Milward" had depicted a working woman reforming a clergyman (see P. Jones 218–19), Gaskell turns in both *Mary Barton* and *North and South* to the reform of the industrialist. The later novel in turn rethinks the nature of this conversion by envisioning a process in which the entrepreneur and workingman "unconsciously and consciously teach . . . each other" (2.26.431).

Consequently, just as *Alton Locke* grants a degree of social agency to the working class, the conversion of which enables the transformation of the elite, so *North and South* envisions reform of the trade union as integral to the reform of the industrial entrepreneur. While Kingsley and the Christian Socialists, who were primarily concerned with sweatshops in London, were envisioning cooperative association as a replacement for Chartism as well perhaps as for trade unionism, Gaskell was in a position to see that in the factories of the north, trade unions were becoming powerful and well organized. Moreover, although relations remained highly contentious, the lockouts of the Amalgamated Society of Engineers in 1852 and the spinners at Preston in 1853–1854 were not nearly as violent or disruptive as the Manchester strike wave of 1842 that lay behind the depictions of the relations between industrialists and working people in *Mary Barton*. Instead of seeking like the Chartists to gain the right to legislate the terms of the relationship between entrepreneurs and laborers, they moved toward the goal, as Patrick Joyce puts it, of gaining "a say in the affairs of the trade" and thus sought not only to obtain higher wages and better working conditions but also to endow workers with "full humanity" as historical agents (*Visions* 111, 104).

Writing at a time when the development of trade unionism was very much in flux, Gaskell seeks to imagine the reform of unions in terms of the model of intercourse between the classes. *North and South* does not, like *Mary Barton*, depict trade unionism or strikes as understandable but irrational responses to economic conditions. Whereas the earlier novel had depicted trade unions as the physical-force consequence of the failure of moral-force Chartism, the later one depicts a union leadership committed to moral force yet unable to control their fellow workers' physical-force response to conditions. It therefore envisions a transformation of trade unionism that, although it does not end strikes or conflict, shifts its emphasis from indirect confrontation to direct personal intercourse.

⸎

North and South responds to Greg's allegation that *Mary Barton* manifests the "delusions of many throughout the *south* of England respecting the great employers of labour in the *north* and west" by making the class discourse pitting north against south—the industrial middle class against the agrarian aristocracy—not the perspective of the implied author but that of the characters in her narrative (Easson, *Critical Heritage* 165). Rather than the novel's unifying point of view (if that indeed is what it provided in *Mary Barton*), that discourse becomes merely one perspective within the novel. The novel thus transposes to its heroine, Margaret Hale, the aristocratic critique of industry that, according to its critics, provided the perspective from which the author of *Mary Barton* portrayed Manchester. Whereas the narrator of *Mary Barton* states that it is no surprise when one sees the "careworn looks, . . . excited feelings, and . . . desolate homes" of the poor "that many of them, in such times of misery and destitution, spoke and acted with ferocious precipitation," it is Margaret who describes seeing men "who look ground down by some pinching sorrow or care—who are not only sufferers but haters" and exhibit a "sullen sense of injustice" (*Mary Barton* 8.126–27, *North and South* 1.10.81). Recognizing that Greg's review employed entrepreneurial discourse in its critique of *Mary Barton*, she similarly transfers his assertion that "a very different feeling now subsists between the employers and the employed from that which once prevailed" to the industrialist Thornton, who contends that "the power of masters and men [has become] more evenly balanced; and now the battle is pretty fairly waged between us" (Easson, *Critical Heritage* 147; *North and South* 1.10.83).[19]

In the first half of the novel, Gaskell stages a series of debates in which the Thorntons and Hales employ their respective class discourses, each of which characteristically espouses values that it establishes through critique of the opposing class.[20] The Hales align the southern gentry with land, religion, literary culture, the old professions, and disinterested leisure, all of which they define against the busy-ness of "trade," while the Thorntons espouse the entrepreneurial ideal, which links together northern industry, innovative enterprise, and energetic productivity, as opposed to the "dull prosperous life in the old worn grooves of . . . more aristocratic society down in the South, with their slow days of careless ease" (1.10.81). Employing discourse characteristic of the political debates that construed social agency as a question of whether the aristocracy and middle class could best govern the nation, the Thorntons criticize the gentry for inaction, while the Hales criticize entrepreneurs for acting without sufficient concern for how their actions affect others.

The fact that both sides in these debates set forth telling arguments but neither builds a stronger case than the other makes these discourses self-enclosed and self-perpetuating. Rather than producing engagement between the two sides, the criticisms made by class discourse merely serve to reinforce the class ideals and identities of the respective speakers. Thornton cannot define the "grandeur" of "toiling" and "suffering" in the north without opposing it to the idleness of aristocratic life in the south. In response, Margaret initially has little to say about the virtues of the south but defends it by attacking the "gambling spirit of trade" in the north, just as she earlier opposes professionals—associated with the "land"— to "shoppy people" (1.10.81; 1.2.19). Each speaks his or her own language so that when John criticizes the south, Margaret replies that he "do[es] not know anything about the South," and when she in turn criticizes the north, he responds that she "do[es] not know the North" (1.10.81, 82). Because each speaks a different language meant to preserve class privilege, they can make no progress toward addressing the real problems of contemporary society.

Consequently, the novel's national narrative, which culminates in the marriage of Margaret and John, does not resolve the conflict between north and south by merging the discourses of the aristocracy and middle class into the "mythic promise of a common language" (Schor 136) but rather by constructing an ideal of "intercourse" in accord with the companionate model of marriage. The marriage of Margaret and John does not mean the end of the "continued series of opposition" that marks their relationship but rather engagement in dialogue that recognizes difference (1.25.197).[21] Drawing on the tradition of the novel of courtship—it is modeled in part on *Pride and Prejudice*—*North and South* makes the disagreements between the hero and heroine the means through which they come to recognize each other as deep subjects with fundamentally different points of view. Whereas *Mary Barton* had been the object of desire who mediated homosocial rivalry between men from the entrepreneurial and working classes, Margaret Hale mediates, and her marriage to Thornton models, the homosocial bond between the entrepreneur and the workingman.

Indeed, considered only in terms of the relation between north and south, the historical frames of the novel's national narrative depict an unequal relation in which the industrial north points toward the vibrant future and the genteel south belongs to the archaic past.[22] The title of the novel is in this respect, as Gaskell herself claimed, inappropriate, for the novel does not ultimately concern itself with the south but rather with how to reform the north, where class conflict involves industrialists and laborers, not the middle class and the aristocracy.[23] The novel thus revises earlier national narratives in which a male travels from a modernizing dominant culture to an archaic and subordinate culture. Insofar as the southern aristocracy continues to constitute the ruling elite, *North and South* reverses this pattern by making the traveler a woman who discovers that it is her culture that has become archaic and is being replaced by the modernity of the formerly subordinate north.

Whereas Margaret initially invokes the benign paternalism of a finely graded hierarchy that Disraeli had contended was fundamentally egalitarian, *North and South* ultimately depicts the southern aristocracy as an archaic feudal order in which the elite exploit the poor. The novel distinguishes the family of Margaret's father, who is presumably from the lower gentry, from the more aristocratic family of her mother, the Beresfords. Drawing on historical narratives that depicted the Commonwealth wars as a conflict between the aristocracy and the rising middle class, Gaskell associates Margaret's grandfather, Sir John, with the monarchy through his daily after-dinner toast, "Church and King, and down with the Rump" (1.5.45). This ritual in turn aligns him with his predecessor, "the last Sir John but two," who, in the manner of a feudal lord, shot his steward for complaining that he racked his tenants (1.16.130).[24] The fact that he racks his tenants, of course, ranks him among the aristocracy who exploit their property for their own benefit and fail in their duties as governors of the people. Accordingly, the novel marks Margaret's shift in perspective on the south by having her make a return visit to Helstone during which she discovers not only that the new vicar is introducing modernity but also, through an incident in which a local woman burns a cat alive, that the south is the site not of reason, culture, and moral superiority but of archaic, irrational, and "savage country superstition" (2.21.390).

The novel depicts Henry Lennox's courtship of Margaret as threatening to entrap her in this archaic culture, as represented by the household of her cousin and alter ego, Edith, who is the daughter of a general and married to Colonel Sholto Lennox. When Margaret says that she likes "people whose occupations have to do with land . . . soldiers and sailors, and the three learned professions," she is employing aristocratic class discourse that constructs the classic professions of the military, law, medicine, and the church in opposition to commerce (1.2.19).[25] Accordingly, Colonel Lennox practices his profession for only a year and a half, after which he spends his time in a "gentlemanly" fashion, sitting "with his wife in her dressing-room an hour or two every day; play[ing] with his little boy for another hour, and loung[ing] away the rest of his time at his club" (2.19.372). The narrator here undercuts aristocratic discourse that depicts professionals as eschewing the profit motive by recasting them in terms of the entrepreneurial critique of the idle aristocracy. Moreover, while aristocratic discourse associated the church, the law, and medicine, which required advanced education, with the ideal of culture, the prestige of the military derived from its association with archaic feudalism.

Accordingly, Edith's family holds a "conclave" in which, in accord with the kinship ideal, they seek to form an alliance that will appropriate her fortune in order to support a nonproductive aristocracy (2.24.417). As a "struggling barrister" who finds his family "frivolous and purposeless," Henry Lennox initially appears to be embracing the middle-class ideal of self-making, but in the latter part of the narrative he courts Margaret because of the "rise, which [her fortune] would enable him, the poor barrister, to take" (1.3.30, 2.22.406, 2.24.415). As Florence Nightingale, whom Gaskell stayed with while writing *North and South*, put it in her recently written "Cassandra," in such a marriage there would be "no . . . unity between the woman as inwardly developed, and as outwardly manifested" (50).[26]

By contrast, the novel depicts the rising middle class as achieving its success precisely through its embrace of egalitarian self-culture. Gaskell sets the historical narrative that aligns the south with feudal monarchy against a narrative in which "men of the same level" had separated into the "different positions of masters and men," creating inequality and "tyranny" until competition among masters enabled working people to gain power so that "now the battle is pretty fairly waged between" them (1.10.83). Thornton embeds his own history of egalitarian self-making within this larger historical narrative. Whereas Harry Carson derives his status from the fortune his father has amassed, Thornton is forced by his father's bankruptcy to become the equal of other workingmen and begin again the process of becoming a master (1.10.84). Whatever the merits of his view "that a working-man may raise himself into the power and position of a master by his own exertions and behaviour" so that "every one who rules himself to decency and sobriety of conduct, and attention to his duties, comes over to our ranks," it constructs an ethos in which the process of self-making ensures that all men are equal (1.10.84).

In keeping with the rise-of-the-middle-class narrative, as we have seen it in novels such as *Barnaby Rudge*, the Hales, as opposed to the Beresfords, reject the genteel status accorded by birth and, along with it, the claims of genteel culture and in its stead adopt the middle-class norm of self-culture. In accord with aristocratic class discourse, Margaret initially associates culture with "the accomplishments of a gentleman" (1.4.39). However, when her father advances the commonplace of aristocratic discourse that literary culture develops one's moral character, Thornton insists that his knowledge of the "Homeric life" had nothing to do with developing the moral integrity that led him to pay off his father's debts (1.10.85). By the time the novel's chief exponent of genteel culture, the Oxford fellow Adam Bell, defends the cultivated ideal of "sitting still, and learning from the past," Margaret and her father have become advocates of the "progress of commerce" who question the idea of sitting "comfortably in a set of college rooms" while one's "riches grow without any exertion" of one's own (2.15.330).

The Reverend Hale nonetheless never fully abandons the claims of culture or the clerical point of view. In some respects, he does break with them. In deciding that he cannot swear to the Thirty-Nine Articles, he dissociates himself from the established church, which was closely allied with the southern aristocracy, and in seeking solace in the case of John Oldfield aligns himself not with Charles II, like Sir John Beresford, but with Cromwell's Puritans.[27] Furthermore, in making the surprising decision to move to Milton Northern and become the teacher of entrepreneurs, he allies himself with the industrial north. However, as his suggestion that literary culture has shaped Thornton's character indicates, Hale remains bound to the genteel ideal, which leads him, just at the moment when Maurice was turning away from the cooperative movement in order to found his Working Men's College where clergy like Kingsley served as teachers, to offer lectures for workingmen on "Ecclesiastical Architecture . . . rather more in accordance with his own taste and knowledge than as falling in with the character of the place or the desire for particular kinds of information among those to whom he was to lecture" (1.18.141).[28] His sudden death suggests that, like the other members of the elder generation from the south—his wife and Adam Bell—he cannot survive the transition to modernity.

In his place, his son completes the shift from gentleman to entrepreneur. Like his father, Frederick comes into conflict with aristocratic authority, a naval captain—and so a member of the genteel professional class—who inflicts harsh discipline on his men in a manner similar to Sir John's treatment of his steward. By taking part in the mutiny and going into exile, Frederick rejects the genteel construction of the military officer as, in Margaret's conception, an aristocratic knight (a "preux chevalier") and becomes instead a "merchant" (2.16.344).[29] Signaling this transformation, he adopts as a pseudonym not the aristocratic name of Beresford, as his mother wishes, but the plebian Dickenson, remaking himself as the son of his father, Richard, but perhaps also of an ordinary Tom, Dick, or Harry.

Margaret Hale similarly completes the transition when, like the protagonists of other national narratives, she inherits property, both the land on which Thornton's factory had stood and the capital wealth that she invests in an industrial enterprise. Unlike Adam Bell, she does not intend merely to live off the rent of her land and the interest from her investments. However, rather than investing in a cooperative like the Christian Socialists or making over the factory into a medieval monastery in the manner of Disraeli's Trafford, Margaret acts not as landowner but as capitalist and invests in Thornton's "experiments." In this respect, she completes the process that transforms the archaic gentry into modern entrepreneurs. At the same time, just as his father's bankruptcy had forced Thornton to become a self-made entrepreneur, so his own bankruptcy brings to an end the older form of industrial relations—as he puts it, he has "to give up [his] position as master"—so that he can begin to develop a new one (2.26.431).

❧

North and South envisions reform of the relationship between working people and industrial entrepreneurs as an analogue to the companionate marriage of Margaret Hale and John Thornton. It shares with *Alton Locke* the attempt to con-

struct social agency that includes the working class, yet by substituting the entrepreneur for the clergyman, it adopts a significantly different stance toward reform.
The Christian Socialist cooperatives involved an alliance between clergy and
working people that promoted an antagonistic relation to entrepreneurs whose
role in economic production it sought to eliminate. *Alton Locke* further displaces
this cooperation onto a brotherhood of clergy and working people who undergo
a conversion that, while it presumably will lead them to reform the entire social
order, disengages them from the immediate concerns of the marketplace. *North
and South* instead envisions a reformed relationship between entrepreneurs and
working people. Moreover, reform takes the form not of religious conversion that
enables the elite clergy and the working people to form a cooperative brotherhood but rather of using cooperation as the occasion for engaging in dialogue
through which they come to a better understanding of their differences.[30]

This conception of social agency implies the development of a reformed trade
unionism. After the failure of the strike, union activity drops out of the narrative, but the fact that Thornton does not expect that establishing "personal intercourse" will do away with strikes implies that trade unions will continue to play a
role in mediating the relationship between industrialists and laborers (2.16.432).
By pushing the union to the background, however, Gaskell is able to explore the
possibilities for alternative forms of working-class agency.

Her representation of the strike reflects contemporary developments in trade
unionism, even as it attempts to explain and resolve difficulties unions continued
to encounter.[31] As noted above, the strikes by the Amalgamated Society of Engineers in 1852 and the Preston spinners in 1853–1854 marked a watershed in the
gradual transition of trade union strategy from the confrontational emphasis seen
in the strike wave of 1842 to negotiation based on a view of industry as a shared enterprise.[32] As unions became better organized and could amass large strike funds
that enabled them to hold out for longer periods of time, they began to use the
strike not as an immediate means of gaining their objectives but rather as a way of
putting pressure on factory owners to treat negotiations as the norm.

In this respect, whereas *Mary Barton* depicts the lower classes turning to
physical-force union activity when moral-force Chartism fails, *North and South*
portrays the union as primarily committed to moral force. As it does with the
critiques of industry and the aristocracy, it shifts criticism of trade unionism from
the narration to characters employing class discourse. The allegations of union
tyranny, which remained a commonplace in the elite press, are repeated by Margaret Hale, and the claim that the laws of supply and demand make strikes futile
becomes, as Nicholas Higgins points out, the biased opinion of a mill owner (Fra-

ser 39; *North and South* 2.3.232). Whereas in *Mary Barton* union members throw vitriol at strikebreakers, in *North and South*, as at Preston, where the leaders advocated *"Peace, Law and Order"* (Dutton and King 127), Nicholas Higgins's union declares that "there [is] to be no going again the law of the land," that there is to be no "noise o' fighting and struggling—even wi' knobsticks. . . . They would try and get speech o' th' knobsticks, and coax 'em, and reason wi' 'em, and m'appen warn 'em off" (1.25.199, 200). Indeed, Higgins not only depicts obeying the law as exerting moral force but also emphasizes how it will make the union's demands more persuasive to the public. By obeying the law, he insists, they will "carry . . . th' public with them" and "show the world that th' real leaders o' the strike were not [violent men] such as Boucher, but steady thoughtful men; good hands, and good citizens, who were friendly to law and judgment, and would uphold order; who only wanted their right wage, and wouldn't work, even though they starved, till they got 'em; but who would ne'er injure property or life" (1.25.200).

However, the novel depicts the union's moral-force strategy as inevitably entangled, like moral-force Chartism, with physical force.[33] The power of the union depends on achieving a unity of purpose that is defeated by the very conditions it seeks to change. Higgins defends the union's practice of sending men to Coventry as a means of making workers join the union by explaining that their "only chance is binding men together in one common interest" because their "only strength is in numbers" (2.3.233). However, dependence on men such as Boucher dooms the moral-force strategy to failure, because it treats fellow workers "as if they possessed the calculable powers of machines" and makes "no allowance for human passions getting the better of reason, as in the case of Boucher and the rioters" (2.3.228). Like *Mary Barton*, the novel depicts Boucher and company as irrational and dehumanized not by nature but by their conditions, yet in this case those conditions include not only unjust wages but also the union, which has "made him what he is" (2.11.294).[34] By titling this chapter, in which Higgins repeats his argument that the only "strength" of the union is in unity, "Union Not Always Strength," Gaskell suggests that trade unionism as currently constituted is, as had been Chartism, ineluctably trapped in the moral- versus physical-force dilemma.

Nonetheless, the novel suggests that although union leaders like Higgins fail to persuade impoverished workers like Boucher to act rationally, they do engage in rational dialogue with entrepreneurs like Thornton. There is no need for an elite to educate men like Higgins in order to make them rational agents. Instead, Higgins and Thornton "unconsciously and consciously teach . . . each other," and Higgins can even claim that he has "improv[ed]" Thornton by speaking his mind to him (2.26.431, 2.15.339). Precisely because one's position in the relationship dictates what one perceives as reasonable—that is, that rationality is always historically situated—Thornton envisions this mutual cultivation as "personal intercourse" that "bring[s] the individuals of the different classes into actual personal contact" (2.26.432).

The novel defines this personal and egalitarian intercourse in which each individual challenges the other from his or her own point of view by distinguishing it from paternalist explanation. Richard Hale fails to recognize that his belief that workers act in "ignorance" that might be overcome if they could "have a good talk [with the masters] on these things" assumes a hierarchical relationship between rational employers and irrational employees (2.3.230). Yet, as Higgins points out when Hale repeats the view that the men "make sad mistakes" in failing to comprehend the iron law of wages, such explanations assume that working people are "such a pack o' fools, that . . . it's no use . . . trying to put sense into [them]" (2.3.229). In place of rational explanation the novel constructs a conception of intercourse that does not seek to achieve a single point of view but adopts the companionate ideal in order to make recognition of difference essential to ongoing dialogue. Although Thornton and Higgins live "by the same trade, working in their different ways at the same object," they discover that each sees the "other's position and duties" in a "strangely different . . . way" (2.25.420). Thus, when Thornton describes Higgins as "my friend—or my enemy" he is acknowledging that their friendship depends on the understanding that they cannot always be in agreement (2.17.361).

This ideal of personal intercourse underlies the conception of the process of reform that Thornton outlines near the end of the novel, when he distinguishes "experiments" involving intercourse in which both masters and workers are rational agents from "mere institutions" in which the master as rational agent acts on behalf of the irrational lower classes (2.36.431). The problem with the latter, he explains, is that "a working man can hardly be made to feel and know how much his employer may have laboured in his study at plans for the benefit of his workpeople. A complete plan emerges like a piece of machinery, apparently fitted for every emergency. But the hands accept it as they do machinery, without understanding the intense mental labour and forethought required to bring it to such perfection." By contrast, his experiments involve choosing "an idea, the working out of which would necessitate personal intercourse; it might not go well at first, but at every hitch interest would be felt by an increasing number of men, and at last its success in working come to be desired by all, as all had borne a part in the formation of the plan." Indeed, the value of this process, it would seem, is not so much the resulting plan but the personal intercourse through which the various parties would become "acquainted with each others' characters and persons, and even tricks of temper and modes of speech. We should understand each other better, and I'll venture to say we should like each other more" (2.26.432).

However, Thornton's description of how he and Higgins established the dining cooperative ultimately reveals the limits of the novel's conception of personal intercourse:

> I bethought me how, by buying things wholesale, and cooking a good quantity of provisions together, much money might be saved, and much comfort gained. So I spoke to my friend—or my enemy—the man I told you of—and he found fault with every detail of my plan; and in consequence I laid it aside, both as impracticable, and also because if I forced it into operation I should be interfering with the independence of my men; when, suddenly, this Higgins came to me and graciously signified his approval of a scheme so nearly the same as mine, that I might fairly have claimed it; and, moreover, the approval of several of his fellow-workmen, to whom he had spoken. I was a little "riled," I confess, by his manner, and thought of throwing the whole thing overboard to sink or swim. But it seemed childish to relinquish a plan which I had once thought wise and well-laid, just because I myself did not receive all the honour and consequence due to the originator. So I coolly took the part assigned to me, which is something like that of steward to a club. (2.17.361)

While this scenario presents Higgins and his fellow workers as agents who make the scheme their own, what Thornton describes is not a discussion in which he and his men work out a plan together or come to learn about their differences. Of course, one might regard this experience as having taught Thornton not to come to his men with a complete plan, but nonetheless in describing the process he still assumes the role of primary agent when he states that he "would take an idea, the working out of which would necessitate personal intercourse." In both cases the men participate, but it is Thornton who initiates the process, a primacy that is reinforced by the paradox that it is he alone who articulates the ideal of personal intercourse, while Higgins nearly disappears from the final chapters of the novel.[35]

The fact that Thornton proposes a consumer rather than a production cooperative further suggests that the "owner of capital" continues to play the primary role in industrial production (1.15.117). Production cooperatives ordinarily appointed a manager—a paid employee, not a capital investor—who performed the organizational functions of the industrial entrepreneur, but while Thornton is content to accept the role of steward to a consumers' cooperative and even to be "only the manager" of a conventional business, it is not clear that he would accept the role of manager of a producers' cooperative owned and controlled by workingmen (2.25.426; see also 2.26.431). Nor does the novel give any indication that he has abandoned his earlier opinion that he cannot conceive what it would mean "for the hands to have any independent action during business hours" (1.15.121).

ᴄ

Both the achievement and the limits of this depiction of social agency manifest themselves in the way in which *North and South* attempts itself to be a social agent. Whereas *Mary Barton* attempted to act directly on its readers, producing sympathy that would lead them to act on behalf of the poor, *North and South* does not encourage its readers to engage in philanthropic activities such as investing in cooperatives but instead seeks to engage them in dialogue by portraying the workings of class discourse. Rather than speaking for the "mute" working class, it defines for the implied author the role of revealing the operations of class discourse so as to create an entrepreneurial class that can enter into dialogue with its employees, thus initiating a process that will produce social reform. In this respect, the novel seeks not only to move away from class discourse opposing the aristocracy to the middle class but also to encourage entrepreneurs to engage in dialogue with the working class. This aim reveals the limits of its ability to function as an agent of reform, however. Although she addresses both classes, she belongs to neither.[36] Precisely by putting herself at a remove from the site of social reform, she avoids the contradiction in Kingsley's depiction of egalitarian brotherhood. Whereas Kingsley critiques the failures of the clergy but nonetheless constructs an implied clerical author who will cultivate a rational working class, Gaskell constructs an implied author who acknowledges that the cultivated elite can do no more than seek to cultivate intercourse between entrepreneurs and workers. From this point of view, the role of the novel is not to inculcate in its readers the superior values of the implied author but to encourage them to engage in dialogue through which they can shape a reformed social domain.

Coda

Rethinking Reform in the Era of the
Second Reform Act, 1860–1867

The project I have undertaken here, of examining how the Victorians understood social agency, was anticipated by William Howitt and George Eliot when, during the era in which the Second Reform Act, of 1867, was under discussion, they wrote historical novels that look back to the beginning of the era of reform and the campaign for the franchise. Just as their predecessors constructed historical narratives that were analogous to or culminated in the present, they treated the earlier era of reform as analogous to the present era, in effect asking what had been learned about agency. These novels, like their predecessors, search for alternatives to the franchise and social class, but my focus here is not, as in previous chapters, on how the novels define these alternatives. Rather, I examine what these novels can tell us about the significance of the Victorian conception of social agency as reform rather than revolution.

While we know little about the circumstances that led Howitt to write *The Man of the People*, its appearance in 1860, together with the novel's implied argument that the people are now educated and should therefore be granted the franchise, suggests that he wrote it in support of the proposal for parliamentary reform advanced that year, the last government-sponsored proposal before 1866. Howitt's novel reaches back not to the era of the First Reform Bill itself but rather to the era of 1816–1817, which initiated the program of parliamentary reform later taken up by the Chartists. Eliot began writing *Felix Holt, the Radical* at the end of March 1865, just a month after the formation of the Reform League (discussed below) and completed it at the end of May 1866, when Gladstone's Reform Bill was being debated.[1] Whereas *Middlemarch* covers the era leading up to passage of the bill, including the last election before its passage, *Felix Holt* is set just afterward, in late 1832 and early 1833, during the electoral campaign for the first reform Parliament.

While both novels are set in the era before Chartism, they draw on parliamentary and Chartist discourses, in particular on the discourse of moral versus physical force. The protagonists of both novels—each based in part on the life of the moral-force radical Samuel Bamford—seek to use moral force and, more particularly, advocate the development of rational decision making through education.[2] Both also attempt to mitigate the effects of their fellow radicals' use of physical force but are arrested and tried by the authorities for what is perceived to be their role as leaders of an insurrection. These plot structures—which recall narratives in which the innocent or those who resist physical force get caught up in mob violence—imply that precisely because moral force cannot be effective without physical force one cannot employ it without being involved in the seditious use of force.[3] In what follows, I examine how this problematic accounts for Howitt's novel's making the case that the people are now sufficiently educated to be trusted with the franchise yet never depicts a rational people, while Eliot's, with its often remarked-upon *conservative* "radicalism,"[4] locates culture, and with it social agency, outside of the political domain entirely. Rejecting political reform as the action of a self-interested class, she constructs agency as self-culture, an "inward revolution" that moves the individual beyond class.

Throughout the 1850s, even as Chartism faded away, various members of Parliament offered proposals to modify the Reform Act of 1832, but none received sufficient support for passage. The government introduced a reform proposal in 1860, but, like its predecessors, it ultimately fell victim to parliamentary infighting. While the US Civil War along with other political factors kept reform off the ministerial agenda over the next few years, popular support for reform began to gather momentum. In April 1864, a largely middle-class group, including many former members of the Anti–Corn Law League, established the National Reform Union with the objective of obtaining suffrage for all males "liable to be rated to the relief of the poor" (*Leeds Mercury* 21 Apr. 1864: 3). In February 1865, the leadership of the Universal League for the Material Elevation of the Industrious Classes, a group of trade unionists and former Chartists, transformed itself into the National Reform League, which aimed to obtain "an extension of the franchise based upon a residential and registered manhood suffrage" (*Leeds Mercury* 24 Feb. 1865: 3). While the Reform Union was better funded, the Reform League had larger numbers and drew on the Chartists' well-established repertoire of contention to bring public attention to the bills that were brought before Parliament in 1866 and 1867.

By 1866, there was widespread support for reform legislation that would extend the franchise without fundamentally altering the makeup of Parliament. Gladstone introduced a bill on March 12, 1866, but a series of parliamentary maneuvers led to the defeat of his government that June. The Reform League mounted a series of public demonstrations beginning on June 29 and culminating in the Hyde Park demonstration of July 23, at which demonstrators, in defiance of a government ban, broke into the park. The Reform League continued to mount demonstrations in the latter half of the year and into early 1867, and on February 23 Disraeli introduced his own version of a reform bill. Although the bill was far from what the Reform League or even the Reform Union desired, they pushed for its passage, and the Second Reform Act became law that August.

What is of interest here, as with the First Reform Act, is not the various contributing factors leading to passage of the act but the way in which the participants explained it to themselves. Not surprisingly, both sides drew on parliamentary and Chartist discourses of the preceding decades, with the important difference that both parliamentary parties now supported limited extension of the suffrage. The concepts of the class as the chief form of actor and exercise of the franchise as the chief form of action remained deeply entrenched in these discourses. The idea of virtual representation of the lower classes by the upper classes largely disappeared, and the Chartist claim that the working classes need to represent their own interests was now widely accepted. All sides agreed that a reform bill was needed because members of the working classes required representation; the only question was how to provide this representation. Even Robert Lowe, the leader of the opposition to reform, implicitly granted the right of representation when he contended that economic prosperity had produced the "spontaneous enfranchisement" of a sizable number of the working classes and that their interests were thus already represented (*Hansard* ser. 3, 182.147).

In accord with the parliamentary discourse that had contended that poverty and ignorance disqualified the working classes from exercising the franchise responsibly, the parliamentary press and proponents of reform now granted that portions of the working classes had become prosperous and educated. In the first debate on Gladstone's measure, for example, Sir Francis Crossley argued that "the Bill of 1832 was not fitted for 1866, as great progress in education, in prudential habits, as shown by the Savings Banks Returns, and in various other respects had been made by the working classes" (*Hansard* ser. 3 182.70). Lowe, speaking in opposition, contended that the majority of the working classes continued to be too ignorant and asked, "If you want venality, if you want ignorance, if you want drunkenness, and facility for being intimidated; or if, on the other hand, you want impulsive, unreflecting, and violent people, where do you look for them in the constituencies?" (*Hansard* ser. 3, 182.147–148). Indeed, the reformers used the argument that the franchise should be extended only to the educated as a way to legitimate limiting the number of voters to be enfranchised. Correspondingly, the *Standard* argued that eliminating certain property qualifications would do away with the "best distinction that can be drawn between those who are and those who are not responsible and independent citizens" (13 Mar. 1866: 4) and elsewhere that, while "the *elite* of the artisans and operatives," who are "as intelligent as the householders between 10*l.* and 20*l.*," would be "a very valuable addition to the electoral body," Gladstone's bill would "bring in a number of ignorant and a number of indifferent men" (16 Mar. 1866: 4). The *Times* similarly argued that "it is for the interest of the State that all citizens who may be fitted by intelligence and character to exercise an independent political judgment, and no others, should come into the pale of representation" (28 Apr. 1866: 11). In sum, education had become the grounds for granting one the right to exercise social agency.

◦～

That William Howitt (1792–1879) should write a novel in support of a new reform bill was in keeping with his long-standing association with radicalism. Although he is mostly forgotten today, he and his wife, Mary, were prolific authors and well connected with literary circles. Indeed, *Howitt's Journal* published Gaskell's early stories.[5] By contending that the working classes have now become educated and can exercise social agency responsibly, his *The Man of the People* employed and itself helped construct the discourse that would legitimate the Second Reform Act. As I discuss below, in its depiction of the events of 1816–1817, the novel employs parliamentary discourse depicting the lower classes as employing physical rather than moral force and thus as unworthy of the franchise that they demand. However, the narrator contends, from the perspective of 1860, that the working classes have subsequently become educated and capable of voting disinterestedly. It is thus integral to the implicit argument of the novel that it portray the working classes of the past as violent and irrational so that the narrator can contend that a change has occurred and a new reform act is needed.

The narrator of *The Man of the People* on several occasions contrasts the impoverished state of the nation in 1816–1817 with the present day. In this respect, the novel's depiction of the past is the reverse of nostalgia; the present, not the past, is the golden age. While he begins the explanation of how the past "was a far

different time from ours" by describing how the governing elites have changed—
they now presumably "listen . . . to the voice of the people, of justice, and of humanity"—he goes on to emphasize the change in the "people," who had formerly
been "uneducated, and therefore excitable" (1.4.108, 1.1.15–16).[6] Similarly, on the
final pages of the novel, the narrator rejoices with his protagonist in the "wonder-
ful progress which his country has made in the science of politics and social existence" and celebrates the "revolution . . . our Sunday schools, evening schools,
national and British schools, ragged schools, mechanics' institutes, lectures and
libraries produced!" (3.15.338–39, 340).

As the latter passage indicates, the novel employs the parliamentary discourse
depicting the people as ignorant and incapable of reasoning: "It was a people,
as yet, ignorant, untrained to mental exercise, liable to be imposed on—in fact,
unapprehensive of its own power—it was yet a people which . . . had shown that,
roused by an infringement of its liberties, it was a terrible and invincible people"
(1.4.116). The reference to "a terrible and invincible people" alludes to the use of
force, but ultimately the novel contends, like parliamentary discourse, that the
people have no real power: because they are "uneducated, and therefore excitable," they are "not permanently strong" (1.4.108). Even Major Cartwright and
Francis Burdett, who favor extension of the franchise, advise Philip Stanton, the
novel's hero, that in his speeches he should advocate the "general necessity of
parliamentary reform," because the people would not be prepared for "universal
suffrage . . . till education had very much further advanced and qualified men to
understand their duty as well as their rights, and to discern their true friends from
their enemies in disguise" (2.11.274–75).

Consequently, the people do not act on the basis of their own rational thought
but are manipulated by demagogues, "the great mass" of men being "ready to
listen to any advocates of brute force, and to follow the most ruinous counsels"
(3.2.49). Stanton himself deems the people "idiots" for "listen[ing]" to the "raving
madness" of leaders who urge an uprising (3.8.171) and elsewhere "wonder[s]" at
the gross stupidity of the men who put their trust in a fellow so ignorant and brutal" (3.8.177).[7] The narrator and Stanton both depict the men as "dupes" (3.9.182,
3.12.262), Stanton insisting that they fall prey to "demagogues" precisely because
they lack education (3.12.262).

In keeping with this use of parliamentary discourse, the novel also depicts the
incapacity to reason as resulting in the madness of revolutionary insurrection.
In keeping with the general principles of the Hampden Clubs, for which he
lectures, Stanton campaigns for "constitutional reform, and parliamentary representation, through universal suffrage" solely through the means of "petition, and

by renunciation of physical force" (2.7.197–98). However, the Spencean wing of the clubs advances doctrines of physical force, asking, as would some Chartists, "Where was the power of moral force without physical force at the end of it?" (2.9.248–49). In the near term, Stanton is able to persuade the people to use "moral suasion in opposition to force" (2.11.308), but in the end the "great mass" of men listen to the "advocates of brute force" (3.2.49) and the Spenceans succeed in shifting the "aim" of the radicals so that they decide "no longer to seek *reform, but revolution*" (3.8.168; emphasis added). The ignorance of the people thus leads them to the use of physical force and disqualifies them from the franchise.

After the failed uprising that ensues, Stanton shifts from giving speeches in favor of parliamentary reform to promoting popular education. Even while he is campaigning for the franchise, he has begun to see education as a necessary preliminary to its possession, for it is "education" that has given "dominance to the few over the almost countless many" and education "alone could turn these 'hands' into heads—could give to these toiling entities the privileges of souls" (3.2.47). Thus his first thought upon learning he has inherited an estate worth £15,000 a year is to "devote" himself to "popular education," which he deems "the only true foundation for national prosperity and political right" (3.12.362). "When they are educated," he concludes, "the people will know their duties and their friends, as well as any other class" (3.12.263).

While the narrator insists that now, in 1860, the people are educated, the novel does not depict the process of educating them. Instead, it displaces the process of educating the people and the resulting preference for the rational use of moral force onto Philip Stanton in a bildungsroman plot in which he becomes educated first about the oppression of the people and then about the necessity of education itself. Although his father, an oppressed younger son of a baronet, becomes an advocate for the people who holds radical views on the corruption of the governing elite, Philip manages to grow up ignorant of the misery of the people (see 1.4.120–22). The young curate Lawrence Hyde must educate him, first by showing him "the great distress" of the "manufacturing districts" and then by providing him with a course of reading in radical literature (2.3.76). While this education initially leads Stanton to join the radical cause that embroils him in the use of physical force, the latter experience in turn teaches him to become a moral-force advocate of popular education.

The effect of depicting the education of Stanton, who already belongs to the educated elite, and omitting the education of the "ignorant" people is to raise the question of whether the people can ever be educated or possess social agency. While Howitt clearly believes that the people should be enfranchised, the unbridged gap between the people as represented in the plot of the novel and the people of 1860 as described by the narrator leaves in place the hierarchy of cultivated elite and ignorant people. Instead of a process in which the ignorant become educated, the novel tends to reinforce the binary that had, in parliamentary discourse, underwritten the exclusion of the people from social agency.

~

We can shed some light on this bifurcation between the depiction of the people as uneducated, and possibly uneducable, and the claim that they are now educated by turning to *Felix Holt*. Whereas the narrator of *The Man of the People* celebrates the education of the people, the narrator of *Felix Holt* never suggests that there has been progress in education. Rather, Eliot's characteristically cosmopolitan narrator questions the reformers' "faith in the efficacy of political change" and implies that in 1866 such optimistic "hope" is no longer widespread (16.179). What dictates this view is not philosophic pessimism but the novel's conception of what constitutes social agency. Like *The Man of the People*, *Felix Holt* employs parliamentary discourse insisting that one must be educated in order to exercise the franchise responsibly, but rather than treating education as the means of obtaining social agency, it instead substitutes education for the franchise, making it the only authentic form of agency. In doing so, it puts into question what constitutes social agency not only by questioning the franchise but also by questioning both the class as social agent and the principle of reform.

In some situations, Felix Holt, like Philip Stanton, appears to regard education as the necessary preparation for responsible exercise of the franchise. When a trade-unionist orator contends that "we must get the suffrage, we must get votes, that we may send the men to parliament who will do our work for us," Holt responds that working people need "something else *before* all that" (30.290; emphasis added). In his contention that "extension of the suffrage can never mean anything for them but extension of boozing" unless they learn to find that "there's something they love better than swilling themselves with ale" and in his plans to "educat[e] the non-electors," Holt would seem to suggest that the "something else before all that" is an education that will enable the working classes to wield power responsibly (11.130, 30.292, 5.73).

Elsewhere, however, it becomes clear that he believes that the franchise is not an effective form of agency and that, rather than preparing them for the franchise, he wishes to substitute education for it. In response to the trade unionist, he argues that "voting" will not do much toward "giving every man a man's share in life" (30.292), and he defines his radicalism by asserting that he "want[s] to go to some roots a good deal lower down than the franchise" (27.264). He never explicitly states what he regards as more fundamental than the franchise, but his constant emphasis on education together with his relationship to Esther Lyon make clear that his desire to "take a little knowledge and common sense to" working men makes cultivation of the self not merely antecedent to the franchise but a replacement for it (5.73).

The novel thus treats the election and education as opposed forms of agency, an opposition dramatized in chapter 11, which depicts Holt's attempts to educate the miners of Sproxton followed by Johnson's attempt to gain their support for Harold Transome's candidacy for Parliament. While Holt wants to "educat[e] the non-electors," Johnson seeks to persuade men who "haven't got a vote" that they can improve their lives by "send[ing] the right men"—men who will "get the law made all right" for them—to Parliament (11.136). He thus urges them to "giv[e] a cheer for" Transome at the hustings, by which he means physically intimidating speakers and voters (11.139). Earlier in this chapter, Holt offers education specifically as an alternative to such election practices. He hopes to "move these men to save something from their drink and pay a schoolmaster for their boys," in which case "a greater service would be done them than if Mr Garstin [another candidate] and his company were persuaded to establish a school" (11.130). Whereas Johnson and Transome offer the men agency only in the form of using physical force to help elect an MP to act on their behalf, Holt suggests that the men can act for themselves by establishing a school on their own. The goal, moreover, is not to educate themselves in order to obtain the vote. In response to the trade unionist who asserts that they "must get the suffrage" so that they can "send the men to parliament who will do [their] work for" them (30.290), Holt replies that they already have agency, that "if you go the right way to work you may get power sooner without votes" (20.292).

Holt argues not only that the people do not yet have the wisdom to vote responsibly but also that wisdom will show them that voting will never achieve desirable change because the franchise as a form of social agency is linked to the class as social agent. Holt concurs with the trade unionist that members of Parliament pursue self-interest, that "men are not ashamed in parliament and out of it to make public questions which concern the welfare of millions a mere screen for their own petty private ends" (30.293). However, he goes on to suggest that the working class is no different, that while there may be thirty men in a hundred who are "sober," the "ignorance" and self-interest of the other 70 percent means that as a class it will not "do much towards governing a great country, and making wise laws, and giving shelter, food, and clothes to millions of men" (30.293, 292). Eliot makes this view even more explicit in Holt's "Address to Working Men" (1868), in which he contends that "any large body of men is likely to have more of stupidity, narrowness, and greed than of farsightedness and generosity" (489). Thus when he says he wants the men to have "another sort of power," he means a power different than the franchise, a power that is not exercised by a self-interested social class but is based on "the ruling belief in society about what is right and what is wrong" (30.292, 293).

Holt's logic implies that it is impossible to educate a class, that it is impossible for a class *as* a class to gain the knowledge and wisdom to act beyond its own interests. Consequently, the men at Sproxton do not take up Holt's offer to be educated and instead accept Johnson's petty bribes. Similarly, at the poll they follow the trade unionist's suggestions that they give a "hint"—the word used by Johnson to suggest physical intimidation—to voters, and proceed to riot on election day (30.291). When the men act as a class, they inevitably resort to physical force because the majority do not have the cultivation to employ moral force. Holt's argument that the majority of the working class is "drunken and stupid" means that even if he did manage to educate a few men, he would not change how they behave as a class (30.294). As his comment that "while Caliban is Caliban, though you multiply him by a million, he'll worship every Trinculo that carries a bottle" makes clear, he regards members of the working class as irrational and liable to being influenced by demagogues (27.264). In arguing that classes act self-interestedly, Holt implies that the class as social agent would always use the franchise in this way, that, contrary to the claims of various classes, none has the privileged capacity to act for the nation as a whole. When he refuses to rise above the working class (see 5.64), he is not arguing against social change but rejecting class as a way of defining that change. Thus he considers it no "virtue" that he does not use his education to enhance his status but insists on cultivating himself in order to advance his "inward vocation" (27.263).

Just as *The Man of the People* displaces the education of the people onto Stanton, so *Felix Holt* displaces it onto Esther Lyon and in turn onto Holt himself. Whereas Holt fails to educate the Sproxton men, he does educate and "change" Esther Lyon (10.123). When he first meets Esther, he is critical of her precisely because she conceives herself in terms of class and wishes to be a lady. Assuming the role of her "pedagogue" (45.435), he follows the Arnoldian program of teaching her to "rise above the idea of class" in order to become her "best self."[8] The result is an "inward revolution" that recapitulates Holt's own "conversion," which has led him to prefer following his "inward vocation" to joining the upper classes (49.464, 5.62, 27.263).[9]

These displacements correspond to the way these novels depict their protagonists as men of the people and simultaneously as distinct from them, as outside of class. Although Stanton acquires the reputation of being a "man of the people" he is not really of the people. It is Lawrence Hyde, the curate who educates him, who is "of the people, not of the aristocracy" (2.3.87). As the OED indicates, "man of the people" can indicate both a person who *comes from* the people and a person who *identifies with* the people. Through his education, Stanton comes to identify with the people, but as he is not "of the people," he acts rather as a demagogue, the "exhorter, leader, teacher of the people" (2.7.201). Not insignificantly, the "people" call him a "man of the people" in response to one of his speeches on behalf of the franchise, but the narrator concludes the novel by deeming him a "man of the people" because of how he has acted "on their behalf," a depiction that distinctly separates him from the people (2.11.290, 3.15.340).

Similarly, Holt, as a number of commentators have observed, does not seem to belong to the working class, even as he insists that he has no aspirations to leave it.[10] In part, as Christopher Hobson points out, this is because he is in the Arnoldian sense an "alien," of the working class but alien to it because he aspires to become his best self (25). The fact that the "conversion" that leads him to this aspiration results from "six weeks' debauchery" implies that he has left behind the merely animal life that he later describes as characteristic of working-class existence (5.62). Just as Stanton is called the man of the people but acts like a demagogue, so Holt wants to remain in the working class but to act as a "demagogue of a new sort; an honest one, if possible, who will tell the people they are blind and foolish" (27.262). While he means to contrast himself with the kind of demagogue who flatters the people and does not seek to change them, he simultaneously distinguishes himself from the irrational people who are susceptible to such flattery. This is consistent with his view that the people would be better off with a school they have funded themselves than with one funded by the governing elite, yet it nonetheless reinstates a division within the working class between the cultivated and the uncultivated that the novel finds no way to bridge insofar as the people seem to be intrinsically incapable of being cultivated.

⌒

In describing the education of Esther as an "inward revolution," the narrator of *Felix Holt* inverts the conventional Victorian opposition between revolution and reform. Whereas parliamentary discourse had depicted revolution as the dangerous undermining of the social order and reform as maintaining the constitutional order, Eliot's novel treats reform as the action of a class that is always limited to its self-interest, in contrast to revolution, which involves a transformation of the self into disinterested citizen. It is this view of legislation and programs of reform as always partial and limited that has raised concerns about how Eliot's novel seems always to forestall the possibility of any kind of action. To take it on its own terms, however, the novel is insisting that there is no possibility of meaningful change, no authentic agency, except through revolution.

Paradoxically, this version of the opposition between revolution and reform underwrites the critical perspective that has led to critiques of the novel's conservatism. While its skepticism about reform has long led critics to claim that Felix Holt the radical is actually a Tory, the novel is radical in the sense cited by Holt that it seeks change at the "root," change that completely transforms social being. In critiquing a liberalism advocating political measures that do not fundamentally transform society, the novel anticipates the way in which much contemporary criticism critiques the liberalism of Eliot's era and our own. The current conception of social agency as revolution leads to critiques of reform measures that do not completely transform the social order as mere palliatives, which ultimately work to accommodate individuals to the existing order and thus are ultimately pernicious.[11]

As with Eliot, however, this dismissal of any attempt at reform as partial and flawed risks becoming an argument against attempting any change at all and, in the name of holding out for revolution, becomes a kind of quietism or conservatism. Perhaps nothing short of social transformation can produce a just society that promotes the flourishing of all individuals, but the history of the last two centuries also raises questions about what constitutes genuine revolution. To many who value literature and culture, Eliot's insistence on inward revolution that transforms consciousness defines the only certain way to achieve such transformation. However, such cultivation of the self requires some means of social intervention, which is why Felix Holt's refusal of reform remains problematic. The history of the Victorian conception of social agency as reform offers us a way of thinking about social agency that can act in relation to present conditions, not merely in relation to a theoretical ideal toward which we might aspire. In this respect, reform can bridge the gap between culture and the uncultivated by accepting that particular actions are self-interested, limited, and flawed but can also serve as a way forward.

Notes

CHAPTER 1: Social Agency

1. The title of the 1832 bill as passed was "An Act to Amend the Representation of the People in England and Wales," but throughout the debates leading to its passage MPs referred to it as the "Reform of Parliament Bill" or, more commonly, the "Reform Bill"; public discussions of the bill, both at the time of its passage and subsequently, almost invariably used the latter term.

2. For example, the *Times* asserted in its leading article of 5 Apr. 1832, that "nearly all the opponents of the Reform Bill . . . denounce the Government measure as pregnant with danger and revolution" (2). See also Wahrman 332.

3. Studies that take this approach are too numerous to cite here. As a stand-in we can note the use of the term in glossaries and encyclopedias of criticism and theory. Wolfreys, Robbins, and Womack succinctly define agency as "literally 'activeness'; more usually used to suggest one's ability to act on the world on one's own behalf or the extent to which one is empowered to act by the various *ideological* frameworks within which one operates" (5; emphasis added). The basic opposition of agency and structure (the "ideological frameworks") can be found in many of the entries of *The Johns Hopkins Guide to Literary Theory and Criticism* (Groden, Kreiswirth, and Szeman; see, for example, the entries on "Feminist Theory and Criticism: 1990 and After" and "New Historicism"). That agency has hardly been theorized or studied apart from ideology is evident from the fact that Wolfreys, Robbins, and Womack are the only authors of such a text to provide an entry on agency. Abrams's *Glossary of Literary Terms*, Baldick's *Concise Oxford Dictionary of Literary Terms*, and the *Hopkins Guide* use the term *agency* within various entries, but none has a separate entry defining it.

4. The definition of agency in terms of ideology theory has dictated that most criticism has focused on the ability to think or know apart from hegemonic structures of discourse, or what Amanda Anderson calls the power of distance. Work such as Anderson's has contributed a great deal to my own analyses, and I see my work as complementing, not challenging it.

5. The best expression of this view, and the one that has influenced me the most, is Raymond Williams's *Marxism and Literature*. While one can find similar views in other Marxist literary critiques (e.g., Fredric Jameson in *The Political Unconscious* 79),

much literary criticism, as I have argued elsewhere, has treated ideology as a fixed entity that predetermines the operations of literary discourse ("What Did *Jane Eyre* Do?" esp. 48–51).

6. I have in mind studies such as Catherine Gallagher's *Industrial Reformation of English Fiction* and Rosemarie Bodenheimer's *The Politics of Story in Victorian Social Fiction*, to both of which I am deeply indebted. Most prominent among other studies of the social-problem novel are Cazamian, Claybaugh, Guy, Lesjak, and Zlotnick. Guy typifies this work in situating these novels in relation to economic discourse; her study is complemented by Poovey's *Making a Social Body*, which focuses primarily on economic discourse and devotes a chapter to Disraeli and Gaskell.

7. See the preceding note. While the canon of what Cazamian called the "social novel" ("roman social") is relatively capacious, more recent studies have tended to confine themselves to what Williams called, in *Culture and Society*, "industrial novels." To his grouping of Gaskell's *Mary Barton* and *North and South*, Dickens's *Hard Times*, Kingsley's *Alton Locke*, Disraeli's *Sybil*, and Eliot's *Felix Holt*, later studies have added Charlotte Brontë's *Shirley*, Charlotte Elizabeth Tonna's *Helen Fleetwood*, Frances Trollope's *Michael Armstrong*, and Elizabeth Stone's *William Langshaw*, all of which merit inclusion because they deal with industrial labor.

8. Epstein, *Radical Expression* 27; Vernon, *Politics* 298. On the importance of constitutionalist discourse, see Vernon, *Re-reading the Constitution* chap. 1; Epstein, *Radical Expression* chap. 1; and Belchem, esp. 6.

9. See chap. 2.

10. As recent work on the history of class (e.g., Cannadine; Joyce, *Class*; Vernon, *Politics*; Wahrman) has demonstrated, the social classes defined by political discourse were only loosely related to the material conditions of the people to which they referred. Even if one questions Joyce's contention that class conflict was not as pronounced or fundamental as previous work has suggested, one can, like Cannadine, accept the principle that class discourse does not necessarily match the realities of material conditions. This argument is analogous to the sex/gender distinction. Just as we distinguish between biological sex as a material reality and gender as a discourse that has a relation to but is not solely determined by it, the material stratification of society is distinct from the discourses of class (see my "What Did *Jane Eyre* Do?" 49–50).

11. Vol. 1, book 1, chap. 2, pp. 171–72. It should be noted that while Blackstone is codifying current understandings, he does not claim that the existing system is perfect and worries that it is insufficiently representative.

12. As Sara Maurer has shown, even as liquid capital increased in importance, landed property retained a powerful hold on the social imagination (10–11).

13. This paragraph also draws on Perkin, esp. chap. 7.

14. On the discursive history of "the people," see Joyce, *Visions of the People*; Vernon, *Politics*; and Wahrman 196–207.

15. Among the few works of criticism to examine the appropriation of radical discourse by mainstream Victorian novelists are Sen's "*Bleak House* and *Little Dorrit:* The Radical Heritage" and Ledger's *Dickens and the Popular Radical Imagination*. In my conception of the dialogic operations of parliamentary and Chartist discourses, I am indebted, of course, to Bakhtin (see esp. 271–73).

16. Trumpener and Ferris both conclude their studies of the national tale around

1830 and do not therefore explore its later history. There are, of course, numerous studies that trace the afterlife of the historical novel in the Victorian era but none that examines specifically the ways that it continues to employ the key elements of the national tale. Corbett has noted that the narrative structures of condition-of-England novels closely resemble those of Irish national tales. However, her focus is on how "class divisions internal to English culture" are "discursively bound within the 1830s and 1840s to the condition of the Irish in England" (85), that is, on nation and ethnicity, while my focus is on how these novels use this structure to represent class conflict. For a reconsideration of Trumpener's argument that Scott's historical novels translated spatial difference into temporal difference governed by a teleology of modernization, see Duncan 98–101.

17. While she does not link them to constitutional histories, Trumpener argues that these genres developed out of Enlightenment political thought, and her analysis throughout treats them as a form of political discourse (137). Scott's *Ivanhoe* (1820), for example, novelizes the myth of the Norman yoke so central to constitutional history. Indeed, *Ivanhoe* begins the process of internalizing the conflict to England. It adapts many of the character groupings and plot elements of *Waverley*, retaining the opposition between nations/ethnicities while internalizing the opposition of metropole and periphery to England, so that the Normans and Saxons are divided socially and politically but occupy the same geographic space.

18. *North and South*'s inheritance from the national tale manifests itself in John Thornton's assertion that northerners have "Teutonic blood," which he opposes to the "Greek" culture of Oxford and the south (2.15.334). As noted above, Corbett discusses the relationship between race and class in these novels, but the focus in her discussion of *North and South* is on the Irish laborers rather than the way class is linked to ethnicity. See also Betensky, who discusses the two-nations trope of *Sybil* and *North and South* as an attempt to envision a "cohesive nation" (60).

19. On equality as a major feature of the companionate marriage, see Stone 217–19.

20. My discussion of companionate and kinship marriage is indebted to Stone. However, I am concerned not with actual marriage practices but with the discourse of marriage that intersects with the discourses of class and gender that novels repeatedly invoked. In short, whether or not there was a historical shift in marriage practices, we can say that the literary tradition repeatedly depicts the companionate ideal displacing kinship unions.

21. I refer to the well-established critical tradition of reading Scott's novels as seeking to find in the archaic past a model of disinterest that can be the means of reforming the self-interestedness of an otherwise superior modern culture. While this reading and its variants can be found in many studies of Scott and the historical novel, most studies focus on the relation of the novels to formal history writing and philosophies of history rather than to the contemporary constitutional histories constructed in political debate. For a discussion that does allude to these contemporary concerns, see Lincoln 4–5, 68–71.

CHAPTER 2: Social Agency in the Chartist and Parliamentary Press

1. Haywood attributes this anonymously published work to Thomas Doubleday (3). It appeared in installments from 19 Jan. to 30 Mar. 1839. For convenience of reference, I cite Haywood's edition.

2. The newspapers I focus on in this chapter—the Chartist *Northern Star* and the

Charter; the *Times* and the *Morning Post*, which supported the Tories; and the *Examiner* and the *Morning Chronicle*, which backed the Whigs—represent this partisan flavor. I have selected this particular group of papers because they were widely circulated and are representative of a range of views. Moreover, the fact that the papers most widely responded to are in this group suggests that each regarded the others as their chief rhetorical foes. The *Northern Star*, for example, very often responds to the *Morning Chronicle* and the *Times*, which it treats as party organs, and the elite press in turn often responded to it. In this context, I would note as well that the *Morning Chronicle* and the *Morning Post* were unabashedly partisan. The *Times* and the *Examiner* took more independent editorial stances, but for the most part during the era from 1837 to 1842 they were aligned with the Tories and Whigs, respectively. The *Times* broke with Tory policy when it came out for repeal of the Corn Laws in 1839, but it consistently attacked the Whig government and generally supported the Tories. Similarly, the *Examiner*, which, of course, had a history as a radical publication, was more sympathetic to the aims of Chartism than was the *Morning Chronicle*, but it also criticized the movement for damaging the Whig government, which it considered more friendly to the working classes than were the Tories.

3. Yeo points out that during the Reform Bill debates the Tories defined the enfranchised "people" as owners of property, not as the entire nation (47). In this discussion I am not concerned with all of the complexities of the concept of virtual representation, especially as found in its chief theorist, Edmund Burke (see Pitkin chap. 8; Judge 97–102), but rather with the rhetorical use to which it was put in parliamentary discourse. See, for example, the *Morning Post* quoting Burke's "Appeal from the New to the Old Whigs" as suggesting that the "wiser, the more expert, and the more opulent" should "protect the weaker, the less knowing, and the less provided with the goods of fortune" (21 Dec. 1838: 2).

4. For the Whigs' official opposition to the principle of virtual representation, see *Morning Chronicle* 17 Feb. 1838: 3, 8 Apr. 1839: 3, 6 May 1839: 3.

5. The previously cited editorial concludes that the working classes are represented by the middle class, which shares its interests (*Morning Chronicle* 5 Sept. 1838: 3). The *Examiner* also invoked virtual representation when, for example, it insisted that the Chartists were mistaken to try their "strength [i.e., arms] against the proprietary interests of the country . . . for the poor have not the power of sustaining any course of action apart from all the proprietary classes" (10 Nov. 1839: 705; see also 2 Feb. 1840: 74).

6. The Chartist press and Chartist oratory repeatedly described the parliamentary parties as "factions" (see *Northern Star* 25 Aug. 1838: 4, 8 Sept. 1838: 8, 22 Sept. 1838: 2–3, 29 Sept. 1838: 4, 6 Oct. 1838: 4, 13 Apr. 1839: 4; *Charter* 27 Jan. 1839: 1, 8). See also the Charter itself (*Northern Star* 16 June 1838: 3).

7. *Times* 26 Sept. 1838: 5. This sentence does not appear in the *Northern Star* report of Fielden's speech (29 Sept. 1838: 6). The difference is probably owing to the fact that these were stenographic reports, but it is nonetheless telling that the term appears in the *Times*, which as a Tory supporter was invested in the principle.

8. The Chartist press often repeated this argument. In one of its first editorials, the *Northern Star* complained that working people were "governed by the opposing interest[s]" of the elites with the result that the laws of the land aim to extract the most money from "those who are not represented" (17 Feb. 1838: 5; see also 28 July 1838: 3).

9. Other editorials similarly indicate the ultimate unity of the aristocracy and middle

class by using a third term that unites them. The editorial "Agricultural and Commercial 'Vampires'" ultimately resolves the difference between the "classes" by depicting them as different varieties of vampire (*Northern Star* 9 Mar. 1839: 4). The *Charter* in employing the phrase "the Lords of the land and Lords of the loom" similarly treats both as aristocracies (17 Mar. 1839: 120).

10. The term "class legislation" occurs over and over in the *Northern Star* and other Chartist papers. It originated in the Chartist press, with nearly all of the earliest instances of its use appearing in radical papers, including the *Northern Star*, the *Operative*, the *Northern Liberator*, the *Poor Man's Guardian*, the *Charter*, and so on. There are more than fifty such instances between October 1838 and November 1839 before it begins to appear in the elite London papers, and then only in reports of Chartist statements. The *Morning Chronicle* printed the term in 1839 (see 27 Nov. 1839: 4) but merely in quoting the Chartists; it became the first paper speaking for the parliamentary parties to take it up as a charge against the political opposition (i.e., the Tories) but did not do so until 1841 (19 June 1841: 4). Similarly, the term first appears in the *Morning Post* in the report of a Chartist speech (22 Jan. 1840: 3); it first uses it in parliamentary discourse, defending the Tories, in an editorial leader in 1842 (14 Mar. 1842: 3).

11. On the use of the language of interest earlier in the nineteenth century, see Wahrman 90–96. The elite press, while focusing on parliamentary politics, treated the parties as proxies for class interests, the Tories for the landowners and the Whigs for commercial entrepreneurs (e.g., *Morning Chronicle* 22 Dec. 1838: 2, 1 Feb. 1839: 2, Sept. 12, 1839: 2; *Morning Post* 10 Aug. 1839: 4). Thus when the *Northern Star* argues that "the Corn Law contest is a mere *party* struggle between the two *classes* of tyrants for the mastery over each other" it equates parties and classes (9 Mar. 1839: 4; emphasis added). Elsewhere it equates the "middle class" with the party in power, the Whigs (22 Sept. 1838: 2–3).

12. See *Northern Star* 2 Feb. 1839: 4, 15 Sept. 1838: 3, 26 Jan. 1839: 4.

13. See Vernon, *Politics* 303.

14. See, for example, *Times* 27 Apr. 1839: 5; *Morning Chronicle* 4 Jan. 1839: 4. Even the *Examiner*, which suggested that once the working classes become educated they should have the right to the vote, rationalized the exclusion of the "poor" from the franchise "on the score of the disqualification of ignorance" (9 Dec. 1838: 769).

15. On the depiction of the Chartist rank and file as dupes, see, for example, *Times* 21 Aug. 1839: 5, 30 Aug. 1839: 5, 12 Dec. 1839: 4, 7 Jan. 1839: 3, 4 Feb. 1839: 2, 17 Jan. 1840: 2.

16. It maintained, for example, that the "populace . . . appear to be stung almost to madness by the treachery of the Whigs, who *were* their teachers and leaders in revolutionary violence, and *are* the most tyrannically harsh in *denying* them, what formerly they led them to *expect*" (18 Oct. 1838: 2). See also 6 Sept. 1838: 2, 18 Sept. 1838: 2, 29 Sept. 1838: 2, 3 Jan. 1839: 2, 9 Aug. 1839: 4, 9 Nov. 1839: 2; *Times* 15 Oct. 1838: 4, 25 Apr. 1839: 4, 21 May 1839: 3, 20 June 1839: 5.

17. In characteristic fashion, the *Chronicle* could read a *Times* editorial as evidence of partisan exploitation of Chartism: the "eagerness with which the Tory press has made the Newport riot a weapon of attack on [Whig] Ministers shows that the party thinks a clever game has been played" (12 Nov. 1839: 2).

18. Tilly emphasizes the idea that the historical literature, even that sympathetic to Chartism, has reproduced this discourse by treating Chartism as symptomatic, as a sign of working-class suffering, rather than a form of political action (24–41).

19. See also 19 July 1839: 2; *Examiner* 20 Aug. 1842: 529, 534. The *Morning Chronicle* more directly depicts men who disrupted anti–Corn Law meetings as "a section of the Chartists . . . which Toryism has pushed forward to do its dirty work" (7 Feb. 1839: 4) and notes that "it has been often remarked that those agitators who first put it into the heads of the Chartists to procure arms and have torch-light meetings were Tories; and the Tory journals did not conceal their joy at the spread of Chartism" (20 Feb. 1840: 2). Once the Tories came to power, the Whig press turned the tables and blamed the 1842 strike wave on the failure of the government to maintain order (e.g., *Examiner* 20 Aug. 1842: 534).

20. The *Chronicle*, for example, complained that "Toryism and Chartism have lovingly made common cause together" in opposition to repeal of the Corn Laws (25 Mar. 1840: 4), and the *Morning Post* traced the Whigs' "alliance with violent men" to the Reform Bill era, when the former sought the support of working-class radicals (3 Jan. 1839: 2). Elsewhere the *Chronicle* claimed that "Chartism is the natural re-action of Toryism, with which for the moment it is in a most unnatural alliance" (3 Jan. 1840: 2). See also 23 Mar. 1840: 2, 20 Apr. 1841: 2, 22 Apr. 1841: 2, 23 Apr. 1841: 2, 24 Apr. 1841: 4; 5 June 1841: 6, 13 Oct. 1841: 2. For the Tory allegations, see *Morning Post* 6 May 1839: 4, 19 July 1839: 4, 22 July 1839: 4, 9 Aug. 1839: 4; *Times*, 19 Nov. 1839: 4.

21. The *Times*, for example, claimed that the "Whig Ministers" were "the actual founders of this Chartist agitation" and were paying them "out of the public purse . . . to agitate for the charter" (21 May 1839: 3), while the Whig press voiced suspicions that the Tories were funding Chartist agitation in order to undermine the stability of the Whig government. Similarly, during the strike wave of 1842 (when the Tories were in power), the *Morning Chronicle* cited evidence of Chartists being in the pay of the Tories for the purpose of disrupting anti–Corn Law meetings (23 Feb. 1842: 5–6, 17 Aug. 1842: 2, 31 Aug. 1842: 2; *Examiner* 20 Aug. 1842: 535, 27 Aug. 1842: 552), while the *Times*, which headlined its reports on the strikes "The Anti–Corn Law League Riots," insisted that the riots were led by "strangers, supposed to be hired by the Anti–Corn Law League" and that there was "no doubt" that the league was "at the bottom of the outbreak" (11 Aug. 1842: 5; see also 12 Aug. 1842: 5, 13 Aug. 1842: 5). For other allegations of Tory bribery, see *Morning Chronicle* 13 Apr. 1841: 3, 23 Feb. 1842: 5, 6; *Examiner* 26 Feb. 1842: 139.

22. The *Times* described Chartist leaders as "insidious and designing demagogues" who "poison the minds of the people" (25 Sept. 1838: 3; see also 11 May 1839: 5, 15 June 1842: 8). The *Examiner* described a Chartist orator as "a spouting demagogue" (26 Jan. 1840: 57), the *Morning Chronicle* referred to "demagogues and their deluded followers" (30 Apr. 1839: 3; see also 1 Sept. 1838: 2), and the *Morning Post* depicted the leadership as a "demagogue tribe" seeking to increase the "numbers of their infatuated dupes" (28 Sept. 1838: 2).

23. The *Examiner* similarly contended that "the Chartist organization . . . neither included the middle classes nor the better part of the working population. . . .They call themselves the masses, but they are no more the masses than the dust in a whirlwind" (10 Nov. 1839: 705), and the *Chronicle* insisted that "the great body of the operatives never were Chartists" (25 Feb. 1840: 2).

24. The press frequently questioned the motives of the Chartist leadership: "There is a very wide distinction between the motives which influence the great mass of our countrymen who now enrol [sic] themselves under the banners of Chartism, and the motives which influence most, if not all, of their principal leaders" (*Times* 28 Dec. 1842: 5).

25. See, for example, *Morning Chronicle* 25 Sept. 1838: 2, 28 Dec. 1838: 3, 27 May 1839: 3; *Examiner* 2 June 1839: 347; *Times* 8 Aug. 1838: 6, 18 Sept. 1838: 6; *Morning Post* 18 Sept. 1838: 2, 22 May 1839: 2.

26. For descriptions of major Chartist meetings as failures, even a "miserable failure" or "complete failure," see *Times* 8 Aug. 1838: 6, 18 Sept. 1838: 6, 26 Sept. 1838: 5; *Morning Chronicle* 25 Sept. 1838: 2; *Morning Post* 18 Sept. 1838: 2, 27 May 1839: 1; *Examiner* 16 Sept. 1838: 597, 2 June 1839: 347. The *Times* suggested that many in attendance at the August 7, 1838, meeting at Birmingham were drinking rather than listening to the orators (8 Aug. 1838: 6); it elsewhere insisted that the large turnout at the September 24, 1838, meeting at Kersal Moor was the result of the leadership coercing factory owners to let men off work and suggested that many in attendance did not take the occasion seriously but were playing "leap-frog" and drinking "potions" (26 Sept. 1838: 5; see also *Chronicle* 28 Sept. 1838: 2; *Morning Post* 26 Sept. 1838: 3).

27. In spite of the fact that the Chartists situated their campaign within a constitutional framework that respects the rights of property, the parliamentary press frequently linked the purportedly revolutionary aims of the Chartists to an attack on private property. The hidden agenda of the Chartists, Archibald Alison contended, was to "pillage all the property of the kingdom, and divide the whole possessions of the wealthy classes among themselves" (294). The papers were quick to interpret damage to property resulting from the Chartist agitations as a sign of a "war against property," and a reporter investigating the Bull Ring riots at Birmingham claimed that "many of the Chartists are Socialists" who aim "by the destruction of property, to reduce all to the equality of property" (*Morning Post* 22 July 1839: 4; *Morning Chronicle* 22 July 1839: 3). To be sure, many Chartists were followers of Robert Owen and Thomas Spence, who had attacked private property, but their main focus was always on parliamentary representation, not on property. Nonetheless, the elite press frequently paired socialism and Chartism in order to suggest that, as the *Chronicle* put it, the movement's "theories" had "nothing whatsoever to do with politics" but were "directed entirely against property" (27 Nov. 1838: 2). On contemporary use of the term *socialism*, see chap. 10.

28. See, for example, an article from the *Weekly Chronicle* stating that while it hoped that a time would come "when the masses in this country may be trusted with the franchise," they had "by their own words and acts . . . done more to convince the most ardent advocates of popular rights of the impossibility of trusting them with it" (reprinted in *Morning Chronicle* 27 Nov. 1838: 2).

29. The *Times*, for example, deplored the Chartists' use of "violent and inflammatory language" (29 Apr. 1839: 5; see also 29 Mar. 1839: 6), and the *Morning Post* criticized the "inflammatory manifesto against life and property" issued by the National Convention (16 May 1839: 4), while the *Morning Chronicle* described a Chartist orator as addressing a "meeting in the usual violent and inflammatory language" (30 Apr. 1839: 3).

30. See, for example, 16 Sept. 1838: 597, 30 Sept. 1838: 614, 31 Oct. 1838: 664–65.

31. However, there is evidence that some Chartists were well aware that torchlight processions contained an element of physical threat; as one of them put it, they presented a "striking and imposing scene" (quoted in Chase, *Chartism* 37).

32. 8 Dec. 1838: 2; see also 25 Aug. 1838: 2, 23 Nov. 1839: 2, 17 Dec. 1839: 2; *Morning Chronicle* 22 July 1839: 2, 1 Aug. 1839: 3, 8 Nov. 1839: 3; *Examiner* 28 July 1839: 465; *Times* 10 Oct. 1842: 4.

33. The *Morning Chronicle* similarly opposed "all theories which would enable poverty and ignorance to give law to the community" (4 Jan. 1839: 2), while the *Times* argued that universal suffrage would result in the "despotism of the ignorant pauper multitude over the enlightened minority of a nation" (27 Apr. 1839: 5).

34. See *Northern Star* 29 Sept. 1838: 6–7, 17 Feb. 1838: 5, 16 Feb. 1839: 4, 27 July 1839: 3, 7 Sept. 1839: 3. The last two articles cited, like other constitutional discourse, invoke the authority of Blackstone. From March 3 to May 5, 1839 the *Charter* ran a weekly series on the right to universal suffrage (3 Mar. 1839: 85, 10 Mar. 1839: 101, 17 Mar. 1839: 123, 24 Mar. 1839: 133, 31 Mar. 1839: 149, 7 Apr. 1839: 173, 14 Apr. 1839: 180, 21 Apr. 1839: 196, 28 Apr. 1839: 213, 5 May 1839: 230). Although the first article employed Paineite arguments for a natural right to the franchise, the next seven articles employed constitutional history (complete with footnoted citation of authorities).

35. O'Connor as reported in the *Northern Star* 8 Sept. 1838: 8; *Charter* 10 March 1839: 101 (see also *Northern Star* 17 Feb. 1838: 5). The articles in the *Charter* cited in the previous note invoked the Norman yoke throughout, tracing universal suffrage to "the constitution raised by our Saxon progenitors" and the present state to encroachments beginning with the "Norman usurpation" (10 Mar. 1839: 101); the editorial leader of the first issue of the paper contends that "the Charter is merely a RESTORATION of principles and of practices which were coeval with the constitution" (27 Jan. 1839: 8).

36. The phrase "repertoire of contention" is from Tilly (see 6–13, 41–48). On the constitutional justifications of these actions, see Epstein, *Radical Expression* 11, 20; Belchem 7. Such appeals are especially evident when, for example, the *Northern Star* contends that in summarily dismissing the Chartist petition Parliament denies the right to petition (11 May 1839: 4; see also 8 Sept. 1838: 8). On claims for the constitutional right of assembly and the right to bear arms, see *Northern Star* 15 Dec. 1838: 4, 1 June 1839: 4, 4 May 1839: 3. As the *Star* insisted (see 27 July 1839: 3, 7 Sept. 1839: 3), these rights had been confirmed by Blackstone, who states that in order to preserve liberty, "it is necessary that the constitution of parliament be supported in its full vigour; and limits, certainly known, be set to the royal prerogative. And, lastly, to vindicate these rights, when actually violated or attacked, the subjects of England are entitled, in the first place, to the regular administration and free course of justice in the courts of law; next, to the right of petitioning the king and parliament for redress of grievances; and, lastly, to the right of having and using arms for self-preservation and defence" (vol. 1, book 1, chap. 1, p. 104). Blackstone does not discuss assembly here, but as he implies elsewhere in this passage, the right to petition was taken to include the right to assemble in order to petition.

37. See *Northern Star* 22 Sept. 1838: 2–3, 4 May 1839: 3, 11 May 1839: 4, 7 Sept. 1839: 3; *Charter* 24 Mar. 1839: 136–137.

38. A condensed version of this thread of my argument has previously appeared in my article "On Chartism."

CHAPTER 3: **Egalitarian Chivalry and Popular Agency in *Wat Tyler***

1. A letter to the *Times* (2 Nov. 1840: 7), a response, apparently by Egan (6 Nov. 1840: 3), and a review of the first number in the *Era* (20 Dec. 1840: 6) indicate that it had recently commenced serial publication. As I have not been able to locate a copy of the novel in the serial format, I cite the first book edition (1841).

2. *Wat Tyler* followed the considerable success of Egan's first novel, *Robin Hood and*

Little John (1840), and Egan continued to be a successful novelist into the 1860s. The novel was reprinted in 1845, 1846, 1847, 1850, and 1851; after that there seems to have been a lack of demand, as no new editions appeared. One indication of its broad circulation is that the late nineteenth-century working-class author William McGonagall wrote a poem, "Grif of the Bloody Hand," based on an episode that appears only in Egan's novel.

3. The tradition begins with medieval chronicles, the first being Froissart, and continues in the various English recensions of the history of Tyler's rebellion in Stow, Baker, Holinshed, and so on. Later literary renditions, including *The just reward of rebels; or, the life and death of Jack Straw and Wat Tyler* (1642) as well as John Cleveland's *Idol of the Clownes* (1654) and *Wat Tyler and Jack Straw, or the Mob Reformers* (1730), continued to treat him as a traitor and a villain in both senses of the word. Later historians such as Hume, though more nuanced, also treated him as a traitor rather than a hero. For a brief discussion of the historical reputation of Wat Tyler and the uprising, see Dunn 149–52; for a discussion of the sources of nineteenth-century representations of Tyler and the rebellion, see Vaninskaya, who also briefly discusses Egan's novel.

4. *Times* 22 Aug. 1789: 2. See also 1 Jan. 1790: 2, 4 Aug. 1791: 2.

5. An engraving of Fuseli's painting appeared in Charles Allen's *New and Improved History of England* (1793), which Egan cites as one of the sources for his novel (ii). Egan illustrated the same scene for the novel (3.9.785).

6. See Storey 253–55. The articles were "Parliamentary Reform," *Quarterly Review* 16 (1816): 225–78; and "On the Rise and Progress of Popular Disaffection," *Quarterly Review* 16 (1817): 511–52.

7. *Northern Star* 20 Apr. 1839: 6; see also *London Dispatch and People's Political and Social Reformer* 18 June 1837: 1; *Morning Chronicle* 9 Mar. 1839: 5; *Charter* 10 Mar. 1839: 101. For allusions to Tyler in speeches given at Chartist demonstrations and in displays of names of, and toasts to, heroes at Chartist meetings, see *Northern Star* 29 Sept. 1838: 3, 20 Oct. 1838: 6, 26 Oct. 1839: 4, 16 Nov. 1839: 5, 27 Feb. 1841: 2. The rise in Tyler's popularity is also apparent from the fact that in the 1830s there were a number of theatrical productions titled *Wat Tyler and Jack Straw: or, The Life and Death of King Richard II* (see *Times* 18 Jan. 1831: 2, 5 Sept. 1834: 2, 13 Dec. 1836: 4).

8. I include within this category both the novels by Chartists identified by Ian Haywood and novels by others that represent Chartism, such as Disraeli's *Sybil*, Gaskell's *Mary Barton*, and Kingsley's *Alton Locke*. For fiction by Chartists, see Haywood, *Revolution in Popular Literature* chap. 6, as well as his two collections, *Chartist Fiction* and *The Literature of Struggle*. See also Vicinus 113–35; and Klaus chap. 8.

9. Admittedly, Tyler only enumerates five, making the sixth a "final" demand. In the histories there are various lists of the peasants' demands. Craik, the most recent source that Egan employed, lists the standard four but then in a footnote indicates one more (on abolition of game laws) added by Tyler.

10. Southey may have invented the detail of King Richard saying the people ought to petition (2.231). This right, which had been established in 1689 by the Bill of Rights, was widely exercised in the eighteenth century, and I have not been able to locate any reference to petitioning in earlier historical accounts.

11. The historical accounts, which provide scant information about Wat Tyler, inform us that he was chosen as leader of the uprising, led his followers to London, where they attacked various individuals and destroyed property, and that, in the second of two

encounters with Richard II, he was killed by the mayor of London, after which the rebellion collapsed. Egan apparently invented Tyler's earlier history, in which he fights side by side with Sir Walter Manny, John Chandos, Edward III, and other heroes of Froissart's *Chronicle* of the Hundred Years' War, on the basis of Froissart's oblique comment that Tyler had done service in France. In the preface to the first edition, he cites as his sources the chronicles of Froissart, Stow, Knyghton, Walsingham, and Holinshed, as well as Charles Allen's *New and Improved History of England* (1793) and Edward Brayley's *Topographical and Historical Description of London and Middlesex* (1810) (ii). In the novel itself, he cites Craik. None of these histories include anything like Egan's account of Tyler's early life.

12. Not coincidentally, Egan's first novel, *Robin Hood*, featured a character from *Ivanhoe*. Various details, in addition to the use of the myth of the Norman yoke, indicate Scott's influence on *Wat Tyler*. The Earl of Tonbridge—a "pure Saxon" who has lost his lands (1.13.134)—resembles Cedric the Saxon, and there is a servant named Gurth (though his name mutates after its first appearance into Gith, suggesting perhaps a typesetting error). The younger Maltravers's pseudonym, Martin du Bois, evokes Scott's villain Brian de Bois Guilbert, and the name Maltravers itself, though historical, echoes that of another *Ivanhoe* villain, Philip de Malvoisin. In the naming of the two chief female protagonists, Violet and Flora, however, he seems to have echoed Rose Bradwardine and Flora MacIvor of *Waverley*.

13. Egan surrounds Tyler with characters who have Saxon or pseudo-Saxon names. Ethelbert, Edric, Guthric, Ulfred, and Ulph (Ulf) are authentically Anglo-Saxon, while Leowulf, Halbert, Bulfric, Grayling, and Rycheart are not Anglo-Saxon but modeled on authentic Saxon names (e.g., Beowulf, Wulfric). Halbert, Benulph, and Hartulf are pseudo-Saxon constructions using Norse or Germanic roots. Editha is a variant of Eadgyth, and Ghita may be an error for Githa, a Danish royal name. Many of these names appear in Craik, who gives Editha as the name of the wife of Edward the Confessor and conflates the names as "Githa, or Editha, Harald's mother" (1:353). Evesham, the surname of Ethelbert and Halbert, is the name of a town in Worcestershire, named in turn for the Saxon shepherd Eof, whose vision of the Blessed Virgin led to the founding of the monastery there. Egan is unlikely to have known the precise origins of these names, but the general trend makes it clear that he meant these characters to be Saxon. In that context, we can note that the village of Brenchley in Kent had its origins in the Anglo-Saxon era and that its name also has Anglo-Saxon roots. I thank Tom Hall for assistance with this material.

14. In addition to the younger John Maltravers's three attempts to kidnap and one attempt to rape Violet Evesham, his father, the elder John Maltravers, and then Grif/ Ogle, both attempt to seduce and then confine Violet's aunt, Editha; Cuthbert du Bois, the cousin of the elder Maltravers, attempts to seduce and then confines Ghita, the mother of Violet and sister of Editha; the soldier Bulfric (who tells the tale of how he had attempted to seduce and molest Katrine, whom he eventually married and abandoned) attempts to abscond with the property of and then to achieve this end threatens the Flemish woman Rubacelle with rape; a group of thieves, among them John Maltravers, who is making one last attempt on Editha, "ill-use" May Farebelle, who lives in the village of the Forest of Dean, where Editha and Ghita have taken refuge (3.2.604); and Thomas de Bampton (one of the commissioners who investigated the peasant resistance to the poll

tax that led to the rebellion [Craik 758]) attempts to seduce the sister-in-law of Rupert, son of the Earl of Tonbridge. In all of these cases, except possibly the last and that of Bulfric, the villain is a Norman and the victim Saxon.

15. As Amanda Anderson has argued, the fallen woman in the Victorian novel frequently depicts the attenuated agency of women (*Tainted Souls* 1–2, 6–9). However, in *Wat Tyler* the figure operates differently in that the women never actually fall, so that while they do serve to indicate the relative agency of its heroes (as they do for heroines in the novels Anderson studies), they also can obtain agency.

16. Violet is ready to leap from a tower in order to escape du Bois but is rescued, and Editha carries a dagger that she threatens to use on herself if Maltravers touches her. The novel reinforces this ultramonogamy by having Halbert and Ethelbert express anxiety that their wives might not have killed themselves rather than be coerced into sexual relations (i.e., raped).

17. There are still other instances of this phenomenon. A Flemish woman whom Wat rescues during the Hundred Years' War falls in love with him (testing his monogamy) and, in spite of the fact that the entirely decent and chivalrous Chandos loves her, swears she will never marry when she learns of Wat's love for Violet. In turn, both Wat and his friend Michael remain steadfastly faithful to their lovers back home, even as the rank-and-file English soldiers think nothing of dallying with French women.

18. The formation of homosocial bonds through the mutual courtship of a woman that both men love was, of course, first discussed by Sedgwick (chap. 1), who in turn adapted Girard's conception of triangulated desire (chap. 1). While I read them in a different context than does Sedgwick, like her I find in them figurations of class and political power. Sharon Marcus's argument that female friendships play a major role in the heterosexual marriage plot complements my argument about the role played here, and in other novels discussed below, by male friendship (76; see chap. 2).

19. On the term *the people*, see chap. 1. Egan does not use the word *people* in terms of class discourse—usually signaled by the term *the people*—until book 3, chap. 10. The class context is also made evident by the fact that many of these instances refer to oppression of the people (see 3.10.790, 794, 795, 796, 799, 11.807, 816, 825, 827, 12.836, 837, 14.858, 861). On the use of the concept of the people as a means of claiming class agency, see Joyce, *Visions* 4–6, and on the way *the people* invokes a dichotomous model of class that seeks to negate the tripartite model, in which agency is confined to the competing aristocracy and middle class, see Cannadine 67 as well as chap. 2 above.

20. The novel here recalls the Chartists' complaint that they had expected that the Reform Bill of 1832 would be the first step toward expansion of suffrage and that the Whigs' claim that it was a final measure amounted to something like a return to bondage. The disenfranchisement of the freeman and return to bondage is the major theme of Mrs. O'Neill's *The Bondman: A Story of the Times of Wat Tyler*, published in 1835, just three years after passage of the Reform Bill.

21. In the medieval chronicles and early modern accounts, there is no connection between the two episodes. Egan was likely influenced by Craik's narrative, in which the Burley episode follows immediately after the assault on Tyler's daughter (758); however, Craik does not suggest that Tyler was discussing the former while the latter was taking place. The Burley episode does not appear in any of Egan's other sources (e.g., Froissart or Stow). Egan is relatively circumspect in his depiction of the assault on Tyler's daugh-

ter, stating only that the collector "swore a fearful oath that he would prove her a liar" and then rushed at her (3.10.797). However, the story that the collector sought to inspect her privates was widely circulated (for a contemporary example, see *London Dispatch and People's Political and Social Reformer* 18 June 1837: 1). Here is Stow's version: "The Tilers wife denied to pay for hir daughter, saying she was under age. Then sayd yᵉ Collector, that shal I soone wit, and toke the mayde violently, and dishonestly searched whether she were of age or no, wherwith the mother made an outcry, hyr husbande being in yᵉ towne at worke" (481). *The Just Reward of Rebels* even more explicitly states that he sought to "see if she had any *pubes* upon her" (A2r). The assault on Tyler's daughter does not appear in Froissart or the other earlier accounts, but some of them do mention the attempts of the collectors to search young women in order to determine whether they were of age to pay the poll tax (see Oman 27).

22. Tyler also exhorts his followers to temper their actions with "moderation, and with every consideration for those whose property our presence may make them believe in danger" (3.12.840). This aspect of Egan's portrayal in particular is indebted to Southey, whose Tyler, as Haywood points out, insists he does not seek to avenge his "private wrongs" but rather the mistreatment suffered by his fellow peasants (1.266; see Haywood, "Renovating Fury" par. 10ff.).

23. Whereas in Froissart, Tyler and his followers behead the archbishop of Canterbury and several other men along with him, in Egan's narrative these executions occur before Tyler arrives on the scene. Similarly, whereas Froissart implies Tyler's presence, if not participation, in the slaying of Flemings and Lombards, Egan has it, per the passage just quoted, that Tyler urges restraint. Not surprisingly, given his representation of Tyler's close relationship to the military command, Egan also omits Froissart's claim that Tyler personally beheaded Richard Lyon, whom he had served in France, presumably in the Hundred Years' War.

CHAPTER 4: Unconsummated Marriage and the "Uncommitted" Gunpowder Plot in *Guy Fawkes*

1. As a matter of convenience and because there is no modern edition, I cite the first book edition, published by Bentley in 1841 immediately upon completion of its serialization in *Bentley's Magazine*, which began in January 1840 and concluded in July 1841 (parenthetic references cite volume, book, chapter, and page). For this edition (and an apparently simultaneous one-volume edition published by Routledge), Ainsworth added a dedication, dated July 26, 1841, and a preface. I have compared the three-volume first edition against the serial numbers and, with one exception noted below (see n. 4), found no differences in wording in the passages cited in this chapter.

2. The *Morning Chronicle* 8 Oct. 1835: 2. Such commentary can be found in editorial after editorial during these years.

3. Lingard's account generally exonerates the Jesuits involved in the plot and contends that their leader, Father Garnet, continued to nurse the hope that he could induce Catesby "to suspend, if not to abandon, his criminal intention" (9.49). He does not go quite so far as to claim they were ignorant of it—as claimed in the dubious confessions of two conspirators—but he does insist that they opposed it and that Garnet did not receive a fair trial (9.44–45, 49–50, 64–65).

4. The text of the first book edition cited in this chapter is identical with the serial

numbers with the exception of the addition of this passage; whereas the general senti-
ment here is present, in *Bentley's*, Ainsworth does not compare bias against Catholics to
that against the Scots, Welsh, and Spanish (*Bentley's* 7 [1840]: 4).

5. While Sharpe offers no explanation for the emergence of Fawkes at the center of
the November Fifth holiday (why Fawkes and not, say, Catesby?), the shift from focusing
blame for the plot on the head of the church to a particular individual is consistent with
his general thesis that the holiday gradually became detached from anti-Catholicism.

6. Ainsworth describes Chetham as a "son to one of the wealthiest merchants of the
town" and "rather above the middle class" (1.1.1.9, 8). I take the latter to indicate the degree of wealth; in terms of nineteenth-century class discourse he is in all other respects
middle class.

7. Ainsworth, who lived near Ordsall Hall, based the Radcliffes on a family of Catholics who were friendly with Chetham and likely knew the Catesbys. There is, however,
no record of their having any connection with the Gunpowder Plot. Viviana is pure invention, and her father, unlike Chetham, Catesby, and Fawkes, is not a historical figure
(the last William to hold Ordsall had died in 1568, nearly four decades before the plot).
Some descriptions of Ordsall Hall repeat the "legend" that the plot originated at the Radcliffes' Ordsall Hall, but I have found no trace of this "legend" prior to the publication of
Ainsworth's novel, so the novel itself seems to be its source. Various gazetteers and other
works published prior to the novel list Ordsall Hall and mention the family but make
no reference to the plot; see, for example, Housman 518. The character of Viviana may
have been suggested in part by the historical Ann Vaux, who, like Viviana, was arrested
for her involvement with the conspirators, released after a short while, and then arrested
again; Vaux does, however, appear as a minor character in the novel.

8. He cites passages from Lingard (9.28, 30–31). However, in the novel itself (and
thus in serialization in Bentley's), he cites Bishop Godfrey Goodman's *The Court of King
James the First* (1839) to document the condition of Catholics, and there is no direct indication that he is following Lingard. Moreover, most of the other quoted material does
not appear in either Lingard or Goodman but does appear in Jardine, who is thus a likely
source. This material includes the epigraphs of books 2 and 3, both from Coke's speech
at the trials (Jardine 2.134, 137), the reference to Camden's remark about Catesby (*Guy
Fawkes* 1.1.3.41; Jardine 2.27), and the "oath of the conspirators" quoted as an epigraph on
the title page (Jardine 2.34). Moreover, many details not found elsewhere, including the
mysterious tolling of a bell when the men are digging their tunnel under Parliament, the
suggestion that Tresham was poisoned, Fawkes's ultimate confession that God did not
support their cause, and so on, appear in Jardine.

9. There are in addition many other references to the oath (see 1.1.8.146, 161, 1.1.12.223,
226, 1.1.14.269, 2.1.20.71, 2.2.2.122, 129–30, 2.2.4.149, 2.2.6.209, 2.2.7.223, 3.3.5.202). The attempt to prevent Monteagle from revealing the plot also revolves around his swearing an
oath (2.2.9.263–67, 271, 274, 276–277, 279, 281). Tellingly, Viviana herself ends up taking
the oath. Both she and her father, though not apprised of the details, become aware that
some kind of plot is in the works. Catesby nearly succeeds in persuading her father to
join the plot, but when he is about to swear the oath, Fawkes intervenes to prevent him.
Yet while he merely needs to promise he won't reveal what he has learned, Viviana, seeking, it seems, to save him from taking the oath, herself takes the oath committing her to
involvement in the plot (see 1.1.13.238, 250–55).

10. As Albert Pionke has pointed out, during the Glasgow murder trials of 1838 the prosecution, employing a discourse that elsewhere manifested itself in anti-Catholic rhetoric, suggested that the trade unions' oaths of secrecy amounted to forswearing allegiance to the Crown (29, 52).

11. As Worth notes, this structure undermines narrative momentum as well, making book 3 quite static (58); I would suggest that Ainsworth risked this loss of momentum precisely so as to achieve the aim of "defusing" the Gunpowder Plot.

CHAPTER 5:   Class Alliance and Self-Culture in *Barnaby Rudge*

1. The satire of the New Poor Law in *Oliver Twist* and his support for Tory factory reforms remind us that Dickens did not always follow the Whig party line. My argument here, however, is not that he seeks to promote a Whig agenda but that he frames his social critique in terms of Whig discourse.

2. Although they were not the first to suggest it, Butt and Tillotson seem to have canonized the assumption that Dickens was depicting Chartism in *Barnaby Rudge* (84–87). Their view has been taken up by Bowen, Brantlinger, Steven Marcus, Pionke, Pykett, Rice, Stigant and Widdowson, and Willis but has been challenged by some recent scholarship, in particular Fleishman, Lucas, G. Spence, and—at exhaustive length—Paz, *Dickens*. As the latter critics have pointed out, the contention that Dickens sought to treat the Gordon Riots as an "analogue" for Chartist disturbances (Pykett 71; see also Brantlinger 95; Steven Marcus 172; Rice 55) either ignores the fact that his choice of topic predates the Chartist movement or implies that he completely reconceived his project. Yet we can take Dickens at his word that his novel "has nothing to do with factories" while recognizing that in depicting the riots he was employing contemporary parliamentary discourse (*Letters* 1:507).

3. Rice suggestively argues that the relationship between Sir John and Maypole Hugh allegorizes the purported Tory-Chartist alliance (66–67). However, while he is correct that the Whig press accused the Tories of supporting subversives and argued that the Chartists were mistakenly allying themselves with a party opposed to its interests, the suggestion, for which he cites no evidence, that the Chartists "assimilat[ed] the anti-Catholic programme of the Ultra-Tories" does not accord with the history of the movement or the rhetoric of the parties involved (64). If anything, the Chartists regarded the antipapist campaign, as did the Whigs, as a matter of political expedience (e.g., *Northern Star* 5 Oct. 1844: 1; see also Paz, *Dickens* 39).

4. As noted below, John Chester is knighted and acquires the title Sir John midway through the novel. In order to distinguish him from his son, however, I refer to him throughout as Sir John.

5. Sir John does not explicitly acknowledge that he has done so, but he implies that he had been able to exploit her family's bigotry when he taunts Edward with the suggestion that he "ought to be so very Protestant, coming [as he does] of such a Protestant family" (15.136).

6. *Guy Fawkes* 3.2.14.83; see chap. 4 above. When Sim Tappertit brings a note containing the imperative "Burn it when you've read it," Sir John, alluding to the similar command at the conclusion of the Monteagle letter, remarks, "Where in the name of the Gunpowder Plot did you pick up this?" (24.203). There is no direct evidence that Dickens read *Guy Fawkes*, but given the fact that he and Ainsworth were friends, that

Ainsworth is known to have read *Barnaby Rudge*, and that Dickens had recently been editor of *Bentley's Magazine*, in which *Guy Fawkes* was appearing, it seems likely he did (*Letters* 2:212). The Monteagle letter was reproduced in Ainsworth's novel (3.2.12.29) in the number published in March 1841, and the allusion to the letter in *Rudge* appeared in the number published May 8, 1841. Of course, Dickens could have learned of the letter and of the suspicions that Salisbury exploited it from other sources, such as Jardine. Wilt has previously noted the Gunpowder Plot allusion, but her contention that Sir John is a conspiring Jesuit—a Father Garnet rather than a Salisbury—is to my mind ultimately unconvincing for a number of reasons, not least of which is her failure to take into account this context (i.e., that the remark that Sir John echoes is made by Salisbury).

7. Folland has previously pointed out that Sir John directs almost all of the actions of the rioters. See also Stigant and Widdowson, who similarly argue that Dickens depicts the riots as a conspiracy organized by the elites who make dupes of the lower classes (27–33).

8. On Dickens's original intention, see Butt and Tillotson 79. The depiction of the rioters as mad has often been noted (e.g., Folland 409). Representative passages include the following: "the mob raged and roared, like a mad monster as it was, unceasingly, and each new outrage served to swell its fury" (49.408); "a bear-garden, a madhouse, an infernal temple" (54.450); "mad for pillage and destruction" (54.454); "mad for destruction . . . rush[ing] to and fro stark mad" (55.460); "mad companions" (59.488); "the whole great mass were mad" (64.536).

9. Whereas the novel draws no direct parallels between the Chartists and the members of the Protestant Association involved in the riots, it does draw on contemporary political discourse in its representation of Sim and the Prentice Knights. Like the Chartists, Sim employs the language of popular constitutionalism, insisting that the Knights do not seek to overturn the constitution but to restore their "ancient rights" (8.77). As Brantlinger has demonstrated, the representation of the Knights also draws on contemporary accounts of trade unions (92–93).

10. Viswanathan assumes that Emma converts, but, unlike *Guy Fawkes*, *Barnaby Rudge* nowhere raises the question of conversion (26). My argument is that the novel's affirmation of the companionate ideal indicates that neither partner needs to convert because the marriage can accommodate difference. Hence, Haredale opposes the marriage not because of the difference of religion per se but because he thinks it will lead to unhappiness for his niece (12.105). Once he determines that she will remain happy, he gives the marriage his blessing (79.657–59). The primacy of happiness of the partners is, of course, one of the hallmarks of the companionate ideal.

11. While my analysis leads to somewhat different conclusions, I am indebted here in particular to the seminal reading of the novel by Steven Marcus (see esp. 184–204).

12. *Morning Chronicle* 25 May 1841: 7, 29 May 1841: 4. On allegations that the Tories were in league with the Chartists, see chap. 2.

CHAPTER 6:   Agricultural Reform, Young England's Allotments, and
the Chartist Land Plan

1. Related traditions of the superiority of the country to the city together with belief in the autonomy of the independent farmer came into play (see Bronstein 1n3; see also chap. 2).

2. On the history of the allotment movement, see Burchardt. On radical programs of agrarian reform, see Bronstein; Chase, *The People's Farm*.

3. Historians generally agree that in his role as leader of the opposition to repeal of the Corn Laws, Disraeli was not motivated by these paternalist principles but by his belief that repeal was a threat to the Tory party and perhaps also by the opportunity to advance his own political career. Nonetheless, as Roberts points out, he was not above invoking the paternalist argument.

4. Subsequent letters appeared in 22 Apr. 1843: 1, 29 Apr. 1843: 1, 6 May 1843: 1, and 13 May 1843: 1.

5. *Northern Star* 2 Nov. 1844: 1. Up to this point, the *Star* regarded the rise of Young England as a sign of weakness in Peel's Conservative ministry and as a positive response to the needs of the working class (see esp. O'Connor's discussion of it in *Northern Star* 14 Sept. 1844: 1; see also 24 Feb. 1844: 4, 3 Aug. 1844: 1).

6. Dickinson, introduction to *Political Works* xii. Note that although these tracts were published in the 1790s, some of them date to speeches Spence had made two decades earlier.

7. In his memoir of Wheeler, Stevens claims that "Wheeler may be said to have been almost, if not entirely, the originator of the Land Plan" (26) and more specifically that "the materials" for *On the Management of Small Farms* "were principally collected" by him and that "there is little doubt that the work in question was a joint production" (25).

8. *Northern Star* 14 Jan. 1843: 4, 21 Jan. 1843: 4. Marshall, whose family's mill was in Leeds, the home of the *Star* until 1844, had written the *Star* about allotments earlier in 1842 (25 June 1842: 6; see also 14 Jan. 1843: 4).

9. The article also criticizes the Owenites for their refusal to support Chartism and failure to recognize the need to gain "power" (i.e., parliamentary representation) in order to succeed with their projects. On O'Connor's efforts to distance himself from Owenism, see Chase, *Chartism* 249–51.

10. There has been some debate about whether the Land Plan represented a funda-mental shift in the Chartist project. Stedman Jones has argued that it shifted the grounds of the movement from the political conception of agency in terms of the franchise to other grounds, including economic ones (167), and it is clear that some contemporaries regarded it as doing so. However, Stedman Jones here relies heavily on Chartism's first historian, Robert Gammage (himself a Chartist who had an ax to grind), whose negative judgments of both O'Connor and the Land Plan have been challenged by recent work on Chartism (see Chase, *Chartism* 13–14, and "Land Plan" 133–34). I would add that O'Connor contrasted the plan with reforms that would address only the economic but not the political issue. These included both competing land projects—allotments and socialist collective plans—and the main projects of the ruling elite, Corn Law repeal and emigration, both of which he criticized for dealing only with economic concerns and not the political. See *Northern Star* 15 Apr. 1843: 1, 22 Apr. 1843: 1; *Small Farms* 124–29.

11. Chase notes that this distinction appeared in earlier radical agrarian discourse (*People's Farm* 143–45).

CHAPTER 7: The Landed Estate, Finely Graded Hierarchy, and the
Member of Parliament in *Coningsby* and *Sybil*

1. The fact that he ultimately leaves his wealth to Flora, his unacknowledged daughter by his mistress, the actress Stella, and cuts off his sons and grandson, merely confirms that he adheres to the kinship model not for the sake of kin but out of his own self-interested motives. Note as well that Coningsby repeatedly observes a lack of domestic warmth in his grandfather, in contrast to what he experiences with the Sydney family at Beaumanoir, which unlike Coningsby Castle, feels like "a home" (4.6.205; see also 4.9.224, 7.5.389).

2. According to the historical accounts that Disraeli gives in the novels, the land obtained through the dissolution of the monasteries had been the basis for the creation of a new group of titled aristocrats, the Whig oligarchy (see *Coningsby* 1.7, 2.1; *Sybil* 1.3, 2.5). He furthermore depicts his Tory contemporaries as members of the Whig oligarchy who have joined the Tories for pragmatic political reasons. As discussed below, the Marney family in *Sybil* follow exactly this pattern (see 1.3, esp. 34–35, 39).

3. Poovey suggests, in reference to the formation of Coningsby's coterie at Eton, that "manly conversation constitute[s] Disraeli's version of a reformed political domain," a domain she links to "homoeroticism" (142). One certainly can discern homoeroticism in the way the novel parallels the courtship of Edith Millbank with corresponding scenes depicting Coningsby's friendship with her brother, and the latter is undoubtedly the more important relationship, but ultimately, I would argue, what is central to the way the novel constitutes Coningsby's political relationships is their homosocial rather than their homoerotic dimension.

4. The following description of Coningsby's desire for companionship manifests the transference of the companionate ideal from the heterosocial to the homosocial context through the characteristic emphasis on equality of intellect: "Often, indeed, had he needed, sometimes he had even sighed for, *the companionship of an equal or superior mind*; one who, by the comprehension of his thought, and the richness of his knowledge, and the advantage of his experience, might strengthen and illuminate and guide his obscure or hesitating or unpractised intelligence" (3.1.139; emphasis added). The wish in this instance is fulfilled by the almost magical appearance of Sidonia later in the same chapter. Similar language marks later scenes describing Coningsby's friendship with Oswald.

5. Epstein points out that the Chartist leadership expected that the proposed strike, although in itself nonviolent, would provoke armed conflict because the government would attempt to force men back to work (*Lion of Freedom* 165–66).

6. Not only is Coningsby the leader of the coterie, but he also lays out its political program when he literally instructs the younger Millbank in quasi-catechetical fashion about his mature views (7.2.371–79). On the reversal of Sybil's views, see 4.15.334–36, 5.1.348–50.

7. It is not clear how much Disraeli knew about the specifics of the Land Plan or O'Connor's attempts to differentiate it from contemporary agrarian schemes. At the time Disraeli wrote *Sybil* (between the middle of 1844 and the end of May 1845), the parliamentary press had paid little attention to the Land Plan. However, the fact that he links Chartism with agrarianism suggests some awareness of O'Connor's scheme, which

had first been announced early in 1843. Moreover, there is some evidence that Disraeli may have encountered it in his research for the novel. In the 1870 preface to the novel, he records that Thomas Duncombe had loaned him the "correspondence of Feargus O'Connor when conductor of the *Northern Star*, with the leaders and chief actors of the Chartist movement" (quoted in Monypenny and Buckle 1:649; see also *Letters* 4:146n2). Given that the novel depicts infighting among the Chartist leadership, it seems likely that what Duncombe gave Disraeli was copies of the *Northern Star* in which O'Connor and his rivals traded accusations with one another (Chase, *Chartism* 236–40). If this was the case, he would certainly have seen O'Connor's many front-page letters touting the Land Plan.

8. A number of commentators have noted that *Sybil* implies the influence of Owen not only in Morley's proposals for workers' cooperatives but also in his strictures against the nuclear family, a key Owenite tenet (3.9.238). The novel links him to Fourier through the title of the newspaper he edits, the *Mowbray Phalanx*, a reference to the Fourierite communities called phalanxes. The Fourier connection has not been previously noted, perhaps because Fourier had little impact in Britain. However, several American groups attempted to establish Fourierite communities, and British radicals, including George Harney, editor of the *Northern Star*, kept abreast of these experiments (see Bronstein, chap. 4). O'Connor's efforts to differentiate the Land Plan from Owenism notwithstanding, Disraeli is not entirely disingenuous in this representation. Wheeler, Harney, and others who assisted him with it and promoted it in the *Northern Star* had been influenced by Owen and Fourier, both of whom contemporaries regarded as socialists.

9. Of course, it was really Disraeli who had been reading Cobbett. On Cobbett's reworking of the myth of the Norman yoke and the general idea that prior to the coming of the Normans land was held communally, see Hill 52. As Alice Chandler has pointed out, the passages in which Walter Gerard discusses monastic property borrow directly from Cobbett (178–80; see also Ulrich 127–28).

10. The importance of this idea to Disraeli's thought is apparent from his frequent use of it, as, for example, in his speech during the Ferrand allotment celebration: "England had once unity of purpose and unity of feeling, because every man filling the position in which he was placed did his duty, encouraged by the conviction that if entitled to rise from the sphere in which he was born, the law permitted him to elevate himself" (*Times* 14 Oct. 1844: 3).

11. See Brantlinger 97; Braun 99; Colón 30. However, as Alice Chandler points out, Sybil's "real inheritance" is not her noble status but "the estate of the poor as it existed in the Middle Ages when both the Nobility and the Church were devoted to securing man's needs" (177). For other fruitful readings of the marriage plot, see Bodenheimer, *Politics* 173–74; Gallagher, *Industrial Reformation* 216; and Ulrich 131–33.

12. For a useful discussion of how Disraeli constructs these estates as alternatives to existing economic structures, see Roy. I would note that although the text does not make it explicit, Oswald Millbank also enacts reform, like Trafford, by modeling his factory on a feudal estate: he has "built churches, and schools, and institutes" as well as "houses and cottages" and has also instituted "a new system of ventilation," "allotted gardens," and "established singing classes" for the sake of the "moral and physical well-being of his people" (4.3.187).

13. Just as he borrows middle-class discourse in order to envision reform of the aristoc-

racy (rather than the rise of the middle class), so Disraeli follows Dickens and Ainsworth in adopting the Whig position of religious toleration, but differs from them in contending that the Tories have historically been more just to Catholics than the Whigs. Eustace Lyle, a Catholic in Coningsby's coterie, thus regrets that his father joined the Whigs when they were promoting Catholic Emancipation, for the Whigs had obtained their estates by dispossessing the Catholic Church during the dissolution of the monasteries (*Coningsby* 3.5.171).

14. The usurpation of royal sovereignty and reduction of the monarch to "Doge" underpins Disraeli's narrative of the "Venetion constitution." See *Coningsby* 1.7.64; *Sybil* 6.6.496–97.

CHAPTER 8: Agricultural Improvement and the Squirearchy in *Hillingdon Hall*

1. In addition to the allusions to *Coningsby* discussed below, which appear on the final pages of the novel, Surtees added to chapter 11 (chapter 9 in serial publication) another allusion to "Young England" (1.11.160), which did not appear in the serial publication (see *New Monthly Magazine* 5 [1843]: 354). The first book publication is dated 1845, presumably early in that year, as the preface is dated October 1844. Monthly installments appeared from February 1843 until June 1844, publication ceasing after thirty-two of what would eventually be forty-seven chapters when the novel appeared in the three-volume first edition. The final chapter in serial publication became the first chapter of the third volume in the first edition, and the twenty-two chapters of serial publication became thirty-two. Because the latter part of the novel did not appear in the serial publication, I have used the first book edition of the novel. References are to volume, chapter, and page.

2. Neumann notes that this is the first of Surtees's novels to have a semblance of a plot (72). The political plot is central from the beginning. Chapter 5 is an extended satire on Corn Law lecturers, and chapters 9 through 13 introduce the Duke of Donkeyton, his model farm, and a house party designed to garner votes in the upcoming election. As I discuss below, the political plot in turn accounts for the courtship plot, which is established in chapters 2 and 4. There is a marked contrast between the chapters involving Jorrocks's relationships with the locals, which remain episodic, and the sustained and interlinked plotlines involving the courtship and political plots.

3. Disraeli makes clear that he intends an anachronism—that is, a depiction of the lower classes in relation to the medieval social order—when Coningsby's friend Henry Sydney claims that he prefers to call them "peasantry" rather than "labourers" or members of the "labouring classes" (3.3.160).

4. It was not until a speech of November 1843, when *Hillingdon Hall* was in the course of publication, that Spencer's position caused major controversy, but he had declared his support for complete repeal of the Corn Laws in a speech in Parliament on August 24, 1841 (Wasson 97; *Hansard* ser. 3, 59.22–24). Other Whig free traders involved with the RASE include Charles Fitzwilliam, third Earl Fitzwilliam, and Henry Moreton, second Earl of Ducie (Goddard 14–15).

5. The story circulates that Northumberland recognized himself and struck Surtees from his guest list (see Gash 94; and Neumann 73). He and Donkeyton do have some things in common; like Donkeyton, Northumberland held the office of lord lieuten-

ant, was "an eternal talker, and a prodigious bore," and "discussed agricultural improvements with his commissioners" but "never got round to carrying them out" (F. M. L.
Thompson). We may thus see a joke when Donkeyton discovers that the "estate" of the
Anti–Corn Law League candidate, Bill Bowker, is located near Sion House, the London
home of the Duke of Northumberland (3.41.180). However, in key respects, notably the
fact that he was a Tory, Northumberland does not resemble Donkeyton. By the same
token, the fact that the novel is dedicated to the RASE leaves little doubt that Surtees
would have been aware of Spencer's views. Indeed, Jorrocks has a nightmare in which
he dreams Spencer had taken him to his seat at Althorp "and kept him on oil-cake till he
declared himself an anti-corn-law repealer" (2.23.136).

6. The assertion "that whoever could make two Ears of Corn, or two Blades of Grass
to grow upon a spot of ground where only one grew before, would deserve better of
Mankind, and do more essential Service to his Country than the whole race of politicians
put together" is made by the king of Brobdingnag in *Gulliver's Travels* (part 2, chap. 7,
p. 126). It is unclear whether Swift originated it or it was already proverbial, but in any
case it had become so by the nineteenth century, and Jorrocks manifests no awareness of
its source. However, the fact that the king says that the man who should make such an
improvement is worth more than "the whole race of politicians put together" coincides
with the novel's general preference for actual farming over political posturing. Presumably part of the joke is that Robert *Smith* Surtees is himself a member of Adam Smith's
"now werry numerous family" (1.16.279).

7. Jorrocks ascribes the phrase to Coningsby, but it is actually spoken by the Tory
operative Taper (*Coningsby* 2.7.129).

8. Jorrocks's comment is apparently intended to suggest that Disraeli had made an
error by setting his steeplechase in autumn, as the main season was in March and April,
but in fairness to Disraeli, some chases were run in the autumn. Although Disraeli drew
on personal experience for many of the scenes in *Coningsby*, others (all of the early
scenes at Eton, for example), were outside his experience, which led him to seek advice
on these episodes (*Letters* 4:120). Nonetheless, there were still anomalies, some of which
he corrected in the second edition (*Letters* 135 and n. 2). For critical comment on these
errors, see Real England, "A Few Remarks on Coningsby," *Hood's Magazine* 1 (1844):
601. It should be noted that anti-Semitism may also play a role in Jorrocks's rejection of
Disraeli (see Gash 29–33).

CHAPTER 9:   The Land Plan, Class Dichotomy, and Working-Class Agency in
Sunshine and Shadow

1. The novel ran from March 31, 1849, to January 5, 1850. It was not republished until
Haywood's edition of 1999.

2. Many of the numbers in which *Sunshine and Shadow* appeared contain O'Connor's
defenses of the plan as it began to fail (e.g., 16 June 1849: 1, 23 June 1849: 1, 30 June 1849:
1, etc.), and similar articles preceded it (e.g., 11 Nov. 1848: 1).

3. Wheeler evinces considerable familiarity with the contemporary novel (29.157,
158), and although he makes no mention of Disraeli the novelist, his narrator does refer
to Disraeli's parliamentary eloquence (21.132).

4. In both cases the narrator depicts school days as idyllic by viewing them through
the lens of nostalgic memory: "'Tis some indefinite recollection of these mystic passages

of their young emotion that makes grey-haired men mourn over the memory of their schoolboy days" (*Coningsby* 1.9.72); "Oh! who does not look back with delight on his boyish days, when life was all enchantment; when, let the kaleidoscope be ever so varied, its colours were always bright, and each new combination more pleasing than the last" (*Sunshine and Shadow* 1.73).

5. As noted in chap. 6, Stevens's memoir claims that "Wheeler may be said to have been almost, if not entirely, the originator of the Land Plan" (26) and that "there is little doubt that [*A Practical Work on the Management of Small Farms*] was a joint production" (25).

6. For discussion of the "flat" characters in *Sunshine and Shadow*, see Mitchell 258 and Seehase 130. In a variation of this view, Plotz cites the novel to illustrate his claim that in Chartist fiction the heroes move from individuality to typicality (*Portable Property* 147–48). It should be noted, however, that he bases his argument in part on the erroneous assumption that the Chartist hero, not his nemesis, is named North.

7. On the way the novel associates Mary with the domestic and removes her from the public sphere of Chartist politics where she and Arthur first meet, see Zlotnick 184–85.

8. See "Chartist Jubilee: Grand Demonstration to the Peoples' First Estate 'O'Connorville'" (*Northern Star* 22 Aug. 1846: 1). The *Northern Star* had earlier made explicit allusion to Old Testament jubilee as restoration of land (4 Oct. 1845: 7; see also 21 Mar. 1846: 1).

9. See the discussion of the Land Plan in chap. 6.

10. Wheeler has many technical limitations as a storyteller, but as I hope should be clear from my analysis, his novel advances a sophisticated conception that self-consciously challenges dominant national narratives. Nonetheless, there has been little in the way of sustained analysis of the novel. The two fullest discussions of the novel (Seehase and Mitchell) are limited by assumptions about what kind of novel it should be, treating it as if Wheeler were trying but failing to write the "proletarian" or "socialist" novel rather than attempting to discover what he was actually attempting to do. Haywood (*Working-Class Fiction*) and Vicinus both provide useful insights into the novel, but neither offers a detailed analysis of the text (for other brief discussions, see Breton and Klaus).

CHAPTER 10: Christian Socialism and Cooperative Association

1. See, for example, Harney's leading articles in the *Red Republican* 4 Jan. 1851: 1, 25 Jan. 1851: 49; the title of the latter, "Social and Political Reform," refers directly to this debate. On the relationship between Jones and Wheeler in this era, see Chase, *Chartism* 353–58.

2. The earliest instance cited in the OED is from 1833. The term begins to appear frequently in the radical press in 1838 and the following year in the elite press. Owen's 1841 congress adopted the term to describe his plan for cooperative associations (Bonner 37; Cole 33). After occurring in the press with considerable frequency in 1839–1841, *socialism* appears less often in the mid–1840s and then begins to appear frequently again in 1848 in reference to France and Louis Blanc's proposals for national workshops. One leading article in the *Times*, for example, contends that "socialism . . . is the principle which now governs France" (17 Mar. 1848: 4). For examples of the use of the term as a synonym for *Owenism*, see *Times* 28 Aug. 1839: 3, 9 Oct. 1839: 5, 20 Dec. 1839: 4; *Morn-*

ing Chronicle 30 Dec. 1839: 2; *Morning Post* 27 Sept. 1839: 2. On the pairing of socialism and Chartism, see next note.

3. For example, *Times* 20 Mar. 1840: 6, 15 Dec. 1840: 4, 22 Jan. 1841: 4, 17 Sept. 1841: 4; *Morning Chronicle* 11 Jan. 1842: 2, 1 Feb. 1842: 2; *Examiner* 4 Mar. 1843: 129; 22 June 1844: 386. While this pairing seems to have meant primarily that they were equally dangerous lower-class movements, not necessarily that they were synonymous, the editors undoubtedly were aware that many Chartists were Owenites and that by pairing them they were suggesting that, like the latter, Chartists were anti-Christian and thus morally suspect.

4. Of the three most important figures, Frederick Denison Maurice was a clergyman and theologian, Charles Kingsley a vicar, and John Ludlow an attorney. Other important figures were the chemist Charles Mansfield, the attorney and author Thomas Hughes, and the attorney Edward Vansittart Neale. Several other clergy, medical men, and scholars were also involved.

5. On the idea that the emergence of liberalism at midcentury involved development of this principle of egalitarian self-culture on the one hand and the anxiety to ensure through an elite that this culture did not become self-interested on the other, see Goodlad viii, 25–29.

6. In one article, Ludlow does invoke Blackstone's contention that one must own property in order to possess a "will" of one's own (3.43–44), but the articles in *Politics* consistently focus on knowledge rather than property as the basis for the franchise.

7. Although Ludlow claimed retrospectively in his autobiography to have this aim from the beginning of the group's existence, I have not found this formulation appearing earlier than Maurice's letter of February 7, 1850.

8. More or less the same was true of *The Christian Socialist*, the weekly the group established in support of their schemes for cooperative associations. Contributions from members of Maurice's circle considerably outnumbered those of Chartist and working-class contributors. In the first volume (it survived for only two), Chartists—Lloyd Jones, Joseph Millbank, Walter Cooper, Gerald Massey, Thomas Shorter, John Bedford Leno, and James Bezer—contributed a total of twenty articles; there are also a few reports on the cooperatives by their managers (one each by Henry James Ballard, James Benny, Joseph Pickard, and William Stork). Of the dozens of other articles, Ludlow contributed fifty-seven, Kingsley twenty-three, and Maurice twenty. For details, see Raven 375–77.

9. For example, in the first dialogue, a Templar who has been to college with Maurice, a silk mercer, and a coal whipper (a large number of coal whippers had been hired as special constables on April 10) discuss political economy with the author. The coal whipper affirms that workingmen suffer from competition; the mercer has developed qualms about it; the Templar, following the tenets of political economy, contends that competition is a law of human nature; and then, in the conclusion, the author intervenes to settle the question by asserting that divine law demands that we resist our competitive tendencies (2.18–21). The second dialogue affirms the principle of cross-class dialogue when "Maurice" explains that his "friends" in *Politics for the People* "wish, if I do not mistake them, to learn of the working men as well as to teach them" and asserts that there "must be as much of mutual confession as of argument" (5.83). Yet there is not much dialogue between the interlocutors (one of whom is a carpenter); instead Maurice develops his views about education in a kind of Socratic dialogue with a fellow scholar and addresses the carpenter merely to seek confirmation of his views. James Spedding

similarly constructs dialogues between a Whig and a moral-force Chartist so that the former always persuades the latter that his own views are more sound (e.g., 9.145–49).

10. The masthead of the *Spirit of the Age*, to which Jones was a major contributor, quoted a passage from Carlyle alluding to Blanc's "Organisation of Labour" (see *Past and Present* 4.3.254) and the second issue printed a review of Blanc's book (1 July 1848: 13). Owen's ideas and writings appeared frequently.

11. Christensen lists Cooper but not Jones among those present at the initial meeting, but his note indicates that the evidence about who was in attendance is not complete (131n28). Given Jones's later role as the major promoter of the Christian Socialist cooperative movement, it is very likely that he was deeply involved from the start, even if he was not present at this meeting.

12. "A Few Words to Parson Lot" (*Notes* 606–9), which responds to "The Long Game: A Few Words to the Workmen of England on the Present Crisis" (*Christian Socialist* 2.55, 15 Nov. 1851: 305–7); "More Words to Parson Lot" (*Notes* 621–23), which responds to part 2 of "The Long Game" (*Christian Socialist* 2.56, 22 Nov. 1851: 321–23), and "More Words to, and Some Words by, Parson Lot" (*Notes* 747–48), which mentions remarks in the *Christian Socialist* on his preceding article (2.58, 5 Dec. 1851: 365) and responds to it by quoting and providing a commentary on a previous Parson Lot article, "My Political Creed" (*Christian Socialist* 1.7, 14 Dec. 1850: 50–51). Parson Lot is Kingsley's pseudonym. As noted above, George Harney, like Jones, insisted that social reform could not be effected without political reform, but rather than critique the Christian Socialists, he promoted a strategy that involved joining with them and others who promoted social reforms as a means of paving the way to political reform. In an article in the *Red Republican*, Harney addressed the relative merits of "Social and Political Reform" and alluded to the efforts of the "Christian Socialists" to promote the cooperative movement (25 Jan. 1851: 49). For a detailed discussion of the exchanges in their respective publications (Harney's *Red Republican* and *Friend of the People*, Jones's *Notes to the People*, and the *Christian Socialist*), see Christensen 226–38.

13. Although few letters survive, there is evidence of regular correspondence between Gaskell and Kingsley. The earliest surviving letters — Kingsley's of 1853 and Gaskell's of 1857 — make clear that they were already familiars (Kingsley, *Letters* 1.370; Gaskell, *Letters* 452). They were aware of each other's work by 1849 if not earlier. Gaskell appears first to have encountered members of the group during a visit to London in the spring of 1849 (Uglow 225). She heard Maurice preach on May 17 and the following day spoke at length with Maurice, Ludlow, and Archdeacon Julius Hare, a close associate of Maurice (Shaen 42–43). There is no mention of meeting Kingsley during this visit, however, and exactly when Gaskell and Kingsley first met or began their correspondence is not clear. A letter of May 17, 1849, indicates Gaskell's familiarity with Kingsley's *A Saint's Tragedy*, which had been published in December 1847, and Kingsley reviewed *Mary Barton* (published October 1848) in the April issue of *Fraser's Magazine* (Gaskell, *Letters* 79; see also 86). Another letter, of 1850, asking a friend to pass along thanks to the Kingsleys suggests that there had already been contact of some kind (*Letters* 129), and her reference to a "note of Mr Kingsley's" would seem to refer to a letter from him (105).

14. Although Chapple conjecturally dates this letter to November 26, 1849 (*Letters* 89), about six months after Kingsley's review, Gaskell's reference, in the same passage, to the Christian Socialists' plans to open a "co-operative tailor's shop . . . in the New

Road, or Tottenham Court Road" (90) suggests that it could not have been written before February 1850. Gaskell was in Manchester that autumn, so it is unlikely that she
heard directly from any of the participants about their plans, and even if she had, it
could not have been any earlier than mid-December, more likely January. The project
of establishing cooperatives was under discussion at the meetings of autumn 1849, but
the group did not make any concrete plans until after the appearance of Henry Mayhew's
Morning Chronicle article on seamstresses, which appeared on December 4. While they
undoubtedly discussed the establishment of a cooperative throughout the month, they
did not decide to go forward until a meeting near the end of December and only worked
out details at a meeting of January 8, 1850 (Christensen 131). Another complicating fac-
tor raised by this passage is that Gaskell refers not to Castle Street, the location of the
first cooperative, but "the new Road, or Tottenham Court Road." This would seem to
confuse the Tailors' Association with the Ladies and Gentleman's Working Boot and
Shoemakers' Association, which was established in April 1850. Finally, the promise in
this same passage to copy out lines from Kingsley may link this letter to another letter,
which Chapple dates to February 20, 1850, in which she says she will copy a "sentence
out of a note of Mr Kingsley's" (105). The context gives no hint about her reasons for
calling Kingsley her hero. Although, as I suggest here, it may refer to his review of *Mary
Barton*, it could, if my reading of the evidence about the dating of the letter is correct,
refer to his response to Mayhew's revelations in his pamphlet *Clothes Cheap and Nasty*,
which appeared in January 1850.

15. See Christensen 260–62. In *Who Are the Friends of Order?* (1852), Kingsley defended the Christian Socialists against charges that their support of the union showed
they were revolutionaries opposed to private property, but he was not concerned there
with the union itself. So long as the others remained active in the cooperative projects,
Kingsley remained involved, but his literary output shifted increasingly to other matters.

CHAPTER 11: Clergy and Working-Class Cooperation in *Yeast* and *Alton Locke*

1. At this time, the first six numbers of *Politics* (including the first two "Letters to the
Chartists") had been published, the most recent on June 3. However, the author of the
letter quotes only from the first number, citing Maurice's article "Fraternity," which it
conflates with Ludlow's article "The Suffrage" and Kingsley's first article, "The National
Gallery."

2. We know of the *Commonwealth* article only from Kingsley's letter. The *Commonwealth* had a very brief existence of two months, and the only surviving copies that I
have been able to locate (in the British Library collection) are the May 20 and 27 issues.
The May 27 issue includes an article on *Politics for the People* ("Mock Friends of the
People.—Well-fed Democracy in Broadcloth"), the conclusion of which suggests the
intention to publish a critique of "Parson Lot" in a future issue (25).

3. The final number appeared in December 1848. As an allusion in *Alton Locke*
makes clear (17.173–74), Kingsley was aware that Disraeli in turn was borrowing from
Cobbett. While the principal allusion here is to *Sybil*, *Yeast* more explicitly takes on *Coningsby*, to which it alludes directly. Cazamian claims that Kingsley wrote a letter declaring that "he had read *Coningsby*, but only after the publication of *Yeast*" (*Social Novel*
342n49), but Kingsley is more ambiguous than this implies: "Many thanks for your most

sensible remarks about 'Yeast.' Quite right; the Prophet is too like Sidonia, but I never read 'Coningsby' till the other day, when the Prophet was months old" (1.191). Given that the 1848 version of *Yeast* directly names *Coningsby*, Cazamian's inference is obviously incorrect. Indeed, the "Prophet" does not appear until the December number (chap. 12), while the text of the novel shows that Kingsley had read *Coningsby* before completing the November number (chaps. 10–11), in which Smith recalls a specific "scene in *Coningsby*" (11.538). Moreover, Kingsley's gloss on the title of his novel, which appeared in the final monthly number, refers to the "rising generation," an allusion to the title and theme of *Coningsby; or The New Generation* (12.690). Most telling are the numerous parallels in plot and structure that I discuss below. Notably, Smith goes through a process of learning about the condition of England in which he is taught by a variety of instructors. Like Coningsby in particular, he loses his fortune and decides to "earn [his] bread or starve" (12.690), though, unlike the former, he does not immediately have that fortune restored him or have a seat in Parliament handed to him on a plate by the father of the woman he loves.

4. Unless otherwise indicated, all citations to *Yeast* are to the 1848 serial publication in *Fraser's Magazine*. Although the 1851 first book edition includes almost all of the original 1848 text, Kingsley made substantial additions to the novel and, most importantly, made significant changes to the conclusion. The few critics who have discussed the novel note that the changes exist but base their analyses on the 1851 text. Note that, owing to the additions, the chapter numbering of 1851 differs from that of 1848. We have no documentation of precisely when Kingsley began working on *Yeast*. On May 22 he wrote to Ludlow about a plan for a tale about a "young squire . . . brought to a sense of his duties, & setting to work" (Martin 92), but, given that the novel began appearing in *Fraser's* just two months later, in July, it is possible that he may have conceived of the novel or even begun writing it earlier in the year.

5. Kingsley's story "The Nun's Pool," which recounts the original episode of the dissolution and the Lavingtons' acquisition of Whitford, not only anticipates the baptismal motif of *Water-Babies* (1863) but also, in the naming of the town Ashy, appears to anticipate the fact that its central character is a chimney sweep.

6. As Peschier has demonstrated, the figure of the Jesuit who disguises himself as an Anglican, ingratiates himself with a family, and secretly contrives to convert them had wide circulation (chap. 4; for the general context, see also Paz, *Popular Anti-Catholicism*). Kingsley would, of course, famously invoke the trope in his accusation that Newman secretly intended to convert to Roman Catholicism but delayed making his intention public so as to bring others along with him (see O'Malley chap. 2, esp. 81–92). That the vicar is a secret Jesuit is evident from the fact that he is hardly conscious himself of his Romanist tendency, even as his true colors reveal themselves in his habit of leading his "friends and pupils" over "to Rome." Consequently, his enemies accuse him of "disguised Romanism" and contend that he is a " 'liar,' 'hypocrite,' 'Jesuit' " (10.533). In one of the 1851 additions, Lancelot's uncle (the father of Luke, who does go over to Rome) inveighs against "concealed Jesuits" who "he suspected" had infiltrated themselves "among his footmen, and his housemaids" (12.277) and expresses the fear that his son would bring in "nuns disguised as lady's maids" to "convert us all" (12.278).

7. This letter is dated only "Thursday," and the editors of *Letters* have placed it in late

1849. Given the contents and the fact that the conclusion published in December 1848 would have foreclosed the possibilities the letter envisions, it seems likely that it belongs to the autumn of 1848.

8. In Hosea, the idea appears to be that the priests are as bad as the people, not that the people are to blame for the failures of the priests: "And there shall be, like people, like priest: and I will punish them for their ways, and reward them their doings" (4:9). As the novel is full of allusions to Carlyle (Lancelot, Paul, and Argemone all appear to be admirers), Kingsley may be alluding to Carlyle's adaptation of Hosea to suggest that an unworthy people will elect unworthy leaders: "Like people like priest; so we may say: Like people like king. The man gets himself appointed and elected who is ablest—to be appointed and elected" (*Past and Present* 1.5.34; see also *Latter-Day Pamphlets* no. 4, "The New Downing Street" 163).

9. Victorian authors frequently invoke the enmity between Cain and Abel—brother fighting with brother—as a figure for class conflict. Carlyle (on whom, see the preceding note) employs it in *Past and Present* 3.2.149.

10. Although we might think of education in terms of Bourdieu's notion of cultural capital, I want to make the point here that the novel allies culture not with industrial or commercial capital but with the power of the aristocracy that originates in their capacity for combat.

11. See Girard chap. 1. In accord with Girard's analysis of rivalrous desire, Alton's initial contact with Lillian mediates George's desire for her, but George's successful rise in turn mediates Alton's desire.

12. Chapter 13, which depicts the abuses of this right at Cambridge, reinforces his claim that the aristocracy who have appropriated it do not deserve it. Kingsley cut out much of this criticism in the 1862 edition, which contains a "Preface to the Undergraduates at Cambridge."

13. Cooper's conviction was for his role in the Manchester strike wave of August 1842, but Kingsley dates Alton Locke's speech about three years later so as to have his release from prison take place shortly before the April 10, 1848, events. For a detailed analysis of Cooper's rhetorical strategies, see Kuduk 167–71.

14. As I have argued elsewhere, Carlyle's conception of guidance allows some limited scope for working-class agency, but it is much more foreshortened than that depicted in *Alton Locke* ("Chartism, Class Discourse, and the Captain of Industry"). While Carlyle envisions the conversion of buccaneering industrialists into captains of industry who lead regiments of workingmen, Kingsley envisions conversion of the workingmen themselves.

15. In the weeks leading up to April 10, Maurice had written to Ludlow: "Meantime, the necessity of an English theological reformation, as the means of averting an English political revolution and of bringing what is good in foreign revolutions to know itself, has been more and more pressing upon my mind. . . . Are not we Atheistic? Is not our Christianity semi-Atheistic?" (*Life* 1.459).

16. In *David Copperfield*, published just a couple of years earlier, David courts Dora Spenlow primarily for what seems to be her beauty or erotic appeal but turns out to be her status and only belatedly recognizes that Agnes Wickfield values him more and herself has superior moral value. The convention is not confined to male protagonists, of course; novels in which a woman is first attracted to the inferior suitor but then marries the superior one are if anything even more common.

17. The importance of this concept for the novel is emphasized by making this term the chapter title. See the discussion of "the natural leaders of the people" in chap. 7 above.

18. This feature of the novel helps to account for the much-discussed inconsistency in the characterization of Locke (see Gallagher, *Industrial Reformation* 89, 96–101; Bodenheimer, *Politics of Story* 136–57; Childers 132–33). Note that we can see a similar pattern in the difference between Mackaye's history and his opinions.

19. See 33.314. Mackaye's fictional birth date is three decades before Carlyle's, so when Mackaye dies, in 1848, he is over eighty, while at this date Carlyle was going on fifty-three. Moreover, the fact that Mackaye's "favourite books were Thomas Carlyle's works" differentiates him from the author, even as it explains the coincidence of their views (6.65). I would also note that the letter from Carlyle to Kingsley often cited in this context does not necessarily imply that Carlyle thought Mackaye was a portrait of himself. Carlyle praises the portrait of Mackaye, but his reference elsewhere in the letter to the "treatment of my poor self" most likely refers to the admiration Mackaye and others have for him, not to Mackaye as a depiction of Carlyle (*Letters* 25.267; see also 212).

CHAPTER 12: Reforming Trade Unionism in *Mary Barton* and *North and South*

1. See my "Social Agency and the Representation of Chartism in *Mary Barton*." As I note there, although the novel explicitly mentions the Chartist petition of 1839, its reference in the same passage to the hardships of 1839, 1840, and 1841 serves to conflate it with the petition of 1842. Most tellingly, Gaskell's depiction of the Chartist petition as seeking to present witnesses to the misery of the people corresponds with 1842, not 1839.

2. This view typifies much of the earlier criticism of the novel (e.g., Craik 31–32; Ganz 69). More recent criticism follows Bodenheimer ("Private Grief" 196); Gallagher, *Industrial Reformation* (75–84); and Schor (15), who have argued for a more complex relationship between the plots (see, for example, Lesjak 34). Nonetheless, even Gallagher depicts the "melodramatic" plot as "suppressing" the "tragic" (i.e., political) plot (78). More recently, Anderson has argued that class conflict, not romantic passion, is the cause of Carson's death (*Tainted Souls* 112).

3. As my interest is in the novels as they were received by the public, I cite the older Penguin edition because it is based on the first edition, the edition that reviewers most likely read. In any case, the editions published during Gaskell's lifetime make no substantive changes in the passages cited in this chapter.

4. There are two complications, of course. One is that although his motives do not concern the romance, they are in part personal, but it is the death of his son as a direct result of poverty rather than the seduction of his daughter that motivates him. Second, although the narrative reveals to the reader the truth that the motive is social, Mary and Jem work to conceal it from other characters.

5. Jem's attitudes are shaped in part by his father, who shows little sympathy for John Barton's views of class. As Bodenheimer has pointed out, the novel distinguishes Barton, who comes from a family already engaged in urban industrial labor, from the Wilsons, who have recently emigrated from the country to the city ("Private Grief" 201).

6. For Barton's invocations of it, see 1.45, 6.104, 9.142, 15.219, and 15.221. The only other character to use it is Job Legh, when he is representing Barton's views (37.455–56). The novel invokes it in only four other instances, all of them epigraphs that anticipate

Barton's views as expressed in the chapter that follows (6.95, 9.140, 15.218, 37.451). In the preface, Gaskell explains her intention as attempting to show why the "work-people" are "sore and irritable against the rich" (37), which, in specific form, is what she does in her portrait of John Barton.

7. As I have argued elsewhere, in this and related respects, Gaskell follows Carlyle's *Past and Present* ("Social Agency" 178). Carlyle had depicted the Manchester strike wave (which, following press reports, he calls an "insurrection") not as an action but as the "inarticulate" expression of workingmen's sense of injustice (1.3.20). For Carlyle they cannot, as John Plotz has pointed out, even speak, let alone act to remedy their situation (*Crowd* 138). Instead, Carlyle insists that the workers do not really want what they are demanding and instead articulates what the workers themselves cannot say by ventriloquizing their demands and interpreting their actions as the "inarticulately" expressed question, "What do you mean to do with us?" (*Past and Present* 1.3.20). On the novel's treatment of working-class agency, see also Bigelow 155–56.

8. I take Gaskell's assertion in the preface that she "know[s] nothing of Political Economy" to mean that she does not fully understand its grounds or the details of alternative views (38). When she states that she knows workers are wrong (3.60), she implicitly affirms that political economy is rational and the workers' views are not, presumably because for the audience she is addressing its rationality is taken as a given.

9. As Bodenheimer has pointed out, the novel does, somewhat at odds with its explicit views, depict the murder of Harry Carson as bringing about the reform of the elder Carson ("Private Grief" 206–7). However, whether the men are merely seeking vengeance or hoping to intimidate the masters into acquiescence, they certainly do not aim to change the masters' point of view by demonstrating to them what it is to lose a child. Indeed, they act as they do precisely because Parliament and the masters have refused to show any sympathy for them.

10. See n. 1. This representation of the Charter leads Sabin to suggest that John Barton does not seem to understand its purpose (52–53).

11. Of course, this phrasing also invokes Carlyle's "cash nexus." Indeed, one could conclude that the ambiguity under discussion here originates in Carlyle's own ambivalent depictions of the alternatives to the cash nexus, which he describes alternately as paternal and fraternal (see my "Chartism, Class Discourse, and the Captain of Industry" 39–42).

12. Audrey Jaffe's discussion of the problematics of sympathy is, of course, germane here. See esp. her introduction and chap. 3, on Gaskell's *Ruth*.

13. A number of critics (Anderson, *Tainted Souls*, 119–20; Betensky chap. 3; D'Albertis 59; Elliott chap. 5) have discussed how Gaskell seeks to elicit reader sympathy and action, but none has noticed the relationship between her aims in writing the novel and her depiction of the Charter.

14. This had been the view of the *Times*, which reported on the strikes under the headline "Anti–Corn Law League Riots" and repeatedly suggested that the league had conspired to provoke the workers into violence in order to pressure Parliament to repeal the Corn Laws (e.g., 11 Aug. 1842: 5). As noted above, at this time the *Times* generally supported the Tories but differed from them on the issue of the Corn Laws by supporting repeal (chap. 2).

15. See Bodenheimer, *Politics of Story* 54–55; Jay, introduction to *North and South* xvii; Shuttleworth, introduction to *North and South* x–xi; Starr 394.

16. See chap. 11. In addition to his review praising *Mary Barton*, Kingsley wrote a letter lauding *Ruth*, and Ludlow wrote a glowing review as well. Over time Gaskell learned more about the cooperatives and other related ventures, and in 1852 she commented on a newspaper account of the annual meeting of leaders of the cooperative associations (*Letters* 195). She probably read *Politics for the People* during its run in May–July 1848, and she certainly read the *Tracts on Christian Socialism* of 1850 as well as the *Christian Socialist*, the periodical that succeeded them and reprinted two of her stories.

17. All citations of *North and South* are to Easson's edition.

18. She does not mention the Working Men's College in her letters, but the fact she was in regular personal contact with the Maurices makes it inevitable that she would have known about it. Maurice proposed the college in early 1854, and classes began that autumn.

19. When Thornton complains that the masters' "doings are sure to be canvassed by every scribbler who can hold a pen," he seems to echo the general tenor of Greg's review (1.15.118). Greg has been proposed as one of the models for Thornton (see Shusterman), but other plausible candidates have been proposed, including James Nasymyth (Chadwick 216–17) and James Wilson (Gill). For a brief discussion that casts doubt on the Greg model and emphasizes the influence of Ludlow and Christian Socialism, see Easson, "Gaskell, Ludlow, and Greg."

20. See Perkin 218–21. The Hales are not aristocracy, of course, but Margaret's mother is the daughter of a knight or baronet, and in all likelihood her father has become a clergyman because he is a younger son from a genteel family. As I discuss in chap. 1, class discourse has to do with identities as much as or more than with material conditions. Thus in spite of the Hales's straitened circumstances, Mrs. Thornton does not hesitate to identify Margaret as aristocratic, claiming that she "comes out of the aristocratic counties" and has an "aristocratic way of viewing things" (1.9.77, 1.23.189).

21. As the preceding citation indicates, my discussion of the novel's depiction of class discourse is indebted to Schor's excellent discussion of its treatment of language; the title of Schor's chapter on *North and South* is taken from the comment quoted here describing Margaret's relationship with Thornton as a "continued series of opposition." Morris similarly suggests that the novel seeks to demonstrate that rational discourse does not necessarily lead to "consensual agreement" and describes the relationship between Thornton and Higgins as "antagonistic friendship" (154, 155).

22. Michael Tomko first pointed out to me the possibility that *North and South* was written in the tradition of the national tale. What distinguishes it from its predecessors is that it maps the cultural or ethnic differences onto the class division between industrial entrepreneurs and rural gentry. As noted in chap. 1, we can see the transition from ethnicity to class when John Thornton opposes the "Greek . . . race," to which the south is allied through its advocacy of culture, to the "Teutonic blood" of the north (2.15.334).

23. There is some question as to whether Gaskell herself proposed this title. We know only that Dickens expressed a preference for "North and South" over "Margaret Hale" and that Gaskell, in retrospect, objected to it, though it must be said, in a rather playful manner (Dickens, *Letters* 7.378; Gaskell, *Letters* 324).

24. Gaskell may here recall Carlyle, who in *The French Revolution* records the abrogation of a law "authorising a Seigneur, as he returned from hunting, to kill not more than two Serfs, and refresh his feet in their warm blood and bowels" (1.2.12). She might also have seen this anecdote in his *Chartism* 10.153.

25. On the classic professions and their association with landed aristocracy and gentry, as well as the rise of the new professions in the nineteenth century, see Larson and Reader.

26. The critical literature has emphasized Gaskell's ambivalence toward Nightingale but has also suggested that Margaret Hale is at least in part modeled on her (see, for example, Morris 155–56; Nord 165–66; Schor 149). It is worth noting that Nightingale's argument against marriage is that, as currently practiced, it does not accord with the companionate ideal except in novels (see 28, 44–48).

27. Oldfield was one of about a thousand vicars ejected from the church following passage of the Act of Uniformity of 1662, which was intended to reverse the elements of dissent introduced by the Puritans.

28. Maurice was probably one of the models for the Reverend Hale (see Sanders 45 and the notes to Jay's introduction to *North and South* 400–401). Thiele points out that by this time the Manchester Lyceum was regarded as failing in its aim of providing instruction to the working class (278).

29. A number of critics have noted the parallels between Frederick's opposition to oppressive authority and the opposition of the mill workers to the masters (Bodenheimer, *Politics of Story* 59–60; David, *Fictions* 14–15; Ingham 61; Morris 146–47; Stoneman 123). Deborah Morse, who provides the fullest and most nuanced account of this subplot, has pointed out that the novel aligns Frederick's violent opposition to the captain with the striking workers' violent opposition to Thornton and that the novel instead supports Margaret's nonviolence. In this respect, the novel depicts Frederick as employing physical force, albeit against an unjust authority, while Margaret and, I would add, Nicholas Higgins employ moral force.

30. In this respect, *North and South* departs from *Mary Barton*, which, in turn, draws on Carlyle's *Past and Present* and, one might conjecture, *A Christmas Carol*. This conversion model lies behind what Edmund Wilson famously defined as the "two Scrooges" of *A Christmas Carol*, which was inspired in part by *Past and Present*, and finds its parallel in what we can call the two Carsons of *Mary Barton*. In each case reform takes a specifically religious form, as we see also in *Alton Locke*. Although Margaret at one point suggests that Thornton's view of his rights is secular (what she calls "human"), he insists that his religious beliefs are simply different than hers (1.15.118). More to the point, he does not, like Carson, undergo a religious conversion or articulate his self-reform in religious terms.

31. Gaskell seldom comments on contemporary politics, and her letters do not mention the Preston strike, but she would have seen reports in the *Times* and most likely would have read Dickens's article on it in *Household Words*. The Gaskells were at this time subscribers to the London *Times* (*Letters* 298; see also 278, 298, 300); in 1854 they were not subscribing to the *Manchester Guardian* (*Letters* 279), and the letters make no mention of the other Manchester papers.

32. Although there has been controversy over whether these strikes mark a radical shift toward a "new model," most historians see in them at least a gradual shift in union

strategies and a decline in violence (See Chase, *Early Trade Unionism* 219–20; Fraser 34–35). On the change as reflected in the Preston strike, see Dutton and King 54.

33. Whereas the novel in other respects draws on the events of the Preston strike, its depiction of the riot at Marlborough Mill forcing the leaders to give up the strike departs from what happened at Preston. Although there was an episode in which a handful of people threw stones at strikebreakers, one of which struck a child in the forehead (Dutton and King 126), the striking workers by and large stayed within the law and there was no "riot." The strike failed for a variety of reasons but not because of this episode or the use of physical force.

34. Here I depart from David, who argues that in depicting the men as animalistic, Gaskell makes the problem their nature, not oppression by the masters (*Fictions* 27). As we have seen, already in *Mary Barton* Gaskell had ascribed violent behavior to conditions created by the masters. The fact that this is the only passage in the novel that employs such descriptions indicates that it applies to Boucher but not to Higgins.

35. Bigelow points out that Thornton adheres to an ideal of "individualism" that "considers all men possessed of the same rights but functions to obscure the continuing power differences created by money, or indeed by creed, race, or gender" (174). I concur with him that the novel goes on to depict Thornton as undergoing reform and abandoning this point of view; however, I would contend that in the passage under discussion here Thornton does not fully escape his tendency to ignore power differences.

36. Although the primary audience for both novels was the educated elite, Gaskell did envision working-class readers. She encouraged the manufacturer Edmund Potter to give copies of *Mary Barton* to his employees (*Letters* 66), and the *Northern Star* praised it in a review of *Moorland Cottage* (28 Dec. 1850: 3).

Coda

1. In part because reform did not become "widely revived" until May of 1865 and in part because she did not begin reading material related to the Reform Bill of 1832 until that month, Fred Thompson suggests that Eliot's original conception involved the Transome inheritance and did not include the reform/radicalism plot (xiii; see also xvii). While the evidence about her reading is persuasive, it is not quite true that debate about reform did not become prominent until May, the month that Edward Baines brought forward a proposal for household suffrage. The Reform Union had been created the previous year, the Reform League was founded early in 1865, and from the end of January there had been a series of meetings to advance reform.

2. Samuel Bamford's *Passages in the Life of a Radical* (1840–1844) depicts his activities in 1816–1821, the first part of which era covers events depicted by Howitt; Howitt was personally acquainted with Bamford and quotes *Passages* in his novel (Woodring 125; Howitt, *Man of the People* 2.9.241–44, citing Bamford 1.5.23). *Passages* is also the first book related to reform and the plot of *Felix Holt* that Eliot recorded reading (*Journals* 124; Fred Thompson xiv).

3. On this linkage in both Chartist and parliamentary discourse, see chap. 2.

4. "Felix Holt the Radical," said Joseph Jacob in 1895, "is rather Felix Holt the Conservative. He is not even a Tory Democrat" (quoted in Bamber 432). See especially Horowitz's "George Eliot: The Conservative," the argument of which is not inconsistent with that of other critics, such as Hobson, who refers to Eliot's "progressive-conservative

politics" (21). See also Bamber 424; Butwin 353; David, *Intellectual Women* 206. Gallagher, "Politics of Culture," and Bodenheimer, *Politics of Story* (esp. 106–8) both seek to complicate this view.

5. On the Howitts' relationship with the Gaskells, see Uglow 115–17, 170–71. There is a record that the Howitts also read Kingsley's *Alton Locke* (Lee 188).

6. See also the passage in which the narrator, after describing the "horrors" of poverty witnessed by the protagonist, concludes: "They who live now in prosperous, improved, enlightened, sympathizing England, can never conceive fully the hard, and dark, and bitter England of that day" (3.12.266, 267). The narrator elsewhere comments that the views of Philip's father, which had been considered "revolutionary, Jacobinical . . . would now be acknowledged as the everlasting truth of the everlasting gospel" (1.2.67).

7. See also passages referring to the people as "maniacs," "demented creatures," "clean mad," and "madmen" (3.8.172, 3.9.192, 193, 195).

8. Felix uses the term the "best self" in a discussion with Esther (27.262). The phrase comes from Arnold, *Culture and Anarchy* (99). On the relation between *Culture and Anarchy* and *Felix Holt*, see Gallagher, "Politics of Culture" 121–27; and Bentley 275–76. See also Bodenheimer on Holt's desire to locate action outside of class (*Politics of Story* 99).

9. See Bentley's excellent discussion of the contradictions within Holt's conflation of self-culture and conversion (279–81). Relevant here also is Gallagher's contention that his conversion has no social determinant ("Politics of Culture" 128). I would link this problematic to the fact that the novel cannot imagine the education of the people, but at the same time the similarity of the inwardness of Esther's education and Felix's vocation suggests that the latter involves a process of educational self-culture.

10. See, for example, Bamber 430. For a general discussion of class in the novel, see also Butwin.

11. See, for example, David, who argues that Eliot's novel "subverts the dominant model of ameliorative change elaborated by organic intellectuals in Victorian England" (*Intellectual Women* 197; see also 205).

Works Cited

Abrams, M. H., and Geoffrey Galt Harpham. *A Glossary of Literary Terms.* 9th ed. Boston: Wadsworth, 2009.

Ainsworth, Harrison. *Guy Fawkes: An Historical Romance. Bentley's Magazine* 7 (1840): 1–10, 107–22, 219–34, 333–48, 441–56, 545–59; 8 (1840): 1–16, 105–20, 217–32, 322–35, 425–40, 529–44; 9 (1841): 1–16, 113–28, 225–40, 329–44, 441–56, 551–56; 10 (1841): 1–16, 105–20, 312–19, 422–28, 529–40.

———. *Guy Fawkes; or, The Gunpowder Treason: An Historical Romance.* 3 vols. London: Bentley, 1841.

Alison, Archibald. "The Chartists and Universal Suffrage." *Blackwood's Magazine* 46 (1839): 289–303.

Anderson, Amanda. *The Powers of Distance: Cosmopolitanism and the Cultivation of Detachment.* Princeton, NJ: Princeton University Press, 2001.

———. *Tainted Souls and Painted Faces: The Rhetoric of Fallenness in Victorian Culture.* Ithaca, NY: Cornell University Press, 1993.

Arnold, Matthew. *Culture and Anarchy and Other Writings.* Edited by Stefan Collini. Cambridge: Cambridge University Press, 1993.

Bakhtin, M. M. *The Dialogic Imagination: Four Essays.* Edited by Michael Holquist. Translated by Michael Holquist and Caryl Emerson. Austin: University of Texas Press, 1981.

Baldick, Chris. *The Concise Oxford Dictionary of Literary Terms.* Oxford: Oxford University Press, 2004.

Bamber, Linda. "Self-Defeating Politics in George Eliot's *Felix Holt.*" *Victorian Studies* 18 (1975): 419–35.

Bamford, Samuel. *Passages in the Life of a Radical.* 2 vols. London: Simpkin, Marshall, 1844.

Belchem, John. "Republicanism, Popular Constitutionalism and the Radical Platform in Early Nineteenth-Century England." *Social History* 6 (1981): 1–32.

Bentley, Colene. "Democratic Citizenship in *Felix Holt.*" *Nineteenth-Century Contexts* 24.3 (2002): 271–89.

Betensky, Carolyn. *Feeling for the Poor: Bourgeois Compassion, Social Action, and the Novel.* Charlottesville: University of Virginia Press, 2010.

Bigelow, Gordon. *Fiction, Famine, and the Rise of Economics in Victorian Britain and Ireland*. Cambridge: Cambridge University Press, 2003.

Blackstone, William. *Commentaries on the Laws of England*. Oxford, 1766–67.

Bodenheimer, Rosemarie. *The Politics of Story in Victorian Social Fiction*. Ithaca, NY: Cornell University Press, 1988.

———. "Private Grief and Public Acts in *Mary Barton*." *Dickens Studies Annual* 9 (1981): 195–216.

Bonner, Arnold. *British Co-operation: The History, Principles, and Organisation of the British Co-operative Movement*. Manchester: Co-operative Union, 1961.

Bowen, John. *Other Dickens: Pickwick to Chuzzlewit*. Oxford: Oxford University Press, 2000.

Brantlinger, Patrick. *The Spirit of Reform: British Literature and Politics, 1832–1867*. Cambridge, MA: Harvard University Press, 1977.

Braun, Thom. *Disraeli the Novelist*. London: Allen and Unwin, 1981.

Breton, Rob. "Ghosts in the Machina: Plotting in Chartist and Working-Class Fiction." *Victorian Studies* 47 (2005): 557–75.

Bronstein, Jamie. *Land Reform and Working-Class Experience in Britain and the United States, 1800–1862*. Palo Alto, CA: Stanford University Press, 1999.

Burchardt, Jeremy. *The Allotment Movement in England, 1793–1873*. Woodbridge: Boydell, 2002.

Butt, John, and Kathleen Tillotson. *Dickens at Work*. Fair Lawn, NJ: Essential Books, 1958.

Butwin, Joseph. "The Pacification of the Crowd: From 'Janet's Repentance' to *Felix Holt*." *Nineteenth-Century Fiction* 35.3 (1980): 349–71.

Cahill, Gilbert A. "Irish Catholicism and English Toryism." *Review of Politics* 19 (1957): 62–76.

Cannadine, David. *The Rise and Fall of Class in Britain*. New York: Columbia University Press, 1999.

Carlyle, Thomas. "Chartism." *Critical and Miscellaneous Essays*. Vol. 29 of the Centenary Edition, edited by H. D. Traill, 30 vols. New York: Scribners, 1899.

———. *The Collected Letters of Thomas and Jane Welsh Carlyle*. Edited by C. R. Sanders, K. J. Fielding, C. de L. Ryals, Ian Campbell, David Sorenson, Aileen Christianson, et al. 38 vols. to date. Durham, NC: Duke University Press, 1970–.

———. *The French Revolution*. Vols. 2–4 of the Centenary Edition, edited by H. D. Traill, 30 vols. New York: Scribners, 1899.

———. *Latter-Day Pamphlets*. New York: Scribners, 1899. Vol. 20 of the Centenary Edition, edited by H. D. Traill, 30 vols. New York: Scribners, 1899.

———. *Past and Present*. Edited by Chris R. Vanden Bossche, Joel J. Brattin, and D. J. Trela. Berkeley: University of California Press, 2005.

Cazamian, Louis. *The Social Novel in England, 1830–1850: Dickens, Disraeli, Mrs. Gaskell, Kingsley*. Translated by Martin Fido. London: Routledge, 1973.

Chadwick, Esther Alice. *Mrs. Gaskell: Haunts, Homes, and Stories*. London: Pitman, 1910.

Chandler, Alice. *A Dream of Order: The Medieval Ideal in Nineteenth-Century English Literature*. Lincoln: University of Nebraska Press, 1970.

"The Charter and the Land." In *The Literature of Struggle: An Anthology of Chartist Fiction*, edited by Ian Haywood, 191–94. Aldershot: Scolar, 1995.

Chase, Malcolm. *Chartism: A New History*. Manchester: Manchester University Press, 2007.

———. *Early Trade Unionism: Fraternity, Skill and the Politics of Labour*. Aldershot: Ashgate, 2000.

———. *The People's Farm: English Radical Agrarianism, 1775–1840*. Oxford: Clarendon, 1988.

———. "'We Wish Only to Work for Ourselves': The Chartist Land Plan." In *Living and Learning: Essays in Honour of J. F. C. Harrison*, edited by Malcolm Chase and Ian Dyck, 133–48. Aldershot: Scolar, 1996.

Childers, Joseph W. *Novel Possibilities: Fiction and the Formation of Early Victorian Culture*. Philadelphia: University of Pennsylvania Press, 1995.

Christensen, Torben. *The Origin and History of Christian Socialism, 1848–1854*. Aarhus: Universitetsforlaget, 1962.

Claybaugh, Amanda. *The Novel of Purpose: Literature and Social Reform in the Anglo-American World*. Ithaca, NY: Cornell University Press, 2007.

Cole, G. D. H. *A Century of Co-operation*. London: Allen and Unwin, 1944.

Colón, Susan E. *The Professional Ideal in the Victorian Novel: The Works of Disraeli, Trollope, Gaskell, and Eliot*. Basingstoke: Palgrave Macmillan, 2007.

Cooper, Thomas. *The Purgatory of Suicides: A Prison-Rhyme*. London: How, 1845.

Corbett, Mary Jean. *Allegories of Union in Irish and English Writing, 1790–1870*. Cambridge: Cambridge University Press, 2000.

[Craik, George Lillie], ed. *The Pictorial History of England: Being a History of the People as Well as a History of the Kingdom*. Vol. 1. London: Knight, 1838.

D'Albertis, Deirdre. *Dissembling Fictions: Elizabeth Gaskell and the Victorian Social Text*. New York: St. Martin's, 1997.

David, Deirdre. *Fictions of Resolution in Three Victorian Novels: "North and South," "Our Mutual Friend," "Daniel Deronda."* New York: Columbia University Press, 1981.

———. *Intellectual Women and Victorian Patriarchy: Harriet Martineau, Elizabeth Barrett Browning, George Eliot*. Ithaca, NY: Cornell University Press, 1987.

Dickens, Charles. *Barnaby Rudge: A Tale of the Riots of 'Eighty*. Edited by John Bowen. Penguin: London, 2003.

———. *The Letters of Charles Dickens*. Edited by Madeline House and Graham Storey. 12 vols. Oxford: Clarendon, 1965–2002.

Dickinson, H. T. Introduction to *The Political Works of Thomas Spence*. Newcastle Upon Tyne: Avero (Eighteenth-Century) Publications, 1982.

———. *Liberty and Property: Political Ideology in Eighteenth-Century Britain*. New York: Holmes and Meier, 1977.

Disraeli, Benjamin. *Benjamin Disraeli Letters*. Edited by J. A. W. Gunn. 7 vols. to date. Toronto: University of Toronto Press, 1982–.

———. *Coningsby; or The New Generation*. Edited by Thom Braun. Harmondsworth: Penguin, 1983.

———. *Sybil; or, The Two Nations*. Edited by Thom Braun. Harmondsworth: Penguin, 1980.

——. *Vindication of the English Constitution in a Letter to a Noble and Learned Lord*. London: Saunders and Otley, 1835.

Doubleday, Thomas. *The Political Pilgrim's Progress*. Vol. 1 of *Chartist Fiction*, edited by Ian Haywood. Aldershot: Ashgate, 1999.

Duncan, Ian. *Scott's Shadow: The Novel in Romantic Edinburgh*. Princeton, NJ: Princeton University Press, 2007.

Dunn, Alistair. *The Great Rising of 1381: The Peasants' Revolt and England's Failed Revolution*. Stroud: Tempus, 2002.

Dutton, H. I., and J. E. King. *"Ten Per Cent and No Surrender": The Preston Strike, 1853–1854*. Cambridge: Cambridge University Press, 1981.

Easson, Angus. "Elizabeth Gaskell, J. M. Ludlow, and W. R. Greg." *Notes and Queries* 236 (1991): 315–17.

——. *Elizabeth Gaskell: The Critical Heritage*. London: Routledge, 1991.

Egan, Pierce. *Wat Tyler*. London: Hextall, 1841.

Eliot, George. *Felix Holt, the Radical*. Edited by Lynda Mugglestone. London: Penguin, 1995.

——. *The Journals of George Eliot*. Edited by Margaret Harris and Judith Johnston. Cambridge: Cambridge University Press, 1998.

Elliott, Dorice Williams. *The Angel out of the House: Philanthropy and Gender in Nineteenth-Century England*. Charlottesville: University of Virginia Press, 2002.

Epstein, James. *The Lion of Freedom: Feargus O'Connor and the Chartist Movement, 1832–1842*. London: Croom Helm, 1982.

——. *Radical Expression: Political Language, Ritual, and Symbol in England, 1790–1850*. Oxford: Oxford University Press, 1994.

Ferris, Ina. *The Romantic National Tale and the Question of Ireland*. Cambridge: Cambridge University Press, 2002.

Fleishman, Avrom. *The English Historical Novel: Walter Scott to Virginia Woolf*. Baltimore: Johns Hopkins University Press, 1971.

Folland, Harold F. "The Doer and the Deed: Theme and Pattern in *Barnaby Rudge*." *PMLA* 74 (1959): 406–17.

Fraser, W. Hamish. *A History of British Trade Unionism, 1700–1998*. New York: St. Martin's, 1999.

Gallagher, Catherine. *The Industrial Reformation of English Fiction: Social Discourse and Narrative Form, 1832–1867*. Chicago: University of Chicago Press, 1985.

——. "The Politics of Culture and the Debate over Representation." *Representations* 5 (1984): 115–47.

Ganz, Margaret. *Elizabeth Gaskell: The Artist in Conflict*. New York: Twayne, 1969.

Gash, Norman. *Robert Surtees and Early Victorian Society*. Oxford: Oxford University Press, 1993.

Gaskell, Elizabeth. *The Letters of Mrs Gaskell*. Edited by J. A. V. Chapple and Arthur Pollard. Cambridge: Harvard University Press, 1967.

——. *Mary Barton: A Tale of Manchester Life*. Edited by Stephen Gill. Harmondsworth: Penguin, 1970.

——. *North and South*. Edited by Angus Easson. Oxford: Oxford University Press, 1998.

Gill, Stephen. "Price's Patent Candles: New Light on *North and South*." *Review of English Studies*, n.s., 27 (1976): 313–21.

Girard, René. *Deceit, Desire, and the Novel: Self and Other in Literary Structure*. Translated by Yvonne Freccero. Baltimore: Johns Hopkins University Press, 1965.

Goddard, Nicholas. *Harvests of Change: The Royal Agricultural Society of England, 1838–1988*. London: Quiller, 1988.

Goodlad, Lauren. *Victorian Literature and the Victorian State: Character and Governance in a Liberal Society*. Baltimore: Johns Hopkins University Press, 2003.

Gore, Catherine. *The Hamiltons; or, Official Life in 1830*. London: Bentley, 1850.

Groden, Michael, Martin Kreiswirth, and Imre Szeman, eds. *The Johns Hopkins Guide to Literary Theory and Criticism*. 2d ed. Baltimore: Johns Hopkins University Press, 2005. http://litguide.press.jhu.edu/.

Guy, Josephine. M. *The Victorian Social-Problem Novel: The Market, the Individual, and Communal Life*. New York: St. Martin's, 1996.

Hansard's Parliamentary Debates. London: T. C. Hansard, 1820–. http://hansard.millbanksystems.com.

Hartley, Allan John. *The Novels of Charles Kingsley: A Christian Social Interpretation*. Folkestone: Hour-Glass, 1977.

Haywood, Ian, ed. *Chartist Fiction*. Aldershot: Ashgate, 1999.

———, ed. *The Literature of Struggle: An Anthology of Chartist Fiction*. Aldershot: Scolar, 1995.

———. "'The Renovating Fury': Southey, Republicanism and Sensationalism." *Romanticism on the Net* 32–33 (2003). Currently available at www.erudit.org/revue/ron/2003/v/n32-33/009256ar.html.

———. *The Revolution in Popular Literature: Print, Politics and the People, 1790–1860*. Cambridge: Cambridge University Press, 2004.

———. *Working-Class Fiction from Chartism to Trainspotting*. Plymouth: Northcote House, 1997.

Hill, Christopher. *Puritanism and Revolution: Studies in Interpretation of the English Revolution of the 17th Century*. London: Secker and Warburg, 1958.

Hobson, Christopher Z. "The Radicalism of *Felix Holt*: George Eliot and the Pioneers of Labor." *Victorian Literature and Culture* 26.1 (1998): 19–39.

Horowitz, Evan. "George Eliot: The Conservative." *Victorian Studies* 49.1 (2006): 7–32.

Housman, John. *A Topographical Description of Cumberland, Westmoreland, Lancashire, and a Part of the West Riding of Yorkshire*. Carlisle, 1800.

Howitt, William. *The Man of the People*. 3 vols. London: Hurst and Brackett, 1860.

Ingham, Patricia. *The Language of Gender and Class: Transformation in the Victorian Novel*. London: Routledge, 1996.

Jaffe, Audrey. *Scenes of Sympathy: Identity and Representation in Victorian Fiction*. Ithaca, NY: Cornell University Press, 2000.

Jameson, Fredric. *The Political Unconscious: Narrative as a Socially Symbolic Act*. Ithaca, NY: Cornell University Press, 1981.

Jardine, David. *Criminal Trials*. Vol. 2. London: Knight, 1835.

Jay, Elisabeth. Introduction to *North and South*, by Elizabeth Gaskell, ix–xxiii. London: Pickering, 2005.

Jeffreys, James B. *The Story of the Engineers, 1800–1945*. 1946. Reprint, New York: Johnson, 1970.

Jones, Ernest. *Notes to the People*. Vol. 1. London: Pavey, 1851.

Jones, Paul Dafydd. "Jesus Christ and the Transformation of English Society: The 'Sub-versive Conservatism' of Frederick Denison Maurice." *Harvard Theological Review* 96 (2003): 205–28.

Joyce, Patrick, ed. *Class*. Oxford: Oxford University Press, 1995.

———. *Visions of the People: Industrial England and the Question of Class, 1840–1914*. Cambridge: Cambridge University Press, 1991.

Judge, David. *Representation: Theory and Practice in British Politics*. London: Routledge, 1999.

The Just Reward of Rebels; or, The Life and Death of Jack Straw and Wat Tyler. London, 1642.

Kingsley, Charles. *Alton Locke, Tailor and Poet: An Autobiography*. Oxford: Oxford University Press, 1983.

———. *Charles Kingsley: His Letters and Memories of His Life*. Edited by Fanny Kingsley. 2 vols. London: Kegan Paul, 1878.

———. "The Nun's Pool." *The Christian Socialist: A Journal of Association* 2 (1851): 13–15, 29–31, 46–47, 78–79, 94–95, 125–127, 142–43.

———. "Recent Novels." *Fraser's Magazine* 39 (1849): 417–32.

———. *Who Are the Friends of Order? A Reply to Certain Observations in a Late Number of Fraser's Magazine on the So-Called "Christian Socialists."* London: Lumley, 1852.

———. *Yeast: A Problem*. London: Parker, 1851.

———. *Yeast; or, The Thoughts, Sayings, and Doings of Lancelot Smith, Gentleman. Fraser's Magazine* 38 (1848): 102–15, 195–210, 284–300, 447–60, 530–47, 689–711.

Klaus, H. Gustav. *The Literature of Labour: Two Hundred Years of Working-Class Writing*. New York: St. Martin's, 1985.

Kuduk, Stephanie. "Sedition, Chartism, and Epic Poetry in Thomas Cooper's *The Purgatory of Suicides*." *Victorian Poetry* 39 (2001): 165–86.

Larson, Magali Sarfatti. *The Rise of Professionalism: A Sociological Analysis*. Berkeley: University of California Press, 1977.

Lathbury, Thomas. *Guy Fawkes; or, A Complete History of the Gunpowder Treason, A.D. 1605; With a Developement of the Principles of the Conspirators, and Some Notices of the Revolution of 1688*. London: Parker, 1839.

Ledger, Sally. *Dickens and the Popular Radical Imagination*. Cambridge: Cambridge University Press, 2007.

Lee, Amice. *Laurels & Rosemary: The Life of William and Mary Howitt*. London: Oxford University Press, 1955.

Lesjak, Carolyn. *Working Fictions: A Genealogy of the Victorian Novel*. Durham, NC: Duke University Press, 2006.

Lincoln, Andrew. *Walter Scott and Modernity*. Edinburgh: Edinburgh University Press, 2007.

Lingard, John. *The History of England from the First Invasion of the Romans*. 13 vols. London: Baldwin and Cradock, 1837–1839.

Lucas, John. *The Melancholy Man: A Study of Dickens's Novels*. London: Methuen, 1970.

Ludlow, John. *John Ludlow: The Autobiography of a Christian Socialist*. Edited by A. D. Murray. London: Cass, 1981.

Marcus, Sharon. *Between Women: Friendship, Desire, and Marriage in Victorian England*. Princeton, NJ: Princeton University Press, 2007.

Marcus, Steven. *Dickens: From Pickwick to Dombey*. New York: Basic Books, 1965.

Martin, Robert Bernard. *The Dust of Combat: A Life of Charles Kingsley*. Edited by A. D. Murray. New York: Norton, 1960.

Maurer, Sara. *The Dispossessed State: Narratives of Ownership in Nineteenth-Century Britain and Ireland*. Baltimore: Johns Hopkins University Press, 2012.

Maurice, Frederick Denison. *A Dialogue Between A. and B., Two Clergymen, On the Doctrine of Circumstances As It Affects Priests and People*. Tracts on Christian Socialism no. 7. London: Bell, 1850

———. *Dialogue between Somebody (a person of respectability) and Nobody (the writer)*. Tracts on Christian Socialism no. 1. London: Bell, 1850.

———. *The Life of Frederick Denison Maurice Chiefly Told in His Own Letters*. Edited by Frederick Maurice. 2 vols. London: Macmillan, 1884.

———. "Recollections and Confessions of William Milward." *Politics for the People* 10 (1848): 161–76; 16 (1848): 257–72.

———. *The Reformation of Society, and How All Classes May Contribute to It*. London: Tupling, 1851.

Mitchell, Jack. "Aesthetic Problems of the Development of the Proletarian-Revolutionary Novel in Nineteenth-Century Britain." In *Marxists on Literature: An Anthology*, edited by David Craig, 245–66. Harmondsworth: Penguin, 1975.

Monypenny, William Flavelle, and George Earle Buckle. *The Life of Benjamin Disraeli, Earl of Beaconsfield*. 2 vols. London: Murray, 1929.

Morris, Pam. *Imagining Inclusive Society in Nineteenth-Century Novels: The Code of Sincerity in the Public Sphere*. Baltimore: Johns Hopkins University Press, 2004.

Morse, Deborah Denenholz. "Mutiny in the *Orion*: The Legacy of the *Hermione* Mutiny and the Politics of Nonviolent Protest in Elizabeth Gaskell's *North and South*." In *Pirates and Mutineers of the Nineteenth Century: Swashbucklers and Swindlers*, edited by Grace Moore, 117–31. Farnham: Ashgate, 2011.

Neumann, Bonnie Rayford. *Robert Smith Surtees*. Boston: Twayne, 1978.

Nightingale, Florence. *Cassandra*. Old Westbury: Feminist Press, 1979.

Nord, Deborah Epstein. *Walking the Victorian Streets: Women, Representation, and the City*. Ithaca, NY: Cornell University Press, 1995.

O'Connor, Feargus. *A Practical Work on the Management of Small Farms*. London: Cleave, 1843.

O'Malley, Patrick R. *Catholicism, Sexual Deviance, and Victorian Gothic Culture*. Cambridge: Cambridge University Press, 2006.

Oman, Charles. *The Great Revolt of 1381*. Oxford: Clarendon, 1906.

[O'Neill, Mrs.] *The Bondman: A Story of the Times of Wat Tyler*. New York: Wallis and Newell, 1835.

Paine, Thomas. *Rights of Man: Part the Second*. London: Jordan, 1792.

Paz, D. G. *Dickens and "Barnaby Rudge": Anti-Catholicism and Chartism*. Monmouth, Wales: Merlin, 2006.

———. *Popular Anti-Catholicism in Mid-Victorian England*. Stanford, CA: Stanford University Press, 1992.

Perkin, Harold. *The Origins of Modern English Society, 1780–1880.* London: Routledge, 1969.

Peschier, Diana. *Nineteenth-Century Anti-Catholic Discourses: The Case of Charlotte Brontë.* London: Palgrave, 2005.

Pionke, Albert D. *Plots of Opportunity: Representing Conspiracy in Victorian England.* Columbus: Ohio State University Press, 2004.

Pitkin, Hanna Fenichel. *The Concept of Representation.* Berkeley: University of California Press, 1967.

Plotz, John. *The Crowd: British Literature and Public Politics.* Berkeley: University of California Press, 2000.

———. *Portable Property: Victorian Culture on the Move.* Princeton, NJ: Princeton University Press, 2008.

Poovey, Mary. *Making a Social Body: British Cultural Formation, 1830–1864.* Chicago: University of Chicago Press, 1995.

Pykett, Lyn. *Charles Dickens.* Basingstoke: Palgrave, 2002.

Raven, Charles. *Christian Socialism, 1848–1854.* London: Macmillan, 1920.

Reader, William Joseph. *Professional Men: The Rise of the Professional Classes in Nineteenth-Century England.* New York: Basic Books, 1966.

Report of the Select Committee on the Labouring Poor (Allotments of Land); with the Minutes of Evidence, Appendix and Index. London: House of Commons, 1843.

Rice, Thomas Jackson. "The Politics of *Barnaby Rudge.*" In *The Changing World of Charles Dickens,* edited by Robert Giddings, 52–74. London: Vision; Totowa, NJ: Barnes and Noble, 1983.

Roberts, F. David. *Paternalism in Early Victorian England.* New Brunswick, NJ: Rutgers University Press, 1979.

———. *The Social Conscience of the Early Victorians.* Stanford, CA: Stanford University Press, 2002.

Roy, Parama. "*Sybil*: The Two Nations and the Manorial Ideal." *Victorians Institute Journal* 17 (1989): 63–75.

Sabin, Margery. "Working-Class Plain Style: William Lovett vs. Carlyle, Gaskell, and Others." *Raritan: A Quarterly Review* 18.2 (1998): 41–62.

Sanders, Andrew. "A Crisis of Liberalism in *North and South.*" *Gaskell Society Journal* 10 (1996): 42–52.

Sedgwick, Eve Kosofsky. *Between Men: English Literature and Male Homosocial Desire.* New York: Columbia University Press, 1985.

Schor, Hilary Margo. *Scheherezade in the Marketplace: Elizabeth Gaskell and the Victorian Novel.* New York: Oxford University Press, 1992.

Seed, John. "Unitarianism, Political Economy and the Antinomies of Liberal Culture in Manchester, 1830–50." *Social History* 7 (1982): 1–25.

Seehase, Georg. "*Sunshine and Shadow* and the Structure of Chartist Fiction." *Zeitschrift für Anglistik und Amerikanistik* 21 (1973): 126–36.

Sen, Sambudha. "*Bleak House* and *Little Dorrit*: The Radical Heritage." *English Literary History* 65 (1998): 945–70.

Shaen, Margaret Josephine. *Memorials of Two Sisters: Susanna and Catherine Winkworth.* London: Longmans, 1908.

Sharpe, James. *Remember, Remember: A Cultural History of Guy Fawkes Day*. Cambridge, MA: Harvard University Press, 2005.

Shusterman, David. "William Rathbone Greg and Mrs. Gaskell." *Philological Quarterly* 36 (1957): 268–72.

Shuttleworth, Sally. Introduction to *North and South*, by Elizabeth Gaskell, edited by Angus Easson, ix–xxxiv. Oxford: Oxford University Press, 1998.

Smith, James. *Remarks on Thorough Draining and Deep Ploughing*. Stirling, 1837.

Southey, Robert. *Wat Tyler: A Dramatic Poem*. London: Sherwood, 1817.

Spence, Gordon. Introduction to *Barnaby Rudge: A Tale of the Riots of 'Eighties*, by Charles Dickens. Harmondsworth: Penguin, 1977.

Spence, Thomas. *The Meridian Sun of Liberty; or, The Whole Right of Man, Displayed and Most Accurately Defined*. London, 1796.

Starr, Elizabeth. "'A Great Engine for Good': The Industry of Fiction in Elizabeth Gaskell's *Mary Barton* and *North and South*." *Studies in the Novel* 34 (2002): 385–402.

Stedman Jones, Gareth. *Languages of Class: Studies in English Working Class History, 1832–1982*. Cambridge: Cambridge University Press, 1983.

Stevens, William. *A Memoir of Thomas Martin Wheeler*. London: Leno, 1862. Facsimile reprint in *Chartism: Working-Class Politics in the Industrial Revolution*, edited by Dorothy Thompson. New York: Garland, 1986.

Stigant, Paul, and Peter Widdowson. "*Barnaby Rudge*—A Historical Novel?" *Literature and History* 2 (1975): 2–44.

Stone, Lawrence. *The Family, Sex and Marriage in England, 1500–1800*. New York: Harper and Row, 1977.

Stoneman, Patsy. *Elizabeth Gaskell*. Bloomington: Indiana University Press, 1987.

Storey, Mark. *Robert Southey: A Life*. Oxford: Oxford University Press, 1997.

Stow, John. *The Chronicles of England from Brute unto This Present Yeare of Christ*. London, 1580.

[Surtees, Robert Smith]. *Hillingdon Hall; or, The Cockney Squire: A Tale of Country Life*. 3 vols. London: Colburn, 1845.

Swift, Jonathan. *Gulliver's Travels*. Edited by Robert DeMaria Jr. London: Penguin, 2003.

Tarrow, Sidney. *Power in Movement: Social Movements and Contentious Politics*. 2d ed. Cambridge: Cambridge University Press, 1998.

Thiele, David. "'That There Brutus': Elite Culture and Knowledge Diffusion in the Industrial Novels of Elizabeth Gaskell." *Victorian Literature and Culture* 25 (2007): 263–85.

Thomas, David Wayne. *Cultivating the Victorians: Liberal Culture and the Aesthetic*. Philadelphia: University of Pennsylvania Press, 2004.

Thompson, Dorothy. *The Chartists: Popular Politics in the Industrial Revolution*. New York: Pantheon, 1984.

Thompson, F. M. L. "Percy, Hugh, third duke of Northumberland (1785–1847)." *Oxford Dictionary of National Biography*. Oxford: Oxford University Press, 2004.

Thompson, Fred C. Introduction to *Felix Holt, the Radical*, by George Eliot, xiii–xxxviii. Oxford: Clarendon, 1980.

Tilly, Charles. *Popular Contention in Great Britain, 1758–1834*. Cambridge, MA: Harvard University Press, 1995.

Trumpener, Katie. *Bardic Nationalism: The Romantic Novel and the British Empire*. Princeton, NJ: Princeton University Press, 1997.

Uglow, Jenny. *Elizabeth Gaskell: A Habit of Stories*. New York: Farrar, Straus, Giroux, 1993.

Ulrich, John M. *Signs of Their Times: History, Labor, and the Body in Cobbett, Carlyle, and Disraeli*. Athens: Ohio University Press, 2002.

Vanden Bossche, Chris R. "Chartism, Class Discourse, and the Captain of Industry: Social Agency in *Chartism* and *Past and Present*." In *Thomas Carlyle Resartus: Reappraising Carlyle's Contribution to the Philosophy of History, Political Theory, and Cultural Criticism*, edited by Paul Kerry and Marylu Hill, 30–48. Madison, NJ: Fairleigh Dickinson University Press, 2010.

———. "On Chartism." In *BRANCH: Britain, Representation, and Nineteenth-Century History*, edited by Dino Felluga. DHCommons, www.branchcollective.org.

———. "Social Agency and the Representation of Chartism in *Mary Barton*." *Victorians Institute Journal* 38 (2010): 171–88.

———. "What Did *Jane Eyre* Do? Ideology, Agency, Class and the Novel." *Narrative* 13 (2005): 46–66.

Vaninskaya, Anna. "*Dreams* of John Ball: Reading the Peasants' Revolt in the Nineteenth Century." *Nineteenth-Century Contexts* 31 (2009): 45–57.

Vernon, James. *Politics and the People: A Study in English Political Culture, c. 1815–1867*. New York: Cambridge University Press, 1993.

———, ed. *Re-reading the Constitution: New Narratives in the Political History of England's Long Nineteenth Century*. Cambridge: Cambridge University Press, 1996.

Vicinus, Martha. *The Industrial Muse: A Study of Nineteenth-Century British Working-Class Literature*. London: Croom Helm, 1974.

Viswanathan, Gauri. *Outside the Fold: Conversion, Modernity, and Belief*. Princeton, NJ: Princeton University Press, 1998.

Wahrman, Dror. *Imagining the Middle Class: The Political Representation of Class in Britain, c. 1780–1840*. Cambridge: Cambridge University Press, 1995.

Wasson, E. A. "The Third Earl Spencer and Agriculture, 1818–1845." *Agricultural History Review* 26 (1978): 89–99.

Weintraub, Stanley. *Disraeli: A Biography*. New York: Dutton, 1993.

Wheeler, Thomas Martin. *Sunshine and Shadow*. Vol. 2 of *Chartist Fiction*, edited by Ian Haywood. Aldershot: Ashgate, 1999.

Whibley, Charles. *Lord John Manners and His Friends*. 2 vols. Edinburgh: Blackwood, 1825.

Williams, Raymond. *Culture and Society, 1780–1950*. New York: Columbia University Press, 1958.

———. *Marxism and Literature*. Oxford: Oxford University Press, 1977.

Willis, Mark. "Charles Dickens and Fictions of the Crowd." *Dickens Quarterly* 23 (2006): 85–107.

Wilt, Judith. "Masques of the English in *Barnaby Rudge*." *Dickens Studies Annual: Essays on Victorian Fiction* 30 (2001): 75–94.

Wolfreys, Julian, Ruth Robbins, and Kenneth Womack, eds. *Key Concepts in Literary Theory*. Edinburgh: Edinburgh University Press, 2002.

Woodring, Carl R. *Victorian Samplers: William and Mary Howitt*. Lawrence: University of Kansas Press, 1952.

Worth, George. *William Harrison Ainsworth*. New York: Twayne, 1972.

Yeo, Eileen James. "Language and Contestation: The Case of 'the People,' 1832 to the Present." In *Languages of Labour*, edited by John Belchem and Neville Kirk, 44–62. Ashgate: Aldershot, 1997.

Zlotnick, Susan. *Women, Writing, and the Industrial Revolution*. Baltimore: Johns Hopkins University Press, 1998.

Index

Acts of Union (1801), 14

agrarianism, 75, 79, 95, 122

agriculture. *See* Surtees, Robert Smith

Ainsworth, Harrison, 22, 99, 214–15n6, 218–19n13; aristocracy in, 53, 54, 55–56, 58; audience of, 35; Catholics in, 50–59, 60; and Dickens, 214–15n6; *Guy Fawkes*, 5, 17, 35, 36, 50–59, 60, 61, 66, 215n10; *Jack Sheppard*, 50; marriage in, 53–57, 58–59; middle class in, 17, 50, 53, 54, 56, 58, 59; political sympathies of, 36

Alton Locke (Kingsley), 5, 17, 139, 142, 149, 150–63, 164, 176, 177–78, 183–84, 230n30; aristocracy in, 153, 156, 158, 159; Chartists in, 139, 150, 152, 153, 154, 155, 157, 160, 161–62, 163; clergy in, 150, 151, 153, 155, 157, 159, 160, 161, 162, 163, 164; poor people in, 152, 157; rationality in, 150, 154, 155, 156, 160–62; religion in, 150, 157, 158, 159, 160, 162, 163; working class in, 150–51, 152, 153, 154, 159, 160, 162, 163, 177–78, 184

Amalgamated Society of Engineers, 129, 131, 132, 140, 178, 184

Anglo-Catholicism, 99, 146

Anti–Corn Law League, 10, 103, 106, 107, 117, 175, 190, 219–20n5

aristocracy, 5, 7, 24, 27, 31, 38, 50, 79, 134; and allotment schemes, 76–78, 79; and class discourse, 11, 12; constitutional histories of, 11; and dichotomous model, 26; and Egan, 40, 41, 45, 46; and entrepreneurs, 9–10; and finely graded hierarchy, 11–12, 17, 77, 78, 142; self-interest of, 61, 85, 86, 87, 104; in Wheeler, 15, 114, 117; Whigs as, 8; and working class, 25. *See also under* Dickens, Charles; *under* Disraeli, Benjamin; *under* Gaskell, Elizabeth; *under* Kingsley, Charles; *under* Surtees, Robert Smith

Arnold, Matthew, *Culture and Anarchy*, 232n

Austen, Jane, *Pride and Prejudice*, 180

Bamford, Samuel, 190

Barnaby Rudge (Dickens), 5, 17, 35, 36, 60–71, 85, 88–89, 93, 170, 182; aristocracy in, 60–62, 63, 66, 68, 69, 70, 85; Catholics in, 60, 61, 62, 63, 64, 66, 67, 68, 69; middle class in, 17, 36, 60–61, 62, 66, 68, 69, 70, 71, 85, 89

Beauchamp, Lewis, 43

Bentley's Magazine, 35, 50

Bible, 143, 156, 157, 160, 172, 173, 226n8

Blackstone, William, 9, 10, 222n6

Blake, William, 37

Blanc, Louis, 130, 132, 137, 138; *L'Organisation du travail*, 131

boycotts, 3, 22, 32, 81

British Quarterly Review, 175

Browning, Elizabeth Barrett, 143

Bull Ring Riots, 23, 120, 207n27

Bunyan, John, 21
Burdett, Francis, 162
Burke, Edmund, 204n3
Burns, Robert, 162, 167
Byron, Lord, 156, 157

Carlyle, Thomas, 16, 134, 143, 148; *Chartism*, 155, 162–63, 230n24; *The French Revolution*, 230n24; and Gaskell, 171, 176, 177, 228n7, 228n11, 230n24, 230n30; and Kingsley, 155, 157, 162, 226n14, 226nn8-9, 227n19; *Past and Present*, 155, 162–63, 171–72, 223n10, 226nn8, 9, 226n14, 228n7, 230n30
Cartwright, John, 162
"Cassandra" (Nightingale), 181
Catholic Church, 52, 53
Catholic Emancipation, 57
Catholic Relief Act of 1829, 50
Catholics, 53, 57, 67–68, 213n8, 225n6; in Disraeli, 99, 146; and Gunpowder Plot, 51–52. *See also under* Ainsworth, Harrison; *under* Dickens, Charles
Charter, 21, 27, 31, 33, 203–4n2
"Charter and the Land, The," 123–24
Chartism (Carlyle), 155, 162–63, 230n24
"Chartist Jubilee" (Jones), 122–23
Chartist Land Plan, 12–13, 16, 95, 99, 129, 130, 216n10, 217–18n7; Chartist Co-operative Land Society, 79; and franchise, 76, 81–82, 123; National Land Company, 80; and O'Connor, 75, 76, 79–82, 115, 122, 123, 129, 164, 216n10, 217–18n7. *See also under* Wheeler, Thomas Martin
Chartists, 5, 6, 8, 15–16, 69, 120, 191, 194; and Ainsworth, 53, 55, 57, 66; and alternatives to franchise, 12, 13; and Carlyle, 162–63, 171; and Christian Socialists, 132, 133, 136, 137; and class, 23–31; and constitution, 7, 32, 34; and Corn Law and New Poor Law, 10–11; and Dickens, 36, 60, 61, 3, 215n9; and Disraeli, 83, 85, 90, 91, 92, 93, 94, 95, 97, 113, 217–18n7; and Egan, 36, 37, 45, 46, 47, 48–49, 50, 66; and franchise, 15, 129; and interests, 25–27, 30, 32; and moral vs. physical force, 12, 21–22, 31–35, 57, 81,

92, 190; newspapers of, 21, 38, 203–4n2; and property, 10, 207n27; and reform vs. revolution, 2–3, 7; and Spence, 80; in Surtees, 103; and trade unionists, 131–32; and working class, 29, 30. *See also under* Gaskell, Elizabeth; *under* Kingsley, Charles; *under* Wheeler, Thomas Martin
Cheap Clothes and Nasty (Kingsley), 139
Christianity, 132–33, 157, 159–60, 163, 164
Christian Socialist, The, 140, 222n8, 229n16
Christian Socialists, 17, 131, 132–41, 224n15; and clergy, 134, 135, 137; and cooperative associations, 129; and Gaskell, 140–41, 164, 176, 178, 183, 184; and Kingsley, 139, 140, 143, 157, 160, 161, 163; and political vs. social action, 137–38
Christmas Carol, A (Dickens), 230n30
Church of England, 52, 99
class, 5, 7, 15, 29, 83, 99, 191, 202n10, 205n10; in Ainsworth, 53, 54; and Chartist discourse, 23–31; and Christian Socialists, 133, 134; dichotomous model of, 12, 24, 25, 26, 27, 45, 87, 94, 97, 98, 100, 114, 117, 133, 134, 142, 151, 152, 164, 166, 167, 168; in Dickens, 61, 63, 68; and disinterestedness, 11, 12, 23; in Disraeli, 13, 77–78, 85–86, 87, 90, 94, 95, 97–98, 100, 151; in Egan, 36, 40, 41, 44, 45, 46, 48; in Eliot, 196, 197, 198; in Gaskell, 13–14, 164, 165, 166, 167, 168, 175, 179–80; in Kingsley, 142, 150, 151, 152; and parliamentary discourse, 23–31; represented vs. unrepresented, 26, 27; and self-interest, 8–9, 10, 24, 26; tripartite model of, 11, 12, 24, 25, 26, 29, 87, 90, 94, 95, 133, 134, 151, 175; in Wheeler, 114, 117; and Whigs, 11, 25. *See also* society, hierarchical model for
Cobbett, William, 162; *History of the Protestant Reformation*, 96
Commonwealth, 136, 143–44
Coningsby (Disraeli), 4, 5, 17, 78, 83, 85–91, 93, 94–95, 97, 98, 99, 220n8, 224–25n3; and aristocracy, 83, 85, 86, 87, 88–89, 90, 91, 94, 95, 101, 103, 104, 113; and Kingsley, 145, 146; middle class

in, 85, 87, 89, 90, 94, 100; and Surtees, 102–4, 105, 110–11; and Wheeler, 113–14, 122; working class in, 85, 87, 94, 100

Conington, John, "The Rightful Governor," 134

constitution, 2, 3, 5, 7, 31–32, 34, 57, 198; in Egan, 40, 41, 45, 46, 47; histories of, 6, 11–12, 13, 15, 33

Cooper, Thomas, 136–37, 144, 223n11, 226n13; Purgatory of Suicides, 154–55

Cooper, Walter, 137

cooperatives, 13, 94, 95, 96, 129, 130, 131, 137; and Christian Socialists, 132, 137, 138; and Industrial and Provident Societies Act, 140; in Kingsley, 139, 143, 159, 160, 178; and Maurice, 183. See also under Gaskell, Elizabeth

Corn Laws, 10, 25–26, 27, 29, 69, 175, 206n19, 219n4; and Disraeli, 216n3; and landowners, 76, 78; in Surtees, 83, 102, 103, 104, 107–8, 219n2

Crossley, Francis, 191

Culture and Anarchy (Arnold), 232n

David Copperfield (Dickens), 226n16

Dialogue between A. and B. (Maurice), 135

Dialogue between Somebody (Maurice), 133, 135

Dickens, Charles, 22, 35, 99; and Ainsworth, 214–15n6; aristocracy in, 60–62, 63, 66, 68, 69, 70, 85; Barnaby Rudge, 5, 17, 35, 36, 60–71, 85, 88–89, 93, 170, 182; Catholics in, 60, 61, 62, 63, 64, 66, 67, 68, 69; A Christmas Carol, 230n30; David Copperfield, 226n16; and Disraeli, 218–19n13; and Egan, 60, 61, 65, 66; and Gaskell, 170, 182, 229n23, 230n30; and Kingsley, 143; middle class in, 17, 36, 60–61, 62, 66, 68, 69, 70, 71, 85, 89; Oliver Twist, 214n1; political sympathies of, 36; and Wheeler, 122

disinterestedness, 5, 22, 37, 48; and aristocracy, 76; of Chartists, 24; and class, 11, 12, 23; in Disraeli, 87, 88, 91, 92; in Eliot, 198; in Howitt, 192; and land, 10, 75, 76; and middle class, 76; and parliamentary discourse, 9; and property, 9,

28; in Scott, 203n21; of Tories, 24, 25–26; of Whigs, 25–26; and working classes, 30, 31. See also self-interest

Disraeli, Benjamin: and allotment schemes, 77–78; and aristocracy, 15, 78, 83, 85, 86, 87, 88–89, 90, 91, 92, 93, 94, 95, 97, 98, 99, 101, 103, 104, 113, 134, 142, 166, 218–19n13; and Christian Socialists, 134; and companionate unions, 15; Coningsby, 4, 5, 17, 78, 83, 85–91, 93, 94–95, 97, 98, 99, 100, 101, 102–4, 105, 110–11, 113–14, 122, 145, 146, 220n8, 224–25n3; and Corn Laws, 216n3; and Fourier, 218n8; and Gaskell, 165–66, 167, 173, 180, 183; hierarchical society in, 17, 85, 87, 89, 90, 94, 95, 99, 100, 103, 110–11, 114, 180; industrialists in, 87, 88, 89, 90, 100; and Kingsley, 142, 143, 144, 145, 146, 148, 151, 158, 159, 224–25n3; middle class in, 83, 85, 87, 89, 90, 94, 100, 218–19n13; monastic hierarchy in, 97, 98–99, 100; and O'Connor, 217–18n7; and Owen, 218n8; Parliament in, 85, 86, 88, 89, 90, 91, 94, 95, 100, 101, 102–3, 111, 113, 158; and Second Reform Act, 191; and Surtees, 102–4, 105, 110–11, 219n1, 219n3; Sybil, 4, 5, 13, 17, 75, 78, 83, 85–87, 90–94, 95–101, 102–4, 113–14, 122, 146, 159, 165–66, 167, 217–18n7, 224–25n3; Times report on speech (14 Oct. 1844), 99; Tories in, 83, 86, 87, 88, 90, 100, 101, 218–19n13; Vindication of the English Constitution, 97–98; and Wheeler, 113–14, 117, 122, 220n3; working class in, 85, 87, 90, 92, 93, 94, 95, 97, 98, 100

education, 133, 190, 192–98; in Disraeli, 88; in Gaskell, 173, 174, 176–77, 181, 185; in Kingsley, 150, 152, 153, 154, 157, 226n10. See also self-culture

Egan, Pierce, 22, 35–36, 170; and Dickens, 60, 61, 65, 66; and Gaskell, 170; marriage in, 39, 40, 41, 42–43, 44–45, 54; names in, 210n13; Robin Hood, 208–9n2, 210n12; and Surtees, 93; Wat Tyler, 5, 17, 35, 37–49, 50, 54, 60, 61, 65, 66, 93, 170, 210–11n14, 211n15

Egan, Pierce, Sr., Life in London, 35

Eliot, George: *Felix Holt*, 17, 189–90, 195–99, 231n1; *Middlemarch*, 189

equality: in Ainsworth, 54; and Christian Socialists, 132; and companionate marriage, 14, 15; in Disraeli, 89, 97, 98, 217n4; in Egan, 40, 44–45, 46, 47; in Gaskell, 167, 172, 173, 177, 182, 186; in Kingsley, 142, 147, 156, 157, 160; and Maurice, 133; and self-culture, 222n5; in Wheeler, 115

Examiner, 25, 28, 30, 32, 203–4n2

Faber, Philip, 146

Fawkes, Guy, 52–53

Felix Holt (Eliot), 17, 189–90, 195–99, 231n1

Ferrand, Busfeild, 77

Ferrand, Margaret and Walker, 77

Fielden, John, 26

Fourier, Charles, 80, 96, 130, 131, 132, 218n8

franchise/suffrage, 1, 2, 6, 7, 8, 133, 170, 197; in Ainsworth, 50, 56; Chartist alternatives to, 12, 13, 15, 16, 115; and Chartist and parliamentary discourse, 28; and Christian Socialists, 132; and constitution, 3, 32; in Disraeli, 94, 95; and education, 190, 192; in Egan, 38, 40, 42, 45, 46; in Eliot, 195, 196; and Howitt, 192, 193, 194; in Kingsley, 142, 147, 150, 154; and land, 16, 75, 76; and Land Plan, 81–82, 123; and legislation, 21, 22; and property, 9, 10; restoration of, 33; and Second Reform Act, 191; and social agency, 3, 5, 16, 75, 76; and Spence, 79–80; in Wheeler, 115, 116

Fraser's Magazine, 139

"Fraternity" (Maurice), 132–33, 136

French Revolution, 37

French Revolution, The (Carlyle), 230n24

Froissart, Jean, 47–48, 209n3, 209–10n11, 212n23

Fuseli, Henry, *Wat Tyler and the Tax-gatherer*, 37–38

Gaskell, Elizabeth, 192; aristocracy in, 175, 176, 178, 179–83, 184, 188; and Carlyle, 228n7, 228n11, 230n24, 230n30;
Chartists in, 138–39, 164–65, 166, 167, 170, 171, 173, 174, 175, 178, 184, 185; clergy in, 140, 176–77, 182, 184; cooperatives in, 141, 164, 176, 183, 184, 187–88, 229n16; and Dickens, 170, 182, 229n23, 230n30; hierarchical society in, 173, 177; industrialists in, 164, 166, 169, 171, 172, 174, 175, 176, 177, 178, 179, 184; industry in, 175, 178, 179, 180, 187; and Kingsley, 164, 223n13, 223–24n14, 229n16; and Ludlow, 229n16; *Mary Barton*, 5, 17, 138–39, 140, 164–76, 177, 178–79, 180, 184, 185, 188; and Maurice, 140, 229n18, 230n28; murder in, 165, 166, 171; *North and South*, 13–14, 17, 140–41, 164, 165, 176–88, 203n18; personal intercourse in, 164, 177, 178, 180, 184, 186–87, 188; poor people in, 167, 170, 172, 173, 177, 179, 185, 188; rationality in, 168, 169–70, 171, 172, 173, 175, 176, 177, 181, 186; religion in, 140, 164, 172, 176, 177; strikes in, 169, 170, 172, 173, 175, 178, 184, 185, 230–31n32, 231n33; trade unions in, 141, 164, 164–65, 166, 168, 169–70, 171, 173, 174, 176, 178, 184–85; working class in, 140, 141, 164, 165, 166, 167, 168, 169, 170, 171, 173, 174, 175–77, 178, 180, 182, 183, 184, 185, 186

Gaskell, William, 177

gender, 14, 67–68, 121, 147, 149, 159. *See also* women

Gladstone, William Ewart, 189, 191, 192

Glorious Revolution, 11, 12

Gordon Riots, 60–61, 62, 63, 64, 65, 214n2

Gore, Catherine, *The Hamiltons*, 11–12

Greg, William Rathbone, 175, 176, 178, 179

Gulliver's Travels (Swift), 220n6

Gunpowder Plot, 51–52, 54–55, 57, 62, 63

Guy Fawkes (Ainsworth), 5, 17, 35, 36, 50–59, 60, 61, 66, 215n10; aristocracy in, 53, 54, 55–56, 58; marriage in, 53–57, 58–59; middle class in, 17, 50, 53, 54, 56, 58, 59

Guy Fawkes (Lathbury), 52

Hamiltons, The (Gore), 11–12

Harney, George Julian, 80, 129–30, 137–38, 218n8, 223n12

Hillingdon Hall (Surtees), 5, 17, 83, 102–12
historical novels, 5, 13–14, 15, 83, 202–3n16
History of England (Lingard), 51, 52
History of the Protestant Reformation
    (Cobbett), 96
homosocial bonds, 15, 40, 44, 61, 69, 70,
    119, 180, 211n18; in Disraeli, 89, 145,
    217nn3, 4; in Kingsley, 146, 147, 151
homosocial rivalry, 15, 91, 167, 180
Household Words, 140
Howitt, Mary, 192, 232n5
Howitt, William, 232n5; *The Man of the
    People*, 17, 189, 190, 192–95, 197–98
Howitt's Journal, 192
Hughes, Thomas, 140, 222n4
Hunt, Henry "Orator," 162
Hypatia (Kingsley), 140

Industrial and Provident Societies Act,
    140
industry/industrialists. *See under* Disraeli,
    Benjamin; *under* Gaskell, Elizabeth
interiority: and companionate ideal, 42;
    and companionate marriage, 14–15;
    in Disraeli, 88, 93; in Gaskell, 168; in
    Kingsley, 158; in Wheeler, 116, 117, 118,
    119
Ivanhoe (Scott), 15, 39–40, 203n17, 210n12

Jack Sheppard (Ainsworth), 50
Jardine, David, *State Trials*, 51, 52
Jesuits, 51, 53, 54, 145, 212n3, 225n6
Jones, Ernest, 129–30, 137–38; "Chartist
    Jubilee," 122–23; *Notes to the People*,
    138
Jones, Lloyd, 137, 223nn11, 12

Kingsley, Charles, 132, 136, 138, 222n4,
    232n5; *Alton Locke*, 5, 17, 139, 142,
    149, 150–63, 164, 176, 177–78, 183–84,
    230n30; and Amalgamated Society
    of Engineers, 140; aristocracy in, 142,
    144, 148, 153, 156, 158, 159, 226n12;
    artists in, 146, 147, 149; and Carlyle,
    226n14, 226nn8-9, 227n19; Chartists
    in, 139, 142–43, 144, 147, 150, 152, 153,
    154, 155, 157, 160, 161–62, 163, 178;
    Cheap Clothes and Nasty, 139; and

Christian Socialists, 224n15; clergy in,
    142, 143, 144–45, 146–47, 148, 150, 151,
    153, 155, 157, 159, 160, 161, 162, 163, 164,
    177, 184; and Dickens, 226n16; and
    Disraeli, 224–25n3; and Gaskell, 164,
    176, 177–78, 183–84, 223n13, 223–24n14,
    229n16; hierarchical society in, 147,
    158; and Howitts, 232n5; *Hypatia*, 140;
    "Letters to the Chartists," 135, 143, 144,
    147, 155–56; "The Nun's Pool," 225n5;
    Politics for the People, 135; poor people
    in, 139, 142, 143, 144, 145, 146–47, 148,
    152, 157; rationality in, 147, 150, 154,
    155, 156, 160–62; religion in, 145, 147,
    148, 150, 157, 158, 159, 160, 162, 163, 178,
    184; working class in, 139, 141, 142, 143,
    147, 149, 149–51, 152, 153, 154, 159, 160,
    162, 163, 164, 177–78, 184; and Working
    Men's College, 183; *Yeast*, 17, 139–40,
    144–50, 151, 159, 176

land, 75–84; and agency, 16; and Corn
    Laws, 10; and disinterestedness, 75; in
    Disraeli, 17, 85, 94–95, 97, 100, 103, 111;
    and franchise, 16, 75, 76; and jubilee,
    122, 123, 221n8; in Surtees, 103, 107, 111;
    and Tories, 8; in Wheeler, 114, 122; and
    Whigs, 8; and working classes, 79
land allotments, 16, 76–79, 99–100; in
    Kingsley, 158; and O'Connor, 80–81,
    82; in Wheeler, 123, 124. *See also* Chart-
    ist Land Plan
landowners, 7, 75, 79–80, 85, 106, 111,
    114–15, 175; and allotment schemes,
    76–78; as disinterested, 10, 76; in Dis-
    raeli, 83, 87, 95, 96
Lathbury, Thomas, *Guy Fawkes*, 52
Leeds Mercury, 190
"Letters to the Chartists" (Kingsley), 135,
    143, 144, 147, 155–56
Life (Maurice), 135
Life in London (Egan), 35
Lingard, John, 55, 57, 213n8; *History of
    England*, 51, 52
Lloyd's Weekly, 136, 143
London and Westminster Review, 25
London Corresponding Society, 79
London Democratic Association, 8

London Journal, 36

love: in Ainsworth, 56, 57; and companionate marriage, 14; in Disraeli, 89, 91–
92, 93–94; in Egan, 42, 44; in Surtees,
105, 106; in Wheeler, 117, 119, 121

Lovett, William, 26

Lowe, Robert, 191–92

lower classes, 5, 10, 28, 29, 59, 79, 114, 134,
192; in Dickens, 61, 62, 65, 68, 69, 70;
in Disraeli, 95, 113; in Egan, 36, 46, 48;
in Gaskell, 171, 177, 184; in Kingsley,
142. *See also* people, the; poor people;
working classes

Ludlow, John, 132, 133–34, 135, 136, 137,
138, 222n4, 222nn6-7, 226n15; and Amalgamated Society of Engineers, 140; and
Gaskell, 229n16; and Kingsley, 142, 143;
"The 'People,' " 133

Macaulay, Thomas, 7

Malthus, Thomas, 109

Manchester: demonstration in, 26; strikes
in, 23, 83, 120, 165, 170, 175, 178, 228n7

Manchester Domestic Mission, 177

Manchester Guardian, 175

Manners, John, 77, 99

Man of the People, The (Howitt), 17, 189,
190, 192–95, 197–98

marketplace, 9–10, 82, 123, 138, 184

marriage: in Ainsworth, 53–57, 58–59;
companionate, 5, 14–15, 42–43, 53–54,
56, 58, 59, 61, 63, 66, 67, 68, 69, 70,
87, 88, 89, 90, 91, 105, 117, 119, 145–46,
147, 149, 150, 158, 160, 166, 180, 183,
186, 217n4; in Dickens, 61, 62–63, 67,
68, 69, 70, 215n10; in Disraeli, 15, 86,
87, 88, 89, 90, 91, 98, 114, 166, 217n4; in
Gaskell, 165, 166, 167, 173–74, 180, 181,
183, 186; in Kingsley, 144, 145–46, 147,
149, 150, 151–52, 153, 154, 156, 158, 159,
160; kinship, 14, 15, 40, 41, 42, 44, 45, 54,
62, 63, 66, 67, 70, 86, 87, 88, 89, 90, 91,
104, 105–6, 117, 119, 144, 151–52, 153, 158,
166, 181; in Scott, 15, 39; in Surtees, 104,
105–6; in Wheeler, 114, 117, 119, 120, 121.
See also women

Marshall, James Garth, 80

Mary Barton (Gaskell), 5, 17, 138–39, 140,
164–76, 177, 178–79, 180, 184, 185, 188; aristocracy in, 175; Chartists in, 164–65, 166,
167, 170, 171, 173, 174, 175; cooperatives
in, 164; industrialists in, 164, 166, 169, 171,
172, 174, 175; industry in, 175; murder in,
165, 166, 171; poor people in, 167, 170, 172,
173; rationality in, 168, 169–70, 171, 172,
173, 175, 176; religion in, 164, 172, 176;
strikes in, 169, 170, 172, 173, 175; trade
unions in, 164–65, 166, 168, 169–70, 171,
173, 174; working class in, 164, 165, 166,
167, 168, 169, 170, 171, 173, 174

Maurice, Frederick Denison, 134, 137,
138, 160, 222n4, 226n15; and Amalgamated Society of Engineers, 140; *Dialogue between A. and B.*, 135; *Dialogue
between Somebody*, 133, 135; "Fraternity," 132–33, 136; and Gaskell, 176, 183,
229n18, 230n28; and Kingsley, 142, 143,
148, 155; *Life*, 135; "Recollections and
Confessions of William Milward," 177;
The Reformation of Society, 133; and
Working Men's College, 140

Mayhew, Henry, 137, 139

Meridian Sun of Liberty, The (Spence), 80

middle class, 1, 5, 26, 27, 78, 134, 171–72,
190; and Egan, 38; in Gaskell, 175,
179–83, 188; and landowners, 7, 76;
and property, 9, 10; and Reform Bill,
7, 24; rise of, 11, 15; in Surtees, 110, 111;
in Wheeler, 114, 116–17, 118, 121; and
Whigs, 8, 25. *See also under* Ainsworth,
Harrison; *under* Dickens, Charles;
under Disraeli, Benjamin

Middlemarch (Eliot), 189

Millbank, Joseph, 137

monasteries, dissolution of, 96–97, 144,
217n2

moral force: in Ainsworth, 56; in Egan,
46, 47; in Eliot, 197; and Howitt, 192,
193, 194; and O'Connor, 49

moral vs. physical force, 16, 31–35, 79;
and Chartists, 12, 21–22, 92; in Disraeli,
92–93; and Eliot, 190; in Gaskell, 170,
171, 178, 184–85; and Howitt, 190; in
Kingsley, 154, 156; and O'Connor, 81;
and Wheeler, 84. *See also* physical
force; physical force, moralized

Morning Chronicle, 2, 24, 25, 28, 29, 30, 31, 36, 69, 137, 139, 203–4n2
Morning Post, 25, 29, 32, 203–4n2

nation, concern for whole, 27, 28, 61, 133, 197; and class interests, 9, 12, 23, 24; in Disraeli, 86, 87, 88, 90; and parliamentary parties, 24, 25, 26; and property owners, 10, 28, 76, 77; in Wheeler, 114, 117, 119, 121
National Charter Association, 129–30, 136
national marriage plot, 13–16, 61, 66, 144, 145–46, 150, 165, 173–74; and gender, 14, 67–68, 147, 159. *See also* marriage
national narrative, 5, 16–17, 39, 45, 53, 62, 68, 83, 104; and Disraeli, 83, 113, 114, 142, 144; in Gaskell, 164, 165, 180, 183; in Kingsley, 142, 151, 164; in Wheeler, 83, 114, 116, 120, 221n10
National Petition / Chartist Petition: of 1839, 1, 2, 10, 22–23, 37, 48, 227n1; of 1842, 2, 16, 23, 164–65, 227n1; of 1848, 2, 13, 84, 113, 115, 124, 129, 139, 170–71. *See also* People's Charter
National Reform League, 190–91
National Reform Union, 190, 191
national tales, 5, 13, 14, 15, 98, 165, 202–3n16, 203n18
Neale, Edward Vansittart, 138, 140, 222n4
New Poor Law, 10, 27, 29, 214n1
Newport uprising, 23, 48, 81
Nightingale, Florence, 230n26; "Cassandra," 181
Norman Conquest, 11, 12, 15, 33, 96
North and South (Gaskell), 13–14, 17, 140–41, 164, 165, 176–88, 203n18; aristocracy in, 176, 179–83, 184, 188; Chartists in, 178, 184, 185; clergy in, 176–77, 182, 184; cooperatives in, 176; industrialists in, 176, 177, 178, 179, 184; personal intercourse in, 164, 177, 178, 180, 184, 186–87, 188; trade unions in, 176; working class in, 176–77, 178, 180, 182, 183, 184, 185, 186
Northcote, James, *Sir William Walworth Lord Mayor of London, Killing Wat Tyler in Smithfield*, 138l, 37
Northern Liberator, 21

Northern Star, 6, 8, 22, 47, 49, 92, 120, 203–4n2, 216n5; and class, 26, 27, 31; and land, 75, 76, 79, 80, 81, 82, 122, 221n8; and moral and physical force, 34–35; and Southey, 38; and Wheeler, 113
Northumberland Society for the Protection of Agriculture, 108
Notes to the People (Jones), 138
"Nun's Pool, The" (Kingsley), 225n5

O'Connor, Feargus, 27, 47, 49, 77, 124, 130; and Disraeli, 92, 95, 217–18n7; health of, 130; and Land Plan, 75, 76, 79–82, 115, 122, 123, 129, 164, 216n10, 217–18n7; and moral vs. physical force, 34, 81; and National Charter Association, 136; *A Practical Work on the Management of Small Farms*, 79, 81, 82, 123, 216n7, 221n5
O'Connorville, 122, 124
Oliver Twist (Dickens), 214n1
"Orator" (Hunt), 162
Owen, Robert, 80, 96, 130, 131, 132, 137, 207n27, 218n8
Owenites, 95, 131, 158, 216n9
Owenson, Sydney, *The Wild Irish Girl*, 13, 53

Paine, Thomas, *The Rights of Man*, 37
Parliament, 51, 76, 78; and Ainsworth, 50, 55; and Carlyle, 16, 171; and class, 23–31, 100; in Dickens, 60, 61, 62, 64; and Egan, 36, 48; in Eliot, 195, 196; in Gaskell, 170, 171, 175; and Howitt, 192, 193; and moral vs. physical force, 22, 31–35, 190; and national marriage plots, 15; and O'Connor's Land Plan, 81; and property, 9; and reform, 1, 2–3, 5, 198; representation in, 1, 6, 8, 16, 21–22, 81; and Second Reform Act, 191; in Surtees, 102, 104, 106, 107, 109–10, 111; in Wheeler, 113, 114, 117. *See also under* Disraeli, Benjamin
Past and Present (Carlyle), 155, 162–63, 171–72, 223n10, 226nn8, 9, 226n14, 228n7, 230n30
Peel, Robert, 100, 101, 102, 110, 111

people, the, 12, 24, 93, 96, 133, 148, 193, 194; and Chartists, 27; cultivated vs. uncultivated, 134; in Egan, 36, 38, 40, 45, 47, 48–49, 211n19; land as stolen from, 79, 81–82. *See also* lower classes; working classes

" 'People,' The" (Ludlow), 133

People's Charter, 6, 13, 32–33, 37, 38, 124, 125, 129–30; demands of, 1–2; in Gaskell, 170, 171; and Kingsley, 138, 154, 162, 163; and moral vs. physical force, 22, 35, 81; and O'Connor's Land Plan, 12–13, 81–82, 164. *See also* National Petition / Chartist Petition

People's Charter Union, 136

Percy, Hugh, 107, 219n5

physical force, 14, 47–48, 55, 56, 57, 60, 65–66; in Eliot, 197; in Gaskell, 168–70, 231n34; and Howitt, 192, 193, 194; in Kingsley, 152, 155, 161

physical force, moralized, 22, 34, 35, 48, 49, 61, 66; in Ainsworth, 17, 36, 50, 56; in Egan, 40, 46, 48. *See also* moral vs. physical force

Plain Speaker, 136

Political Pilgrim's Progress, The, 21

Politics for the People (Kingsley), 135

Politics for the People (pamphlets), 132, 133, 134, 135–36, 137, 143, 144, 156, 229n16

poor people, 77, 78, 90, 94, 97, 133. *See also under* Gaskell, Elizabeth; *under* Kingsley, Charles

Practical Work on the Management of Small Farms, A (O'Connor), 79, 81, 82, 123, 216n7, 221n5

Preston spinners, 178, 184, 185, 231n33

Pride and Prejudice (Austen), 180

property, 1, 28, 42, 54, 158, 183, 204n3, 207n27; in Disraeli, 95, 96, 122; and Reform Bill, 9, 10, 75, 76; in Surtees, 103, 104; and Tories, 8, 24; in Wheeler, 114, 122

Protestant Association, 60, 64, 215n9

Protestants: in Ainsworth, 53, 55, 58, 59; in Dickens, 60, 61, 62, 67, 68; in Disraeli, 99

Purgatory of Suicides (Cooper), 154–55

rape, 41, 42, 54, 67, 210n14, 211n16. *See also* seduction

rationality: in Carlyle, 155; and Chartists, 32, 92; in Dickens, 62, 65, 66, 68; in Disraeli, 93; in Egan, 36, 40, 48; and lower classes, 10; and Ludlow, 133; and property, 28; and working class, 29, 30, 31, 66, 197. *See also under* Gaskell, Elizabeth; *under* Kingsley, Charles

"Recollections and Confessions of William Milward" (Maurice), 177

Red Republican, 130

Reform Act of 1832 (Reform Bill), 1, 2, 38, 75, 100, 189, 190, 191, 211n20; and class, 7, 8; and constitution, 5, 6, 12; in Disraeli, 83, 94, 97; and middle class, 11, 24; passage of, 13, 15; and property, 9, 10, 75, 76; and social reform, 16; in Surtees, 104–5; in Wheeler, 116, 118; and Whigs, 29

Reform Act of 1867, 1, 2, 189, 191, 192

Reformation of Society, The (Maurice), 133

Reform League, 189

revolution, 2–3, 6, 7, 46, 189, 193, 198–99

Reynolds's Miscellany, 36

"Rightful Governor, The" (Conington), 134

Rights of Man, The (Paine), 37

Robin Hood (Egan), 208–9n12, 210n12

Rochdale Society of Equitable Pioneers, 131

Royal Agricultural Society of England, 16, 78–79, 103, 107, 108, 109, 111

Scotsman, 24, 28

Scott, Walter, 203n21; *Ivanhoe*, 15, 39–40, 203n17, 210n12; *Waverley*, 13, 14, 15, 39

seduction, 39, 42, 166, 167, 168, 210–11n14. *See also* rape

self-culture, 222n5; and Christian Socialists, 134; in Dickens, 66, 68, 70, 71; in Disraeli, 88; in Eliot, 190, 196; in Gaskell, 174, 182; in Kingsley, 142, 149–50, 152, 153, 155, 156, 160; in Wheeler, 116, 117. *See also* education self-interest: in Ainsworth, 55; of aristocracy, 61, 85, 86, 87, 104; of Chartists, 32; of class, 8–9, 10, 24, 26; in Dickens, 64, 65, 85; in Disraeli, 85, 86, 87, 104; in Egan, 42, 48; in Eliot, 190, 196, 197, 198, 199; in Jones, 138; in Kingsley, 159; in Scott, 203n21; in Surtees, 104, 122. *See also* disinterestedness

self-making, 9–10, 11, 15, 88, 117, 167, 174, 181; in Dickens, 68, 70

Shorter, Thomas, 137

Sir William Walworth Lord Mayor of London, Killing Wat Tyler in Smithfield, 1381 (Northcote), 37

Smith, Adam, 109, 173, 220n6

Smith, James, 107–8

social agency, defined, 3–5, 6, 22

socialism, 80, 94, 95, 96, 97, 130, 131, 132, 137. *See also* cooperatives

society, hierarchical model for, 25, 146, 151. *See also* aristocracy; class; Disraeli, Benjamin; *under* Gaskell, Elizabeth; *under* Kingsley, Charles; *under* Surtees, Robert Smith

Southey, Robert, 209n10, 212n22; *Wat Tyler: A Dramatic Poem,* 37, 38, 39

Spence, Thomas, 79–80, 81, 122, 123, 194, 207n27; *The Meridian Sun of Liberty,* 80

Spencer, John, 107, 219–20n5, 219n4

Spirit of the Age, 223n10

Standard, 192

State Trials (Jardine), 51, 52

strikes, 22, 32, 35, 81, 165, 206n19. *See also* Manchester; Preston spinners

Sunshine and Shadow (Wheeler), 5, 17, 80, 83–84, 113–25; Chartist Land Plan in, 17, 84, 113, 114–15, 120, 122–25, 216n7, 221n15; Chartists in, 83–84, 113, 114, 116, 118–19, 120, 121; working class in, 113, 114, 115, 116–17, 121, 122, 123

Surtees, Robert Smith: agriculture in, 17, 83, 103, 103–4, 106–9, 110, 111–12; aristocracy in, 83, 102, 103, 103–4, 106, 107, 109–10; and Disraeli, 102, 219n1, 219n3; hierarchical society in, 103, 110; *Hillingdon Hall,* 5, 17, 83, 102–12; and Young England, 219n1

Swift, Jonathan, *Gulliver's Travels,* 220n6

Sybil (Disraeli), 4, 5, 13, 17, 75, 78, 83, 85–87, 90–94, 95–101, 167, 217–18n7, 224–25n3; and aristocracy, 85, 86, 87, 90, 91, 92, 93, 94, 95, 97, 98, 99, 104, 113, 166; and Gaskell, 165–66; and Kingsley, 146, 159; middle class in, 83, 85, 87, 90, 94, 100; and Surtees, 102–4; and Wheeler, 113–14, 122; working class in, 85, 87, 90, 92, 93, 94, 95, 97, 98

Times, 2, 10, 30, 31, 32–33, 75, 203–4n2, 228n14; and finely graded social hierarchy, 25; on French Revolution, 37; and property qualification, 28; and virtual representation, 24

Tories, 8, 10, 24, 29–30, 78, 175, 191, 203–4n2, 204n3; and Ainsworth, 50–51, 52, 55, 60; in Dickens, 60, 61, 69, 214n1; as disinterested, 24, 25–26; "No Popery" campaigns of, 36, 50, 52, 55, 60; in Surtees, 83, 104, 106, 109–10, 111; and working classes, 10, 25. *See also under* Disraeli, Benjamin

Tracts on Christian Socialism, 229n16

trade unions, 13, 16, 17, 129, 137, 178, 190; development of, 131–32; in Eliot, 195, 196, 197. *See also under* Gaskell, Elizabeth

Universal League for the Material Elevation of the Industrious Classes, 190

upper classes, 1, 35, 59, 122, 143, 154, 170–71

Vincent, Henry, 11

Vindication of the English Constitution (Disraeli), 97–98

Walworth, William, 37

Wat Tyler (Egan), 5, 17, 35, 37–49, 50, 210–11n14, 211n15; and Dickens, 60, 61, 65, 66; and Gaskell, 170; marriage in, 39, 40, 41, 42–43, 44–45, 54; and Surtees, 93

Wat Tyler (Southey), 37, 38, 39

Wat Tyler and the Tax-gatherer (Fuseli), 37–38

Waverley (Scott), 13, 14, 15, 39

Wheeler, Thomas Martin, 15, 218n8; Chartist Land Plan in, 17, 84, 113, 114–15, 120, 122–25, 216n7, 221n5; Chartists in, 83–84, 113, 114, 116, 118–19, 120, 121; and Disraeli, 220n3; and Land Plan, 216n7, 221n5; *A Practical Work on the Management of Small Farms*, 123, 216n7, 221n5; *Sunshine and Shadow*, 5, 17, 80, 83–84, 113–25; working class in, 113, 114, 115, 116–17, 121, 122, 123

Whigs, 11, 27, 29–30, 50–51, 78, 117, 171, 191, 203–4n2; in Ainsworth, 36, 52, 53, 54, 55, 58, 59, 60; in Dickens, 36, 60, 61, 69, 70, 214n11; as disinterested, 24, 25–26; in Disraeli, 86, 87, 217n2, 218–19n13; and middle class, 8, 25; "Ministerial Plan for Parliamentary Reform," 2; newspapers of, 203–4n2; in Surtees, 83, 102, 103, 104, 106, 107, 109–10, 111; and working classes, 10, 24, 25

Wild Irish Girl, The (Owenson), 13, 53

women, 67–68, 147, 149; in Egan, 39, 40, 41, 42, 44, 46, 211n15. *See also* gender; marriage; rape; seduction

working classes, 1, 2, 10, 17, 38, 50, 77, 155; and Christian Socialists, 132, 133–34, 135–37; and constitution, 32; in Dickens, 61, 66, 68, 71; and disinterestedness, 30, 31; as educated, 192–95; and education, 191–92; in Eliot, 195, 196, 198; in Howitt, 192–95; incapacity of, 28–29, 31; and O'Connor's Land Plan, 79, 82; and the people, 12, 27; poverty and ignorance of, 28, 31, 191–92; rationality of, 29, 30, 31, 66, 197; representation of, 5, 191; strikes by, 23; and trade unions, 131; and Whigs, 24, 25. *See also under* Disraeli, Benjamin; *under* Gaskell, Elizabeth; *under* Kingsley, Charles; people, the; *under* Wheeler, Thomas Martin

Working Men's College, 135, 140, 183

Working Tailors' Association, 139

Yeast (Kingsley), 17, 139–40, 144–50, 151, 159, 176; aristocracy in, 144, 148; artists in, 146, 147, 149; Chartists in, 139, 144, 147; poor people in, 139, 144, 145, 146–47, 148; rationality in, 147; religion in, 145, 147, 148; working class in, 139, 147, 149

Young England, 16, 75, 76, 77, 78–79, 134, 146, 219n11; and Disraeli, 17, 83, 88, 95, 99, 100, 101; in Kingsley, 158; and Surtees, 83, 102, 111